COMPANY OF REBELS

COMPANY OF REBELS

Elizabeth Lord

Severn House Large Print
London & New York

This first large print edition published in Great Britain 2006 by
SEVERN HOUSE LARGE PRINT BOOKS LTD of
9-15 High Street, Sutton, Surrey, SM1 1DF.
First world regular print edition published 2004 by
Severn House Publishers, London and New York.
This first large print edition published in the USA 2006 by
SEVERN HOUSE PUBLISHERS INC., of
595 Madison Avenue, New York, NY 10022.

British Library Cataloguing in Publication Data

Lord, Elizabeth, 1928-
    Company of rebels. - Large print ed.
    1. Tyler's Insurrection, 1381 - Fiction
    2. Historical fiction
    3. Large type books
    I. Title
    823.9'14 [F]

    ISBN-10: 0-7278-7503-5

Printed and bound in Great Britain by
MPG Books Ltd, Bodmin, Cornwall.

To Elizabeth and Walter Bain
with my deep thanks for inspiring me to
write this book

Prologue

It had been the dream that awoke John Melle, sweat standing cold on his forehead.

A dream of thundering hooves on dry mid-summer turf, of brilliant morning sunlight glinting off silver helms and the metal headguards of the warhorses, giving them the look of demons; of four hundred lances lowered as one at the waiting peasants who gripped their own sharpened staves, ancient bows and rusty pikes, more in terror than any hope of fending off the charge.

The barricade of chained farm carts being swept aside like chaff to the wind as the destriers seemed to fly on wings over the heads of the rebels. The knights leaning low, iron gauntlets wielding double-edged swords as deft as if scything through wheat, peasant blood splattering the gleaming armour of well-trained men.

John Melle felt the lance bite into the small of his back, saw the warhorse above him, its eyes bloodshot behind the sockets of its headguard, glimpsed the eyes of its rider glowing hatred behind the visor, saw Death descending through his own scream of pain...

★ ★ ★

7

The room was dim and still. The glimmer of dawn across the Thames marshes was easing through the narrow slatted window under the low eaves.

Sitting up on his pallet, wincing at that old wound stabbing at him with the sudden movement, the old blacksmith could just discern the humped shapes of his grandchildren under their coverlets – two girls of nine and eleven, and young John just eighteen. None of them had stirred, so his scream must only have been in his mind.

From the room below came the murmur of women's voices. His wife and widowed daughter-in-law were at their morning chores. Even as he became aware of them, his wife Alice called gently up to him.

'John, are you stirring?'

'Ay,' he mumbled, but delayed the effort of rising, his head thick from too much ale the night before.

It had been the first day of May. Young folk had jigged to old Adam Coupier scraping away on his rebec while his pockmarked son beat time on a tambourine. A May Queen had been crowned – a pert little wench who'd later made off into the trees with her young consort while the rest of Fobbing Village primed itself for a thick head in the morning on home-brewed pudding ale, heavy stuff that was so moreish.

For most folk, yesterday had marked the end of frugal spring and the promise of summer's plenty. For himself it merely marked

8

another year to add to his growing store, no longer filled with promise, each an immutable maggot sucking what little vitality remained to him.

By day his still muscular arm rose and fell to the clang of iron, but no one except Alice knew the toll it took on him. There was a time when he'd have been down to the White Lion tavern after his work to slake a blacksmith's roaring thirst. These days he looked more to his bed and a posset of warm ale and herbs to sooth aching joints and that dull, annoying pain in his chest.

A squawking from below interrupted his thoughts. Alice was shooing out the hens that came to scratch up her earthen floor for the mites her broom had disturbed.

'John?' he heard her call up again, her voice shrill. 'It's getting light.'

'Ay, woman, blast you!' he growled down irritably.

She wouldn't retaliate but go quietly back to her task. There had never been any high words between them in all their forty years together. But like all meek and mild folk, mildness was her strength. Growl as he might, she would have her way.

Hawking on night phlegm, he clambered to his feet, struggled into his rough woven tunic and dragged on loose woollen hose, thrusting his feet into scuffed leather boots. Stomping past young John's pallet, he prodded it with his foot.

'Time you roused yourself too, you lazy

wight! Sprightly younker like you should've been up an' about well afore me.'

As the mound under the cover groaned to show itself awake, John clambered stiffly down the ladder to the room below, the warm odour of yesterday's baking wafting up to greet him, mingling with the dankness of musty thatch from the room he'd just vacated.

He didn't acknowledge his wife as he made towards the door to the yard. After forty years under the one roof what was there to say? She'd not been a beauty, her face full and flat from the start, but there had always been a tranquility about her for which John thanked God. His father could have chosen a shrew for him, or one with a harelip or a wall eye.

In the yard he passed Joan, his daughter-in-law, mother to young John. She was coming from feeding the sow whose litter, when slaughtered and salted later in the year, would get them through the next winter.

'Good morning, Father.' There was no smile with the greeting. Bleak with the loss of her husband – his eldest son – from the ague twelve months ago, she'd become sour, her face lean and bitter, and she wore her widow's hood like a hair shirt.

'Time that lad of yours were up and about his work,' John growled in reply. 'Seems I'd be better off employing some journeyman than that lazy wight.'

'He'll be up,' she called after him. 'The boy needs his sleep.'

John turned and glared at her. 'He's eighteen, woman! No boy. But I'll make a fine smith out of him yet. Make him strong, like his father...'

The words choked in his throat at the memory of Robert, broad of chest, with arms like the bole of a young oak – a man of iron. To think a simple ague could have taken him. Resolutely, John thrust aside the memory.

'Your son's hands are more black with soil than honest soot, digging in the earth like a peasant,' he railed. 'Ever dreaming of being a yeoman instead of following his proper trade like me and my father before me, respected by all. It's time he was a man, time he wed and proved himself a man.'

Even as he spoke, he heard his own father's words almost to the letter. Christ! Forty-odd years ago it had to be, the year of the great uprising over that accursed poll tax.

That was the year John had turned his eyes on the comely Marjory Reede, as did most of the village lads, but as she had her eyes turn-ed on his friend, Tom Baker, he'd remained silent.

It was also the year that his deep friendship with Tom Baker had grown to become a talking point with the village gossips, who maintained that at eighteen he should have outgrown such unnatural affection for an-other lad. So much so that his father, fearing he might not be as he should, had been in a devil of a haste to find him a wife, prove his son's manhood and settle the gossips once

11

and for all.

Turning painfully away from his son's widow, John stomped across the yard to relieve himself by the midden. The yard was still in shadow, shielded by the smithy and shaded by the great oak under which he and Tom as lads would loll out of the midday heat of summer and gaze over the marshes. That was until his father, the smith, goaded him back to the forge and Tom's father, the baker, came to drag his own son back to his oven.

Fobbing Village stood on a long, low promontory jutting out on to the marshes like an island in a motionless sea. This morning the marshes lay in shrouds of thin, flat mist that stretched away to where the Thames Estuary lay in pewter stillness.

On the far side of the river, the hills of Kent were mere smudges of darkness blending into the morning haze, but on the Essex side, the slopes of Hadleigh stood sharp against the luminous eastern sky with Hadleigh Castle in black relief.

Nearer, Fobbing Church was tinged with pink. The village was stirring, dogs barking as people opened their doors for children and night soil pots to be put out of the house.

Having relieved himself, John made for the water butt by the open-fronted smithy to plunge his head into the icy water, the cold shock making him gasp. Refreshed, he set about coaxing the warm forge back to life. The charcoal was glowing bright before young John came bleary-eyed and breathless to set out the tools.

John couldn't help noticing how reluctant his grandson was. For him, working with iron was his life. It was a joy to watch metal begin to glow, first dull crimson in the breathing flame, then orange through to yellow and almost white heat, but not too malleable for his hammer. He knew exactly when to draw it from the charcoal to place on the anvil. With young John as striker, the ingot thinned to a narrow strip, and under his own expert hammer, fashioned sometimes into a finely curved scythe or a knife for skinning an animal or butchering meat, sometimes a trivet or part of a gate. Beating, turning, plunging the hot metal into the trough of cold water to temper it, the steam hissing, iron baptized by water, hardened for its new life – just as young John must be hardened, if by God's grace he was given time enough to harden the boy.

The ingot then went back to the flames to be withdrawn and hammered with a rhythmic double beat, first on the anvil, then on the implement. Man against metal. Iron tempered to obedience with sensitive strength. But his joy was short lived. The pain in his chest caught him without warning, almost as if the Devil's hand was gripping him.

'Christ above!' he swore loudly. 'Damn this!'

With a terse word to his gaping grandson to get back on the bellows, he took himself to the open front of the smithy to recover a little,

13

waiting for the charcoal to glow bright again as good an excuse as any. The smith standing at his entrance was a signal for anyone passing to stop and exchange a few words, but though several neighbours were about now, he just hoped they'd be too busy to pause and chat. When the pain was on him it was difficult to be civil.

It was then John noticed the stranger, an elderly man on an elderly nag ambling at such a weary pace as to be worthy of notice. Had travelled far by the looks of him.

A stranger in Fobbing was no great thing. They'd see an occasional wandering friar or hedge priest, or merchants coming to buy the succulent cheese made from ewe's milk for which Essex marsh villages were famous, a steady trade going on down by the wharf with Fobbing Creek connected at high tide to Holehaven and across to Kent. There was the odd pardoner with his bits of parchment that for a price would secure an easy road to Heaven. For a bit more cash he'd allow one to touch a holy relic – a finger bone of St Peter or a splinter from the True Cross. John dismissed it as rubbish.

'Blessed St Peter must have had a dozen hands, the number of his finger bones I've seen, and the True Cross must be as big as a church, the splinters that have come off it these many years.'

This stranger, however, was different to any other. An elderly man dressed like a youth – bright-blue cape, particoloured hose and

14

doublet, a high-crowned hat with a brilliant red feather – yet he rode such a decrepit old nag that people stared at him as he passed. It was almost as if he was trying to be noticed.

But it was the way he returned John's stare, the lips behind the thin beard twitching for a moment as if in recognition, a slight reining of the horse so that the animal lifted its head and faltered in its gait. Then the weather-beaten face turned away, the grip of the reins loosened and the horse continued as though it hadn't lost a stride. So mystifying was the moment that John continued to gaze after him, but the man didn't look back.

Young John's voice startled him out of his trance. 'These embers are glowing bright enough now. Shall I stop?'

His grandfather swung round on him. 'God's curses! If they're bright enough, then bloody stop, you clodhead!'

John turned back to the stranger, but he'd disappeared. Where to? If he'd spurred his horse to a gallop he couldn't have reached the trees to the north of the village, certainly not as far as the manor. If he'd entered one of the tenements, his horse would be tethered out front. John shuddered. It was as if the Devil had spirited him away.

He was left uneasy for the rest of the day, all the while the man's face haunting him as vaguely familiar. Then at supper, as Alice was putting a dish of baked herring in front of him, his thoughts suddenly came together.

'God's bones, I do know the man!'

15

Alice stared at him as if he'd gone mad. 'What man, John?'

John ignored her, talking to himself. 'But after all these years it can't be possible.'

'What man are you speaking of?' Alice asked again, and again was ignored.

'He wouldn't dare return here. Why should he?' Then it came to him so abruptly that he thumped the table and leapt up, startling his family, and made for the door, flinging it open and striding off, leaving it flapping.

John and Anna Hacche's tenement stood a short way down the line of cottages to the north of the village, some two hundred paces from the smithy and not far from the miller's house. A rickety fence extended some way past it with a gate that usually lay open to allow access to the small bakehouse, but tonight the gate was shut. The stranger's horse had to be inside.

John hesitated before the door, staying his hand raised to thump on the wood. What if he were wrong? And yet he had to make sure that the man he'd seen this morning was the same man he'd not set eyes on these forty years.

Taking a deep breath, he gave a couple of thumps on the wood with the heel of his hand. There was no response. No chink of rush light or tallow candle pierced the cracks in the door's rough planking or that of the window shutters. The silence within was complete. And yet he could swear someone

16

was in there, on the other side of the door, listening, waiting.

It brought a presentiment of peril so strong that he found himself glancing about, caught by a fear of being observed. Taking hold of his nerves, he knocked again, this time more firmly.

'Tom, I know you're there,' he hissed. 'D'you remember me, John Melle?'

There was movement, as light as the scratching of a mouse, then John Hacche's voice. 'What d'you want, Master Melle?'

'Thomas Baker,' John replied, now convinced he'd been right.

For a moment there was silence again, then Anna's voice, small and timid, said, 'My father fled this village forty-two years ago, as well you know, Master Melle. For fear of his life. Before I was born.'

'And now returned,' John said. ''Twas him I saw this very morning.'

'You were mistaken,' was the reply. 'Please, Master Melle, go away.'

'I mean him no harm,' John whispered. 'But I know he's there.'

He waited for a response. He could hear voices, low and sibilant in argument. Then, cautiously, the door opened just a crack to reveal Anna's small oval face, chalk-white in the half darkness.

'What do you want of him?'

'To speak to him. Nowt more'n that.'

Her face suddenly disappeared as though she had been plucked back by something

17

behind her. Just as suddenly an arm was extended through the aperture and John found himself seized by the front of his tunic and pulled bodily into the house, the door closing quickly behind him.

Released, he stood blinking in the gloom relieved only by the tiniest flicker of an all but moribund fire in the hearth. No one spoke. His eyes slowly adjusting to the meagre light, he began to make out a group of six children, Anna's children, whimpering slightly and huddled together by the ladder to the upper chamber. Anna was standing to one side, her small figure rounded by childbearing. The stocky figure of her husband stood beside her and a little removed from them stood the tall, lanky figure of the stranger, owner of the arm that had jerked him into the house.

The stranger moved forward and took John's arm again, this time with a firm gentleness.

'My dear old friend,' he said quietly. 'Come to the hearth and we'll talk.'

That voice spanned a desert of forty-odd years, yet to John it was as though he'd heard it only yesterday.

What a strange evening it had been, at first fraught with fear, then filled with the joy of reunion, and then it had dissolved into sadness that even now was tearing at his heart.

John clung on to a rail outside Ralph the carpenter's house, his head hanging over it, his breath gulping in great drunken sobs. The

18

ale had been the strong, heady stuff that only a baker's wife could brew. And he, poor fool, had thought the evening turning merry. If only he hadn't asked the question that had plagued him all evening while his old friend Tom Baker related his adventures since his flight from the gallows.

Tom had fought in France, but with the uneasy peace after Richard II's marriage to the seven-year-old French Princess Isabella in 1397, he'd ceased soldiering and had settled in Flanders, never daring to return home. By the time Henry V invaded France to crush them at Agincourt, Tom had been too busy with his bakery in Bruges to become a soldier again.

John had been enthralled with his stories, yet beneath the camaraderie John had detected anguish. Finally he had burst out, 'Why do you risk all to come back here? Don't you know the danger that still awaits you? Your insult to Sir Gildeborough's family has not been forgotten or forgiven.'

Tom had gazed at him, his eyes gentle in the firelight, the way John remembered they'd once been when full of bright enthusiasm. The smile, too, was gentle though now toothless. 'Would you deny me a last sight of my daughter before I die?' Those words had pierced John's heart.

Who knew if Anna was his true daughter or not? That Tom should assume so had torn at John's breast, as the recollection was doing now. Was she his or Tom's? Looking so like her mother, who could say? But soon it wouldn't matter unless they met in Heaven.

Hot tears dribbled down John's bearded cheeks while Tom's voice pounded in his befuddled brain.

'I've a stone growing in my belly, John. Nothing can be done. Good doctors in Flanders have prodded and probed, administered their leeches and potions and yet still it grows, like the Devil's child in a witch's womb. Soon it'll be as large as a babe ready for birth. But this child will devour me unborn and with such agony as I dread to bear. Already it gnaws at me like a serpent. Nay, John, I would suffer it no longer. I would have an end to it.'

Anna had broken down in tears, fallen at his feet, her head upon his thin knees. 'I shall care for you, Father. From my birth I've not known you. Now you return to tell me you will die soon. I will nurse you.'

Tom had touched her greying hair that had once been golden and lustrous like her mother's, the comely Marjory whose golden tresses and azure eyes had captured both his and Tom's heart.

Tom had stroked her hair, pouring all the love that his exiled years had deprived him into that caress. He'd never seen his lovely Marjory grow big with child, never knew that she had died giving birth. He smiled tenderly down at Anna.

'Nursing would only draw out a life with which I have already done,' he said, giving a hollow chuckle. 'Three score years and two is a good way towards our allotted span. I've fulfilled a long-held desire to see my daughter and am now content for God to do with me as He will. By His grace I escaped my executioner all those years ago. I have no complaint now that He sends me to my rest at last.'

The words tore at John's heart. That the once handsome young wight should come to this!

His stomach heaved. He hung over the pole, bringing up the ale, weeping aloud with each retch while Tom's quiet voice echoed in his head. 'I tell you, John, I'd sooner endure the gallows than end my days supping pap and letting forth my bowels like some babe. No, John, I've other plans.'

This had been said as he'd seen John to the door, closing it so that Anna shouldn't hear. Strange, he hadn't felt that drunk then, only moved by grief as Tom gripped his arm.

'Tomorrow I keep an appointment in Brentwood where word of my visit has gone before me. I made certain of that as I came through nearby Corringham on my way here. Whence I go from there, God only knows, but I shall not be coming this way again, nor any other way on this earth.'

'But did you not know the King finally granted amnesty to all who escaped?'

Tom had smiled sweetly. 'Not all. Anna told me I am one who was listed as having been executed, but the clerks were so confused by the great numbers to be tried that their lists

21

got muddled. She told me that many were fined but I am still on a list of more than two hundred wanted by the hangman, a list that will last until all are dead, for all King Richard himself is dead. There are families with long memories of the wrongs done to them. The family of our manor lord, Gildesborough, still hunts me more than forty years later.' Tom gave a mighty sigh. 'Well then, they will not have long to wait for their revenge.'

The grip had tightened on John's arm. 'If you still love me, old friend, I have a boon to ask of you and little time to ask it. The hounds are baying for my blood in Brentwood. You must not fret for me. I am in the singular position of choosing my own quitting of this life. I am in terror of the end that awaits me if I fear to take it by the throat now, yet I dare not end it by my own hand and be forbidden ever to beg my way out of Purgatory. I will let others do the task for me and send me decently to Paradise. I've seen to it that I am already shriven and in a state of grace. Those who seek me do not know the service they do me.'

He had suddenly winced at the pain in his stomach, grunting back the agony with an effort. Recovering, he had fumbled with a purse at his belt and pressed it into John's hand.

'Here. Money to guard my daughter against the loss of her home through my death, for surely it will be confiscated, I being a traitor.

You know that with her mother dead, my parents reared her. When they died Anna and her husband paid the re-entry fine. But as my father's heir, it might be assumed to be my property and, as with those taken in felony, be forfeit. I would not have her suffer through my cowardice. This time the re-entry fine would be so great as to leave her homeless. This money is for the re-entry fine but I cannot give it into her hands and distress her further, and I don't know what manner of man her husband is. He might fritter it away, though he seems honest. But you, John, I trust – old wounds apart.'

John had cried out, 'For God's sake, Tom, take the money back. Escape while you have the chance!'

'Would you have me linger and suffer a slower death?'

Dear God, that he would not, but he'd been unable to reply as the purse was pressed even more firmly into his hand.

'I am content, John. Now go home, dear old friend. Farewell, John. Old sores forgotten, and God go with you.'

Tom had slipped quietly back into the house and, knowing the door would not be opened to him again, John had lurched away, defeated and heartsick.

His vomit sour in his mouth, he clung to the rail. In his chest was a bitter pain that grew in intensity, making him gasp. 'Ah, Tom!' he cried out loud in the darkness. 'See what a heartache you've given me.'

23

Cold, clammy sweat had broken out on his brow. He let go of the pole and tried to pull the hood of his tunic over his head, but his arms felt too heavy to lift. All his strength seemed to be ebbing away. He had to get home. Alice would tend whatever ailed him.

On trembling legs he reeled down the centre of the road. Those on their way home from the White Lion saw him and laughed – the old blacksmith drunk as a lord. A fine head he'd have in the morning.

Through mists of pain he heard his own cry: 'In God's name, help!'

Someone was coming. John, his grandson? No, it was Tom. He felt an overwhelming wave of relief. Tom had changed his mind. John's legs buckled under him, the ground coming up to meet him, but Tom was hurrying to catch him...

It was young John who caught his grandfather, but the old smith saw only his dear friend, handsome and full of the eagerness of youth, coming towards him on a bright spring morning, bursting into his father's smithy to tell of the arrival of the people's priest, John Ball, ready to rouse the people against the cursed Poll Tax.

One

Well before Tom Baker came rushing into the smithy that morning, a mare had kicked out while being shod, breaking Adam Melle's arm.

'I told him he should use a restraining frame,' John Melle said to his younger brother Ned out of their father's hearing. 'That mare was in season and naturally irritable.'

Ned sniggered. 'Do you think he'd heed you? More think the Devil to wear a halo. I've heard him say many a time that the day he needs to use a frame will be the day he takes to his bed.'

John eyed their father cautiously, aware of his present mood. 'It was not his fault. It was that child whooping past. He was taken by surprise. He's as strong as a bull usually.'

And so he was. Ruddy-cheeked with a tawny bush of a beard to make up for a balding pate, Adam Melle's biceps were as thick as a man's thigh, and beneath the aging could still be seen as a handsome man. John was like his father had once been, although at nineteen he didn't yet possess a beard but had a mass of fair hair.

John felt some sympathy for his father. Humiliated before his sons as he suffered his arm to be set between two splints of wood by Ralph Reede the carpenter, John had watched him bite back his groans so as not to be further humiliated.

By noon on this fine day in May, with hardly any work done so far, Adam Melle was in no mood for an exuberant Tom Baker bursting into his smithy gabbling about some priest coming to tell Essex folk how bad was their lot.

'I know how bad my lot is,' Adam growled from his seat of pain on an upturned cask, nursing his throbbing arm while his two sons did what he should have been doing.

'With tithes and fines and now this new Poll Tax, I know it without some accursed hedge priest coming here to tell me. And now this broken arm to add to it, God's curse on it!'

'This is no hedge priest, Master Melle—' Tom began, but was stopped short by a bellow.

'Do you not have your own work to do without disturbing these two sluggards from theirs? Get off with you!'

Ned smothered a giggle but John felt angry. Tom was his friend, his close friend, enough to be almost more of a brother than Ned. Yet gossips were trying to put a wedge between that friendship with their nasty suspicions. And what had his father done to settle their gossip? Paid eight shillings – eight shillings! Nigh on two months' wages – as merchet to

26

Walter Bole, a serf from another village, for that man's plain-faced daughter Alice to be wedded to his suspect son.

John felt he'd never forgive his father for that, but short of forsaking him there was little he could do about it. Wed now to the flat-faced Alice, the close friendship he and Tom had shared would never be close again. What angered John was his father's attitude towards his friend even though Tom didn't seem put out by it. Tall, slim, fine-featured, his blue eyes glowed with open sympathy for the older man's misfortune this morning.

'I heard from my father and came here to express my regrets,' he said evenly.

Adam was not appeased. 'You did not! You came here to babble of this hedge priest.'

'This is no hedge priest,' Tom said again. 'He is John Ball who comes to champion the poor, and tomorrow he'll be at Horndon, speaking against the Poll Tax. I heard it in Dame Wodelarke's alehouse.'

He was stopped with an impatient wave of Adam's uninjured arm. 'Your father must be addle-brained giving you leave to go listening to ale-gossip down at Dame Wodelarke's.'

'No ale-gossip, Master Melle. Father would go himself to hear John Ball but he must bake bread for the manor. He agreed to let me go and I thought if you could perhaps spare John...'

'God's truth!' Adam started up from his seat only to sink back with a groan, nursing his arm. 'Don't tell me who I can and cannot

27

spare in my own smithy. I've enough to put up with, rot it, without green boys of twenty summers disrupting my work and priests stirring honest folk to discontent.'

'There's already discontent,' John cut in.

'And growing daily,' Tom added, his eyes bright and fervent. 'From demands that keep us all impoverished. You know, Master Melle, the tithes you pay keep the clergy fat, and fines keep our manor lord in rich clothes.' He began counting off on his fingers. 'There's avesage for feeding pigs in manor woodlands on acorns our lord doesn't use. There's quit-rent for work we fail to carry out on the manor...'

'I know all that,' Adam growled, but Tom wasn't done.

'There's merchet for marrying a woman belonging to another manor, and chevage if he wishes to leave his manor and work else-where, and if he leaves without permission he is branded. There are entry fines and com-mon fines – it goes on and on. Now yet another Poll Tax, the third in two years, just so King Richard's uncles can pay for their wars with France.

'And how does your John Ball mean to change it?' Adam challenged, spitting con-temptuously on the earth floor. 'Insurrection, is that what he preaches? Handing out arrows for fools like you to fire?' He shifted uncom-fortably, knowing he was in danger of being drawn into a political argument, but he couldn't help himself. 'This has all been said

28

before. We all know of a grasping lord and a fat clergy. But in such zeal to put it right, you forget the bailiff or the reeve or the ale-taster – common folk too, but with a bit of power – ain't above squeezing an extra penny from their neighbours to line their own purses. And don't forget, alongside fat clergy there be many a poor parson with not enough benefice to keep his house mended after his bishop has taken his share of tithes.'

John risked interruption. 'Our own parson's house leaks from so many holes in his thatch. His fence is half down and lets in every pig in the village to root up his cabbages while he's at mass.'

Ned gave a chuckle. 'Ole Jack Straw never was one with hammer and nail—'

'Keep a respectful tongue in your head, younker!' Adam rounded on his sixteen-year-old son. 'The man's name is Rackstrawe. And it's Parson when you speak of him. And don't bend that brow at me,' he added as Ned scowled, 'else you'll feel my fist across it!'

'Folk mend his house when they can,' Tom put in hurriedly. 'He's well thought of in his village. No high and mighty manner about him, no hunting with hounds as some clergy do. He lives frugally but keeps a good table for hungry wayfarers as comes to his door. Yet his house could fall down for all the Bishop of Westminster cares. It's of such injustices that John Ball will speak, I'm sure, and tell us how we can remedy them.'

Adam snorted. 'Will he tell me who does

my son's work while he's away being preach-
ed to about things that can't be changed?'

'But they *can* be changed.' Tom's blue eyes
shone with conviction. 'Great crowds gathered to hear him speak against Robert Hales,
the King's treasurer, and against Archbishop
Sudbury, and the King's uncles, John of
Gaunt and Thomas of Woodstock, who own
the very lands we in this village till. All of
them are authors of this newest Poll Tax, the
highest one yet.'

'But this recent one,' Tom reminded them,
'you can't turn away from its unfairness.'

John expected his father to lose his temper
at the lad's rudeness, but instead he sighed
heavily, shaking his balding head.

'I like it no better than the next man. This
time it's three groats on everyone over fifteen,
working or not – my wife, Ned, John here and
his wife, his sister not yet turned fifteen, my
old mother who does nowt but sit by the
hearth all day, mumbling, contributing
nothing. Fifteen shillings I am being ordered
to pay. I spend my days working my guts out
and still pay rents and fines and tithes, but
this new tax will all but finish me.'

'What will it do for those already impoverished?' Tom asked. 'They could be flung out
of their hovels.' He was on the balls of his feet
with enthusiasm. 'John Ball will show us how
to solve grievances as have been growing
since the Great Pestilence when the Statute
of Labourers was set up to curb demand for
higher wages. We know of landowners who

pay double the old rate for labour, but woe to the common man caught leaving his manor to work for them. He'd be branded and all his possessions taken from him.'

John stood listening in awe. His friend had learned his letters some years ago, helped by the priest before Parson Rackstrawe. He had a quick brain and knew a lot of things John didn't even know existed.

'You see, Master Melle,' Tom was saying, 'how important it is to change such things? It must begin somewhere and John Ball is the one to show us how, perhaps at Horndon tomorrow. We must be there to hear him. If you would consent to John being there...'

Exhausting his arguments, Tom fell silent while John held his breath for his father to respond, which he did in a torrent. 'What is all this? Ned, back on them bellows! And you, young Baker, back to your father's business and leave me to mine. I've a pair of hinges to finish afore noon on bailiff's orders from the manor.'

John gazed after his friend. What an easy stride Tom had. What a squire he'd have made had he been high-born. But though his father was a master baker and, like his own father, enjoyed respect and an income better than most of his neighbours, by no stretch of the imagination could they be deemed wealthy.

As a young boy, Tom's fascination with church books had prompted old Father Giraldus to teach him his letters and even approach Tom's father to let him enter the Church. Hugh Baker had been happy to agree and the priest began making arrangements to seek a patron who would pay the substantial sum required. But the old priest had died and the then lord of the manor, one of the great Bohun family, had considered the loss to himself of a potentially skilled baker and had terminated Tom's hopes. He would have made a fine priest, but now he was set to be a baker like his father, and had been married these last few months to the comely Marjory, whether he'd wanted to or not.

It had all come from a bit of pleasure on Plough Monday. Despite the freezing weather, they'd slunk off to a barn. Shaking her pouting breasts at every lad in the village, John was sure Marjory had slunk off to that barn with many of them in the past. But this time she'd been discovered, with Tom, which had shocked John, never thinking him to be like that. It had felt like a betrayal at the time.

Marjory had been called on to confess that she was no longer a virgin and had named Tom to cover all her other discrepancies. Shamefaced, he could hardly deny that he'd taken full advantage of her favours, and in order to save her the awful humiliation of being paraded through the village for fornication, he'd allowed himself to be wed to her. He then had what all the lads in Fobbing had drooled over, but John got the impression that, married, Marjory's ardour wasn't what it had been previously. But Tom was besotted and it didn't occur to him that he'd struck a wedge between the deep friendship he and John had shared from childhood.

How he managed to get through the day was beyond John. With his father bellowing at him, the heat of the forge adding to the heat of the May sunshine and the air hanging heavily as if waiting for a storm, he worked on.

The thought of Tom going off to Horndon tomorrow was a torment. Several times he came close to asking for permission to go, but each time his courage failed him.

As the day wore on it became clear that half the village was going, and that he could be the only one – besides his injured father and maybe a few of the older men – to be left behind.

Ned, too, was looking agitated. What if Ned was the first to ask and gain his father's sanction while he was ordered to work on? Someone would have to be left to work on. He'd have to get in first. As they were damping down the hearth for the evening John plucked up courage.

'I'll work thrice as hard on the morrow,' he added.

His father's lip curled derisively as he supervised the stacking of the blacksmith's tools into boxes or on hooks lining the soot-grimed timber walls of the smithy.

'Would you have me fined at next manor court for plying my trade on God's day?'

John had forgotten. Tomorrow was Sunday.

All would be in church, except for those going off to Horndon. 'I'll work thrice as hard on Monday then,' he said hastily. 'That I promise.'

'And I promise you will,' Adam said, spitting into the dying, charcoal. 'But why only on Monday, pray? Why not Tuesday or Wednesday?'

Adam Melle wasn't unaware of the excitement gripping Fobbing Village all day. Folk going by his smithy would usually stop to exchange a few words if he wasn't too engrossed in his work. Today, with him sitting on a barrel unable to lift a hand to his tasks, they stopped without exception. Did he know of the planned visit to Horndon? Had he heard that the priest John Ball would be coming to talk to the people of Essex? Did he plan to go, especially as he was now handicapped by his broken arm and could do nothing in the smithy? He could safely leave his sons in charge, couldn't he? What did he think John Ball, now being called the people's priest, would have to say? So it went on until it was all he could do to keep his temper, a temper that sat just beneath his skin at the best of times.

Each time his reply became more and more gruff until he burst out to one unfortunate, 'God's teeth, man! Ain't I got enough pain with this arm wi'out adding to it, bumbling along roads? No, I won't be going, nor will my sons!'

When John had the temerity to approach him again for permission to go with the other fools, it was the last straw. His refusal should have been sufficient, but it wasn't.

'This family should be represented,' the boy persisted, but Adam knew what was really in the lad's mind – to be with his beloved friend, despite the two now being married. John clung to that other one like a maid to a man; it wasn't right.

'You said yourself,' John whined, 'you cannot go with your arm, and Ned isn't near old enough to take in all that will be said. So shouldn't I go? I'm as oppressed as any, having to pay a poll tax on a wife now.'

Adam rounded on him. 'You pay the poll tax on your wife? Christ's wounds! I've had to loan you the three groats for her from my own purse, and when will I see that back?'

John should have been warned, but youth heeds no warnings. 'I'll pay you back,' came the retort. 'Do not fret on that score.'

'I trust I'll not have to,' Adam shot back, trying to compose his temper by staring out at the yellowing sunset that hinted of an end to this spell of fine, warm weather. 'The woman be your wife, your responsibility, and until I get my money back you will work twice as hard for me.'

'I didn't ask to be wed,' John said, his voice raised.

'But brought it on yourself for all that,' Adam said without turning away from the sickly sunset.

'How so?'

'You know well enough, how so.'

'Ay, I know well enough the old women who see little good in anything that is honest and true. I know the thoughts put into a father's head as might never have entered it, and about his own son, too. I know what they read into mine and Tom Baker's comradeship, may their evil tongues rot in their foul mouths!'

Adam heard the tools John had been gathering being hurled into a box by the wall. 'Given time, I could have found a comely wife. I might even have taken Marjory Reede had I not been saddled with a wench whose face is more like a cow's arse than anything I know.'

Adam turned on him, his glare silencing a giggle from Ned. His voice was low and dangerous. 'Have a care, John. You speak of a good woman who is pure and chaste in thought and deed, and a good, obedient wife, unlike Marjory Reede whom your *good friend* Tom Baker licked after.'

John had gone silent. Ned was busying himself packing up the tools far more industriously than he'd done for months. Adam felt sarcasm creep into his words.

'What did you expect, then, with gossip gone ahead of you? Find yourself some wealthy heiress to wed, mayhap the sister-in-law of Thomas of Woodstock, the little Mary Bohun. Might she have been more to your taste, my lord?' He touched his forehead in

36

mock obeisance. 'Why not become lord of the manor while you're about it, so highly prized are you by the fairer sex, I must say!'

His acid humour suddenly fell from him like a discarded cloak as he saw defeat in his son's face. He bore John the love of a father, as he bore all his children. John was a hard worker. He didn't deserve this.

He moderated his tone. 'Listen to me, John. I did what I deemed was right. I am smith in this village, respected even above Hugh Baker – certainly above our miller whom all detest for his short returns when grinding folk's grain, and they bound by manor law to go to him and no other. Barring our parson, who all love, and our bailiff, who all fear, I'm held in high esteem. And one day, John, so will you be. Nothing must mar that. Do you understand?'

He saw John's miserable nod but found himself hating the winning.

Completely dejected, John closed the top and bottom halves of the doors fronting the smithy and followed Ned and his father through the yard to the house. With Ned going on ahead, the aroma of supper hastening his feet, John's father hovered, waiting for him to join him. When he did, to John's surprise the man put his free hand about his shoulders, his head bent, his gaze trained reflectively on the ground.

'Don't let there be dissension between us, John,' he said in a quiet tone. 'We have

37

enough of that all around us. And Alice, I would you look upon her more favourably. Ay, she be plain, I know, but she is a better wife than all the Marjory Reedes of this world. I have a fear of wenches such as Tom Baker has taken for a wife. The Devil lurks within too fair a woman and I can foresee trouble going ahead of that one. Your Alice will be a sweet and loyal wife to you, always, a helpmeet, and a good mother to your children. Mayhap you were too young to wed, but what's done is done, and what I wish to say is, for the sake of your standing in this village, get her with child soon.'

His hold on John's shoulder had tightened, preventing John making any protest. 'This talk of your Alice is not what's on my mind, but rather this business of John Ball. I'm not agin what he preaches, but his venom disquiets me. I may seem an old fool to you, John, but I mind the unrest there is around these days. I too have a desire to make things right, but the old can only look back. 'Tis the young as must go forward, rise up and change what us old ones thought could never be changed.'

Adam's pace slowed even more, his arms still about John's shoulders. 'Dwelling upon that,' he said slowly, 'I've decided you should go and hear what the priest has to say. Ned and I will manage here wi'out you. There'll be few folk left here as will need my services. Tomorrow there'll be more of Fobbing in Horndon than in Fobbing itself.'

38

He gave a low chuckle as they reached the house and took in a deep breath of the succulent aromas wafting out to greet them. 'God's bones, but that herring pie do smell fine. Your Alice's, I vow. Your mother sets a good table but that wife of your'n, young as she be, outcooks her when it comes to herring pie!'

Two

With what seemed the entire village making its way down towards the church and east through the villages of Corringham and Stanford-le-Hope to the market town of Horndon, John took leave of his family.

Ned was looking surly, required to stay and help their father, while their sister Cicely hugged John as though he was never coming back. Few people ever went far from their villages. Alice was hanging back, shy of saying farewell to her husband before others, but John hardly noticed; his eyes were on Marjory and Tom, further along the road, saying good-bye to each other, Tom pressing her fingers to his lips as though indulging in courtly love.

Seeing John, he waved, kissed Marjory's hands in a final farewell and began making his way down the street towards John.

'We are off then,' he said cheerily, his handsome face eager as others flooded past them.

'So it seems,' John answered. 'Like an adventure.'

From the corner of his eye he saw Marjory beckoning to him. Her action looked to him to be urgent and as two friends of theirs came abreast of them, taking Tom's attention, John hurried off towards her.

'Make certain my Tom is safe while away,' she whispered when he reached her. She was gazing up into his face in a way that made John feel strange and his heart started to race.

'Safe?' he echoed stupidly. 'What could befall us on such a fair day?'

'I do not know,' she said, her voice husky. 'Who can say?' Her eyes were a limpid green. He hadn't realized how green they were, reflecting the morning light off the fields behind the cottages. 'Our lords are not gullible,' she went on. 'Surely they must know of John Ball's coming, or be blind and deaf.' She caught her lower lip between her neat white teeth. 'Trouble could arise so easily. Please, John, look to his well-being ... And to your own too.'

Small and slender, she wore her simple brown kirtle as elegantly as any gentlewoman in an embroidered mantle. Her golden hair was plaited, caught with frets over each ear while a small linen fillet and veil formed a perfect frame for her delicate features.

The sight made John breathe heavily and as she lifted her small oval face to brush his cheek with a grateful kiss, he stepped back quickly, praying that no one had noticed this unseemly act towards a man not her husband. Her slender hand held towards him now was almost flirtatious, her gaze seductive enough to set him trembling and he shot a glance towards Tom, but he was still talking to his friends. As though drawn by the glance,

41

Tom looked up and, seeing him with Marjory, gave him tight smile. Had he seen what had gone on and read it correctly?

John's face flaming with guilt, he hurried back to him. God, if Tom were to know the sinful thoughts that had crossed his mind just now of her lying beside him. May God forgive me, he prayed as he acknowledged Tom's smile with his own and had Tom fling his arm about his shoulder, the way he used to do before marriage pulled them apart.

'Is all well with you?' Tom asked, noticing his tight expression as they moved off with the others.

'Why shouldn't it be?' John snapped and his friend fell silent.

A deep, gruff voice behind them swept away John's thoughts of his friend's wife.

'What think you the priest will have to tell us?'

Turning towards the voice, he saw the long-chinned, weather-beaten face of Walter Gildeborn, the man's gait slack-limbed as he came alongside. When not doing service for the manor, the shepherd worked for his brother, William, a franklin of comfortable means, owning a stock of cattle and some seventy sheep.

Seeing John's expression, he looked closely at him. 'Why so surly? All I asked was what you thought John Ball might have to say.'

John forced a smile. 'Nowt as we don't know already,' he answered.

It was true. The lists of taxable polls had

42

been submitted earlier this year, every list well short of names, for who'd be stupid enough to declare every single member of a family that was too old, too addle-brained or too crippled to work? In some cases the lists had been almost too short to be acceptable. Yet surprisingly they had been accepted, and everyone had relaxed for a while.

Now the authorities had caught on, the authenticity of those lists finally challenged when it seemed that a good third of the population had mysteriously died or moved to places unknown. Yet even now it was possible to fob them off with some plausible excuse for an absent poll in the family. In fact, defaulting had become a game, and those around John chuckled knowingly. But Tom didn't laugh.

'None of us knows so much,' he said quietly, 'as we don't need to know more. Doubtless we shall be told this very day, something we *thought* we already knew but didn't.'

Tom's sober wisdom made John feel unaccountably annoyed with him. 'We can still tell him a thing or two!' he retorted sharply.

'Ay,' agreed Wat Gildeborn. 'Many as be ill used by them as look to grab every penny when already wealthy.' Warming to his subject, he fell into step alongside the growing knot of friends. 'Take old Dick Haggepound – him as lived down by the wharf. Him hardly cold in his grave and along comes our bailiff demanding heriot of his widow to swell the purse of Thomas o' Woodstock as lord of

43

this manor.'

'We heard,' someone said. 'But it's always been done.'

Wat ignored him. 'Claiming old Dick's best beast as heriot. His best beast! It were his *only* beast. His widow left wi'out, and for why? Because he'd deprived his lord of his paltry service by dying!' Gildeborn shook his head in disbelief. 'And she still must pay mortuary, the Holy Church assuming a man never paid *all* his tithes when he lived and thus claims its mortuary when he dies, no matter how poor. How will his poor widow cope?'

'Well, she can't,' John put in. 'Our parson helps with food as best he can, he with barely enough to feed himself after helping the needy.'

'Our absent lord could do with taking lessons from our parson.'

'What's this about our absent lord?'

Will Randere had come up behind the group, bow legs making him smaller than the others. Yet for all his shortness, the eel-catcher had such a handsome visage and sensuous eyes that few women failed to simper as he savoured every curve of their bodies. Nearing forty, already twice married, his present wife was nineteen but had already borne him two children and was again pregnant.

Wat Gildeborn gave him a long-toothed grin. 'I was saying our absent lord be rich beyond dreams yet still grabs more from us. Marriage to that Bohun heiress brought even

44

more wealth to our absent Earl of Buckingham. Do any ever see him? He hardly knows this village even exists, yet is always ready to receive. 'Tis said he owns a bed worth a hundred and eighty pounds. More than the value of my brother William's land, beasts and chattels all put together.'

'Would I could marry into wealth,' the man in front said, glancing over his shoulder at them. A bondsman of no means at all, Ralph Peteman should have been tending his lord's fields but had absented himself without the bailiff's permission, so eager was he to be at Horndon today.

Will Randere hawked and aimed a gob of spittle into a ditch. 'And be wed to that haughty, cold Bohun fish? Give me a poor but hot-breathed wench any day!'

'Speak for yourself!' retorted the broad-faced bondsman. 'I'd take wealth before any hot-breathed wench.' He hitched up his homespun tunic to display threadbare braies underneath and lifted a much-mended, hobnailed shoe while he smirked at Will. 'I wager a king's ransom you would too if you had a choice.'

'A king's ransom? You couldn't wager a Grey Friar's fart!' He grinned at the guffaws around him, Grey Friars known for their extreme poverty.

Wat Gildeborn remained baleful. 'Eleanor de Bohun with her estates like Pleshey and her only seventeen, and Woodstock now Earl of Essex and Hertford by marriage to her, as

45

well as already being Earl of Buckingham, conferred on him by his nephew, our own young King Richard.'

'How can you know so much?' John asked.

'My brother William. He is well able to read and reads widely.'

'Hmm,' muttered John, thinking of Tom who also knew his letters. Striding beside the others, he became aware of how silent Tom had become. Not arguing or joining in with the continual wisecracks – it wasn't like him.

'What ails you?' he asked eventually as they neared Corringham. This hovering guilt he'd felt since leaving Fobbing made his tone sharper than he meant it to be. He moderated it quickly as Tom looked questioningly at him. 'Why so brooding?'

'There's nowt ailing me,' came the reply, dismissive and short, only serving to heighten John's sense of guilt.

'I'm sorry if I spoke impatiently to you earlier.'

'Did you?' Tom countered. 'I didn't notice.'

But he had noticed. For why fall so strangely silent, and why the need to lie about it now?

John gave a nervous laugh. 'Probably all the excitement. And this oppressive heat.'

He glanced up at the sky that had taken on a burnished haze. He needed something to take his mind off that earlier episode. 'Looks like this fine weather will break soon in a fair old storm.'

'Ay, it does.'

46

Tom's easy reply finally put to rest the guilt John had been feeling. More relaxed, he joined in with the lively conversation and general joking as the easy stride of men used to using their feet took them swiftly towards Horndon.

Their numbers had swollen considerably on passing Corringham and Stanford-le-Hope, swollen even more by folk from the marsh villages of Mucking, Linford and even Tilbury. With every step the way became livelier and noisier.

John gazed about in excitement. 'I've not seen as jolly as this since our last May Day, and that only half as jolly.'

'We're bound to see more once we reach Horndon,' laughed Randere, licking his lips at the sight of two young girls. 'Like them two pretty wenches for instance. Might even find one like them to dance a tune to me,' he added, winking.

'And what about your wife?' Tom reminded, knowing what he meant.

'Ah, her!' Randere smirked, then burst out laughing. 'What she don't know won't fret her.'

'You're a lecherous old dog,' Tom told him as they strode away. But Randere gave another loud laugh. 'You say that, Tom Baker, but I knows one or two as finds a little such temptation to their liking.'

They finally emerged from a covering of woodland to a lane that climbed up to a large number of dwellings huddled about a timber

47

church. Horndon. Nearby, beneath a stand of oaks, a crowd was gathering, with people converging from all directions.

'Come on!' yelled Gildeborn. 'We must move fast or lose a good view.' Those around had already broken into a run, some more fleet than others.

'Where be ye from?' hailed a long-legged man over his shoulder as he passed – a fisherman judging by the smell that followed him.

'Fobbing,' John called out, struck by the broad accent. 'And you?'

'Kent,' the man shouted back, slowing a little so that John could catch up with him. 'Did bring meself across,' he panted. 'We in Kent be as equally oppressed as ye in Essex.' With that he put on a spurt, putting distance between himself and the Fobbing groups.

Not to be outdone, they lengthened their stride, waving aside a beggar without which no gathering would be complete, his clawed hand outstretched for alms.

Reaching the edge of the throng, the lanky Wat Gildeborn elbowed his way in, followed by his companions and reaping some abuse from those who'd been there for ages. From Orsett, Ockendon, Barstable, Childreditch they'd come, and while waiting, men had met others they'd never seen in their lives, talking as old friends, their babble a deep, rippling, unbroken murmur. After a while, as they continued to wait, John found himself talking to another smith from Thurrock while Tom

48

had discovered another baker from Billericay to the north and who even bore the same name as he, Tom Baker.

There were even soldiers in the crowd, who'd fought in France and bore their scars proudly, telling of old campaigns, knowing their value but now merely manor workers tied to their work and to low pay. 'No one cares that we must meet the inflated price of food and such,' one remarked bitterly.

The murmer began to die down, slowly, like a breeze falling away. All eyes had turned in one direction as though on a command and the mass began to surge forward.

Wat Gildeborn, head and shoulders taller than most men, pointed excitedly. 'He's coming!'

Taller even than Tom, the gangling shepherd had seen where the crowd had fallen back before two riders. John was only just able to see, but little Will wasn't faring so well.

'Can you see anything?' he pleaded.

'There are two of them,' John obliged. 'One brown-robed on a small shaggy horse. The other more rough-looking, riding a larger mount. They're both dismounting. The one in the priest's robe must be John Ball. Ah, he's now stood up on something so we can all see him.'

'I still can't,' came Will's plaintive voice. 'What's he like?'

Tom lifted his voice above the now roaring, excited gathering. 'He's talking to the fellow

49

that was riding with him. 'An ugly devil, scarce fitting, I say, to be companion to a priest.'

'Never mind the companion,' shrieked the exasperated Will. 'What of the priest?'

'He's large, heavily built.'

'His face, man, what do it look like?'

'Hard to see from here.' Tom stretched himself taller, eyes narrowing in an effort to focus better. 'Seems he doesn't have the pallor of a priest. More a peasant hue. A large nose. Heavy chin. Ah, he's thrown back his cowl. Dark hair, tonsured like a priest's...'

'He *is* a priest,' cried John. 'What else could be expected?'

Tom scowled at him as though insulted, but he quickly became good-natured again. He even laughed. 'If you were to hoist Will Randere up on your broad shoulders, John, I wouldn't have to go on describing him.'

'I can hardly move,' retorted John, taken by surprise by the brief scowl, 'much less find room to hoist him up.'

'*Someone* assist me,' came a desperate cry. 'Else I'll suffocate here!'

Laughing in spite of himself, John flexed his broad shoulders and strong arms to push away those pressing around him and with Tom's help got Will precariously on to his shoulders, immediately rewarded by a reek of fish from his shoes and chausses.

The priest had lifted a hand for quiet. Instantly a hush scythed through the throng and he began to speak.

50

'You know me?' The voice was bell-like. It rang in every ear as audibly as if he was standing beside each listener. The crowd responded as one man.

'Ay, we know you, John Ball.'

'Then John Ball, sometime priest of St Mary's of York,' he sang back, 'and now of Colchester, greeteth well John Nameless and John the Miller and John the Carter...'

'As though he addresses us personally,' whispered Tom with pride.

'...and biddeth ye beware of guile in borough, and to stand together in God's name, and biddeth Piers Plowman to go to his work...'

'Who's Piers Plowman?' queried Will from his perch.

'From a poem of the commons,' Tom supplied, the only one able to read. 'By Langland, also a priest—'

'Stop y'mouth!' Wat Gildeborn interrupted, elbowing him. 'Hark to what's being said.'

'...and chastise well Hobbe the Robber...'

'Sir Robert Hales!' Tom cried, unabashed by Wat's earlier interruption. 'He talks of Hales who robs us all with his taxes.'

'...and take with ye John Trueman and all his fellows, and look that ye shape to one head and no more.'

A roar of approval greeted him. Everyone understood what shaping to one head meant – the young King Richard, a fair, fourteen-year-old boy who had their sympathy, surrounded as he was by counsellors who

51

robbed in his name, and uncles who would rule in his stead given half the chance. For this reason they particularly detested John of Gaunt, whom they suspected as being the prime candidate.

'One head!' came the response. 'We'll not be robbed by grasping advisers!'

'John Ball doth know you all.' So great was the noise that the priest had to raise his voice to get above it. 'And he doth ye to understand that he hath rung your bell. Now, right and might, will and skill, God hasten ye in everything.'

The crowd roared its approval as the voice rose above it. 'Ay, good people, matters goeth not well in England, nor shall do till everything be common. And that there be no villein nor gentleman, but that we be all united together.'

'Ay!' Nigh on a thousand united voices was like the crash of a great wave against a cliff.

'And that the lords be no greater than we be.'

The crowd swayed like a huge, heaving beast, bellowing agreement while the priest spread his arms wide as one crucified, the gesture done to embrace them all.

They in turn took note of the coarseness of his garments, as old and shabby as theirs, allowing them to identify with this man, a man of the cloth who understood their plight, would not look down his nose at them as though their poverty were of their own doing. Here was one to whom they could bring their grievances, who would do something for them at last, a leader. The noise died away. They stood, waiting.

Attuned to their mood, he lowered his tone though not its power. 'Have we deserved to be kept thus in servage?' he beseeched, and ripples of agreement moved through the crowd like corn bending before a breeze.

'We be all come from one father and one mother, Adam and Eve. Then whereby can they say they be greater lords than we be, saving by that they cause us to labour for what they dispend?'

Fervour began to break out. 'Ay, they grind us down into the very soil we till for 'em!' came a voice not far from John. Then another voice nearby, 'It be us as fill their fat purses – by our sweat!'

The cry was taken up immediately by others. 'We'll have no lords over us! Have at them! Kill every last one!'

'No!' cried the priest, again and again until the chanting subsided. 'Let us go to the King. He is young and fair. Show him what servage we be in and how we would have it otherwise, or else provide the remedy ourselves. If we go together, then all manner of people that now be in bondage will follow us and be made free. Show the King that we will have some remedy.' John Ball's tone became low and ominous. 'Either by fairness or otherwise.'

At the threat his audience began to look apprehensively around. Calls for violence issued from the safety of a crowd carried a certain amount of anonymity. The same uttered by that single, clear voice to any happening to be on the perimeter, whether by intention or accident, lay any one of them open to a charge of treason, a hanging penalty.

Not only that, there could be a bailiff or a constable in their midst, set to inform against them. As far as could be seen, no one was making any suspicious exit and with the priest speaking again, their attention returned to him.

'John Ball doth know your grievances, but it is not yet the hour for us. When the hour comes, then shall ye all hear my bell. For it shall peal forth loud and clear to tell ye what shall be done.'

There came frantic cheers. Tom called to those around him, 'He is getting down. He is leaving.'

John almost tumbled Will Randere off his shoulders as the tight-packed throng began to sway to make a path to let the priest through. His companion could be heard above the hubbub. 'Give way there! Give way!'

Within arm's reach of the Fobbing men, the rough-faced companion to the priest appeared, mounted now, working a swathe through the masses. Behind him on the lowlier beast came John Ball. His large sandaled feet, sticking out from beneath his robes, looked almost ludicrous. His head was now cowled and bent low, but from beneath the bushy brows his eyes surveyed the face of each man

54

he passed. And what eyes. Piercing grey, they seemed to penetrate the very soul as though claiming it absolutely.

As that glance touched John, he felt suddenly powerful, as though there was nothing he could not achieve had he the mind to. Glancing at Tom as the priest moved on, the way closing up behind him, he saw Tom's blue eyes shining with the same optimism.

It was the same with everyone: Wat Gildeborn, the hard-nosed shepherd; Will Randere, the salacious little eel-catcher; Dick Wodelarke, who enjoyed his ale as had his now dead father; Henry Sharpe, the wheelwright's rabbit-toothed son – a host of faces from Fobbing Village mingling with those of many others, all influenced by the same wondrous spell, that from henceforth life would be better.

Like a river bursting its banks the crowd began to flow after the departing priest, first a trickle then a surge, everyone streaming downhill in his wake. But already he'd put distance between him and them, his figure bent over the small, bony horse, his rope sandals kicking its flanks.

One by one the pursuers slowed to stand gazing after the two until they were lost amid the trees. An overwhelming sense of anti-climax settled over John as he too came to a halt. After a moment Tom heaved a tremendous sigh.

'Ay,' John said slowly, attuned to the sentiment neither of them could express.

Listening to the priest he'd firmly believed that this day would begin a righteous crusade against oppression, but now they were all just standing there wondering where all the fervour of only a moment ago had gone.

'What now?' queried Will, succinctly summing up all their feelings.

John glanced back to where their saviour-priest had disappeared. His gaze settled on the midday clouds heaping pile upon pile along the horizon to the southwest. All morning the sun had been struggling against a thickening haze. He turned away, aware that the air had become unbearably heavy and completely still. He nodded towards the crouching mounds of cloud.

'If naught else,' he said slowly, 'we'd best turn for home afore that storm gives us all a soaking.'

Moving off downhill until gaining the highway leading to London, the band of Fobbing men turned east along the tree-lined road that would take them home, all of them certain that they wouldn't see the priest again. Empty words, that was all they'd been, spouted to empty air.

Three

With the fading of a lurid evening glow the first growl of thunder was heard, an ominous, protracted roll as that of some hellish wagon being towed.

As night closed in, eerie flashes lit up the solid clouds that had crouched sluggish but gradually growing above the horizon throughout the afternoon. Now the low rumbles crept inexorably nearer with seemingly unbroken booming that made John's flesh creep. It was as though God was voicing his displeasure at the work they'd been about that morning.

Praying the storm would pass to the north, John went to bed to an uneasy sleep, dreaming of being pursued by riders bent on hunting him down as a traitor, ropes and disemboweling knives in their hands, until with a fearful crash the hand of a rider smiting him down made him leap awake in terror.

John heard Alice beside him scream and, thinking her caught as well, grabbed at her. But the terrifying crash had been the long-awaited storm breaking directly overhead. Alice was shaking. Sitting bolt upright on their sleeping pallet, she'd let the coverlet fall from her naked breasts, slack for all her youth, as with each new thunderclap she crossed herself.

' 'Tis just a thunderstorm,' John said irritably, still shaken by his foolish dream.

The lightning had become continuous, the thunder hardly given time to diminish before the next rocked the house. He could hear rain pounding on the shutters and hissing on the thatch above their heads. Within a few minutes every tenement would be awash if the torrent kept up, the occupants putting tubs and buckets where the rain penetrated any weak spots in the thatched roofs.

John shuddered as he remembered what day it was. Sunday thunder – ever a presage of ill fortune, according to the old wives. Quickly he and Alice dressed, ready to put out tubs should they be needed, although Adam Melle's thatch was always kept in good order.

John could hear him cursing, sleeping awkward with his injured arm throbbing, and now disrupted from the light sleep he had managed to find. Ned was already rekindling the hearth to bring light and warmth against the sudden cold a storm brings. He too was moaning over his disturbed sleep as he ignited a rush light or two.

In one corner Cicely crouched in fear until scolded into action by her mother as the first drip of rain splashed on the earthen floor near the hearth beside which the old grandmother still lay snoring, oblivious to everything.

His father's voice was raised, bellowing that he would have the guts of the thatcher who hadn't made sure of his work. 'Good money I paid him,' he roared. 'Tomorrow I'll have him back to do a proper job, and not pay him one more penny for it.'

His tirade was interrupted by a frantic hammering on the door accompanied by a man's voice crying out. As John opened it, to be met by a vicious blast of wind-borne rain, Will Randere's brother Dick fell into the room, his narrow face streaked with rain and wet soot.

'God save us, John! We be struck!' He was waving towards his home that lay along the steep slope leading to Fobbing Creek. 'The house has fallen down!' he was yelling. 'My son ... trapped ... dead ... In Christ's name, help us!'

Dragging on hoods, John and Ned were out immediately, making towards Dick's ruined tenement. They found others already waiting there.

John Sharpe, the wheelwright, was straining on a heavy iron lever wedged under the bough of the great fallen elm that had been struck by a bolt of lightening and crashed into the house. Ralph Reede, the carpenter, was sawing at the huge bough that had Dick's young boy of thirteen trapped by his legs.

While Ralph worked, with someone on the other end of his double-handled, wide-toothed saw, others were madly clearing away parts of the collapsed wall and stiff bunches of thatching, splintered timbers, soaked wattle and slimy limed daub, their efforts impeded by the tangle of smaller branches and wet foliage and the unremitting downpour.

As the child lay inert, his eyes closed, his rain-soaked face ashen, John and Ned together pitted their considerable combined strength against the weight of the great tree. By luck it proved to be balanced in their favour and as others came to add their strength, slowly tipped just enough for them to start dragging the child clear, producing screams of pain and a cry of relief from his distraught mother.

'Oh, thank God! He is alive! My boy is alive! Please don't hurt him!' But there was no time to be gentle.

'Make haste,' John gasped, clenching his teeth as he strained his muscular arms against the tree's now dead weight as it stuck. 'Pull! For God's sake, pull!'

Any minute the huge elm would defeat them and fall back, in its altered position crushing the boy's chest. More men had joined them, together managing to hold the tree for a few more seconds while the limp body was dragged free, the boy having fallen unconscious and making the job easier. The tree then groaned and fell back with a tremendous *thrrump*, sending shivers through everyone.

The child being unconscious made Old Mother Harelip's task of manipulating broken bone and crushed flesh back into place that much easier.

'None but the good God Himself will ever make that leg straight again,' the old healer hissed when the child was carried to a nearby house. 'But with my skills 'twill mend fair enough.'

'He'll not suffer the loss of the leg then, Old Mother?' Dick asked.

'Nay, not with the herbs as I shall lay on it come the morrow.'

'Thank God, through Jesus Christ, our Lord,' whispered the boy's mother as she clasped her hands together.

'Thank God?' Her husband gazed through the tenement door towards his ruined home, wild flashes of lightning revealing its splintered walls and the toppled elm in one great tangle. The long rolls of thunder seemed to echo the sarcasm in his voice. 'Thank God? Do we thank Him for our broken home which must be built all afresh? And where do we find the means to rebuild it, pray?'

Parson Rackstrawe had arrived as the boy was being borne into the neighbour's house. He looked up from comforting the mother and her now conscious, whimpering son and went to lay a comforting arm across the shoulders of the embittered father.

'A house destroyed can be rebuilt,' he said gently. 'A life destroyed, never. Rather than blame Him for the damage to your house,

61

praise Him that your son's injuries will be no more than a crooked limb. Cheer yourself now. I will give you and your family food and shelter in my parsonage while your house is being rebuilt. You know full well that folk here will help in its rebuilding. You have no need to worry for anything.'

Moved as he was by his parson's generosity, Dick's bitterness lingered. 'If God be so merciful, why send a bolt of lightning to strike my home, injuring my son? I've ever been pious. I pray earnestly in holy church every Sunday. I do no ill towards any neighbour and look diligently to the welfare of my family. I do not beat my wife. Yet He punishes me...'

'Do not judge God,' Rackstrawe reprimanded, cutting through the man's outpourings of sorrow and blame. 'There was tempest ever before He created man, for He made the firmament first. The man who sets his house up beside a great elm must expect calamity if that elm be struck. So do not set yourself so high, Dick Randere, to presume God selected *you* from others to punish. Many as I can name would better reap His retribution yet go unscathed. In Isaiah it is written, "*woe unto them that decree unrighteous decrees ... to take away the right from the poor of my people, that widows be their prey, and that they may rob the fatherless.*"'

Amid the general distress of this night, Rackstrawe's quoting went largely unnoticed, but John suddenly saw the man in a new

62

light. It was the fierce way he'd said it, quoting from the Bible, yet it seemed to have been aimed specifically at their lords and masters. But before John could form any real opinion of the man, Old Mother Harelip gave a thin chuckle.

'Ay, Dick Randere, you'll be going to church to give thanks e'er the morrow comes, but don't forget, I be the one as sets them bones, so you give thanks to me as well, Master Fisherman, with a free and goodly helping of your next catch, eh?'

The crone's jest at least broke the tension. With the sky breaking and greying in readiness for dawn, one by one the wet, bedraggled helpers left after enquiring if there was anything more the family needed, somewhat relieved when they shook their heads.

'Three hours from now,' John said as he returned home with Ned, Tom and his father, 'our church will be packed with folk glad to have been spared Dick Randere's misfortune.'

'Mayhap his brother will be there too,' Tom remarked. 'Seldom do we see him in church, more occupied with tupping that young wife of his, despite her well into bearing his next child.'

John felt equally at fault. Apart from chatting to neighbours – church being a duty, but more a social event than a pious one – he found the mass utterly boring, having to listen to Latin gibberish that no one understood. Today though, he would go, if only to

63

study in a new light the man intoning it. Why had he quoted Isaiah with such vehemence? It was obvious that it hadn't been solely directed at Dick Randere, but held some deep bitterness.

For one so loved by his parishioners, no one knew much about him. He had never referred to his past life. He'd appeared one day in the village after old Father Giraldus died, looking more like an anchorite, a religious recluse, than a priest.

Thin as a pole, hollow-cheeked with deep-set eyes, he looked as though he hadn't had a good feed for years. But his tonsure was the smallest John had ever seen on a priest's head, as though at the slightest whim he would allow the hair to grow over the shaved patch. Nor did he always wear a priest's robe, but would sometimes be seen striding through the village in a stained gipon, a tunic such as country folk wore, with ragged hose and ankle boots similar to theirs. He'd often be seen practising archery at the butts as many a man did. Sometimes he'd be out on the marshes with Will Randere, bare legs clung with mud, helping him catch eels.

In church, in his priest's robes, his sermons were as forceful as any orator in high dudgeon. He could hold the attention of everyone, as he was entertaining and frequently politically provocative.

Today, as John returned home thinking of the venom contained in what the parson had said, he was more puzzled than ever by him.

'It does look a sorry sight by daylight,' Tom remarked, taking in the village as his and John's families walked to the church, along with practically the entire community.

John nodded, taking in the homes of their neighbours, some lining the street, others dotted about behind them. All had suffered in last night's storm one way or another. Everywhere bedraggled thatch hung down – almost to the ground on some. Storm ditches were overflowing and in the road, ruts had become so filled with water as to become elongated deep pools in which ducks paddled. Leafy branches, torn and splintered, were strewn all over and in the fields young seedlings lay waterlogged, sticky Essex clay soil pounded flat by the weight of the rain.

'It looks like extra fieldwork for many poor souls,' Tom said over his shoulder as he turned into the church, Marjory close behind him.

John, entering just behind him, merely grunted, already made ill at ease as Marjory turned her green eyes and slow smile on him, her gaze lingering too long for his peace of mind before she turned away to mount the two shallow steps into the building. He hoped his family, coming up behind him, hadn't noticed the flirtatious way she had looked at him. He was glad when she went off with some of the women to find an unoccupied bench along the walls.

Some folk were standing around, others

sitting on the floor with their backs to pillars. Chatter filled the nave as they waited for Parson Rackstrawe to enter, bringing them all to their feet. Tom had to raise his voice above the low rumble of men's voices, the laughter of women and the shrill crying of babies as John came to join him.

'This could bring us a poor harvest if replanting isn't done quick. Wait too long and that clay will set as hard as rock. Too soon and it'll be heavy slough and nothing will take hold in it.' Tom's expression was one of sympathy. 'There'll be little time given to them to replant their own tofts.'

'It'll mean a hungry winter,' said John.

'Especially if it follows as bad as our last one,' Tom added.

'A godforsaken winter that was,' agreed John, looking round the rapidly filling nave. 'Rain, day after day,' he went on. 'Corn mildewing in sacks. Apples rotting in barrels.'

'Yet still tithes and taxes are expected to be paid,' Tom said grimly. 'Even if folk starve and be thrown out of their homes for being unable to pay. That's why we were at Horndon yesterday. So don't anyone say that storm was retribution for our going there.'

'There's some as are saying that,' John said, beginning to ease his way towards the front of the nave to be nearer when Rackstrawe arrived. 'What good did we get out of it?' he added as Tom followed him.

'Perhaps peace of mind,' Tom answered. 'Perhaps determination to have the right to

66

feel at ease with ourselves this morning in this place.'

It was a beautiful church to be in, not poky as many were, but a place to make a heart fill with pride. The bright chancel had been built fifty years earlier. The little chapel, its painted carving of Our Lady with the infant Jesus on her lap, was bathed in soft colour from a small window of stained glass. The fine wall paintings fresh with colour were a never-ending source of interest during the service when the meaningless Latin began to pall.

The tower was old, the original nave even older, with a double splayed window that Tom had learnedly said was Saxon. It was now divided from a newer nave by a double arch, one with a stone head of a sweet-faced saint at its centre, the other with a stern, bearded king.

It was a comforting place to be in, yet today John could not feel at ease. The times, possibly, and the storm. But more unsettling was the presence of Tom's comely wife. Did she know that the way she looked at him was throwing him into confusion? He felt she did. But why do it? She didn't seem discontent with her husband, so why cast about for some diversion, if indeed that was what she was doing? Or was it just his own imagination, his sinful lust? For no matter how he tried to deny it, this squirming, curling sensation remained low inside his stomach, prompting his member to rise and harden as he tried to turn his mind from the vision of him and she lying together, her body...

'Why so glum?' Tom's voice startled him so that he gasped.

'Why should I be glum?' he countered tersely, almost angrily.

Tom gave a laugh. 'Come, you stand all silent and glowering. It weren't you had your house ruined and a child hurt. So what ails you?'

'Merely recalling the storm,' John lied. 'Displeasure of our deeds yesterday, thinking us equal to our lords who are by birth of good blood—'

Tom's loud laugh interrupted him. 'Are you bewitched or sommat?' Suddenly the humour fell from him. 'Think on it this way, John. If it were God's displeasure, upon how many was that storm visited? On our lords, too, remember, their fields equally ruined, they put to extra cost replanting 'em. Might that storm easily be a warning to them of their own guile?'

John hadn't thought of it that way, but was still unconvinced. 'It were us as suffered flood and ruin. Our privileged masters suffered not a stone of their fine houses loosened. Their tenants will toil to save their harvest and replant at no extra expense as I can see.'

'Think on it another way then,' Tom said congenially. 'I read that when the Conquerer came to England, a great plumed star were seen to cross the heavens and thought to be an evil sign, the Normans affrighted and begging the invasion be delayed. But Harold had also seen that long-tailed star. So who can say who that portent was for? Don't fret yourself, John. Them Normans were alarmed for nothing. And so are you. I will swear on that by all that's holy.'

Even over Parson Rackstrawe or John Ball, it was the practical words of his dearest friend that gave John the most comfort and he felt a profound depth of loving gratitude towards him as he turned his attention to the entrance of their parson.

Four

It turned out there had been informers at Saturday's meeting after all. Otherwise how could their bailiff have known of it?

He'd been absent that day at his master's castle at Pleshey handing in his quarterly accounts to Steward Somenour. He would surely have been unaware of his absconding field workers during those few hours, especially as the storm would have obliterated any of their work had they completed it. They'd felt fortunate in this at least. Yet he'd discovered their knavery for all that.

'Someone had to have been there,' Wat Gildeborn surmised as on Monday evening the bailiff came marching down the centre of the street towards Fobbing Church accompanied not only by Hugh Elyot, the constable of their hundred, but also another from Horndon.

Everyone knew what that meant and came out of their doors to follow reluctantly as he took up a position in front of the church. There was a fine open space there where the street forked. In front of the impressive flint and rubble-stone church tower that reared above the squat tenements with their rickety,

70

leather-hinged doors and their narrow, un-glazed windows with only wooden shutters to keep out the weather, he took up his stand, a fine stage for oratory. With legs splayed he stood, a squat and portly despotic figure, the constables on either side of him as folk gathered to hear what he had to say.

Rycard, who took his orders from the steward under whom their lord's demesne was managed, was regarded with dislike, apprehension and contempt. Dislike for his overbearing manner, that of a petty tyrant; apprehension because his appearance usually heralded an unpalatable task for someone or reprimand for some oversight or small mis-demeanour, and veiled contempt for his air of self-importance and wont to play lord of the manor.

Today he would have put a cock pheasant in the shade. A pleated, knee-length surcoat of green brocade, long-tailed, scalloped sleeves, cerise hose, and on his head a bright-blue capuchan twisted into a fashionable shape and fastened with a silver brooch.

'Prideful arse!' Adam Melle growled as he came to a halt in the village square. John grinned and made his way to where Tom stood with his father, glad to see no sign of Marjory. Most had left their womenfolk behind in the house, they having better things to do than listen to Master Rycard spouting.

Tom's hands were still covered with flour. 'Now what does he want, I wonder,' John said.

71

'I've a feeling we know already,' Tom replied ominously.

While Rycard surveyed the forty or so faces with an imperious eye, he held out a hand to receive a roll of parchment from Hugh Elyot without once taking his eyes off his audience, proceeding ceremoniously to unroll it. Finally he glanced down at it.

'Walter Gildeborn, Henry Sharpe, William Randere, Dick Randere,' he recited, rolling each name around his tongue like a sweetmeat, 'John Melle, Thomas Baker, Robert Bat, Richard Elys, John Rede, Ralph Peteman, Richard Wodelarke...' The list seemed never-ending, but by the time it was exhausted they all knew its purpose. 'These persons,' continued Rycard after a dramatic pause, 'to be at a manor court in the church nave on Tuesday before Pentecost, this fourth year of lord King Richard the second.'

'What for?' someone bellowed.

Rycard didn't look up. 'For attending an illegal meeting at Horndon on Saturday last to hear—'

'Who says it was illegal?' came a cry. Again it was ignored.

'To hear an heretic address by John Ball, a priest of Colchester, intending to incite ill will against government and our lord King Richard...'

'We did go out of idle interest.' Tom's clear voice rang out like a bell. 'What harm in that, Master Rycard?'

This time the bailiff had his attention fully

claimed. He glared at the heckler as Tom's father pulled his son back by the shoulder, hissing for him to guard his tongue.

'Harm enough,' Rycard returned. 'Harm enough to disturb the peaceful business of this manor, to the concern of your lord.'

'When was he last here to be concerned by anything we do?' called Tom. 'More likely he'll be feasting in the Welsh Marches or wasting treasury money on expeditions to France.'

'Have a care, young Baker,' Rycard warned, but Tom wasn't finished.

'He can't even be bothered to provide us with a proper tenant lord to protect us from grasping bailiffs and stewards.'

'I said have a care!' came a second warning. That, too, was ignored.

'When do we even set eyes on our present so-called tenant lord? Sir John Gildeborough be too busy enjoying himself in his own estates away from here to bother with us.'

'I speak on behalf of Sir Thomas of Wood-stock.'

'And make haste to inform him of us.'

'It is my duty to report to him all that occurs in his demesne.' Rycard again bent his head to his parchment and began to read out loud. 'Further, they did attend the aforesaid meeting without his consent or that of his officers.'

'Sounds like bailiff made that 'ere document up to suit hisself,' jeered Wat, head and shoulders above those around him. 'How

73

long did it take you to compose it then?'

Amid hoots of laughter, Rycard struggled manfully on. 'Thereby, I say, thereby forsaking their custumal duties upon the lord's demesne to the jeopardy of the hoeing and weeding of his crops.'

'What does it matter?' Tom challenged, shaking off his father's restraining hand. 'That there storm flattened all them seedlings whether or not they'd been tended, our work all wasted and our work all undone. And another thing, Bailiff, for us as pay quit-rent, we're free to go wherever we choose, so long as it's not to work outside our manor, and you know that full well, *Master Bailiff.*'

Ignoring his father's warnings, Tom had pushed to the front to say his piece, Rycard glowering at him from just a couple of feet away.

'I would advise you,' he said slowly, 'to heed your father, Thomas Baker. Manor custom will be observed.'

'Ay, manor custom, not splitting hairs over sommat that storm would have undone anyway. 'Tis already understood seedlings are to be replanted.'

'Rightly it is understood, young man. But attending a meeting – an *illegal* meeting ... None sought my permission.'

'Your permission? You weren't here for us to ask your permission.'

'Your reeve was here. He would have advised you against the folly of leaving manor duties unattended. Folly serious enough to

74

have disturbed Sir John Gildeborough from his own duties.'

'And who raced to inform him?' Tom turned to address those behind him. 'This stinks of someone seeking reward at our expense – as always.'

John began to feel worried. Their bailiff was beginning to seethe. He had no doubt expected some sort of discontentment, but now his integrity was being insulted and that he would not tolerate. He was glaring at Tom.

'Be careful, Tom Baker,' he warned. 'I could make things very hard for you – for any who fail to respect their superiors.'

Tom swung round at him. 'Superiors?' He gazed about as though seeking someone. 'What superiors, pray?'

He was being a fool. John shouldered his way through the gathering and grabbed his arm. 'Watch yourself, Tom. This is no Colchester Fair to be playing the jester at.'

Dick Elys had also pushed his way through. His thin chin was thrust forward on his scrawny neck as he regarded John. 'Nay, let him have his say.'

Tom's father shoved forward to catch hold of the skinny serf. 'You stick your advice up your arse, Dick Elys! My son don't need your help to make a bigger fool of himself than he already is.' Turning to the bailiff, he made an appeal. 'My son be maggot-brained, Master Rycard.'

Rycard was not to be propitiated. 'He'll be even more so when he pays a sturdy fine for

75

today's insult to an officer of the manor.'

'He do apologize,' entreated Hugh Baker.

'I do not!' yelled Tom. Again he addressed his neighbours. 'Our bailiff grows fat on fines he exacts from us. If truth be known, part of it goes into his own purse.'

Certain of this bit of truth, a few fists began to be shaken at Rycard, who responded by sweeping an imperious forefinger back and forth over the crowd.

'Any violence,' he blustered, 'and it will go ill for you all, with extra weekwork, and on top, a fine. Perhaps even a flogging for those inciting it.'

This stayed them a moment until John called out, 'What weekwork?'

Rycard recovered his composure. 'Your steward agrees that any work left undone on a manor until its tenant or servant feels fit to complete it should count as work not done at all.' He broke off as the gathering began to press forward, angry at this new outrage. 'Hold! I say hold! You cannot gainsay manor law.'

'That's not manor law,' Wat yelled at him. 'That's your law.'

'You can't enforce it,' yelled John amid a dozen supporting voices.

'I can, and will!' Rycard shouted back.

Tom almost had his face in his. 'You are a mean man, Simon Rycard. You're nowt better than us but you lick-spittle to your superiors for favour and to better yourself at our expense.' Ignoring the menacing staves of the

76

two constables, he went on, 'Storm damage will be put right, but that and no more. You cannot ask it.'

'Weekwork will be honoured!' cried Rycard, his round face bloated in rage.

'And whence comes the new seed?'

Rycard began imperiously to roll his parchment with an air of finality, avoiding Tom's eyes. 'That is not my concern.'

'It *is* your concern. Our manor lord will have to feed us if he does not provide the seed.'

'This is all by the by. Meanwhile, those named on this list will appear in court...' His words were drowned out by a roar of protest. Rycard's voice was a squeak as men began to advance. 'Constables! Hold them off!'

But despite their staves, both were overwhelmed, Rycard seized by the flowing sleeves of his houppelande to find himself being propelled away from the square towards one of the filthier ditches. Another step and he'd have been up to his knees in stinking night soil from piss pots emptied daily into the ditches, only a little diluted by last night's rain and the earlier storm. It was a yell from Parson John Rackstrawe that rescued him.

Rackstrawe had been out on the marshes with Will Randere and his eel traps. With a stipend of just eleven pounds a year, from which he had to keep his church in repair, pay for communal bread and wine and candles, as well as give traditional hospitality and alms to

77

those in need, even the lowly, staple eel came very acceptable. He'd been coming up the steep winding path from the wharf when he heard yelling. Breaking into a run, Will lolloping behind with his half-filled lidded willow baskets of squirming eels, he was in time to see the bailiff teetering, open-mouthed with horror, on the edge of the ditch opposite the church.

'What in the name of God is all this?' he thundered, bringing them to a halt. With Rycard still on dry land, everyone turned to stare at the tall, thin apparition with his clothes covered in mud and bits of seaweed, more like the manifestation of some sea god than the vicar of holy church.

He came storming towards them as Rycard was hastily pulled to safety and tried to regain his breath, his dignity and some of his bombast. Straightening his blue capuchan on his head, Rycard strode forward. 'I thank sweet Jesus you arrived in time to save me from these knaves.'

Whatever else he was trying to say was drowned in protest as villagers made for their parson with their own version of what had been going on. But Rackstrawe was not a man to take sides.

Tall and dour, he thrust aside their cries, regarding them as a stern father might. 'My parishioners manhandling an officer of the manor under the very walls of the holy church! Off to your homes to think on what you were about to do.'

'Father,' Rycard began, stepping forward, but he too was rounded upon.

'Master Rycard, your official duty here seems to be done. I bid you God's blessings.'

'But, Father...' The sharp grey eyes turned on him, stopping him mid-protest. The priest seemed to tower over his short, round stature.

'Is it not enough that these good people must be brought to court for their petty misdoings? Must you add to their woes? You set yourself too high, Master Rycard. I advise you to examine your own motives, for God sees all things and knows all hearts and His fearful judgment shall fall upon low and high alike. Think well on that, Simon Rycard.'

Even as the bailiff quailed, he made one last attempt to bluster before stomping off with his constables, a baleful glare focused upon the one who had prompted the villagers into action in the first place.

'Remember, Thomas Baker, I have marked you. It will go hard for those who stir others to violence.

But Tom was in high spirits. 'You stirred it, your lordship, not I.'

A mocking bow brought hoots of laughter and a few cat-calls. From that moment he became their champion, their acknowledged leader. But John felt a prickle of fear run through him over Tom's uncharacteristic lack of wisdom. He'd stuck his neck out too far today.

The sky might have been wrung bone dry

since that storm. Sun-baked, the previously soaked claggy earth was now set with a cap of iron against which hoe and spade rang in a bid to keep the soil open around tender shoots of wheat and rye. While once-elongated pools in rutted roads shrank, stagnated and dried, the sweat of those toiling in the fields all day poured off them like rivers.

Any fortunate enough to be able to pay quit-rent to avoid fieldwork began giving his neighbour a helping hand in his tiny croft between following his own trade, just to help keep that neighbour from starving come winter.

News had it that John Ball's call for unity against oppression was having its effect on every quarter; in Fobbing it was more united antagonism towards their bailiff, their eyes on Tom Baker to lead them in humbling the man in whatever way.

'Did you know,' Will Randere's young wife told another as they drew water from the village well by Iron Hatch, 'he refused my husband's brother a miserable bit of timber to mend his house the elm tree fell on. The timber he asked for has been stacked unwanted against one of the manor barns for years and will certainly rot away before long.'

Word of it coming to Rackstrawe's ears, he was seen making his way to the bailiff's home by the manor house. Soon afterwards, Dick Randere was allowed to take what timber he needed, for a small price. Cheaper than he'd have paid for better quality, it still emphasized their bailiff's meanness.

'If he be awkward over a bit of ole wood,' Walter Coupere remarked over a pot of ale, 'how's us going to prevail on him for leniency at manor court for going off to Horndon?' The leathery features wrinkled dolefully; he too had left the cutting of willow wands for manor fencing to hear the priest of Colchester.

'Do you expect leniency, then?' queried Dame Wodelarke as she served them more ale. 'You're all going to be announced as being in error, but then most of us are, one way or another, all the time.' Her fat cheeks squashed by the tight old-fashioned wimple she constantly wore, she beamed at her customers. 'I be paying fines at every court we hold, just for *selling ale*. Our manor lord do indeed make a good profit out o' me, by God! Lord bless us, 'tis us as keeps the manor going!'

Laughing raucously, she refilled the mugs to the very brim from a great leather jug held in one podgy hand – strong, for all her girth – her other hand held out for the money.

'In truth, a man can no more leave his work undone to go off on his own pursuits without permission than a lord can ignore the demands of *his* overlord to whom he must pay homage. In truth we all be in bondage in this world, high and low alike.'

Her wisdom didn't help. 'Bailiff will be making a fine profit from us,' Wat Gildeborn grumbled as she went to serve other

81

customers. 'I lay odds he'll be calculating how much he can keep back for hisself.'

'Not with Steward Somenour there,' Dick Elys reminded.

Wat gave a contemptuous laugh. 'Robbers, the lot of 'em.'

John had come to join them. 'The Hallmote will have to be conducted on manor customs, and not as our bailiff thinks fit.' He took a deep draught of his ale, cool and sweet after a day's work at the forge with his father's arm still not set enough for use. 'We elect the tithings to see fines are fair and square.'

He looked at old Walter Coupere. 'You're one of the chief pledges and so see things are fairly administered at manor court, and are liable to fines, same as us all. Our bailiff has to recognize view of frankpledge and that makes it less easy to rob us.'

Dick Elys gave a disparaging snort. 'Ay, for normal fines, entry fines and the like. But we did cry out against bailiff hisself and he ain't one to forget an insult. There'll be some hefty fines this time, and he'll make sure he gets a bit for hisself.' He swiveled a sly look toward Tom who all this time had been sitting saying nothing. 'There were some I'm thinking as spoke up a bit too hasty for our own good that day.'

'All this talk of Simon Rycard!' Tom burst out, the first time he'd spoken in ages. 'What I need is another ale.' He raised his voice. 'Mother Wodelarke, fill all our pots afresh, if you will.'

This brought smiles from around the stained wooden table, all accusations forgotten at having their pots filled at Tom Baker's expense.

Five

With the manor court only a week away, it seemed that even before they presented themselves, condemnation was being visited on the villagers from a far more powerful source.

'If the Almighty's judgment is upon the rich as well as us,' John said as the hot, dry weather following the storm continued, 'then it's a very strange one, they taking their ease in warmth and laziness while we sweat our guts out in this heat. And that's not all.'

Since the storm, ague had crept off the marshes, a dozen victims now laid low by fever. Dick Randere's injured lad's leg had become as puffed as a pig's bladder, and Old Mother Harelip had to be called in. Tom's father had developed an abscess on his neck the size of an oak apple, requiring the old crone to draw and cut it to release the evil yellow pus within. Children had broken out with the scaly itch on face and hands known as dry-scall. It had the look of leprosy though more a nuisance than harmful, usually linked to this time of early summer when last year's fruits were exhausted and this year's not yet ripe.

Mother Harelip was kept busy with her potions and salves. But for her, whose gape lip and impeded speech put terror into tiny children, things could have been a lot worse. But even she couldn't allay the general unease as the day of the manor court loomed.

Marjory Baker made a point of voicing her own uneasiness to John, stopping him in the street the evening before the court sitting. 'John, will you stand by Tom tomorrow?' she pleaded, slim fingers closing on his upper arm as though feeling his biceps below the coarse linen.

'Of course I will,' he said, wanting only to get away from her.

Her hold on his arm did not lessen. 'Our bailiff is looking to blame him for stirring others to violence.'

'You mustn't worry,' he said sharply, looking around in case anyone saw them.

Her touch was unsettling him, putting all sorts of thoughts into his head. He should have moved away but he couldn't. Her green eyes were wide and apprehensive, their gaze seeming to melt inside his. 'I fear for his wellbeing. Would you caution him against recklessness?'

Before he could answer, a sigh escaped those pink, pouting lips, like a woman being fulfilled by a man. He'd listened to Will Randere speaking of how that sounded – he wouldn't know himself, having not yet fulfilled Alice.

'I'll do what I can,' he said gruffly. He saw

85

her close her eyes.

'I am full of fear and in need of comfort, John. Comfort as Tom cannot give me for he would laugh at my fear. But I feel that you understand how full of anxiety I am, John.'

As she moved closer, he put a hand out to stop her. 'I shall watch out for him as you ask,' he said, easing her fingers from his arm as gently as he could and striding off.

Had anyone been watching the small drama, they standing so close to each other, she with her face raised to his? It was very likely. The very doors of gossips had eyes. They missed nothing.

He gave a brief backward glance. She was still there, a small, slim, lonely figure, a wraith in the quiet twilight, her brown kirtle merging with the drab colour of tenements and dusty street. It was as if their parting had left her lost and forlorn, a fact anyone watching could interpret just as they wished.

All evening he couldn't wipe the sight from his mind. Even as he lay beside his wife, having gone through a brief parody of copulation with her, dutiful rather than pleasurable, aware that his mother lay awake listening and hoping that her daughter-in-law would soon be with child, he thought of Marjory.

He'd tried to pretend that Alice was Marjory, but those slack breasts would never be like the firm, pouting mounts that strained at Marjory's bodice, giving but one thought, that a single tug of the lacing would make

86

them leap out at him like small wild creatures suddenly released. It was only that thought that stiffened him enough to enter Alice, who sighed in delight of her strong husband, no doubt counting herself fortunate to have such a one.

As Alice slept the sleep of the content, he ventured a hand to touch her belly, feeling suddenly sorry for her and dislike of himself. But feeling the slack, yielding flesh he quickly withdrew his hand. He could imagine Marjory's to be as firm as a fresh apple. Yet following on from the imagery came reality – Marjory was a rare beauty, but frail, narrow-hipped, not shaped for childbearing, and wasn't that what life was about, to beget children to see yourself secure in your old age?

Children took away loneliness when one partner passed away as must always happen. Passion was one thing, but companionship was what should be looked for. If Marjory thought to cuckold Tom, might she not one day do the same to him? Besides, any thought of cuckolding Tom made him cringe.

Odd that Marjory, who professed to be so in love with Tom, had not yet conceived after all these months, a young wife always eager to proclaim her good news to her neighbours. But neither had Alice any good news of her own yet, though in her case the fault was his, as he was seldom able to rouse himself with her and her passiveness in bed instilled him with no surging need. But once he fulfilled his role as he should, those wide hips of hers would quickly respond to his seed.

Feeling a sudden and deep sorrow for Tom and gratitude for his own wide-hipped, full-breasted wife, he vowed earnestly not to let his thoughts be impaled upon the forbidden beauty of Marjory Baker. Turning towards Alice, he laid a comforting arm about her slack-fleshed body, but Alice slept on, breathing steadily, each breath producing a slight snore, and finally he too slept.

The nave packed, Rycard and his steward came to the trestle table, the babble of conversation dying away in anticipation of the coming proceedings.

They began benignly enough with the usual common fines: neglect of a ditch needing to be cleaned out; a squabble with a neighbour causing disturbance to others; William Gildeborn, freeman, needing to purchase some more land giving oath of fealty to his lord with the appropriate relief fine. They passed without much notice, as more interest centred on Tom Baker, who would be their spokesman when the real business began.

Tom's father had been seen outside the porch arguing with his son, Tom shaking his head at his father's counselling, all drawing comfort from it.

'Him'll make bailiff look a right fool in no time at all,' chuckled old Crookback Rediere to John, having overheard the stand Tom was making. John hardly acknowledged him. The old man was addle-brained anyway and hardly able to tell sunrise from sunset. It was Tom who would be drawing his attention this morning.

'Take care how you address Simon Rycard,' John warned him as they came to stand with others in the body of the church.

He might have received a response from him but their bailiff was already rapping on the table for silence. Everyone was here: women, their children growing restive and having to be cuffed by their mothers, babies whimpering, having to be given the breast to hush them, though one refusing to be placated rent the air with its howls.

Simon Rycard's bloated face creased in distaste as the odour of seventy-odd villagers, unwashed from their labours and crammed into one building, greeted his nostrils. On the right of his table stood the tithing men, called here to present their erring neighbours as was manor custom. Today they looked shame-faced, reluctant to speak against their own friends, many of them among those who had insulted the bailiff.

He'd heard one mutter to another, 'It ain't right for us to stand up and declare against them as did nowt but seek just rights.' Well, he'd give them 'just rights'! Stand up they would or be fined for concealment in failing to present the transgressors.

The court began by dealing with the smaller matters: John Jollylock, ale-taster, for not performing his duties correctly – amerced two pence; that old idiot Rediere for letting his hovel down by the wharf fall into disrepair, it being his lord's property after all – two pence.

Rycard was growing weary of this petty stuff. He had a toothache, had suffered its nagging all week rather than submit to the briefer agony of having it being drawn by the smith. This interminable court wasn't helping, damnation on bad teeth and ignorant peasants!

His tongue worrying the rotting tooth, he surveyed the throng. Filthy, all of them, grime under their fingernails, mouths revealing blackened or missing teeth. Some were more presentable, like the baker and his son, the young man clean-limbed, clean of face and hands – and just as well considering he baked bread for the manor. Nearby was his ever-constant companion that even marriage hadn't managed to separate entirely. He was slightly shorter and, although the grime of a smith showed on him, John Melle still had a wholesome look to him, fair-haired, ruddy-faced.

Rycard delicately picked his tooth with a little finger, hastily removing the finger as the tooth responded with a stabbing pain. He smirked as he cast his eyes over the rest of them. Yes, they'd follow Tom Baker like sheep, seeing a leader in him. Even now their eyes were turning to him. They'd follow any man fool enough to stick his neck out at authority. There they were, ignorant, heavy-lipped, vacant-eyed, illiterate, envious, greedy, every-one out for himself – this was how he saw them, little better than animals, most of them.

He flicked a flea from a brocaded sleeve. These stinking rustics were running alive. His wife, Beatrice, spent many a night turning his clothing after he'd been in contact with these people, flicking the things into the fire, but these people let them run alive.

He was beginning to feel impatient. How much longer before they got to the real reason for this court today, to see Tom Baker squirm? The crowd were respectable enough now, each man bobbing his head, each woman dropping a curtsey. But behind the fawning he saw rebellion, envy of his position. If they but knew how he loathed being chained to this backwater, how he longed to become a steward of some large and busy manor. He was sick of facing the grumbles and sour looks of those of this tiny village at having to pay their ordinary fines.

But today a thread of confidence ran through their obsequious bows and curtsies. It was in the way Dame Wodelarke had spoken back at him where normally she'd have shrugged at the two-pence fine for sell-ing ale, which had become more payment for a concession than an amercement. When she'd also been amerced for selling it contrary to the assize, she'd let fly, her coarse voice raised.

'How so? I sell good ale at the regular price.

91

All here know I never give short measure.' He'd thumped the table to silence her but she refused to be.

'Master Jollylock should be in mercy, not I,' she'd screeched. 'Your ale-taster accuses me because I made him pay for his samplings. He looks for samples near enough to be a quart and hints of bringing me to court if I refuse to give it. So I charged him and now he brings me to court.'

'If he'd done his duty properly,' Rycard had told her, 'you might have looked more closely to the quality of your ale, allowing its strength to fall. Amerced three pence.'

He'd looked at the chief pledges, they hardly able to look at the woman, to ask who was next present, but before they could reply, her strident voice had rang out, 'Who else says my ale be weak?'

It ended up in a battle of wits. 'Sir, forbear,' she'd bawled. 'I sell good ale. All here be witness to that.'

Upon which he'd thundered, 'If you gainsay this court's decision once more, you'll be paying a far larger fine, so have a care.' He saw all eyes swivel towards Tom Baker, expecting him to spring to her defence, but he'd remained silent. Rycard couldn't help but smirk.

Without warning Simon Rycard then turned to the business of the assault on his person. Again all eyes turned to Tom. Now would be the time. None could say whether it was a good or bad thing that he conceded to his father's counsel to hold his tongue as each was fined sums ranging up to forty shillings. Had he raised his voice it could have been worse. But that was of little comfort. Outside, Tom reaped baleful looks, his brief standing as a leader over. Only their reeve, Nicholas Ocford, had a smile for him.

'I overheard steward advising bailiff against his plea for imprisonment – that a fine need suffice. "What if our manor lord comes a-visiting," I heard him say. "Who'll tell him the only baker skilled in making such delicious pies and pasties as ever I've tasted in all my years at Pleshey Castle has been sent to prison and his lordship must be content with second best. Young Baker's father cannot touch his son's skill. I'd not wish to be the one to tell him," I heard him say to bailiff, and he look askance at him and said, "Unless you'd care for the privilege of telling him." And what could bailiff say to that?'

The reeve chuckled and gave Tom a taunting poke with a forefinger. 'You be fortunate, young Baker, to be that cunning as to know yourself worth your salt. And sly enough at keeping a still tongue in your head.'

Tom didn't answer. 'I wasn't thinking of my position,' he said to John later as they made their way down the steep path to the alehouse for a much needed drink. 'I thought only that speaking out would cause more uproar to the jeopardy of us all. Simon Rycard has enjoyed enough revenge for one day.'

A bend in the path brought the mudflats into view, the creek full at high tide. Small barges were being loaded with wool and ewe's milk cheeses. Overlooking it, the alehouse sat rickety but enticing to throats parched by the stress of the size of fines exacted today.

'Forty shillings!' Tom muttered as they entered and sat at a table already occupied by some of their friends. 'Where do I find such a sum?'

'Where will any of us find it?' John said, steeling himself to face his father's wrath when he finally went home.

'Better to have been sent to prison,' Tom said caustically as Dame Wodelarke came to serve him. 'My father would be short-handed but there'd have been one less poll tax for our family to pay.'

The alehouse was nearly full with men, today mostly silent with their own thoughts, none of the jolly uproar that usually filled the room.

'Thirteen shillings and fourpence,' grumbled Dick Elys. Sucking his rabbit teeth in frustration he regarded Tom across the table. 'Four marks, and all I did were touch his accursed sleeve!'

'You did more than mere touch it,' John said in Tom's defence when Tom refused to be drawn.

'And I did but shake a fist,' added Ralph White, the thatcher's son.

'Right under his nose,' John reminded.

Ralph ignored the remark. He glared at

Tom, their fallen leader. 'We trusted you to stand up for us. Seems we were mistaken.'

Tom refused to be provoked as he quietly put down a coin for the pot of ale that a tight-lipped Dame Wodelarke thumped down in front of him. It was John who rose to the bait.

'I didn't see any of you declaring the fines to be unfair. Nay, like the cowards you all are, you were waiting for someone else to say it for you.'

'Nor did we see you ready to stand up, John Melle,' Ralph shot back at him.

'Maybe not, but I'm not blaming someone else for my own lack of courage. You put him up as your leader. You didn't ask, you just assumed. As for me, I shall pay my fine as best I can, and not lay blame at another's door.'

He received a sneer. 'No doubt smiths and bakers have no trouble finding a few marks that for other men be a prince's ransom. Them as have no scruples at turning a few pennies to their advantage.'

John leapt up from the rickety table, almost upsetting everyone's ale. 'You accuse my father of cheating his neighbours?'

Ralph quelled before the broad chest and thick arms. 'I didn't say that, John.'

'Say it then, say my father be dishonest!'

Tom put a hand on John's arm. 'Nay, sit down, John. We're all in bad humour today.'

Breathing heavily, he sat as Dame Wodelarke came waddling over to see what the ruckus was about. Tom waved her away with a disarming smile while Ralph White gazed sullenly into his half-empty ale pot. But he was not ready to give up so easily.

'And who made us ill-humoured today? With respect,' he eyed the young smith warily, 'we did look to Tom Baker today as spokesman. Maybe we were wrong, not asking aforehand. But we were goaded in violence last Monday by Tom's own words and are now all fined for it.'

'We shouldn't have baited our bailiff,' put in Dick Elys sadly.

'No one asked you to,' John shot at him. 'Don't blame Tom here for his wisdom in silence when none of you sprang to his aid.'

His words brought another sneer from Ralph White.

'I might have guessed you'd defend your close friend. Too close, I've heard say, you and he.'

John kept his eyes down, gazing into his ale. 'Ay, I can see how loyal you all are!' he said bitterly but at Tom's warning cough, fell quiet.

Trudging back uphill with several others, Dick Elys lifted his salient features to the arid sky and heaved a great sigh.

'Seen a black ole ram tupping a ewe yesterday. Could mean a few hot and dry months ahead of us.'

Ralph turned to give him an enquiring glance, having slowly recovered his composure. 'Never heard of that sign afore.'

'Nor I,' laughed Elys. 'But if it were a sign o' dry weather, it could be proper welcome, I'd say.'

'Fool's arse,' Ralph burst out. 'What good will dry weather do for our empty bellies next winter?'

'Nowt as I know of,' Elys replied blithely. 'But I was thinking what a wondrous providential thing it would be if all became so dry that manor house were catched alight by all this heat and all records of fines and the like blaze along with it. A proper welcoming sight that would make.'

Suddenly everyone was gazing at him, seeing his round blue eyes grow serious. The rabbit-toothed grin took on a significant twist. In that moment minds began to visualize some less natural cause for parchments to go up in flames and all their names along with them.

Although his supposition reaped no verbal suggestion to assist divine providence as they parted company to go off to their individual tasks, a seed of speculation had been planted in everyone's mind.

Six

'Little use looking at me to pay your fine!' His splinted arm held close to his body, Adam Melle stomped off across the yard to the house.

From the smithy, Ned watched him go. 'He do not mean it, John,' he said. 'He'll give in rather than see you suffer. I'm with you, if he ain't.'

Dragging off his leather apron, John gave his young brother a rueful grin. 'He's with us, Ned. Only more cautious, being old.'

Ned gave a morose shrug. 'It matters little now the Colchester priest has been excommunicated, thrown into gaol by the Archbishop of Canterbury. So much for leading us to seek the King.'

John made no reply. While Ned damped down the dying fire for the evening, he sought the cooler air of the open forge front, leaning on the rail where horses and oxen would be hitched to be shod and bargaining done. From here he had a good view of much of the village. Tom's house was a little further along the road with the mill set back some way behind it. A little further on, the bailiff's house and the manor house were just beyond the bend in the road and obscured by its orchards.

On either side of the smithy were the wheelwright's workshop and the carpenter's. Opposite, but some way down from him, stood the church and the priest's house. After that, the road sloped down to the wharf and the marshes. Beyond them the Thames could just be discerned, reflecting a deep-red sunset – another fine, dry day tomorrow. He recalled Dick Elys's words and smiled to himself.

In the fading, fiery light, folk were making their way home from the manor fields. Their short, double-handed hoes on their shoulders, they trudged in twos and threes, weary feet stirring the dust. From the carpenter's shop came the sound of hammering and Henry Sharpe's fine voice raised in intermittent song, the man still engrossed in his work despite it being dusk.

Will Randere and his brother were taking some of their catch up to the manor house, no doubt for the steward and bailiff to take full advantage of in their lord's absence. As Will came abreast of John he hailed him. 'Saw Wat Gildeborn out on the marsh with his sheep. Asked if I'd be at Dame Wodelarke's later on. Said it were special I be there, and you too, and a few others, and Tom too. Someone there as you might care to meet.'

He gave a meaningful look as he trudged on past, leaving John frowning. No name mentioned, just that knowing look. He gazed towards a group of children playing a noisy

99

game of hot cockles – one boy blindfolded by having his hood reversed across his face, his hands out behind him while each slapped them aggressively, he having to guess who did the slapping.

Agnes Lyghtfoot had come down the street to shake her fists at them. 'My man be sick in his bed,' she yelled, 'and is not better for your blessed shouting.'

Nothing as John could see was dire or sinister about this evening, so why Will's odd behaviour as he'd passed him?

He saw Parson Rackstrawe come to stand outside his house. He was brushing dirt from his hands after working in his glebe. John saw him look up at the fine blush in the west as though judging what weather tomorrow would bring, probably thinking that a little rain wouldn't come amiss for his cabbages and onions. He glanced John's way and threw him a brief wave before going back into his house.

Tomorrow was Sunday. Folk would go noisily to church, the one diversion in their humdrum lives. What did they pray for? Rain – gentle rain for the beans and onions in their tofts; that next winter might not be as wet as the last one had been when hayricks lay so sodden they had rotted, giving no fodder to feed their remaining thin-shanked beasts; for improvement to their lot; for a more lenient manor court, a more clement lord? Pray the tax commissioners at this moment traversing the country checking on those suspected of falsifying their tax returns, hopefully might leave Fobbing out of their prying?

John's lips curled. As much for himself as others, pray God help us rather than us having to summon the courage to seek our own salvation.

The priest of Colchester had had them all believing they had found a saviour, a leader; that with him at their head they'd soon be pounding on the gates of London demanding to see their fair young King Richard who would listen to their grievances and put all aright.

And if he couldn't, or wouldn't, then John Ball with all his followers would topple those authors of this latest Poll Tax, Archbishop Sudbury and Treasurer Hales and all their crew. Then the commons would be masters over their grasping lords and call the tune.

But it hadn't happened. John Ball was in prison. Now, without a leader, it was all coming to nothing. A sharp female voice brought him back to the present. He turned to see his sister standing inside the smithy, hands on hips in remonstrance.

'Father says to come in to supper. He tells me to say he has waited long enough for you and Ned to come in.'

Cicely would not see her fifteenth summer for another month yet but was already a woman, the bodice her mother had sewn for her earlier this year pulling across firm young breasts.

The narrowing waist and the broadening of

her hips that she'd waggle, testing her new womanhood, had every lad ogling her. Her long fair hair hanging free the length of her body, as with all unwed girls, was held in place by a plaited linen chaplet into which she had woven a few wild flowers. Full of self-confidence, her pert young face lifted tauntingly at him. 'I have a mind to tell Father that I caught you idling while Ned does the work.'

John's lips tightened. 'Tend your own business!' he retorted.

'I am tending it,' she laughed and, turning on her heel, ran back to the house, leaving them to finish off and wash their hands in the water butt before following the appetizing aroma of stewed salt pork, cabbage and onions wafting towards them. John's mouth was already watering.

Near the house Swain the dog leapt on his chain, whining in anticipation of scraps soon to be thrown to him. John bent and briefly patted his head on the way in. 'In a while, old man.'

With the aroma of food mixed with the fatty odour of lighted rushes dipped in mutton fat to make them burn long and well, John took his place at the trestle table, bowing his head in a brief thanks to God for the bounty.

'You left all tidy?' growled Adam.

John looked up from his trencher of stale bread on to which Alice was ladling succulent gobbets of pork. The trencher he'd eat afterwards, soaked with meat and vegetable juices.

'Have me and Ned not yet proved ourselves capable enough these two weeks since your mishap?'

Adam frowned. 'It'll take more'n two weeks to prove yourselves fine enough to match a practised smith as is more'n twice your age, so keep them high opinions of yourself to yourself till you can be.'

John glanced red-faced at Alice, feeling put down in front of her, but she kept her eyes lowered as she poured ale into wooden mugs for them all whilst Cicely placed bowls of whey for the two younger children. It angered him that his father constantly belittled him in front of Alice. It was as though he looked for ways to make him appear of no consequence in her eyes.

His appetite waning, he chewed morosely on a piece of barley bread from the woven osier basket Alice had put in the centre of the table. She showed great skill at bread-making, young as she was, her bread seeming to stay fresh and moist much longer than his mother's. But his mother showed no jealousy – in fact encouraged her in all things. Of course, as the new daughter-in-law she was a boon to the older woman, now able to sit back a little from her life of labour and give more attention to the old grandmother, his father's mother, which was as it should be.

He looked up and saw Alice smile uncertainly at him, seeing that he wasn't enjoying his meal, and to please her he fell to eating again. Good food should not be wasted, although his father was a man of substance as this table bore witness to.

As smith to this manor, Adam Melle had free use of charcoal from its woodlands, its plough for his own holding. All depended on him for their tools – the thatcher, the wheel-wright, the carpenter, the manor lord himself. Despite Ralph White's remark that a smith might well exploit the needs of others, Adam Melle had never cheated anyone, many a time waving aside payment from an impoverished widow whose holed pan or broken pot hook needed mending. It was by honest work and fair dealings that he put food on his table. If only he could find it in himself to deal more fairly with his eldest son...

'You're not eating, John,' his mother's voice cut through his reverie. 'Alice prepared this herself. Do it not please you?'

It was an accusation. John forced a smile. 'It do please me, and very much.' Seeing the anxiety on Alice's face, he added for her benefit, 'I was deep in thought, nothing more.'

Adam belched loudly. 'Time you ceased being deep in thought and put your mind to getting your wife with child. Seems her monthly cycle be upon her again. My advice, put a stop to it by putting a babe inside her.'

'Hush, Husband!' Agnes hissed as Alice's cheeks began to turn deep crimson in embar-rassment. 'It is their business.' She broke off to slap Cicely's arm, the sharp sting stopping the girl's giggle. 'That's for your foolishness!'

All her children had felt her hard hand at one time or another and she hadn't mellowed with age. Wiry, stoop-shouldered, her hair grey, hidden by the loose linen hood she always wore, she still commanded obedience and respect from them all, including her husband. She turned to him now, her face hard.

'And let there be an end to your coarse tongue at this table. Leave your son alone if he wishes to be with his thoughts awhile.'

'Little time for thoughts,' Ned muttered, digging into his supper. 'What with bailiff worrying us to do them coulters and the plough not needed for many months yet. We sorely miss your strong arm, Father.'

'Which reminds me,' Agnes said, 'Mother Harelip did press me with some new salve to hasten that arm's healing.'

'I'll suffer no more concoction from that witch,' Adam growled. 'She with her brews and balms.'

'She healed Dick Wheler's broke leg last spring. Broke that leg so bad he thought to go hippety-hop the rest of his life.'

Adam took a draught of his ale. 'He went hippety-hop afore that.'

'It could have worsened. He walks well enough now for one his age. And after taking her brews, Tom Gower's cough were cured.'

'It were Dame Wodelarke's brew as cured that.'

'Be that as it may,' she stated firmly as she

got up to ladle broth from the pot hanging over the hearth into a bowl for the old grandmother huddled on a stool by the fire, even though it was a hot and close evening, fixing a spoon between the clawed hands. 'I shall rub the balm on your arm for you.'

'Let Alice do it,' he said testily. 'Your hands were ever too rough.'

'And what makes them so?' she challenged, returning to the table.

'May I have a sip of your ale, Father?' asked Agnes's youngest boy, Adam, just seven years old, while his five-year-old sister took up the cry, but their mother silenced them both with a single look.

These were probably the last of her brood. She was nearing the end of her childbearing days – perhaps thankfully so, for these last few years had seen the fruits of her womb stillborn, all her goodness used up, preventing any more strong children. Of her fourteen only five had survived; God had seen fit to take back the rest for one reason or another. But John could see in the way she looked at Alice, she was hoping there could be a grandchild for her to croon over before long.

'I heard Master Gildeborn found one of his ewes lying dead over on Hawkesbury land,' Ned was saying through a mouthful of bread. 'Just its head and feet left. Even its fleece gone. Seems the animal as ate it, ate the fleece as well.'

'A two-legged beast!' His father gave another loud belch, his stomach full. 'Dis-

106

charged soldiery, most like. Many wander the byways nowadays with no means of livelihood. That's what them cursed wars wi' France has done for us – given us a new breed of vagabond.'

Agnes went to get the pot of Mother Harelip's ointment from a niche by the hearth while Alice and Cicely began clearing away. 'I wonder Master Gildeborn didn't raise hue and cry on finding the carcass.'

'What point?' Adam sneered. 'It had been dined off and the feasters well gone, time he found it.'

Bored by the conversation, John got up from the table. He was itching to know the reason for Will Randere's message and that meaningful look.

'I'm of a mind to stroll down to Dame Wodelarke's,' he said as casually as he could. His reward was an exclamation of disgust from his father.

'A fine brave lot as gather down there these days. Go then, fill your belly wi' poor ale and your head with idle boasts of fools rather than staying here and fill your woman's belly with a child. I swear this barrenness of hers is no wit her fault. Seems you've more liking for that Tom Baker than for a decent woman.'

At the door John turned on him, his eyes blazing. 'Say no more on that, Father! You've humbled me enough tonight in front of my wife. And to allude to my friendships in that manner...' He broke off for a second, almost beside himself with sudden rage. ''Twas you as saw nowt but ill in it, and you as pushed me into marriage. I never wanted it, not so soon. But you let your hand be guided by the tongues of worthless old women and wed me with such haste to a—'

This time he broke off, seeing bleak dismay in Alice's face and his anger fell from him like a limb snapped from a tree. 'Forgive me, Alice,' he whispered inadequately, 'I did not mean to ... I wouldn't hurt you...'

He was only making matters worse. Tears had filled her eyes. They slipped slowly over the rims to slide down her full cheeks. Not one sound did she utter and it was the very silence of her misery that tugged at his heart, leaving him wishing he had torn out his tongue before uttering such cruel, thoughtless words. Yet the presence of his family looking on would not let him stride to her and hold her to him and beg her forgiveness.

Instead he turned and fled into the night, lashing out at Swain, catching him on the muzzle as the animal leapt eagerly on the end of his chain to greet his young master. A little later he'd be sorry to have taken out his wrath on a dumb animal wanting only a pat on the head, but at this moment remorse was for that which was beyond rectification.

The vespers bell had long since tolled. Those answering its summons had now returned to their homes to close their doors and shutter their windows against the night. Shafts of fire glow and rush light pierced chinks in the doors and shutters to give

108

enough light for those still abroad to see their way.

Parson Rackstrawe was standing outside his church door as John approached, taking in the still air before retiring to his house. Tall and monolithic in the strange light, his iron-grey hair cut square across a flat forehead, his cheeks grooved on either side of a thin prominent nose and thin colourless lips, he might have been carved from stone.

Seeing John, the statue came to life and beckoned to him with a long, authoritative forefinger. 'A word with you, John Melle.'

John hesitated. 'I'm going down to Dame Wodelarke's to meet...' He broke off, remembering Will Randere's sly look.

'A word on your neglect of late of holy church,' the other went on.

John frowned. He did not go to vespers, and true, he had sometimes missed Sunday mass, but there was no call to be upbraided here in the street. The clear voice, accustomed to being heard above the chatter of an inattentive congregation, now echoed down that street for any who wished to hear and smirk. John moved towards him, sullen and angry. First from his father, now from the priest. He was a married man, so why was he being made to feel like a chastised boy?

The cold grey stare was slightly above his morose one. 'I grieve to see you making haste so often to be away to the alehouse after mass, John Melle.'

It was grossly unfair. He was as attentive as

109

any and had made his last confession only two weeks back, not that long ago. He began to protest but was cut short.

'I grieve, too, that your contemplation this eve was not directed to attending vespers but to sampling Dame Wodelarke's brew.'

John maintained tight-lipped silence. Even for a priest Rackstrawe was going too far. The grey figure leaned towards him. His voice fell to a whisper as if to impart the threat of Hell's fire upon this wayward soul.

'Then pray God your companions there are guarding their tongues. I have but a moment ago marked a man making towards the ale-house – a wayfarer by his dress. But I have seen him before and not in these parts. I think him to be other than he seems. It could be he is one of Simon Rycard's hirelings, but I think he may be something more.'

'I don't understand,' John said, but the parson cut in.

'Your friend Tom Baker is there even now, and we know our bailiff would see him close fettered as our John Ball now is, in Maidstone Castle. Though, pray God, we'll see the good priest released soon enough by his loyal followers.'

It was hard to believe what he was hearing. Was this the same man who a moment ago had been upbraiding him for his spiritual laxity?

'You stand for John Ball?' he cried out.

'Hush!' Rackstrawe looked hastily about. 'You'll hear from those you are meeting tonight of certain plans regarding that release. But now you must hurry and warn them of an eavesdropper.'

He moved back and his clear voice rang out again. 'I shall overlook your persistent absence and expect to see you among those at mass on the morrow.'

With that he turned sharply to stride off along the diagonal path towards his house.

Seven

John sped down the steep wharf path to where the alehouse overlooked the creek, a few deserted fishing boats lying askew on the mud awaiting the next tide.

Their dark shapes seemed all the more silent for the laughter and merry chatter emanating from the flimsy structure, all the more remote for the cheery light pouring through its open doorway and unshuttered windows. The whole place appeared innocuous and jolly as always. Rackstrawe must have been mistaken.

Ducking under the low lintel, he stood gazing about the single long room. A narrow gallery ran along the furthest wall where sweet herbs hung from the rafters and sacks of barley lay waiting for mashing. The narrow guardrail made a fine roosting place for Agatha Wodelarke's several chickens who found the grain easy pickings, and their droppings had been known to land in the open casks immediately below where she continuously dipped her great leather serving jug.

Even so, her ale was thick and strong and moreish and, as she'd pointed out more than once, who could find fault with its flavour –

112

and what did any chicken of hers eat but good, wholesome barley? The stranger who came to sample usually stayed to drink, even bailiff himself, and the ale-taster certainly took himself more than a small sample, and none had died from it yet, so what harm?

At the centre of the room the hot embers in the great hearth had been allowed to die down on this warm evening and served now merely to give a more ruddy glow to drink by. Men sat about on upturned tubs with larger tubs for tables, their shadows cast along the ruby-tinted plastered wattle and daub walls.

From the semi-gloom of one far corner a voice hailed him above the general chatter. 'Ho there, John! Over here, lad!'

He recognized Will Randere's voice and made towards the group. Tom was there, so was Wat Gildeborn and his brother William, and a lean, heavily bearded man he'd never met before, a man in his forties, perhaps.

'This is Master Tripat,' Wat announced as John came to sit with them. 'Lately a long-bowman of Lord Thomas of Woodstock's army, but once of this village some twenty years ago.'

'No longer a soldier then?' John queried sociably as their hostess came to pour ale for him and he dropped his penny into the fat palm.

In answer to his question, the man held up a hand that would have held the arrow steady on the string. Both forefinger and index finger were missing at the second joints.

'A Frenchman's halberd,' he chuckled. 'Went down wi' a French arrow in me chest – lived to tell the tale, but these chopped as neat as a trotter off a pig afore the Frenchman himself went down to one of our own arrows. I were one of them as was not as lucky as them that could hold up his two fingers to the Frenchmen!' The throaty voice held a Kentish accent.

'Not much fighting the French now,' John observed, drinking deep.

'Not since our Earl of Buckingham's fruitless expedition there wasted even more of our Treasury's coffers. That's what you're paying for, wasted ventures such as what cost me my two fingers and livelihood as a soldier, poor as it was. Three months' pay I'm owed but will never see a penny of it. Yet it's the likes of us as must pay for such follies as our King's uncles see fit to indulge in.'

'Which brings us to the point of this meeting,' Will broke in, a little too stridently for John's peace of mind after the way the man had looked at him this afternoon. 'Master Tripat comes hotfoot from Kent and brings us news of—'

'I was going to bring my brother Ned tonight,' John interrupted loudly. 'He did ask to come, but my father would have none of it. Lad's too young, he says.' He gave a great laugh, aware of the bewildered and irritated looks he'd provoked from the group. 'But what I say is it's never too early for a lad to enjoy the taste of good ale.'

Whilst they'd been talking he'd taken a moment to glance around at the customers. He recognized all by sight with the exception of two – one a wayfarer in a travel-stained cloak and hood, possibly a tinker needing shelter for the night though usually tinkers slept under the stars. He looked harmless enough as he sat chatting with two locals, quite openly, before retiring to the barn next to the alehouse to sleep.

The other stranger sat alone near the door, not far from John's group. A peasant, he appeared ordinary enough, yet there was a doubtful look to the well-worn clothing, as though it had never been on his back until this day. It looked wrong somehow. After years of wear a man's clothes become like a second skin, each crease, each irregularity of his body, the way he carries himself, causing those who know him to identify them with the man himself even if he is not wearing them. This man's clothing did not belong to him.

Will retorted angrily, 'What's up with you, John?' But John laughed even louder, slapping Will on the back as though he'd cracked a joke. Then like Parson Rackstrawe had done earlier, he leaned close, bringing his voice down to a whisper.

'Keep your eyes down. Our parson alerted me on my way here of one of bailiff's spies possibly being here. It seems, too, our parson be sympathetic to John Ball's cause. The stranger sits just behind us by the door. Now, all laugh out loud as if I've just imparted some great joke.'

Tom was the first to recover, bursting out laughing and rolling back on his tub, the easier to catch a glimpse of this apparent eavesdropper, his glance moving on as if he hadn't seen the man at all.

'Afore God, that were a good'un!' he roared as the others, catching on, also burst out laughing. 'Who's got another?'

'I've one,' cried Tripat and bent forward, the others doing likewise. 'Where is he?' he hissed.

'By the door, alone,' John said.

Tripat turned his head slightly. 'I see him. Now listen, this must be done quickly. In Kent this day I spoke with one Abel Ker of Erith. He and a small band are recruiting sympathizers of the Colchester priest. Like you here, the Kentish folk are heartsick of being bled dry by taxes and say enough is enough. But they cannot rise alone. They need the support of Essex, Suffolk and Norfolk if they are to succeed in putting an end to the oppression of those who cannot be bled one drop more.' With this he leaned back with a burst of laughter. 'A good one, eh?'

On cue they burst into loud guffaws, bringing their hostess waddling over, her fat face squashed by its old-fashioned wimple, full of eagerness.

'That sounded a merry old joke,' she wheezed, a veritable store of jokes herself, most of them coarse, which suited her

116

customers down to the ground. 'I've a saucy one to tell while I pour ye all another good measure.'

John looked up, wondering how to be rid of her as quick as possible. 'We'll have your ale, Mother, but our jokes be too coarse for such delicate ears as yours.'

'Gar! I hear far worse in this place. Have you heard the one about the rooster as hadn't got a—'

John stared into his pot as she began to fill it. 'To the top now,' he ordered rudely. 'Don't stint it, good mother.'

She paused on the very brink of her story to glare down at him. 'Stint it? *Stint it?* Why, I couldn't get another drop in that 'ere pot. What d'ye mean, stint it?'

John forced an insolent chuckle. 'I've seen it overflow other times.'

She looked as though she were about to pour the jug over his head. 'I've never stinted anyone. By my arse, it be our blasted manor court as put doubt into everyone's minds. When have I ever given short measure?'

'Never, Mother, never,' Tom butted in, touched by her distress. 'John here was jesting.'

'Then tell him to keep his pissed jests to himself,' she retorted as the pennies were dropped into her palm, leaving her to waddle off indignantly, calling over her shoulder, 'That be the last joke I share with any of you.'

Left to their business, Wat Gildeborn leaned close. 'There'll be a knife in our friend's guts

117

come dawn,' he hissed malevolently.

'Nay,' Will whispered. 'What has he to report? We waste time, Master Tripat. What plans are being made over the river?'

'Ker and his men are to cross the Thames to raise an army from Barking district,' Tripat said. 'With them they will return to march through all the townships from Dartford to Rochester, swelling their numbers on the way. Those unwilling to join will be intimidated until they are. Then we make for Canterbury to release our priest, John Ball, who'll lead us to London in a great company. Like myself, Ker was a soldier in France, and knows what he's about. But all this must be timed right. Those on this side must rise at the exact time as those in Kent, otherwise...' He broke off. 'Laugh! For God's sake, laugh!'

The stranger was almost on top of them, dawdling, apparently intent on his empty mug. As they burst out laughing he called out, 'Good Brewster, another draught of your excellent brew if you will.'

This action confirmed their earlier suspicion. None need leave his seat to be served. Thumping the table with the empty pot was sufficient to bring the ever-attentive hostess hurrying with jug slopping in her haste to collect another penny. It had to be a ruse to catch what they'd been saying. But little good it did him as Dame Wodelarke was on him immediately, her jug at the ready.

'I've not seen you here afore,' she said sociably as she poured. 'Where be you from,

118

then?'

It was good to see the man caught on the wrong foot. He ran a tongue across his lips. 'I am ... seeking a nephew of mine hereabouts,' he faltered.

'Oh, I might know him, sir,' she said readily. 'Few as I don't know around here. What be his name?'

He was busy fishing in his purse for money for his refill. 'I doubt you know him. He abides Corringham way. I paused here to wet my throat.'

The woman regarded him with some surprise. 'It be a mite late for to go on to Corringham now. Road ain't safe for travellers at night. But I have a warm barn and yonder peddlar'll be good company for 'ee.'

'It is of little consequence,' returned the man, his speech unlike that of any peasant John had heard, being moderately refined. 'I have a horse and it is but a mile or so to Corringham. Thank you for your draught.'

John slyly eyed the man as he went back to his seat. How come a ragged peasant, speaking as well as any lord, be riding a horse about the countryside after sunset? And intimating himself to be a stranger, how come he knew how far Corringham was from Fobbing?

He sat now with his back half turned from John and his companions, staring through the door on to the dark world outside as though mesmerized.

'Do you think he heard any of what we were

119

a-saying?' queried Will.

'If he did, he won't get far with it,' Wat vowed menacingly.

'He looks a-feared of us somewhat,' said Will.

'He have a right to be a-feared,' Wat said. 'Come morning he might not have his life to be a-feared about.'

John felt his stomach crawl at talk of killing. 'Bailiff will be alerted for sure,' he said, 'if his man comes not back to him with some report.'

'Rather than be alerted by the spy hisself,' Gildeborn said. 'Keep an eye on him lest he slips away. Meantime, we'll hear more of what Master Tripat has to tell us. And no more pretend merrymaking. Time is short.'

Obligingly, Tripat leaned forward. 'Five days from now a certain Thomas Bampton, a commissioner, comes to Brentwood to make enquiry into the collection of poll tax in the Hundred of Barstable, of which this village is part. And you know full well that he has already collected what you consider is due and should be acquitted of it, for all 'tis held by the commissioners to be a fraudulent return.' He leaned even closer. 'Therefore, you have the right to present yourselves to make protest against this unwarranted inquiry.' He seemed to know their rights almost as well as a commissioner might.

'Raise the folk of neighbouring villages,' he went on, 'to add to your protests, so making such a mighty tumult as to bring even more to our cause. Then in all haste return from Brentwood to light a beacon here on the hill of Fobbing, by which Kent will know Essex has risen. Messengers will be sent all over the county to alert folk from every corner. I leave it to you to elect leaders.'

They looked at each other in common query. How would they choose leaders? It was Will who voiced the obvious.

'Tom here spoke us for us in front of bailiff that first time.' He looked ingratiatingly over at Tom. 'All did expect too much of you at manor court. We now know you was cunning enough to keep silent and not involve us all to our detriment. Now we understand. What say you, Tom?'

Tom shook his head, hard put to find words of protest, while John looked on in alarm, seeing them like wolves with their eyes on the baker, slavering over a kill. And when Tom voiced his refusal, would they see no wrong in again damning him for a coward?

Will Randere was having all the say here – let him put his courage where his mouth was; let him volunteer to be spokesman, leader, if he dared. John was about to put these sentiments into words when Gildeborn caught hold of his arm.

'The spy!'

They looked round in alarm at the empty chair. On their feet instantly, they rushed out, startling everyone. Wat had already slipped his knife from its strap across the top of his pouch. Outside they cast about but there was

121

no sign of the man.

Wat moved fast. 'Come on!'

With him they ran up the wharf path, peering between the tenements for movement. By the church they paused, breathless, but still no sign.

'Spread out!' Wat hissed.

'Nay, stay together,' Will Randere said. 'He may be lying in wait for us.'

'He be lying in wait for no one,' said William Gildeborn flatly. 'No point hunting about in the dark. Our fox is back in his hole.'

His tone hid despair. He'd been a fool to let his brother talk him into coming here this evening. But maybe it was not all his brother's fault. Though he was wealthier than some petty lords, he was forbidden a lord's privileges and bore their contempt. He was weary of hearing his issue referred to as his brats, his wife treated little better than a common wench, himself being regarded as an ignorant rustic. It was time things changed.

The searchers stood uncertain what to do. 'What now?' John asked. Already he could feel a traitor's noose about his neck. 'Maybe if we depart to our homes and deny...'

Tom shook his head. 'We should seek our parson's counsel,' he said, taking command of the situation. 'If he be for John Ball, he will help us.'

With returning hope they stared towards the ramshackle cottage beside the imposing structure of the church. Thin shafts of light glimmered through the closed shutters. With a brief glance at each other, they made across the parson's glebe towards the hatched door.

It was as though he'd been expecting them. Hardly had Tom raised his arm to thump the wood with the heel of his fist, the door opened. In his dusty brown robe, Rackstrawe let his deep-set eyes flicker over the group.

'Inside, all of you!'

Bundled through into the long, single room they stood, breathing heavily, while he closed the door, dropping a bar across it.

He turned to them. 'Ye marked well the bailiff's man, then?'

'Ay, but he slipped away while we was talking,' Wat grated. 'We gave chase but lost him in the dark.'

'Then he's already reporting what he heard.'

'He heard nowt,' said Will Randere. 'From the moment John here brought warning, all six of us kept our voices low.'

'All six?' queried Rackstrawe. They glanced at each other in the dim rush light.

'Where be Tripat?' John burst out.

'He were with us,' Tom said. 'He came up the wharf road with us.'

'Well he ain't here now,' John returned.

Rackstrawe looked anxious. 'Can it be our brave emissary from Kent is in the pay of another?'

'How so?' demanded Will. 'He spoke of the Great Company.'

'So I understand. Yet I'm beginning to doubt the veracity of his errand – a displaced soldier of no use except as a messenger of Master Abel Ker, also a soldier who might know him only casually. Who knows if he has interests in none other than profit to himself?'

They were looking at their parson in amazement. 'You know of Master Tripat?' Will asked, then grew defiant. 'You have no reason to doubt him. He comes from this very village. He left to be a soldier when I was but twenty, and now returns, maimed and useless.'

'And so would find a few marks of use in his purse for a small favour, passing on information of treasonable sentiments this night to any who'd give his right arm to see young Tom Baker in jail, as we all well know.'

'Not so!' cried Will. 'I know him to be right honest. I mind his father was wheelwright here afore any here present were born. I mind folk spoke highly of him. You've been here only two year, Parson, and heard nothing of past folk in Fobbing. The son of old Hugh Tripat as was once a reeve here, be honest as the day be—'

'And what is honest?' the parson cut in. 'To you I am honest, yet you know nothing of my life prior to my coming here. There is many a dishonest priest. I may take you for an honest man, yet I do not know your innermost secrets but what you say at confession.' He gave a deep sigh. 'Think on what you mean by honesty and trust no one, especially in these times, which could cause your neck to be stretched should our cause fail. Trust no man unless he be our dearest friend, and even then...' He broke off, seeing a look pass between John Melle and young Baker, the young smith's face puckered by a sudden frown.

He continued quickly. 'We all be frail, my friends. Remember St Peter and our blessed Lord at Calvary.' Recovering, he grew more brisk. 'I know only that a certain person would be at the alehouse tonight to instruct you on what, as plain men, you must soon do in support of Kent. I know his name but of himself I know very little and cannot trust him until he proves himself trustworthy. I knew another would be there, perhaps in the pay of Simon Rycard, or someone far more sinister. But this deed, vanishing into the night along with Rycard's man, is not to my liking at all.'

'Then why're we standing here yabbering?' cried Wat discourteously. 'We came to you for advice. What do you advise we do?'

'To make yourselves scarce,' came the reply. 'At least until we know more. Go across the marshes to Bawley's Mill by Haven Hole and remain there until the true commons have arisen and it is safe for you to venture forth and mingle with those making for London. I will let your families know where you are.'

Tom regarded him curiously. 'I crave pardon for any disrespect, but for a poor village parson you do appear to have great knowledge of what is being planned.'

A cunning expression flitted momentarily

across the usually stony features. 'It wouldn't benefit you to concern yourself with my doings. I am priest of this parish. That is all that need concern you. Now go, all of you.'

A rattling of the door made them start.

'Who can it be?' whispered Will, transfixed with fear. But Rackstrawe acted immediately.

'Quickly – into the loft.'

The loft was little more than a platform under the roof along one wall, gained by a wooden ladder. Once up there, they backed into its deepest shadows as best they could while Rackstrawe went and opened the door to the caller.

There was no raucous demand for entry as they'd expected, only a bewildering silence. The parson called up to them, his tone light, even amused. Warily they crept forward to peer down into the room below. There, staring up at them, on his bearded face a look of grim satisfaction, stood Tripat. Firmly grasped between thumb and the two remaining fingers of his right hand was a knife on whose blade blood was already drying.

'Our spy'll not be reporting anything to-night, nor any night,' he said dispassionately as he spat on the blade and wiped it along the palm of his hand, in turn wiping the hand down the side of his tunic before returning the weapon to its pouch.

Slowly they descended the ladder. No one questioned where he'd hidden the body. By the time their bailiff realized what had happened, the commons would have risen, leaving him powerless to do much about it.

'Best we be off home then,' Tom said after a moment or two.

Nearing John's home, Tom bade him goodnight, but John caught his arm. 'Watch yourself, Tom, with them lot,' he warned. 'They be using you. They cast about for a leader where none of them have the guts for it.'

In a brief gesture of affection, Tom put an arm about his shoulders. 'Don't worry, dear friend. I be as cautious as any when it comes to handing out brave deeds. We need tact, not blood and thunder and killing. In time proper leaders will appear – men of wisdom and learning who'll go to our King peaceably on our behalf and put our petition afore him.' Dropping the arm from John's shoulders, he gave a low laugh. 'For now, I've more pressing business wi' my sweet Marjory. And you to your Alice, eh?'

John watched him stride away, aware of the heavy thumping in his chest enough to bring on a sick sensation. Tom and his sweet Marjory. Himself and Alice, while all the time his mind filled with thoughts of the way Marjory had looked at him, not once but many times these last weeks, making him feel sick from these vivid imaginings of holding her in his own arms.

Eight

John's house was in darkness. All were in bed, as if expressing displeasure with him this evening. Only the embers in the hearth still glowed, the big iron pot of water suspended above it from a pot hook.

By the glow he could just distinguish the wooden bench, stools, board and trestles stacked against the wall for the night. From his parents' pallet along the other wall came stentorian snores, backed up by the wheezing of his old grandmother huddled as near to the embers as she could without her wrappings being singed, so hard was it to warm her old bones. Cicely and Ned, being more agile, could mount the ladder to the loft above, sleeping with the two younger children. It was damper up there but young bones were not so bothered with that.

Creeping to his own pallet, he stood a moment gazing down at its occupant. She was lying on her back. Her mouth agape, her snores were soft and regular. Pushing away comparison to his vision of Marjory Baker, he began slowly to get out of his clothes, unbuckling the leather belt from his hips, pulling off his russet gipon and hood, easing

128

off the felt leather boots and dragging each leg free of his chausser and breech cloth. Whereas in winter he kept most of his clothing on for warmth, he slipped carefully in beside her, naked. Only high-born folk looked for night garments.

Careful though he was not to wake her, she turned towards him, the straw filling of their pallet rustling.

'You be late coming home,' she sighed and he caught the faint trace of stale breath. How could he make love with that in his face? But that was unkind. Everyone's breath grew stale in sleep.

'Why so late?' she asked sleepily. There was no reproach in her tone but he'd expected none, so mild a soul was she.

'I had business,' he said brusquely. 'Go to sleep.'

She slipped into silence, her breathing growing heavier, and was soon snoring so loudly that he nudged her slightly, hoping to reduce it. Instead she awoke with a start.

'What – what is it, John?'

'Nowt,' he muttered.

She lay quiet for a moment then snuggled against him. 'Would you put your arm around me, John?'

'The hour's late. I'm tired,' he mumbled.

In the darkness he knew she pouted. 'High time you did caress me, John. Will you not now, just a little, for I be in fair need of my husband.'

It was a rebuke, though gently spoken. How

129

could he not do her bidding? Dutifully he slipped an arm beneath her head, laying the other across her naked body. Her breasts gave gently beneath the weight of his hand, giving him an impression of pigs' bladders half filled with water, hating such a thought.

He let the hand lie motionless as though he'd drifted off to sleep, but she stirred impatiently, running her short, broad hand, one already roughened by work, along the flesh of his stomach. 'John?'

'Huh?' he snorted, pretending to come awake.

'You fell asleep, John.'

'Did I?' He gave a mighty yawn. 'I must be very tired.'

She was holding his hand firmly against her breasts, squirming a little in an effort to entice him. Suddenly she ceased moving.

The hand holding his against her breasts loosened and fell away and he heard her tremulous whisper, 'I be sorry, John, that I do not please you.'

He came alive, instantly full of remorse. 'You do please me,' he lied.

He knew she didn't believe him. 'Ah, John, dear, would that I was more comely. Then you would find more pleasure in me. But I was not born comely.'

In the face of such quiet anguish, he half sat up. 'You must not put yourself down. You have a nature many women lack – kind, gentle...' He wanted to go on but couldn't, it sounded so false. He fell back, defeated. 'It

130

may be that it is not you, but I who is wanting. Maybe the gossips are right – I cannot find pleasure in any woman.' But this too was proved a lie as the lithe shape of Marjory Baker flashed through his mind. 'If my father be right that I tend towards unnatural...' He broke off. Could lusting after the wife of his dearest friend equally be called unnatural?

'Don't say that, John!' He felt her wince. 'You be as good and proper as any man, and I love you so. 'Tis a noble thing for a man to have affection for his friend. I hear tell that our own King Richard do hold such an affection for the young Earl of Oxford, Robert de Vere, which do cause folk to speak slightingly of it, or so I heard from a wandering friar as came by just lately. But if for a king, why not for any man?'

'The King be but a boy of fourteen,' he interrupted gruffly. 'I be a man who should find comfort in a wife.'

'Then find that comfort,' his father growled from the far side of the room, 'and let us get some bloody sleep!'

Cringing, he fell silent, but Alice had determination on her side.

'Now is the time,' she whispered. 'Don't fret, John, if you fail with me, for men cannot always be lusty and ready every time, and you mustn't count it against yourself if you fail to rise.'

She kept her voice low from the half-awake man their voices had disturbed. 'Most like it is the fault of the woman for not stirring her

131

man enough and I be not that much skilled in these things.'

'That's not so,' he hissed, turning towards her, but she put a gentle finger to his lips.

'I need to tell you, John, I count myself most fortunate to have a husband both young and handsome. My father thought only to find me some aging widower as had need of someone to cook and clean and rub his old bones for him. Or someone bent and bowed who could get himself no more than a plain wife.'

It slay him that she saw herself as such and on impulse he drew her to him. 'Alice, take no heed of looks. You are the kindest, mildest of souls, and I would have you above any ravishing beauty with a sharp tongue and shrewish ways. And I *will* prove it this very night.'

But it wasn't to be the night for him to rise, even though he conjured up the one who plagued his every thought, even though he visualized the slack body he held to be firm and slender beneath his hands, even though he pushed himself between the plump legs imagining them to be vibrant in readiness to receive him, his member remained poor and limp as one on his death bed.

Sickened and angry with himself, he finally turned from her, hearing her soft voice his ear.

'Do not count it against yourself, Husband. It may be next time, when you are not so weary. I be content enough.'

Comforting words, except that as he lay with his back to her he felt her body shaken by suppressed tears.

Morning saw the conspirators at mass. Of Tripat there was no sign.

'Must have left for Kent,' Tom mused. 'I wonder where he hid the body?'

He and John stood with their families in the cool nave, pleased to be doing little with their time. John saw Tom fondle Marjory's hand as she clung on to his arm, but her glance was towards John. He glanced guiltily down at Alice. She stood beside him, not touching him. She looked downcast though she smiled towards one or two other women with whom she had become friendly when drawing water from the village well, that den of gossips. God forbid any of them had noted the look Marjory had just given him.

'I wonder who he was,' Tom was saying. 'And if he had a wife and children.'

John came abruptly to himself. 'Who?'

'He who met Tripat's knife last night.'

'You should fret,' John said callously, his mind on his own problems. The events of last night seemed a long way off, a dream, a thing that had happened to others. Had he really conspired to treason last night, chased an informer, seen the man who had done away with him wipe that bloodstained knife on the palm of his hand?

'I slept little last night,' said Tom, 'thinking of his woman widowed, his children fatherless, left unsupported. I fear I displeased my Marjory with my worrying rather than enjoying her embrace. All right long I dreamed of that woman's man lying dead somewhere and her unknowing.'

Mass had begun, its unintelligible intonation in John's ears as he lingered with uncharitable gratification on Tom's inability to please his wife. It made his failure with his own wife seem less weighty.

'Men die every day, leaving widows,' he said as they came away. 'Why fret over the fate of an informer?'

'I care not about him but them he might have left behind,' Tom said. 'But apart from that, what if the body be found and traced to us?'

This was more practical. 'It wouldn't be the first time a wayfarer travelling alone at night has fallen foul of robbers. He stated his intention to Dame Wodelark for all to hear. We've nowt to worry about.'

'And his horse?' asked Tom. 'Robbers would have taken the horse. What if he hadn't time to unhitch it from behind the alehouse? What if it's still there?'

It was a thought, a dread one. Anyone making enquiries would come to the conclusion that this hadn't been the act of robbers who fade away into the night, never to be found.

Making excuses to their families, the two hurried down the wharf road. The horse was indeed still there. Quickly, Tom unhitched it, smacked its rump and together they watched it amble away.

'If it's found now,' Tom said, 'all will think it escaped those who took it.' Which was a great relief to them both.

On the Tuesday Simon Rycard was seen visiting the alehouse to quench an apparently urgent thirst and was heard to enquire casually if any strangers had passed through the village of late. He was told by the innocent alewife of one who had insisted on going on to Corringham after dark, his enquiries reaping little more than raised eyebrows at this strange interest in travellers. Strangers came and went, and who cared so long as they dropped by to swell her purse and were peaceable?

Also on Tuesday, Parson Rackstrawe was noticed departing Fobbing on his scraggy old mare, dressed for travel, making towards Corringham but bound for a journey well out of the area.

From the forge, John noted with a grim smile that at least the wheel of events was beginning to turn as he watched the man go, guessing he'd be making for Tilbury. Soon after, Wat Gildeborn came to say that Rackstrawe had told him to pass on the message that he was bound for Kent to speak to a certain Walter of Rochester who was holding forth about crushing dues exacted on the common folk by landlord, Church and government.

'The man's a tiler by trade,' he said. 'And takes his surname from his trade, being known locally as Wat Tyler.'

John was shoeing a black palfrey belonging to Steward Somenour's long-nosed wife who'd come to stay awhile with Dame Rycard at the manor. The young groom was lolling by one of the uprights of the open-fronted smithy. If the lad overheard what was being said he could carry it back to those only too eager to know what was going on. As is often said, small mouths fill big ears.

He carried on working, keeping his voice low. 'Did Rackstrawe say the purpose of his meeting with this Wat Tyler?'

Gildeborn too kept his voice down. 'Only that the man at this moment is raising an army of common men – a great company, it is being said.' He watched, mesmerized, as John hammered the shoe into shape, the sparks leaping dully from the heated iron. 'They say he be well seasoned in the French wars, like Dick Tripat. Them's what we need, seasoned soldiery.'

Ay, thought John as he took the hot shoe to seat it on the animal's hoof amid clouds of smoke from the burning horn, seasoned soldiers as leaders, not gentle-hearted bakers of pies who, because they speak up once afore their neighbours, must be pushed forward as scapegoats to lead where lesser men dare not.

Not yet satisfied with the fit, he took the shoe back for reheating. His father would have done it in one go. He was glad the man wasn't sitting here watching him, making him feel inadequate.

'All are beginning to talk of the great company,' Wat went on under cover of the hammering and filing. 'We'll have a proper reckoning when we all go to meet old Bampton in Brentwood on Thursday.'

'Not so loud,' John warned, the hammering having stopped. Bent over the hoof to file at the pared horn, he jerked his head towards the groom still leaning apparently idly against the wooden upright.

In particoloured livery of plum and saffron, the youth had one leg crooked, foot flat against the timber while he nibbled at a thumbnail and gazed out upon the world.

'Best say no more,' John warned and Wat fell silent while the other continued to trim and file the hoof.

Little more could have been said anyway as Adam Melle came stomping from the house and into the smithy, irascibly nursing his arm, to see how his son was doing. He glared at the gangling man who looked to be disrupting his son from his work.

'Have you business here today, Master Gildeborn?' he enquired, his tone polite enough, for any potential customer was money not to be turned away and Wat Gildeborn might have been waiting to have a new shepherd's crook made after the black mare had been dealt with.

'Not today,' Wat replied respectfully. 'But I shall be bringing a snapped crook for your

137

services tomorrow.'

'Then we shall see you on the morrow.' He lifted a hand in brief dismissal and Wat quickly took his leave.

The groom having left with his mistress's palfrey, John and Ned settled down to the rest of the morning's work, their father supervising. The village was quiet in the heat, most workers gone to the fields to keep the baked soil open. By midday it had grown so hot that their father took himself into the cool of the house to nurse his frustrations at not being able to work. Alice came with a jug of ale and a platter of bread and cold meat, which they took to the shade of the oak tree.

The meal done, they were about to return to their work when they saw Dick Tripat heading towards them from the direction of Brentwood. Sweat stained his clothing and poured from his forehead into his beard. He was shouting as he ran.

'If you've polls undeclared, get 'em out of sight! A tax collection comes this way, making enquiries!'

John was on his feet in an instant. 'Ned, get our old grandmother out of the house and under the woodpile by the midden.'

Ned hesitated, his sixteen-year-old head not entirely taking in the urgency of the situation. 'She'll suffocate from the stink. We ain't cleared it of night soil since father got his arm broke.'

Despite the urgency, John couldn't help grinning. 'Then our fine visitor will keep a respectful distance, won't he?'

While Ned went to warn their father and Tripat alerted the rest of the village, he ran to the nearer fields to spread the news, they in turn passing it on to others. By the time the investigator arrived, not one unaccountable poll remained to be found.

In a scribbler's flat hat and dark gown, he rode a sleek cob. He was alone, so sure of his position. These people were too simple to know the difference between what was official and what private.

People were hurrying in from the fields. He smiled slowly. News of his coming had travelled ahead of him as he'd expected. Nevertheless these might be the ones he would catch out, unprepared. He was sure he would find a few extra names to present to Sir Thomas Bampton, thus getting into his good books – maybe even being promoted.

Long enough had he been an underling, bowing and scraping to those who saw themselves as his betters. It wasn't as if he didn't know his letters and was wily with it, just the sort of person they needed, yet he was still accounted little better than the rustics he despised.

He deserved better, and this whim of his of coming here unannounced and catching these rustics out would stand him in good stead with Bampton, he was sure.

Nine

John watched, apparently unperturbed, as the collector approached.

The sallow face bore an expression of importance, the thin mouth confident, with a self-satisfied smile. This man was no fool. He had the look of someone who knew his job, able to winkle out a hidden poll or two. They in turn knew that he was aware of every cunning contrivance of theirs to hide an undeclared relative. It was going to be a battle of wits, as always. Strange though, that the man was unaccompanied by bailiff or constables. Was his visit entirely official?

'That there cob of yours looks to be losing a shoe,' John called out as he came abreast of the smithy.

The man looked at him as if he were an idiot, beneath contempt. 'Your bailiff appears to be absent. Where is your reeve? I need a spokesman to call all these people to the village square.'

John shrugged. 'I know not where our reeve is either.' He saw the man's lips tighten, the first sign of indecision. The man should have brought constables with him. It was odd.

'Then I will make my own announcement,'

the man said and, raising his voice to those now standing at their doors, he began to read from a scroll he produced from the sleeve of his houppelande.

'Sir Thomas Bampton, steward of the manor of Havering-atte-Bower and justice of the peace for the county of Essex, commissioned to make inquisition into certain non-payment of taxes, commands every township in the Hundred of Barstable to make diligent enquiry and give reply to Sir Thomas at Brentwood on the thirteenth day of this month where they will pay the new subsidy to be levied from them to make reparation for the money in default.'

Their reaction was as he had expected. 'Tell your Lord Bampton we've already paid our taxes.'

But he knew his job. He presented an oily smile of sympathy. 'Good folk, I have my duty to do, whether I like it or not, and must carry out my duties to the best of my ability.'

As expected, he was met with jeers and cries to carry his duties out elsewhere. He stood his ground as they began to gather. The protests would die away soon and they would stand shuffling their feet before his official presence. Just so long as he maintained a lack of aggression.

But he'd reckoned without the tall, upright young figure, his clear, handsome features intelligent. 'My father be baker in this village,' came the clear tones. 'Respected by bailiff and steward. He was one who represented

141

this village in making declaration and paying the tax asked at that time – afore Plough Monday, this very winter. As far as this manor is concerned, we have paid our tax in full.'

John had come to stand shoulder to shoulder with Tom. 'My father be smith to the manor, an honest man, once a reeve here, and would not cheat on his dues to any authority.'

Even as he spoke, John felt his insides quail, knowing that his own grandmother crouched behind the midden, that honest smith making sure she with her muddled old brain didn't creep out again to go back to her hearth. Holding tight to his courage, John fixed the investigator with his glare.

'You challenge my father's honesty?' He had the satisfaction of seeing the oily face blench.

'I believe you all to be honest, but I have my orders and must carry them out or be relieved of my duties and become unemployed. I've no wish to discredit any of you. I'm here merely to ensure all is correct and I promise I shall depart as soon as possible. But I must go from house to house as bidden by orders of Treasurer Hales himself. Who am I to decide whether it is right or wrong?'

Before his entreaty, fists were slowly lowered, anger dissolving into sullen resignation as the gathering stepped back for the man to pass. Beginning at the manor end of the street, he marked off names in each of the tenements he entered.

John and several others remained where they were. 'I've no wish to be there when he gets to ours,' he remarked. 'He knows who I am and I will not answer to him as though I were a grovelling peasant. Let him come to me if he wishes.'

Standing in the heat of a May sun they could see the man proceeding from house to house, leading his cob to tether it outside each one.

John found himself holding his breath as his own house was entered, his mind on the undeclared poll even now concealed behind the midden.

For a long time nothing happened. The time began to draw itself out, yet the man had spent just as long in other houses. Suddenly a piercing screech issued from the yard. John started as though struck. The old lady had been discovered. Why had his father chosen this occasion to be dishonest?

He started forward along the street to be met by his mother flying out from the toft, her kirtle held clear of her feet, her grey hair – always so neatly bound beneath her linen coif – now streaming about her anguished face, her mouth wide open in terror.

'John! Ned! Oh, come quick!' she cried as she saw them. John caught her as she all but fell into his arms. 'Violation – ah, St Eloi! That Devil's spawn...'

As she sank down almost in a faint, John held on to her. Her screams had brought everyone running to see what was wrong. They stared as he shook her to bring her to her senses.

'What violation?' he demanded.

'Cicely. Oh, God forgive us! He did demand to learn her age. I told him she was but fourteen still, but he said she looked more sixteen. I told him some maids do develop earlier than others, but he said he would know for himself, and he did...'

John held her tight as she sagged again. 'He did what?'

'Oh, sweet Jesus,' came the sob. 'He put his hand on her breast, she struggling, and he said he would test her age for himself. Before I could stop him he lifted her kirtle. I saw her lower parts exposed to his filthy eyes, his hand on her and she crying out.'

Again she sagged but recovered without John's help, her face now twisted with a mother's fury. 'I upped with an iron cooking pot I had been holding and brought him a great knock on the head. He ran out of the house leaving Cicely and the children dolouring and Alice trying to keep me from running after him.' Tears were streaming down her lined face. It was then they saw the bright splashes of blood on her dark kirtle and sackcloth apron. 'I'm certain he's dead. There is so much blood...'

'Not you, Mother?' John gasped in disbelief and horror.

She turned her eyes up towards his. 'Your father. He came running from the midden to our cries and I cried to him from the door that Cicely be violated. He snatched up a hammer lying against the smithy wall and

144

caught him in the yard and with his good hand brought it down on that vile knave's pate. Merciful God, you know his strength. Great gobs of brain flew everywhere.'

It was all too much for her. She closed her eyes and sank at last into a faint.

While men rushed to the smithy yard the women carried her into the carpenter's house next door, lamenting more for their own selves than the stricken, for not only was the smith as good as dead when his deed was discovered, the whole village would come under vengeful authority. Woe to any who did not set up hue and cry, deemed to be as guilty as the culprit if they didn't. Yet though they knew they were heaping trouble on themselves, not one went running off to the bailiff's house to raise alarm. Bailiff wasn't there but his wife was and she would send a messenger galloping off to alert him to bring constables to arrest the smith and that must not happen.

The brothers burst into the yard only to be stopped short by the sight of the dead man, his skull a bloodied mess, their father still holding the rusty hammer. He looked completely dazed. Cicely was crouched by the house door, shaking as though from the ague, both fists clenched tightly against her cheeks, her eyes wide and staring. Bending over her, Alice was trying to give comfort. The two younger children were huddled together, both crying, while on her hands and knees the old grandmother had crept from

145

behind the dung heap to stare enquiringly, grinning, her wits unable to grasp anything.

Seeing the body, Ned had covered his head with his hands, crying, 'Dear Christ, have mercy on us!' John stood unable to move as behind him the necks of the villagers craned to see more.

It was Tom who, despite his father's warning, went and gently removed the hammer from the smith's palsied fingers and put it to one side. In the same quiet manner, he told Alice to take the two children inside, then went and lifted the sobbing fourteen-year-old Cicely and led her inside as well.

Returning, he reminded the onlookers drinking in the grisly scene that should Bailiff come by on his way back to the manor their presence might be misconstrued. Within minutes the area was as empty as an apple barrel in April. Only Wat Gildeborn stayed, offering help to hide the body.

'None will betray you to Bailiff,' he stated as, urgently, they found sacking to wrap the body in. 'They won't want to be questioned why they didn't run to the manor to report this on the instant of knowing it.'

'Where do we put him?' John asked, too numbed by what had happened to be able to think two minutes ahead.

'Bury it out on the marsh. It will never be found,' Wat, the practical-minded shepherd, said grimly, and with this they all agreed.

Grabbing two spades – all they could carry with the body as well – they left Alice and

146

Tom's mother to swab the yard free of blood. With Ned taking care of his still dazed father, the three men lugged their limp and heavy burden to the rear of John's house and down the sloping meadow behind it.

'We must find a spot along Fobbing Creek,' Wat said, puffing under the awkward weight.

John's heart was thumping madly. He felt sick with fear at all that had happened. For some reason he recalled Marjory's face in the crowd, her pleas to Tom that it wasn't his business and to come away, ignored.

'What if the tide uncovers it?' Tom asked.

'The mud's soft and deep there. Easier to dig.'

'We should take it further out on the marshes,' John managed to say. 'No excessive high tide there to overflow and uncover it later.'

They fell silent, engaged in negotiating the sloping meadow that finally flattened out to marshland. In the stillness their laboured breathing sounded too loud. Passing behind the church they finally gained level ground, making the going easier, but now they were exposed.

'If Dick Tripat were with us,' John said softly, 'he'd a' known where to hide this. Where did he go after alerting us?'

'To Vange and West Leigh in case the scribbler went on there.'

'This one'll go nowhere now,' Wat observed dryly, but John was in no mood to jest. Something kept making him glance up at the

147

church tower as they struggled on past it. A square, stone structure, rising higher for being on a high promontory, it could be seen from miles away, and was a fine lookout.

They struggled on, choosing the firmer tussocks of grass amid the mud to make the going easier. Finally finding what seemed a suitable spot, they laid the body down and began digging. And perhaps it was his imagination but all the time John kept feeling eyes were watching them.

'I wonder where Bailiff is?' he asked at one point.

'He weren't at the manor,' Tom supplied. 'When I delivered bread there this morning, one of the scullions said he'd gone down to Corringham to do some business.'

John stopped digging for a moment to stare at him. 'You gave us to believe that crowd of gawpers would bring him running.'

'But it did shift 'em.'

Despite everything, John grinned while Wat's chuckle briefly broke the silence of the marshes. Even so he was still uncomfortably aware of the great square church tower looming over them, even at this distance. From it a man could see in every direction.

Several times he glanced towards it, but behind its battlements there was no movement. Yet its looming stillness was awesome. He kept thinking of the young groom who had lounged by the front of the smithy this morning apparently paying no attention to anything. Had he been paying attention to work being done, it would have been more natural. Listeners often look quite innocent, gazing off into the distance while their ears waggled. Had he gone off carrying tales?

Casting his thoughts aside, John bent to his task of digging, stripping off his sweaty gipon. His tensile muscles rippling, he made the clods of mud fly, the grave deepening swiftly.

With the hole already filling with brown salt water, they rolled the body in at last, hurriedly piling back the clods and finally clumps of marsh grass to disguise the spot. John donned his tunic, which immediately stuck to his sweating torso, and together the three men started on their way back, each with enormous relief and John deeply grateful for their generous help, given with no thought to their own safety.

Soon they would be up the steep meadow and to the safety of their own village. He'd felt far too exposed out on the flat marshes. They were even laughing in their relief when Tom pulled up sharply, his head lifted towards the church tower. Laughter instantly breaking off, they followed his gaze in time to see a small figure flit between the merlons, its particoloured tunic as inescapable as the plumage of a popinjay.

Reaction was instant. Up the slope at a run, leaping hummocks, the thorns of low brambles and small blackthorns unheeded, they reached the churchyard, bounded through it, rounding a corner of the church as the lad appeared from the porch, breathless from his scamper down from the tower.

Seeing them, he gave a terrified squeak, streaking as fast as he could to escape, but the gangling shepherd's legs were long and the lad found his tunic grasped, bringing him to such an abrupt halt that his slim body was almost pulled off its feet.

The other two ran up but stopped suddenly. Approaching them from the Corringham road, riding his fat horse, was Simon Rycard. Helpless they watched as the boy, tugging himself free, sped up to the bailiff, pointing in their direction, yammering hysterically.

'Christ! We're dead!' John gasped.

Gildeborn was more positive. 'No more faint hearts – take 'em both!'

Not pausing to question, all three rushed forward, Tom catching the bridle of the startled bay while Wat flung himself at its rider, hauling him from the saddle.

'Get the boy!' he yelled to John as Rycard hit the ground.

Rycard's shrieks ended in a gurgle as his captor's sinewy arm came about his throat. John was finding it hard to control his own squirming captive, squealing like a caught piglet. 'What d'we do with 'em?' he panted.

'Slit their gizzards.'

Trying to soothe the frightened horse, Tom turned on him. 'Use your wits. We've enough trouble without looking for more.'

'There'll be trouble—' began Rycard, only to be cut off by increased pressure on his windpipe.

'What's to be done with 'em?' John repeated. He felt almost sorry for the lad, who was rapidly dissolving into tears.

Tom was stroking the animal's quivering flesh, slowly calming it. 'Until we can all go to confront the King's commissioner in Brentwood, we must hide – take these two with us so as not to raise the alarm before then.'

Emboldened by the hope of being spared, Rycard immediately rasped out a threat. 'When this lad fails to return and Master Somenour comes to enquire where he is, your skins will not be worth the price of a bean.'

'Quiet!' Wat gave the man's throat another jerk. 'Or I'll skin you of yours for less than the price of a turd.'

'Someone must send word to Steward that the boy's been taken ill,' Tom said thoughtfully as he tethered the horse to a nearby branch.

'Ill with what?' John returned. 'He'll still come looking for him.'

Tom thought again. 'A murrain. That'll keep him away. None will venture here with rumours of plague. Hopefully his wife and Bailiff's will leave too, thinking Bailiff be also kept away by the news for the sake of his own skin.' It was fanciful thinking, but the best any could come up with.

'We could make for Bawley's Mill,' John suggested as their priest had advised earlier. 'We'll have to bind these two so they don't escape.'

A few villagers had begun to venture out.

151

Tom's father was hurrying towards them, his face ashen as he reached his son. 'For the love of God, Tom, this isn't your business. Your wife awaits you at home, all trembling and frightened. Come away. Our good bailiff will surely overlook...'

'That I will not!' stormed Rycard, his words serving to leave Tom with no alternative but to remain with the others, even strengthening his resolve.

'John has been my closest and dearest friend from boyhood,' he said, looking at his father as though he was the child and Tom the parent. 'What concerns him concerns me, for good or bad. What's more,' he lifted his voice to include all those who now stood about, 'this deed concerns us all. We're all implicated whether we like it or not. In this, and larger matters,' he added significantly. They knew what he meant.

'Quit all that gabble,' Wat cut in roughly. 'I'm tired o' hanging on to this fat-arsed fool while you argue about what's what. 'Tis help we need now, Master Hugh Baker, and if you're fretting on your son's safety, then listen to him. Go on, Tom, tell them, but no more preaching.'

Tom shot him a look, then turned back to the growing crowd of villagers. 'First, get rid of Bailiff's horse, Father. Second, alert the villages hereabouts for men to meet at Pitsea. There we'll gather our own Great Company and go to Brentwood together to meet Thomas Bampton. This is the plan set

152

by them in Kent. We are to raise an outcry in Brentwood, from where we march to London to set all aright. Kent will be doing likewise. John Ball will be freed from Maidstone Castle to lead them.'

The crowd suddenly heartened, there was little his father could do but nod his assent to his son's request. Tom was again their leader and they hung upon his decision.

'Right then. A rope for these two. Bound well apart so no conspiracy can pass between them and unbind each other when no one is looking.'

No longer in fear of their bailiff, they set to work. The boy they bound lightly, the bailiff less so, enjoying his winces and leering into his face, their insolence perhaps a little rash, Will Randere running up to do a taunting jig in front of the bound man. Only Tom seemed to be keeping a sense of proportion, John was glad to see, even regarding Rycard with respect.

'We mean you no hurt. When this business at Brentwood begins, you will both be freed, for you can do us no harm by then.'

'Harm?' bellowed Rycard, his face suffused at the indignity of having his arms bound to his sides, his wrists tied in front, for they would be going across mud and water-filled channels and no one wanted either captive to fall on his face with his hands bound behind him.

'I shall have you before the assizes for this. I'll have you drawn on a hurdle and hung,

Thomas Baker. I'll escape before you ever reach Brentwood and then watch out, you ill-bred scoundrel, you snot-nosed serf!'

Swift as lightening, Wat's knife was in his hand, held to the man's nostrils. 'Call us serfs one more time and I'll slit that fat nose of your'n.'

Tom pushed away the knife. 'There'll be no blood-letting.' He turned to the onlookers. 'We need five or six to come with us to safeguard these two.'

Every man, young and old, pressed forward, obliging him to make choices. It was difficult, but he finally picked the younger men with alert enough minds to keep watch over their charges and be sure-footed on the slithery terrain.

'Dick Wodelarke – one,' he counted. 'Henry Sharpe – two. Dick Elys – three. John Reede – four. Tom Fuller – five. And Ralph Peteman – six. The rest of you as wants to meet up at Pitsea, be there first light on Tuesday.'

'What about me?' demanded Will Randere above the murmurs of disappointment. 'Have I not been in this all along? I've been out on them marshes all my life, catching eels. Or think you now as I be too old for this, you young puppy?'

Tom looked apologetic. 'I know your worth, Master Randere. But we cannot take all. You must understand that some men of trust have to be left here to convince any as may come to investigate the disappearance of these two that all is well.'

But Randere wasn't ready to understand. 'I know every twist and turn of them saltings like the back of my own hand. And mark this, Tom Baker, the tide'll be on the turn within an hour – did you give mind to that?' He gave a triumphant chuckle as he saw Tom's face drop. 'Nay, you didn't. But I did. It runs quick twixt Haven Hole and Canvey Bank, and them mud creeks will take you up to the waist if you slip in some unseen channel – a man could drown for sure. But wi' me leading the way, we'll make Bawley's Mill without mishap. Go wi'out me and you'll all be caught by them tide creeks.'

To someone like Randere, knowing the tides was as much a clock as the sun's crossing of the heavens. Twice a day Fobbing Creek filled from the vast tide of the Thames Estuary, a little later each day as the moon moved, easy for any Thames-side man to calculate, and Tom immediately felt embarrassed before them all, his authority undermined, especially seeing the man's smirk.

John had also seen the expression and went to his friend's aid. 'The creek will fill come nightfall. We can row down to East Haven under cover of darkness, better than being spied walking out there as plain to see as flies on a sweetmeat.'

'Ay, you do that,' scoffed the eel-catcher. 'You wait around, giving these two the chance to slip their fetters and make off. You go now across the marshes or not at all. But wi'out me,' he stabbed his narrow chest with his forefinger, 'you'll end up a-floundering afore you get anywhere near Bawley's Mill.'

Tom drew himself up. 'Very well, what's one more man?'

'And I lead.'

There was no more to say. Tom stepped back, surrendering his short-lived leadership, but John could only feel glad. It was a huge responsibility for Tom to have taken upon his shoulders and he thanked God that by Will Randere's arrogant intervention, all that responsibility had been taken from him.

Ten

Flushed with his own success, Will was issuing orders. Five to precede the prisoner and five to the rear; he would lead, picking the route; all to travel in single file; food to be brought along, enough for two nights; every man to arm himself with a weapon of some sort.

John felt the prickle of disdain. For all he was glad to see Tom relieved of an unenviable honour, the manner in which it had been done was hurtful.

'Let him stick his neck out,' he said quietly to Wat Gildeborn out of his friend's hearing. 'We'll see how much of a leader he is when we confront Thomas Bampton.'

'Let's get across them marshes afore we think of confronting anyone,' Wat said. 'I'm at ease out there with the sheep, but with just us twelve it will feel mighty different, lonely somehow.'

Now they were out here, John knew what he meant. After all those who had seen them on their way, it did indeed feel lonely. Alice had come to bid him an anxious farewell. Dame Wodelarke had been there warning her son to take care of himself, as had the mothers or wives of most of the twelve.

He'd watched Marjory Baker clinging to her husband's arm, and as he ran a hand over her veiled hair, had lain her head on his shoulder in a loving way that to John had looked totally convincing, until she had come over to him to say, 'Look out for him, for my sake, John.'

He'd assured her he would, but her hand on his arm had moved gently along the muscles beneath the sleeve. Against his will, the sensation had stirred him, had angered him, too. No accidental touch, she'd known what she was about. She was a witch, yet such a desirable one. He'd tried to pull away, yet his whole being had seemed to be burning and throbbing and he'd felt dizzy as though from too much ale.

He'd forced the question from between dry lips. 'Why are you doing this?'

'I've always wanted you, John,' she'd whispered, still smiling as if at a friend. 'But your father had you married, and Tom was found with me, the two of us compelled to wed.'

He couldn't help it. 'Have you no love for him at all?'

'He is the gentlest of men, yet I confess it was you as I had always wanted.'

'Then why did you lay with him in that barn?'

'Because...' But there had been no chance for her to answer as Tom came hurrying towards them. Laying an arm about John's shoulders, he had smiled down at the sweet face of his wife, his expression so open that John had cringed inside himself.

'Enough of bidding Godspeed, my love,' he'd said evenly. 'We are ready to go.'

The pace had been brisk to begin with, going down the sun-baked meadow, its turf already yellowing, and out on to the marsh edge, the ground still firm where sheep could be left to themselves to graze on sweet pasturage.

Away from the village the silence had descended. A skylark singing its heart out unseen in the hazy blue made the sense of loneliness even more acute, leaving a man time to think.

John's mind refused to leave him in peace for thinking of the way Marjory had accosted him – and worse, his reaction to it. God forbid Tom should ever find out that he was being virtually betrayed by the man he saw as his truest friend. Automatically he made a small, surreptitious sign of the cross then gave a start as he heard Tom's voice in his ear.

'What's this? Crossing yourself? Take heart, John.' He gave him a playful push. 'Nothing will go awry. Soon we'll be home again, masters of our own fate.'

Their own fate! What fate lay in store for him and Tom? The years ahead were unthinkable if their friendship were to be ruined. Again he vowed to keep distance between himself and his dearest friend's wife, and again he crossed himself in hope of God to help him in his vow.

'That's twice now, John! What's ailing you?'

John ignored the tinge of humour in the tone. 'Nothing. I am worried about them two,' he said, indicating their prisoners. 'They could escape.' It was as good excuse as any. 'I'll be glad to reach old Bawley's place.'

It was two miles to their destination as the crow flies, but twists and turns of the narrow creeks, the mud wet and soft from the previous high tide, could add nearly another mile. They'd have to move to beat the next tide. Once there they'd be able to breathe again, even though the mill itself was in a sad state and offered poor shelter.

The air, dry as dust over the land, was pleasantly moist here, the rays of the afternoon sun moderated by a faint sea breeze, its tang refreshing. Walking at a good pace, they'd begun to shout foolish jokes at each other. Already they'd forgotten the spattered brains of Bampton's man.

None seemed to comprehend that until the gates of London were opened to them and their King confided in and brought to see their plight, such acts as they had committed would be seen as treason. Until this uprising reached a successful end, no one could rest easy.

'What d'you think London will be like?' Dick Elys's question broke through his thoughts.

Wrenched back to his surroundings, John answered, 'I've never been there so I can't say.'

160

'I hear it has churches with spires all made of gold and castles with towers of gleaming white stone.'

'Don't believe tales told by wandering friars,' laughed Tom Fuller from the back of the column, the quiet of the marshes making their voices carry.

Elys ignore the big, jolly man. 'They say lords and ladies prance in the street every holy day. They dress so brightly it blinds the eye. Or so I've been told,' he added defiantly as Fuller gave a great belly laugh.

'Well, I can believe it,' John Reede said, walking just ahead of John.

John said nothing, but stared at the broad young back. How unlike Marjory – his sister and Tom's wife – he was. Strongly built, blue-eyed, brown-haired and robust whereas she was slight, her skin smooth and pale, her hair like sheer gold – and those green eyes of hers, that could all but drown a man's very soul in their liquid depths.

'It ain't all fine folk and fine castles,' Dick Wodelarke called back over his shoulder. A huge grin wreathed his round, florid face. 'There were a merchant last year as paused at my mother's alehouse. He said he'd been to London. He said the houses were of sturdy wood but so close together that a man could lean from his window and shake his neighbour's hand opposite.'

'It be like that in Brentwood,' called Henry Sharpe from the very rear. 'I've had call to go there now and again, and not for a king's

161

ransom would I fancy to live there with its stinks. Give me the clean air of our village every time.'

Dick Wodelarke was talking over him. 'So close set them houses, I was told, that the sun don't touch the streets, which are strewn with dung and slops as dogs and pigs and rats feed off. Not such a fine city as I want to see.'

'If ever you get there to see it!' shrilled Simon Rycard vehemently. 'And if you do, it'll be plagued by more rats than it ever saw ... Aah!' His words ended in a cry as Wat swung round and cuffed him across the mouth.

John too drew a shocked breath. 'Have done!' he called. 'In God's name, why spoil the story Dick were telling us?'

'This bailiff spoilt it, not I, with his insults. I made sure he doesn't do so again so freely, that's all.'

'He is still our bailiff,' Tom reminded in support of John, 'and worthy of some respect.'

'Respect!' Wat spat into a muddy channel. 'For this puffed-up lump of sheep turd? He would have you rotting in a dungeon if he had his way. And you speak of respect?'

Well ahead of them, Will Randere paused to look back at them all. 'God's wounds! What's all this dawdling? If we be caught by the tide we'll have to turn back.' With that he resumed his march, forging ahead, picking his way along the drier tracts.

Tom grinned. 'Go on then, Dick, with your

162

tale of London.'

Dick immediately warmed to his story again. 'This merchant, he did speak of food, such as none here has ever tasted, he said, cookshops by the dozen, pies and pastries sold in the very streets, filled wi' meats and savouries, or pies filled wi' apples or cherries wi' honey poured over 'em. Sweetmeats spiced with ginger and saffron. And custards made of egg yolks and cream, rich wi' clove and nutmeg and cinnamon, spices from far off...'

'Have done!' Ralph Peteman called back to them. 'My mouth be fair watering.'

Tom spoke in a faraway tone. 'When our former manor lord, Sir Geoffrey Bohun, were alive, he would furnish my father such ingredients as you spoke of, Dick, for his entourage when he visited Hawkesbury Manor, and my father made such fare with them as would put them cooks in London to shame.' He sighed loudly. 'Not so today, with our present lord, Thomas of Woodstock, ever absent, leaving his bailiff free to use most of his manor's allowance on hisself...'

'Liar!' yelled Rycard, fighting his bonds. 'Foul lies!'

Tom gave a terse laugh. 'You dressed in that fine cotehardie, in this heat too, and fine rings adorning your fat fingers, my God, you are so badly served on Woodstock's allowance.'

'They are honestly come by.'

'The Devil's arse, they are!' cut in Gilde-born.

163

'A bailiff doesn't have it all his own way,' Rycard protested manfully. 'Should the target of produce not be met, he must make good the deficiency out of his own purse. Each Michaelmas I must make audit. Each spring I must prepare an interim statement. Any shortcomings I have to make good.'

'At the expense of us customary tenants,' interrupted Fuller. 'With fines and homages and tallage. I vow a quarter of it never sees the inside of our manor lord's coffers with him not here to check on it. Seems we pay to line your purse, Bailiff.'

'You'll pay,' blustered Rycard. 'You'll pay for this day's outrage. Not by fines, but by seeing the inside of a dungeon. I'll see there be a branding or two, even a hanging, for why did this lad cry out murder, and you chasing him? I shall get to the bottom of this. I will indeed.'

He looked so ridiculous, belligerent, red-faced, puffing as he slithered along, his hands bound, his richly draped clothing bespattered with mud, that John couldn't help a chuckle. Beside him, the lad still looked fresh, somehow able to keep the mud from clinging to all but his shoes and the lower part of his hose.

Around thirteen perhaps, he'd no doubt been taken from his home and wealthy family to spend his young days in service of even richer families. It enabled him to better himself and, though harsh, had to be good for him. John felt suddenly sorry for him. How lonely he must have felt leaving those he'd loved to serve some lord. On impulse he drew his knife from his belt and severed the lad's bond.

'Hold!' Wat demanded instantly. 'What're you doing?'

'It can do no harm,' John told him.

'He can escape.'

'And get lost?' To make his point, John swept his gaze over the saltings. The sun cloaked in a heat haze, nebulous and undefined, the humid haze had settled, obscuring the Kentish Downs on the other side of the Thames and the gentle rise of Hadleigh on the other. They now walked in a world without horizons, as though they were floating. 'Where would he go?' John asked, leaving Wat to hold his tongue.

Their bailiff wasn't so silent. 'I demand to be loosed, too,' he shrilled.

John was about to threaten him with having his face pushed into the mud if he didn't shut his mouth, when a shout came from Will Randere.

'I see the mill!'

Through the haze the broken form of the mill could be seen about another half-hour's walk on this increasingly difficult terrain. But the pace quickened, risking a slip into a gully, all of them eager to reach their destination and have done with negotiating these meandering, ever-narrowing banks of spongy cord grass and sea twitch.

A curious silence had descended that was not entirely from the dying of conversation –

165

a silence peculiar to any foreshore dominated by a large tidal range. Without the lapping of water, or the sound of breeze in a tree, it was an atmosphere of unreality. There *were* sounds – the barely audible sucking of air trapped beneath the mud disturbed by their passing, the plop of a cockle snapping shut its shell at their approach, a faint haunting mew of a distant curlew, the far-off cry of gulls squabbling over a dead fish at the water's unseen edge – but they were sounds that did no more than accentuate this sense of complete isolation.

'One thing,' Ralph Peteman said, so suddenly in the eerie hush that everyone started. 'This mist'll hide us from any as may come looking for us, if they are.'

The observation was the opposite of reassuring. What if they should flounder into some bottomless mud pan and become trapped and at the mercy of the incoming tide? Even as they contemplated that awful possibility, the mud in the deepest pans began to stir. Hardly noticeable at first, just a thin lay of water appearing as from nowhere, not sweeping in, not even a trickling, but an insidious, wetter gleam to the mud, deepening even as they looked.

A shudder of the unknown flickered along John's spine. While he and those of his village lived so close to this estuary, few found any reason to venture far enough out on to the mudflats to experience this tenacious grip as the foot sank into the slithery, slime-coated, grey-brown mass before finding a solid base. Perhaps Randere did. An eel fisherman, this was his world and in him they must trust.

The dim shape of Bawley's Mill was now only ten minutes away, yet seemed more out of reach than ever. Floating in a now clammy mist it had the look of a decayed tooth in the naked gums of the flats. The sun hardly pierced the thickening fog now. Even the gulls had ceased to squeal. The depressions were already filling. John shrugged off his fear and trained his eyes on Will walking confidently ahead. It was as well he was leading them.

Indeed, soon they were moving up out of the tidal mire, feeling dry land beneath their feet. Climbing the wide embankment that followed the East Haven to Pitsea, its well-trodden path dotted at intervals along its length with the low cottages of fisherfolk, they were soon crowding through the cottage door that the insane old miller was holding open for them, gleeful to find himself with company.

Eleven

Weary though they were from trekking such terrain, the miller's one room, ten paces by six, gave a dozen men little chance of comfort for the next two nights. By Thursday morning they were famished, Bawley not having the means to feed himself properly, much less all of them as well.

Simon Rycard, now untied but still closely guarded, spent his time haranguing his captures with dire retribution, but the young lad, who said his name was Robin, adapted very well, seemed happy to be with them and as excited by the sense of adventure as any youngster would be.

At first light they thanked old Bawley for his hospitality, not that he comprehended, and turned their faces to Pitsea with its promise of some decent food at last. How to get there had already been agreed, Will Randere now fully in charge, putting Tom down yet again for assuming they'd travel by road.

'On foot we've no escape from any as might pursue us, as well they might,' he sneered. 'We go by boat. I've seen two good-sized ones by the mill wall – old, but watertight. That way, if any come looking for us afore we reach

Pitsea, we'll be out in the creek and can make for Canvey flats where they can't follow, thence to Pitsea by way of other creeks. Knowing these parts, I know what I'm about.'

Everyone agreed it was the right strategy. To John's rancour, Tom was outvoted and ignored as they pulled away in the half-light, energetically bending to the oars, the filled creek as friendly to them as the mudflats had been forbidding.

By the time the sun was up they had reached Pitsea to find a hive of activity, men armed with an odd assortment of weaponry such as they could find. Longbows, of course, which many a rustic possessed and regularly practised with at the village butts, and a few halberds maybe last used by an older generation at the battles of Crecy or Poitiers. One had even found a battered helm and a rusty hauberk to wear. All carried a knife of some sort.

Will gave a derisive chuckle. 'Seems they be all prepared for some sort of battle. What battle? We'll run that slimy commissioner out of Brentwood and back to London with his tail twixt his legs without need of weaponry.'

There was a festive air about the place, men in merry mood, children skipping around their feet, women with the hems of their greasy kirtles tucked into hempen belts to free their feet for walking back and forth. Little more than a sprinkling of fishermen's cottages, Pitsea stood back from the creek upon slightly rising ground, safe from inundation by flood and high water during gales. It didn't even boast a proper church like Fobbing, just a wooden structure perched on a knoll. Its population hardly totalled thirty souls, yet today the place was bursting with folk. Hugh Baker had done a good job alerting neighbouring villages. Most of the able-bodied of Fobbing were here – as well as Corringham, Stanford-le-Hope, Mucking, Linford, Vange – and must have been congregating for the last twenty-four hours until there was hardly room enough to squeeze in one more arrival.

'There must be several hundred there,' John said as the boats ground on to the hard and their occupants scrambled out, pushing the bailiff before them, his hands again bound, though young Robin had become one of them and went free as he pleased.

'And have most like devoured all there was to devour in this goat's hole of a place,' Wat said sourly. 'And us with our gills sticking to our ribs.'

'Who's your spokesman?' enquired a scrawny-necked fellow with black stumps for teeth.

John automatically glanced towards Tom, but Will instantly thrust out his stubble-chin. 'I led my lot across the marsh after we took our bailiff and this stripling captive afore they could run squawking of what they knowed.'

The man and those around him looked grim. 'We heard,' he said. 'Just as well you fled. I be from Corringham and one of the

170

steward's varlets came through on his way to Fobbing yester-eve, said he were enquiring after a lad sent with a palfrey of the steward's lady to the smith there. They found the palfrey but no lad. This be he?' He glanced at the boy whose eyes shone with excitement of this occasion.

'Ay,' John replied before Will could say anything.

The man looked at him. 'You the smith as we heard struck down the commissioner's scullion as vilely assaulted your sister?'

Wishing he'd not been so quick to speak, John glanced towards the bailiff but he was out of hearing. Not wanting to implicate his father, he evaded the question.

'The varlet as came through your village?' he enquired, keeping his voice down. 'Likely he informed the steward of the lad being missing. We gave out that the boy had been stricken with a fever.' He felt sick for his father's safety. 'Would that I knew where our steward is now.'

The man revealed his black stumps in a grin. 'Wouldn't rightly know. But I know where his varlet be.'

'Where?' John's sinking heart leapt to see the man's grin widen. 'Your prisoner?'

'Nay, joined us of his own free will. As he was leaving, I said to Dick Jolyman here,' he indicated a broad-chested man beside him, 'I said, "Ask him if he wants to join us," and Dick said, "I've already asked and he don't." So I said in the varlet's ear, "Well, if he don't

171

then he's likely to leave here without his head, ever he puts a foot in that stirrup." And I made to take a swing at him with this sword.'

To demonstrate, he drew a sword with a dull blade from a shabby scabbard and brandished it, making those around him leap back. 'So he joined us,' he concluded with a rasping laugh as he ran a stubby thumb along the sword's blunt edge. 'Happen you might be a bit of a sword-smith as well as a black-smith and sharpen this for me?'

'I'd be glad to,' John said, but the man gave him a quizzical look. 'I'm a mite surprised you're not spokesman here, Smith, instead of this weasel.' He grinned as Will scowled. 'No offence, neighbour,' he said rudely. 'Doubt-less these good folk have their reasons for choosing you, though I'd have thought a smith or one of them other two tall'uns.'

He nodded towards Tom and Wat Gilde-born and, sheathing his sword, strode off, leaving John to mull over that last remark. Finally he could stand it no longer. Having to nurse their hunger before the lingering smell of cooking and a futile desire for a draught of ale, for it seemed the place had already been virtually eaten empty and drank dry, he turn-ed on Will, resentment pouring out in a flood.

'You were quick in stepping forward, weren't you? None as I know chose you by name, but you insisted on leading us to Baw-ley's Mill. None elected you spokesman for us at Brentwood. Tom here is the better man, and you know it.' Even as he spoke he knew

172

the last thing he wanted was Tom to be marked out yet again. Tom had said nothing, but Will gave a sly look, his thin lips curling.

'I tell you why I be the better man. I'll lay a gold coin to a grain of sand there's none of you be not famished to the backbone and wi' this village stripped bare by them as arrived afore we.'

The squint eyes in the weather-beaten face twinkled with cunning. 'While you was all snoring last night, I went about my business. In this bag of mine be victuals enough to fill all our bellies. I kept these until we were proper in need of 'em.'

Untying the string around the leather bag, he thrust his hands in and dragged out two large, fat, glistening eels, still squirming. 'What say you now?' he challenged as he held them aloft.

'You godforsaken rogue!' Wat burst out. 'You let us row all that way with our guts a-rumbling like thunder and not say a word?'

'Right.' Will sniggered. 'And what would you have done? Lit a fire in the boat? Well, get a fire started and we'll have us a fine meal and be filled ready to march to Brentwood. You too, Bailiff.'

'I'm eating none of your filthy peasant fare,' returned Rycard. 'By the mass – I'd soonest eat the dirt at my feet.'

'Help yourself,' giggled Will, man of the moment.

In a pot loaned by a local fishwife, they watched the eel as it stewed. For three pence

173

she also provided a third of a stale quartern loaf and a dozen oysters – small, gritty and at this time of year of doubtful quality – all of it an exorbitant price, but one they willingly paid out. People weren't stupid. They knew how to make a profit.

The oysters helped flavour the broth, making a grand feast for hungry men. While they ate, their eyes searched the crowds for others they knew, in turn spotted and hailed. So many from their own village were here, from poorest cottars like Robert Batt and John Mott to Will Copyn, their hayward, and John Kirkby the forester and old Nick Ocford, their reeve.

John had glimpsed his brother Ned among the faces. Clambering to his feet he was soon after him. 'What brings you here?' he demanded. 'You should be at home and looking out for our father. He could be in danger should someone come.'

'None will come,' Ned said. 'No one knows and them as do will not dare to say anything after all this time, or be in error. And they all know what that could mean for them. No one's interested in having pots mended.'

Dragged back to his brother's friends, Ned fell to dipping a finger in the succulent broth and sucking the juices while John questioned him further.

'How is our father?'

Ned continued to lick until given a portion. 'Back to hisself again. But his arm pains him. The exercise with our sister's assailant

174

did jar it.'

'How is Cicely? And Alice and our mother?'

'She seems recovered. Alice is better at comforting her than Mother, being nearer her age. Alice is full tender and caring. And Mother is back to attending our grandmother, who sees it as normal a day as any gone before.'

'And the others?' John cast a cautious glance at Tom who was busy talking to some of their friends. 'Tom's wife – she must be concerned for him. Is all well with her?'

Ned looked at him, bewildered, then shrugged. 'As far as I could tell.'

'No message from her? For Tom,' he amended hastily, seeing the perplexed frown deepen. What was he thinking, questioning Ned in this way? 'No matter,' he said and became very busy prodding the charred remnants of wood further into the dying fire.

A stir among those around them took Ned's attention from his brother. As if by common consent, instinctive as the singular wheeling of a flock of pigeons, the aimless wandering of this great gathering began flowing in a definite northward direction.

Will was on his feet. Wiping greasy fingers on an equally greasy tunic, he hitched his leather belt to an easier position on his hips, the leather bag lighter of the now consumed eels.

'Come on, lads,' he ordered. 'Us o' Fobbing began this business and it will be us as will head this march.'

175

His fast, nimble feet hurrying them on, they were soon at the front, their bailiff tethered in their midst, though young Robin, having found a companion in Ned, skipped alongside him free as a bird.

'His home is in Oxford,' Ned supplied. 'He hasn't seen his family since he was six years old. Think of it, John. I already miss my village and I've been gone only one day. He were but seven when he were sent to Pleshey Castle to be instructed on becoming a squire, as are the sons of many well-born folk. I'm heartily glad I weren't born of wealth if that's what happens.'

John was eying the lightly built lad. 'You and your mistress were a ways from Pleshey to be in Fobbing without her husband, our steward.'

The delicate elfin face smiled back at him. 'Steward Somenour's lady was on pilgrimage to Canterbury and I required to go with her as page, along with others. She had arranged to rest at Fobbing Manor by invitation of your bailiff's wife for a night or two.'

With all that had happened one couldn't be too careful, but the boy's open looks revealed no subterfuge.

The way ascended gently northeast out of Pitsea to disappear into heavily wooded country, the men with twenty miles ahead of them glad to reach shade.

Before the trees closed in, John cast a glance at the column behind him. With the narrow

176

lane obliging men to walk singly or in pairs, their numbers looked far greater than they actually were. It was like seeing a long, snaking caterpillar, early morning sunshine emphasizing its dull colours of russet, brown and grey, its stiff hairs the points of lances and pikes, longbows and staves that seemed to protrude along its back with menacing intent for all the merry chatter that floated up.

Travelling west on the road known as Smythes Strate, part of a road that ran from London to Hadleigh Castle, took them some two miles through unbroken woodland, finally coming out on to the open fields of the manor of Bottelers. A few women who had been hoeing came hurrying to meet them.

'You to Brentwood?' one called, leaning on her hoe. 'Our men are ahead of you, started out afore dawn. Our manor lord gave leave for some to make representation on our behalf, but more'n he knows went with 'em, their real purpose to tell the King's commissioner, more forceful like, as us here have already paid our dues in full.'

'We'll give him his dues orright,' one of the marchers laughed. 'We'll send him back to London quicker than he left.'

'And where you be from, lad?' a thin, elderly woman asked John as he passed her. Quickly he told her and found her walking beside him.

'Fobbing, eh? Be your manor lord one o' the King's uncles, Earl of Buckingam?'

'He's lord of a great many manors, old mother. Ours is just one pinch of what he owns.'

'A pox on him, I say.' She spat on to the sun-baked road. 'Him and that other one, John o' Gaunt, the Duke of Lancaster. It's my belief they both plan to rule this land, using our king, that golden boy, for their own greedy ends.'

'Ay, but young King Richard have us to watch out for him,' said the younger women who'd come to join her. 'Great Edward's grandson is our king by right of God and the untimely death of his father, the Black Prince, Edward, Prince of Wales.' Her voice was vibrant. She was obviously proud of her knowledge. 'We'll have no John o' Gaunt ruling us in his name. 'Tis as John Ball says, when the time be right the commons will go to our young king and open his eyes to what's going on, and to our needs.'

'And what we start in Brentwood this day,' Gildeborn's voice lifted for all to hear, 'will echo through this land and down the ages. Will it not, lads?

'Ay, it will!' came a chorus of voices.

It was an exuberant, thirsty crowd that poured into the tiny village of Bertlesdon. A little stone church perched on a small round hill to give it a sweeping view of the flat countryside, a few cottages, one or two freemen's farms, and that was all. Even the alehouse was merely a single-roomed cottage, identified

178

only by its ale-stake, a small bush stuck on the end of a pole outside the open door.

A dumpy little man hurried out carrying a huge leather jug brim-full of his somewhat thin brew, his dumpy wife having appeared clasping no less than ten wooden mugs to her large heavy breast. Neither looked at all prosperous, their clothing worn and full of holes.

Amid jesting and laughter, pennies were dropped into the pouch at her thick waist, a few, like the leering Will Randere, dropping theirs down her deep cleavage and receiving a light-hearted slap on the hand for their audacity.

'This is the life,' sighed Wat, sinking down beside his brother Will and taking a long draught that set his Adam's apple leaping like an agitated frog. 'Just to sit here and not have to gaze at sheep.'

His brother nudged him and pointed to distant field. 'Look, Walter,' he said slowly. 'Sheep.'

For a moment Wat regarded them. 'Ay, but them's not ours, Will.'

Will Randere did not laugh with the others. 'We ought not dally overlong here. Look at 'em all.' He pointed to the lounging groups, laughing, exchanging vulgarities with the villagers, some wandering off to obey nature's needs, unaware they were being spied upon by a small group of maids from behind a cottage wall. An older woman spoke sharply to them and, shamefaced, they moved away.

'You'd think we be going to some fair to look at 'em all,' Randere said sourly. 'All this lolling about won't get us to Brentwood, and there's a way to go yet. Time we arrive others would have chased that royal commissioner back to London and we'll miss out on all the credit.'

'Is that all you're keen on?' Tom asked, fixing him with a look. 'A bit of credit? I thought we were to Brentwood to state our grievances and put all wrongs to right. Not to hold ourselves up to empty fame.'

'All this did begin in Fobbing,' said Kirkby. 'We should have some of the credit.'

'Why?' Tom shot at him. He sat upright. 'This isn't about this village or that proving itself better than another. This is about folk trying to lift themselves from the mire in which our lords would like us to remain.' Into the silence that followed that statement, he added, 'We go honestly to Brentwood to state our case.'

There came a derisive chuckle from Tom Fuller. 'You're fooling yourself, ain't you? It's true we be going to meet the commissioner to say we've paid in full, but we all know there's many an old mother, an idiot sister, a spinster aunt as has not been revealed, supposedly died in the last twelvemonth, or a son supposedly fled the manor to work elsewhere. We ain't being too honest about that and by the rood the Commission knows it too, and this Bampton is no fool. Either we pay up or send him packing. So don't you go talking

180

about honesty, Tom Baker. And if there's a bit of fame at the end of it, then let us have our part in it, I say.'

Tom's face had tightened and he leapt to his feet, dragging the speaker up with him. John leapt up too. It wasn't like Tom to go thumping into a man, but it looked like he was about to do so now.

'Tom, no!'

John's cry stayed Tom's hand for long enough for Fuller to twist from the grip on his gipon. Just then Ned and his new friend Robin came running up.

'Some are beginning to move off,' Ned called. 'We'd best be going, too.'

Tom stood for a moment as everyone got to their feet. He was breathing heavily. John had never seen such a change come over his friend. Usually so mild, he suddenly seemed another person.

'Yes,' Tom said slowly, looking at Randere. 'We'd best go, or we'll miss all the fun.' The sarcasm that rang in his voice wasn't like Tom either.

Passing village after village, most of their route was shaded by wild woodland, the long straight path beneath the trees still damp from that great storm, with slimy puddles where the sun hadn't penetrated the foliage.

Some of the chatter had died away and John came alongside Tom to whisper in the eerie silence, 'I'll be heartened to see habitation. If I were alone here I would think as some evil

181

could well leap out on me.'

Tom's chuckle fell dully on the moist air that smelled of dank wood and moss. 'Well, you're not alone, John. We're all together to keep them evil things at bay.'

'We're here,' Randere put in importantly, 'to keep that pox-ridden Bampton at bay, and a fart to your evil things!'

This said, he strode on ahead on his bent legs, looking less a leader than anyone John could imagine. He was indeed having trouble keeping up with this eager company, whose pace hadn't diminished even after all this walking.

Twelve

The sun was well high by the time they passed Ingrave, their destination but a few miles further on. Several hundred men, having slept rough in fields that night, were more in a truculent mood than jocular, but they cheered as the road widened to become more than a mere cart track and began filling with people on their way to Brentwood, many with goods on their backs, others in small oxcarts, it being market day.

'Not far now, men. We'll soon be eating well and drinking well. And maybe we'll sleep wi' a wench tonight in a comfortable bed.'

John saw Will Randere's eyes light up at that thought, making him look away contemptuously.

'Are you some of those attending the Commission?' enquired a rider on a fine horse as they reached the crossroads at the north end of the town. A surcoat of tawny velvet and a high-crowned hat of good-quality beaver proclaimed him a merchant of some wealth as he rode in front of two heavy carts full of woolsacks drawn by two pairs of oxen, his cartmen looking well fed and sprightly.

The man's enquiry was one of pure curiosity, but coming from one of better standing than them it met a surly challenge from Will Randere. 'What's that to you, then?'

The merchant reined gently. 'I do not think Sir Thomas Bampton was expecting so many of you,' he said quietly, his accent strange to the Thames-side villagers.

He'd addressed the remark to Tom rather than Randere, Tom having smiled up at him in a friendly way, compensating for Will's hostility.

'Seems he'll be in for a surprise, I think,' Tom answered amicably, and then just as amicably asked, 'Has he many soldiers with him, do you know?'

'That I don't.' The merchant lifted a hand to stroke thoughtfully at his neatly forked beard. 'He has remained within the tollbooth these three hours, not showing himself to any that have already arrived, and I must admit I am sure many more are here than he did expect.' He gave a small smile. 'Well, good day to you,' he said and moved on ahead.

If the man had glimpsed their bailiff still bound in their midst, he'd said nothing, but Tom suggested they untie him.

'What for?' challenged Will, glaring at him as though his leadership was being usurped.

'Because should he be seen fettered, Bampton will call his soldiers out for sure.'

Even Will could see the sense in that. Begrudgingly he allowed Rycard to be freed. 'But keep a close eye on him lest he cry abduction,' he warned.

'I've no need to cry abduction,' Rycard

gloated, confident now that he was free. 'When his lordship learns how you have ill handled an officer of your manor – and he will – then we will see who are the masters.'

'Hold your tongue, Bailiff!' snarled Wat Gildeborn behind him, cuffing the man across the head, but Simon Rycard was feeling bold now.

'Sir Bampton has obviously been alerted to the great number of men coming here. Before this day is out, I warrant those of you not lying dead in Brentwood will be awaiting a hanging for treason, for there is an army concealed to receive you, mark my words.'

His threat prompted guffaws, but John felt the laughter a little hollow. But within moments of entering the main street, John's anxiety was dispelled at the sight of so many folk. The place was alive with people buying and selling, with carts and livestock, as well as those who had come here to meet the King's Commission.

A group of pilgrims, each with a staff, scrip and a small bundle of personal belongings, hovered around the chapel of St Thomas Becket. Having paused at the chapel to offer silver for their souls' sake, their faces reflected an eagerness to be off on the next stage of their journey to St Thomas's shrine at Canterbury.

The marketplace itself was in an open square at the far end of the little town. There, stalls were loaded with local produce, cheap trinkets and cloth, and the noise of barter and

185

bargaining reached the new arrivals' ears above the din of cartwheels and the cries of stallholders, squawks of chickens and the quacking of ducks, their heads protruding from slatted crates.

Opposite the chapel an entertainer juggled with firebrands watched by a thin circle of onlookers, some children doing their best to make him drop one of his flaming sticks.

Opposite the marketplace stood the two-storeyed timber tollbooth where the court of wayfarers was held – the *pieds poudrés*, as it was known, with power to deal with the numerous scuffles and fights that accompanied market day, and to administer punishment. In front of the door a trestle table had been set up ready to receive the moneys still purported owing from the last poll tax demands. The table was deserted, its surface bare.

'The sight of us has frightened them off,' someone laughed as they hurried to join those already milling about the tollbooth and making no attempt to conceal their animosity.

The numbers were growing by the second. Soon the crowd would take over the entire open space, ousting the stallholders who would see trouble coming and pack up hastily.

Five people had emerged from the tollbooth. Three were in dark clerical garb, each embracing a bundle of parchments. The other two were the Justices of the Peace to whom

186

the men were expected to make answer.

The smaller man was Sir Thomas de Bampton. Elderly, rotund, his surcoat of sombre brown brocade was trimmed with squirrel fur as was his square hat.

The taller, angular, heavy-chinned man, whose large, firm mouth was surrounded by a close-cut beard, was Sir John Gildeborough, lord of the manor of Wennington, a man who had recently added land in Fobbing to his many other acquisitions. Visibly younger than Bampton, he obviously favoured bright colours. His plum-velvet pleated surcoat, particoloured with saffron, was short and in keeping with the current fashion of the wealthy. A jewelled leather belt nipped in the waist and the conical plum and saffron velvet cap was set at a jaunty angle. Though younger and renowned as a fair-minded judge, he was nevertheless a strict one.

From the side of the building two serjeants-at-arms had come to take up positions on either side of the small group. Seeing only two, John had a creeping suspicion that more were concealed as he moved forward the final few yards to come to a stop just in front of the table, he and some of his companions having somehow pushed to the front for a better view.

Bampton was thumping the table with a mallet to bring everyone's attention to the commencement of proceedings. He seemed little perturbed by the numbers confronting him.

'Good people...' he began, his voice pitched high to reach everyone.

It was then that Simon Rycard's voice rang out from somewhere in the crowd, despite being close-guarded as Randere had ordered.

'My Lord de Bampton!' His cry was instantly stifled, though Bampton did not seem to have heard it anyway.

'I command you to know that I am Sir Thomas de Bampton, steward of the manor of Havering-atte-Bower, a justice of the peace appointed by our Lord King and his government to make inquisition this day into the most recent collection of poll tax in the County of Essex and certain flagrant evasions arising therefrom.' He held aloft an unrolled scroll, its huge seal dangling.

'This is the Commission sent to me to raise all moneys in default, and I thereby command you all to make diligent inquiry among yourselves, to give me your reply, and to pay your money without more ado, by order of the government of the Lord King Richard.'

There was not one cry of protest as he finished speaking, though John could see men looking at their neighbours, willing each to be the first to speak out. What had happened to all that bold talk – or had it only been vain glory and bluster? It had all come to nothing. In a moment or two, men would start coming forward, humbly making excuses for their oversight in paying the taxes. Yet he was as faint-hearted as any of them.

For guidance, he looked towards their self-

188

appointed leader. Randere had the receipt for previous payment clutched in his hand. He met John's glance and looked away. His small stature protecting him from notice, he was even easing his body back between those behind him, seeming to melt into the crowd. Tom had also noticed and had rounded on him before the man could completely disappear. Contempt was written on his face, but his voice was quiet.

'I could have told you what would happen, right from the start.' With that, he plucked the receipt from the other's hand and stepped forward clear of the crowd to stand isolated before their Justices.

'Here!' His voice rang out. He held the receipt aloft. 'Here, Master Bampton – a receipt for tax collected, in full.' Calling the man Master Bampton, rather than Sir, was insult in itself. 'A receipt from you afore Epiphany by the village of Fobbing. And I daresay there be like receipts in every village in this hundred.'

Bampton had sat down after his announcement, and now regarded the upstart with a harsh frown. 'By what right do you come forward?'

'By right that I am spokesman for the village of Fobbing.'

Bampton leaned forward over the table. 'By what name are you known?'

'By the name of Thomas Baker.'

'Then, Thomas Baker, do not come leaping at me with your worthless bit of parchment. I have bidden all here to make diligent inquiry among their fellows as to the honesty of their returns – returns that are in grave doubt and are therefore the reason for this sitting.' He was addressing them all now. 'I therefore bid them to say their names to my clerks and make true payment of tax. Nothing more is required of them.' He returned his attention to the man standing rudely before him. 'So there is no need for you to postulate before me—'

'There is every need, Master Bampton!'

It seemed to John that Tom was being deliberately insolent, addressing him as an equal. John saw him hold the receipt out at arm's length, almost under the man's nose. Perhaps he was trying to regain his leadership and put Randere down, but why with such force, allowing himself to be marked out like this? Where was the mild-mannered man that John knew?

'We have paid!' he shouted.

Bampton was beginning to lose his temper. 'I told you, young man, do not flourish bits of rubbish purporting to be receipts that no doubt you cannot even read.'

'We've paid, Master Bampton,' Tom repeated, while behind him came murmurs of encouragement. 'Full, fare and square, as this receipt shows. And I do know my letters, sir. This is an acquittance from yourself, which means we need pay no more. Nor will we!'

This last flagrant rebut of their lordship's integrity brought shocked silence from those at the table. Gildeborough's thin, hard lips grew harder. Bampton's fleshy cheeks grew florid. From the crowd broke ragged cheering that quickly became a roar of approval, everyone gathering courage from their new leader. Now they were one.

Emboldened, several moved forward to range themselves alongside Tom. The cry was being taken up: 'We'll pay no more!' This soon became a chant. A huge body of men was pressing against the flimsy table, which wobbled precariously. In alarm the clerks leapt up, sweeping ledgers and documents into their arms like mothers protecting their children.

The huge crowd swept forward. The two serjeants-at-arms clutched at their scabbards, awaiting orders to draw sword. Both Bampton and Gildeborough were up on their feet and calling for order, trying to avoid violence. Two swords against a mob, poorly armed as it was, would be as effective as tickling an ox with a feather.

Bampton's raised voice could hardly be heard as he held up his arms, ineffectually patting the air with the flat of his palms. 'Hold! Hold I say, else I'll have you all arrested!'

'You'll arrest no one, Master Commissioner.' Tom's voice rang close to John's ear, but his words were lost as Bampton signalled in panic to the serjeants-at-arms, who immediately spurred their mounts into the crowd, swords drawn.

191

It was too much. With a deep-throated roar, the mob closed about both animals, grabbing at them, the first few going down with sliced faces and arms from the frantic sweep of the swords, but the rest overwhelming both horses and riders.

The table had given way in a splintering of wood. The terrified clerks dropped their bundles and fled as scores of feet trampled the parchments. Before the officers could do more damage, billhooks caught their sword arms, hooked into the surcoats over their protective hauberks, and both men were hauled from the saddle into the melee.

Unbelievably, they were allowed to struggled free, the main objective being to destroy the Commission and send those entrusted with it back to their overlords. Murder would have defeated their cause before it had even begun. This was the message that had been spread by all, and every man saw its worth.

But neither of their lordships stayed to be certain of that. As stones came flying at them, they turned and ran to their horses tethered behind the tollbooth. Seconds later they were galloping off down the long, straight road south of the town, heading for London, followed at a distance by their unseated bodyguards and the three terrified clerks, a host of ruffians in their wake, ripping the official documents to shreds as they went.

It was over. The task was completed. Now let them in London know that they were not dealing with mere gullible subjects but with men who knew what was unfair and refused to be treated that way.

But now it was all over there was a sense of anti-climax. Only one way to stop that – celebrate. The mob broke up to roll about the town boasting of their victory and what they would do in London, looking for something to quench their thirsts.

Amid the celebrating, John looked about him, frowning. 'Where's our bailiff?'

The group of Fobbing men ceased slapping each other on the back as young Robin pointed timidly northward. 'I saw him making his way out of the throng while all were closing in upon their lordships.'

Wat gave the boy a smack across the ear, making him yelp. 'Whyn't you raise an alarm, you young brat? Or were you in mind for him to slip away?'

The lad glared at him in resentment. 'If that were so, would I be here telling you now and not be off with him? There was such a clamour I could not bring your attention to his going.'

'None of your stinking lies—'

'Leave the lad be,' Elys cut in. 'Ain't his fault. We should have kept a better eye on that slippery toad. What's done is done.'

'You say that!' John flared at him. 'My father could be at risk from what this young spy told Bailiff.'

'Only if he told him what he *thought* he saw.' Wat took the lad viciously by the same ear he'd just clouted, making him squeal. 'You had time to blurt what you *thought* you'd seen us doing. What did you tell him?'

The boy twisted in pain. 'You were on me before I could say—'

'Don't gainsay me, younker! Skulking on them battlements. You saw something to the disadvantage of us, spy.'

'I saw nothing—' He squealed again as his ear was twisted. 'I went up to see what great distances could be viewed. I saw men digging, burying something. I do not know what. When you all looked up, pointing towards me, I took fright.'

'So why go crying to Bailiff, you weasel, if you saw nowt?'

'I thought you intended to molest me. When I saw your bailiff, I ran to him to save me. Before God, I swear that was all.'

'Why didn't we think to question this young devil afore?' Elys said.

'And have Bailiff smell a bigger rat than he already had?' Tom's soft question drew their eyes to him, realizing the danger of saying too much before the lad. But John's mind wasn't so easy.

'Our bailiff did seem alarmed. Perhaps the boy did have time to alert him of...'

'Of what, John?' His friend's warning voice cut through what he had been about to say. 'Us burying a dead animal? Had we not taken them both captive, we'd have been obliged to show Bailiff what we'd buried and been delayed from our main purpose. We'd have

194

been apprehended for burying that deer, poached to supplement a poor tenant's larder, food being thin on the ground this year. And we all know poaching brings sentence of imprisonment. What say you, lad?'

He patted the lad's shoulder while, glad for a spark of kindness amid all this sudden hostility, the boy nodded his head in gratitude, convinced now as to what he had seen.

With Bampton chased off, his Commission thrown to the four winds, there was no holding back the jubilant crowds.

Two fieldworkers had mounted the officers' abandoned horses, riding up and down the main street, bowing and gesturing like knights and falling off in the process, resulting in some bloody noses as others tried to take their place.

Men were roaming about bragging, calling to the townsfolk to join their cause, which had gone a little astray, with whole groups of villagers splitting up to fall into taverns demanding ale and wine by the cask, refusing to pay, and by weight of numbers getting away with it. The day was theirs. They were the lords.

The market stalls had closed. Some diehard stallholders had already had theirs knocked flat, their goods trampled and kicked about the square by men growing increasingly drunk, squabbling and fighting. Some of the wealthier townspeople were seen leaving for nearby South Weald and safety while others had closed their shutters and bolted their doors.

As evening closed in, leaders counted for nothing, everyone seeing himself a leader as he swayed and staggered about the town, ale dribbling down his beard, a great wooden mug in his fist whilst he let water against any wall he pleased.

The Fobbing men, too, had split up, Randere the first to go, stomping off to find a choice whore for himself. Tom, the Gildeborn brothers and John now sat in one corner of the marketplace eying the revellers as they pranced up and down with linked arms, singing at the top of their voices while local harlots hung on their shoulders. John was glad he had insisted on Ned and young Robin staying here with him. Ned had protested, looking for some fun, and Robin had looked downcast, but John had remained adamant.

'There's enough trouble at home without you getting into more here. I don't want you to face our father when we return with a black eye and cut lips – or worse.'

He was now certain they would return home. No one was going to march on London. No one was going to lay his grievance at the feet of the young King Richard. No one was going to do anything about the Poll Tax. This was as far as it would go. It had all collapsed.

'It don't even trouble them,' he said to Tom, 'that Bampton could return with an army. There could be a hanging or two by this time tomorrow – and for what? Half a day's glory without purpose.'

'All I yearn for now is to go home to my sweet Marjory,' Tom said.

The mention of her name brought a sudden picture of her into John's head. The small stature, the glowing golden hair framing that pale, heart-shaped face, the green eyes – oh, those green eyes – and her touch, the small hand on his arm, testing its strength, caressing, like the touch of a lover...

Shocked at himself, he forced his mind away from the vision, hearing Tom saying, 'She must be fretting, not knowing how I am or where. Now I must return home to tell her that her fretting was for nothing, that at no time was I in danger, that all I did was sit on a market corner and watch men making fools of themselves.'

No danger? John felt anger bubble up inside him thinking how Tom had stepped out from a mob of well over two hundred men, making himself a marked man.

He thought too of himself, his family. With their cause fallen into ruin, his father was now at risk of being pointed out, taken and hung for the murder of a government official.

'I cannot return home,' he said huskily. 'Not openly. Not with the others.' In the fading light he saw Tom turn and glance at him, the look on Tom's face showing him there was no need to explain.

'Nor can you,' he went on. 'You should never have given your name to them Justices.'

Tom mulled that over for a moment or two, then said sadly, 'We'll get a message to your father to flee,' and John knew it would be a while before Tom would see his sweet Marjory, and the guilt he felt about his own secret thoughts of her was like iron pressing on his breast.

'Or perhaps we can get to him in secret,' Tom added hopefully with Marjory still on his mind.

'Get to who in secret?' Wat asked, overhearing.

There was no need to reply as a party of drunken merrymakers went lurching by, diverting his attention. John turned back to Tom, his voice low.

'You know you've reaped Bampton's displeasure – could even end up swinging at the end of a rope...' He stopped in horror at the evil thought that shot like the fiery hand of the Devil through his brain. With Tom gone, what of him and Marjory? He'd swept the unspeakable thought out hardly had it formed.

'Tom, you've got to flee!' There was something like panic in his voice. 'They have you well marked. It'll be you they come seeking, not that drunken lot, damn 'em! And damn you!' A sudden rage consumed him, not so much at Tom but at himself. 'Damn you, Tom! What right had you to go leaping in and declaring against what can't be changed, assuming we were all behind you? No one asked you to. Damn you for what you've put us in, all of us now in danger.'

Tom was regarding him in silence as his tirade wasted itself and he was left panting from his anger. Wat and William Gildeborn and the two young boys had come to stand gaping, as had a few who'd overheard his outburst.

Tom's eyes seemed to be boring into his, for a moment seeing inside his head, almost as though he knew what thoughts lay there. Did he know? Had he seen the small exchange that had passed between his friend and his wife? John felt himself shudder. Then the expression faded, to be replaced by a devil-may-care look as if nothing untoward had ever been uttered.

'Then there's no point sitting round here dolouring over spilled milk. Life's too short. Might as well join others in such disport as we can, while we can, for we'll all be dead afore too long.'

And he was off, striding along the main street towards the nearest tavern leaving the others to follow if they wanted as he linked arms with a line of singers, even breaking into song himself.

'Bring us in no mutton, for that be seldom lean,
  And bring us in no tripes, for they be seldom clean.
  But bring us in good ale, boys, bring us in good ale.
  For our blessed Lady's sake, bring us in good ale...'

199

Thirteen

John found himself draped, limp as a ten-day-old cabbage leaf, over a cask in a silent market square. It seemed that only a moment ago there had been laughter and song and brawling. Now all was quiet with a fierce sun beating down.

He stared about, trying to focus. A few folk wandered aimlessly about. A dog was scratching itself, another sniffing at some horse dung. It all looked rather forsaken as John tried to remember last night.

All that came to him was the dream, the nightmare – Tom finding him closeted with Marjory, drawing a knife to plunge into his deceitful friend's breast while Marjory cried to him to let Tom die so that they could be together ... The dream had switched to him trawling through the marshes trying in vain to find Tom...

John looked up to find Tom standing over him with a wooden mazer of water in one hand and a mug of ale in the other.

'Here!' Unceremoniously the water was dashed full in John's face, bringing him gasping and spluttering to a sitting position, uttering a string of oaths at the pain ripping through his skull as the mug of ale was thrust into his hand. Oaths cut short, he crammed the mug to his lips and took several gulps.

'God's bones!' he gasped as he came up for air. 'I did need that.' Unsteadily, he got to his feet.

Wat Gildeborn was sitting on the ground nearby, knees drawn up to support his elbows, his head buried in his hands.

Nearby his brother William, a man of sense and substance, stood with his shoulder against a wall, a faintly amused smile quirking at the corners of his mouth. No sick head for him this morning, ever careful with his drinking.

Wat mumbled into his hands without looking, 'What day is it?'

'Friday,' Tom told him, against the wall. 'Friday morning.'

'There are bells in my head.'

'The matins bell coming from South Weald.'

Wat looked up, squinting, the morning sun hurting his eyes. John saw he had a large swelling beneath one eye. The sight at last awakened recollections of last night – the tavern, an argument with a local man about the disturbance to his town, Wat sending him sprawling and a fight issuing with onlookers yelling encouragement and punching the air with their fists.

A knife had been drawn, which Wat swiftly dealt with by clouting his assailant with his forehead to leave him with a nose that would never be firm and straight again. Wat had gone roaring off, bleeding lip, bruised cheek and all, followed by a crowd of supporters. John now also recalled that he'd not seen Ned and his young friend.

To his enquiry Will Gildeborn said, a little unkindly, 'You should have kept an eye on the lad instead of drinking yourself silly.'

'Ned will come to no harm,' Tom quietly put in, casually leaning his weight against the wall, but John turned on him in sudden anger. Tom was always far too sure of himself.

'You say that! He could be lying somewhere with a knife in his guts.' A snatch of his dream came whirling back. 'Both could have been waylaid by robbers. But what do you care?'

He saw a glint come into Tom's eyes at such unfairness, but his voice remained unruffled as if he were fighting to conquer some sort of rancour within him. There was something odd about Tom lately.

John saw him heave himself away from the wall. 'Bad tidings travel swift,' he said, terse enough to leave John wondering if in his drunken state last night he'd babbled something he shouldn't have. Marjory seemed to be haunting his every thought as the days went by, and now his dreams too.

'How so?' John challenged, more aggressively than he meant to.

'We've heard nowt as could make us think him harmed.' The reply now controlled. 'Even in this town a crime would be noticed by someone. You worry needless, John. He be nigh sixteen, almost a man. Most likely he and the other lad are with some of our neighbours even now.'

'So you say.' John knew he was being unreasonable but found it hard to stop. 'You always have something to say – a salve for every sore. What makes you so high above the rest to be so certain...' He stopped himself in time, aware that some demon inside him had been about to open Tom's eyes to certain facts about his wife. It left him quaking inside knowing how near he'd come to that insanity. It couldn't go on like this. He had to put thoughts of her aside, never dwell on her again.

Tom was looking at him enquiringly. His look had changed, becoming kindly enough that a moment later he might have broken down, except that they were interrupted by a stranger coming up to Tom and putting a heavy hand on his shoulder, making him swing round defensively.

'Be ye Thomas Baker of Fobbing? A baker there?'

John eyed the man in alarm. A thought sped through his head that this was someone in the pay of authority sent to bring him to account for felony.

He glanced about for the man's henchmen. There were none. Then the fool would stand no chance making an arrest with him here to defend Tom. He would knock the man down and drag his friend away. But he mustn't jump to conclusions.

'Who are you?' he demanded.

The man grinned, showing rotten teeth. A man authorized to make an arrest would not look like this. John relaxed a little but was still on his guard. The man's fiery beard was shot through with grey, as was his patchy hair. Now John noticed that his leather jerkin smelled of fish.

'If you be of Fobbing,' he said, ignoring John's question, 'doubtless you know of Rackstrawe?'

'Our parson?' Wat was up off the ground, his tone incredulous. His brother had also come forward.

'You know Parson Rackstrawe?'

The man grinned in amusement. 'Parson Rackstrawe, is it? Well, whether you call him parson or no, or whether you call him Rackstrawe, we in Kent know him as Jack Straw, and I daresay it be close enough.'

'What of him?' asked Tom.

'Are ye Thomas, baker of Fobbing?' the man repeated.

'I am.' He ignored John's warning hand. 'What do you want of me?'

The man gave a nod of satisfaction. 'I'm here at your ... ah ... your parson's bidding. You and your companions, if they are trustworthy, are to follow me.'

With that he shambled off, not turning back to see if they followed. With a moment's hesitation they made after him, John a little reluctantly, imagining Ned coming back here to find him gone.

They were led down an alley running off the main street, then into an even smaller one at right angles to the first. A few paces along the man ushered them, very much on their guard now, into a small stableyard. John turned instantly to face their guide.

'What is this place?'

'As ye can see,' the man grinned. 'All ye need to know is that John Ball hath rung our bell.'

It was Tom's turn to be suspicious. 'John Ball lies in Maidstone gaol.'

'Not for much longer,' came the reply. 'Jack Straw says ye are to spread John Ball's signal to as many villages and townships as ye are able. I hope all can ride wi'out falling off?' He chuckled at his own jest, directed at common men more accustomed to using their feet to get from place to place. 'Now is the time to say.' He swept a hand towards the dim stalls whose occupants peered over the open half of the hatches, occasionally tossing their heads and snorting.

The men looked at each other questioningly. Three of them could ride fair enough, but Tom was the doubtful one. The baking of bread had very little to do with the need to ride a horse. He was contemplating the large, spirited animals with apprehension, but the stranger allowed none of them the opportunity to negate or confirm an ability to ride.

'Enlist whoever ye consider able to spread our message with all haste. An army of commons must be raised. All must join. How it is

205

done will be your concern.'

'What if some refuse?' Tom asked.

'Accept no refusal unless he be near to dying in his bed.'

'There are some as will have other plausible excuses,' Tom said, but the man had an answer for that, too.

'A threat on his life, even his house, will cause him who is loath to follow come leaping to your side. Our army must number thousands else our cause is lost. Now, up with you all while I go to the rest of my business. They're saddled and ready.' At the gate he paused. 'Ah – I all but forgot. Jack Straw ... I do beg your pardon – Parson Rackstrawe –' he gave a small, mocking bow – 'bids you to light a beacon on Fobbing Mound so them in Kent will know Essex is risen. We must all rise as one at the exact moment. But make sure ye have an army to match the great company as Kent will muster.'

They watched him slip out into the alley, leaving them to stare from one to the other.

'One of us must stay to rally them in this town,' Tom said, taking command. 'I've little skill with a horse. I daren't try to mount any of them great beasts. I'd be on my arse ever a foot touched the stirrup. I'll seek another to take my place as messenger.'

John's protest was instant. 'You imperil yourself by staying here. The King's Commissioners will return with men to arrest the ringleaders, of whom you are one. We must choose—'

'God's blood!' Wat burst out. 'We've no time to draw straws! Let him stay if he wants.'

Thrusting the others aside, he made for one of the stalls, savagely flinging open the lower hatch to grab the bridle of the biggest animal, a large grey. As it rolled wild eyes and pulled back with an alarmed snicker, he yanked its head down with all the strength of his lanky body to lead it out.

'We must make a plan,' Wat said, assuming authority by virtue of the size and strength of the horse he'd chosen. 'No point all galloping one way. I'll go to the northwest. John to the southwest...'

'Southeast,' John corrected curtly. He'd not be ordered about by yet another self-styled leader. Too many were ready to assume that role, like Will Randere, only to relinquish it like a hot stone at the first hint of danger. 'And then to Fobbing to light our beacon.' A small, evil voice in his head told him exactly why he'd suggested that; a voice he desperately fought not to comprehend. 'Being as I'll be in that part of the county,' he finished lamely.

Wat gave him an impartial look. 'I leave you all to argue it out atwixt you. But time's pressing.'

He swung his long body into the saddle with a certain amount of grace, but there ended his horsemanship. At the first feel of a rider's weight, the horse snorted, flung up its head and danced sideways all around the yard while Wat, letting out great oaths and bellows, tugged on the reins.

His brother regarded his antics with amusement. 'Have a regard for that beast o' yourn. He'll be little use to you if you go pushing him to his limit, all lathered and blowing afore you finish rousing all north Essex.'

Wat's reply to this was another string of curses aimed at his mount, now at the point of getting the better of its rider. With two of them running to open the yard gate wider, he tried thumping the animal's flanks with vicious heels, making little impression on the beast and flicking the reins like a goodwife shaking her table linen. The grey, seeing the double gates opening wide, responded so suddenly and with such power that Wat was almost thrown backwards as man and horse swept out of the yard.

'If he ever stays on it,' his brother muttered sagaciously towards the empty opening. Chuckling, he turned to John for his choice of steed, but when John shrugged in wordless impartiality, he chose the roman-nosed skewbald for himself.

John watched him mount, reining in the animal with a hand as adroit as any knight. A franklin, a man of substance, he was well used to riding and could match any of lesser means but who by virtue of his high-born lineage called himself his lord and master. From his saddle he looked down at the other two. 'There were men here from Ingatestone, Stock and from Bocking well past Chelmsford to the north. They were returning home this very morning with news of yesterday's victory. I shall ride first to Ingatestone to ensure they dispatch messengers further afield, thence to Danbury and Maldon and as many townships atwixt the river Blackwater and the River Crouch as time allows.'

'And I'll get messengers to the southwest,' Tom promised as William leaned down from the saddle to clasp each briefly by the hand.

'God guard you both.'

'Godspeed,' returned Tom as, leaning low over his mount's neck, Will Gildeborn swiftly departed.

Left alone, John regarded him anxiously. 'I'm loath to leave you here, Tom. If anything should befall you...'

Tom smiled reassuringly. 'Nothing will befall me. I shall guard myself well until you return with an army. Meanwhile I shall search for Ned and bring him safely to my side.'

John felt the gratitude flow through him like honey, yet the bee had a vicious sting. 'John, if you can, if there is time, convey my fond love to my wife, my heart desiring for her.'

Regarding his friend, John felt his gaze waver. 'I will,' he said curtly.

'Say how my heart aches for her. Tell her I am well and in no danger, that I yearn to be with her and will soon be.'

'That I will.' Even as he uttered the promise, a sick thumping had begun in his breast. He was vile. Such thoughts as came upon him were vile and they must be slaughtered ever he reached Fobbing. This he promised. His throat constricted suddenly. He laid a hand over that which still held his. 'God guard you well, Tom.' He could hardly speak for emotion. 'I couldn't bear ... Tom, should others show hunger for leadership, then by Jesus, let them eat!'

To his relief Tom threw back his head in a peal of laughter. 'I've had my fill of such fare, I think. So rest easy, my dearest, truest friend. Ay, the best friend a man could ever have, one from boyhood, the sort that doesn't die.' He gave him a small, embarrassed shove. 'Now get you gone. May our Blessed Lady grant you swift return with a great army at your back. Make haste now.' He stood back while John chose the quieter of the two animals – a deep brown one with a shaggier coat and broader girth than the other, and possibly less excitable.

Swinging himself up revealed how deceptive were appearances as he was forced to tighten his knees against its ribs and, holding the reins firmly, talk as soothingly to it as he could until it ceased gyrating and settled down with its head in the general direction of the exit, pawing the ground to be off. He shouted to it and it leapt forward.

John's last glimpse of Tom was of him standing alone in the stableyard, his hand raised in farewell, as he turned the horse to the left.

Bending to avoid catching his head on several low, overhanging eaves while the horse's hooves splattered through alleys full of kitchen refuse, he was glad to break out on to the main street and sunshine. There was little sign of yesterday's disturbance. Folk going about their normal business looked at him as he galloped by, but no one seemed hostile.

Once out of town he thought of the seriousness of his errand and drove the horse to even faster speed, realizing his folly only when foam spattered across his face. They had a way to go yet and the day again promised to be hot. He eased to a canter as the road narrowed, the forest closing in again, cutting off the sunlight.

He'd never been alone before – not truly alone. Working, sleeping, there was always someone close by, a constant presence that he took for granted. Lack of privacy was not a bother. Isolation belonged to hermits, anchorites, not ordinary folk, not even lords and ladies, who shared their castles with all their retinue and family. Perhaps those like Will Randere, wandering the lonely marshes or alone in a small boat on the estuary, knew isolation, but normally it was a comfort rather than an aggravation to have folk constantly around. What point to life if there was no one to hail, none to hail back? People were made to live together.

John felt his skin creep at this silence. He longed to be out of this shrouding greenery and breathe again the open air, an uncluttered horizon of marsh and estuary all around, hear again the sounds of his own village. Those who spent their lives ever surrounded by forest were welcome to it.

But soon he passed his first fellow traveller, a man with a great bundle of faggots on his bent back. Being given a sociable wave, he was soon hailing more people and minutes later swept into Ingrave Village, feeling in better heart. They knew all the news of Brentwood, being so close, and so without stopping he spurred his horse on through yet more wooded terrain.

Billericay, too, had been alerted. 'And we've sent word on to Ramsden Bellows and Downham and the Hanningfield Villages,' he was told as he paused to quench his thirst with a mug of ale given free before turning south for Ramsden Crays. It was heartening to find so many aware of the rebellion in Brentwood.

With Wickford leaving to spread the news to those along the Crouch, he headed southeast, moving ever nearer the coast. The mudflats of Foulness preventing any further progress east, he turned south, fording the muddy Roach towards Shoebury on the furthest point of the Thames Estuary. From there he would have to double back along the river and finally reach Fobbing by nightfall. The sun directly overhead saw him riding stiff and saddle-sore into Shoebury, having covered the best part of thirty miles. In contrast his horse seemed as fresh as when it started out, cantering down the narrow street catching everyone's interest.

Helped painfully from the saddle and guided to one of the tenements, folk crowded around the open door while others ran to fetch workers from the fields and shoreline. Seated at a table, he was handed a trencher of stewed eel and lamprey by a florid-faced goodwife.

'Ay, get that down you,' she said as he tucked in, not having eaten properly since the night before. 'You must be famished.'

But decency told him to consider her poor circumstances and stop before too much went out of the stewpot meant to feed her entire family. She went to find her man, leaving several children watching him eat.

In one corner sat an old grandfather. Thrusting aside a couple of chickens with the end of his crutch, he got up, grunting at twinges of pain. Leaning heavily on the roughly fashioned implement, his limbs grossly misshapen from aging joints attacked by a crippling disease that had also deformed his fingers into claws, he hobbled to the table, curled both claws around the jug of ale and took a deep guzzle.

As the woman returned with her husband, the mug was hurriedly put back on to the table, the old cripple tottering back to his corner like some maimed spider, but not before she'd seen him.

'Father! God save us! Ain't you had enough this morning wi'out sneaking ale and food from our guest? There be little enough for

213

us...'

She caught her words too late, realizing she'd betrayed her poverty. Quickly she turned to John with a disarming smile revealing decaying teeth, childbearing having robbed her of good health.

'He be an old dotard. We have enough in this house for all, but he be that drouthy for ale, I must needs withhold it from him for his own good.'

Having corrected a humiliating situation she stepped aside for her husband to sit down beside John, who put his half-empty trencher to one side. When he left, no doubt it would go back into the stewpot.

John's host introduced himself as John Hurt, leaning on the table to hear about Brentwood before taking him outside to acquaint him with a man whom he presented as his elected lieutenant.

'John Syrat,' he announced as the squat, heavy-browed man with a sprinkling of fish scales glinting in his black beard came forward to grasp John's hand. 'A fisherman. But a fine longbowman, too.'

'We've many good men here as can handle a longbow,' Syrat said. 'Plenty o' practice wi' them Frenchy raiders sneaking over to these parts. Keen of eye, we be, and as good a match for any trained soldiery.'

Another joined them, a man with more hair on his chin than his head, calling himself Tom Hilleston. He'd mustered a small army of villagers armed with shackforks, staves, sickles and treasured longbows, all ready to set off for Brentwood. John held up a restraining hand.

'No good each village making its own way to Brentwood in dribs and drabs; we must have one army.' Quickly he told them the plan. 'Make for Pitsea so we can all march together at the appointed time.'

He'd have liked to leave, but he was their hero, expected to remain at their head to Southchurch to swell their forty by a like number, over eighty men in all. Among them was their bailiff, who for some reason of his own had elected to join them, proof that this army would not be composed solely of poor peasant and fisherfolk, but men of standing – a fine boost to morale.

John found himself joined by a heavy, bull-faced man incongruously riding a slim palfrey that was more suited to a lady, having helped himself from the manor stables after intimidating the steward into saddling it for him.

'Ralph Spicer is the name,' he stated. 'Lately a miserable tenant of this manor, now a knight. See, I have a sword.' He brandished the weapon obviously taken from the manor along with the horse. 'Pity there were no war-horse in the stable, but this beast will suffice for a fine knight such as I.'

John laughed. 'You're lacking a helm to be a true knight.'

Hearing it, someone nearby ran up with a small leather bucket. 'Here, sir knight – you need a helm? Stick this on your head. And here's a knight's crest to put atop it – a fine pig turd!' The jester neatly forked up a partly dried pile of pig dung with his shackfork, dropping it on the upturned bucket where it adhered in all its glory.

Falling in with the ribaldry, Spicer thrust the helm, crest and all, over his head, the bucket covering his face. 'How do I see where I'm going in this,' he boomed out from its depths.

'Skewer a hole in it, silly arse!' said a voice with such droll patience that everyone around broke into laughter.

Spicer lifted his helmet to nod at the joker. 'Ah, it is Will Croume – a chandler by trade, but now captain of my hordes. When I find a destrier fit to carry a fine knight, you can have this one and be my squire. Then we shall see who be the gentlemen!'

The chant was instantly taken up: 'When Adam delved and Eve she span, who was then the gentleman?' And they all marched joyfully to Pitsea.

Fourteen

It was good to be alone again after the multitude they'd found gathered at Pitsea, the word of the uprising having gone before him.

John had been astounded at how many people had managed to arrive so quickly and could only surmise they'd been told by those returning to their homes immediately Bampton had made his escape that something more was afoot.

There had not been enough food to go round for so many and when a man called John Glasiere of Rochford arrived with a wagon of food intended for his own contingent, it was set upon by hordes of hungry men, the food demolished as if by packs of ravenous wolves. Scuffles had broken out, food trodden underfoot and wasted as men fought. Christ Himself would have been hard put to divide those loaves and fishes among such as them. Yet they had finally settled down with their ill-gotten gains, the aroma of cooking rising into the evening air along with talk of forcing their King's sympathy, of hoisting the heads of his uncles on pikes on London Bridge, of burning the houses of the rich to the ground, the cause already looking

217

to deteriorate into anarchy and bloody devastation with man at his most vile.

How would the good John Ball view all this, John wondered, and then he'd remembered that Kent must be alerted, and quickly, and that a beacon was to be lit. He was glad to get away and be alone again. He now saw there was something to be said for being by oneself so as to think straight.

It was late as he neared Fobbing. With the instinct of most Thames-side dwellers, he could judge roughly what hour it was by the salt breeze that sprang up on most fine early summer nights after the last glow along the western horizon faded, almost as accurately as a monk's candle-clock. It was a little under an hour to midnight. Folk would be snoring in bed.

Refreshed from its short rest in Pitsea, his stalwart animal was covering ground at a marvellous pace, its breath snorting in and out as regularly as its hoofbeats.

'Make haste, Halberdier,' he urged, inventing a name for the animal. As if approving of its new name, it lengthened its stride without once breaking rhythm, its hoofs pounding on the dark, dusty road to Fobbing.

The village lay in darkness, but one dim glow remained at the far end, from Dame Wodelarke's alehouse. John felt a warm feeling at coming home. It seemed hardly credible that he'd sat in that place only four days ago with its homely, comforting fireglow reflecting shadows along its uneven limewashed walls; only three days since the killing of the commissioner's man and the capture of their bailiff. Where was the bailiff now? Was he already here, waiting to leap out?

John felt a shudder pass through him, already heartsick for his father's well-being. He alighted and walked Halberdier quietly past the manor hall. No glimmer of light penetrated through the trees shielding the building from the roadway. Yet Rycard must have got back by now. Even on foot he'd had a night and a day and much of the afternoon of his escape to get himself back here – unless he'd been waylaid by robbers, clubbed to death for his fine clothes. But his lady must have sent word to Steward Somenour of her husband's disappearance. Maybe he was here, with men, waiting. Yet all was as tranquil as any warm night, with crickets chirruping under stones and in cracks, an owl hooting and another answering it. Even so, John walked Halberdier quietly past the mill and Tom's house.

Resisting the temptation to turn into the yard of his own house, wanting so much to have them all awaken to the joy of seeing him safe and sound, he moved on, past the darkened church and its small cottage in which their parson no longer resided but waited across the river under the name of Jack Straw, awaiting the glow of a beacon that would tell him that Essex had risen.

A twinge of excitement stirred John's

219

stomach. With it fear fled and, thrusting caution aside, he made down the wharf path to Dame Wodelarke's. Tethering Halberdier, he hurried inside.

Rush light had been extinguished, leaving only the fireglow. Only three customers were left at such a late hour: old Walter Coupere, Edmund Horn, who was too crippled to have gone to Brentwood, and Dick Randere, still too concerned about his son's smashed leg to go off with the others.

Half-drained mugs limp in their hands, they sat talking, nodding languorously at each other's words, having reached that sentimental stage of inebriation that does no ill. On a stool beside her kegs sat their hostess, her body hunched in weariness, her podgy hands lying flaccid in her lap, palms upward, her ale-splashed red bodice carelessly agape to reveal an expanse of pendulous breast. Her eyelids drooped sleepily, but while a man had a penny for ale she would spurn her bed to serve him.

At John's entry all four looked up with mild interest. Seeing who it was, stupor vanished. While her customers continued to stare without focus, Dame Wodelarke came awake to bounce up from her cask as though stung.

'Young John Melle – by all the saints!' She picked up a mug and hastily filled it from a nearby leather jug. 'Here – get this down. I'll not charge you. You look as though you need it. What news?' she pressed as he drank deep. 'We've heard nowt since everyone left for

Pitsea. What did you do with our bailiff? And did you put that old rogue Bampton to flight? Was any hurt? Is my own son safe?'

John laughed easily now as more questions came flooding. It was obvious their bailiff hadn't returned or she wouldn't be pressing him on that point.

'We put the commissioner to flight orright,' he told her gleefully. 'He ran like the frightened rat he was, and his clerks after him.' Quickly he told her all that had occurred and that her son was well the last time he'd seen him. Then he let his merriment die away.

'But there are things to do. All Essex is aware of the rising and will muster. I have orders to light a beacon alerting Kent of our triumph so that we can march together to London, them on that side of the river and us on this side, two prongs to confound any of London's defenders.'

'A beacon?' Her florid cheeks were bright with excitement. Quickly she readjusted her wimple and tightened the laces of her bodice. 'This very night? But all be asleep. At least...' She tilted her head in the direction of the three still sitting bemused by John's entrance.

'Then we'll raise every one,' he said. 'They must build a bonfire on high ground by the church and light up the sky for a dozen leagues around.'

She caught his arm in sudden fear. 'What if your beacon alerts others as well as Kent?'

He knew what she meant. 'Too late for any to do mischief. We are weightier in numbers

221

than our lords, even wi' soldiery behind 'em. This will be a mighty rebellion.'

Soothed, she followed him out, leaving her three customers to their drinking. By the time the bonfire had been allowed to die, her alehouse would be nigh overflowing with dry throats to be quenched, and already she was making a mental calculation of her stock and the resultant healthy state of her coffers.

While other fists thumped willingly on doors throughout the village, John's concern was for his family. It was good to see all of them safe, they in turn relieved to see him, his father clasping his hand in glad reunion.

As Alice ran to throw her arms about his neck in an open demonstration of joy, because he was smitten by guilt in failing to share her feelings, he made an effort to return her embrace convincingly. It was cruel; all he could feel for her was duty and an engulfing sadness for them both as finally he took her arms from his neck to go outside where the village street was now thronged with people as though it were midday.

As the first brands were thrust on to the beacon pile, the isolated flames came quickly together until they burst through the top of the dry timber in a roar of crackling that flung up sparks as fire lit the sky, the night erupting into brightness, picking out figures leaping and prancing with glee. His family helped to heap fuel on to the blaze and he could see Tom's parents doing exactly the same, but there was no sign of Tom's wife.

For an instant it crossed his mind to go and seek her, wherever she was, but he swept the wish away as quickly as it had come and applied his mind to watching for any answering blaze from the Kent side. The heat was roasting his face. Needing to avoid it, he moved back slowly until he finally found shadow and coolness. For a moment or two he stood taking in deep breaths of cool, refreshing night air.

A hand on his arm made him catch his breath and turn sharply with an instinct to defend himself. But it was no enemy who stood there – he found himself staring into Marjory's face, the distant flicker of firelight making her features dance.

'John...' Her voice was low and musical. 'Do you have any news of my husband for me?'

With an effort he recovered his wits. It was hard to control his voice. 'He's well,' he answered as evenly as he could. 'He thinks of you constantly. He asked me to...' He let the message die away, unable to form the words of love that Tom had requested he convey on his behalf. He knew that if he were to repeat them they'd be his own words, from his own heart. Instead he stood like a dumb fool, staring into her eyes while she gazed back at him, their depths appearing innocent. But were they really so innocent?

The voices from the fire's circle seemed to be receding, his world narrowing to include only her. The thumping of his heart was beginning to suffocate him and all he could

223

think was that nothing mattered beyond this tiny world that comprised only the two of them.

'I miss the comfort of a strong arm about me, John,' he heard her whisper.

'He'll be back before you know it.' But even as he spoke, the small hand on his arm was drawing him, unresisting, further from the light and into the cool depths of shadow. Such a gentle pull as he could so easily have shaken off, but he no longer seemed to have any will to do so.

'Soon you will be away once more and I shall be alone...' She let her voice fade as several thorn bushes on the slope of the meadow hid them at last from sight. His body was on fire, yet he trembled as she sank down on the dry grass. Like a sick man he had dropped on to his knees beside her, but there was strength in him as urgency overcame him and he began feverishly to drag her skirt back to bare her long, slim legs drawn up, parting readily for him.

She was already sighing as though he were inside her. Her warm female scent flooded his nostrils, pouring into him and sweeping away all thought but one as he leant over her, his need driving him savagely into her, grunting with the repeated efforts, hearing her gasping with joy.

It was over far too quickly. His need and the danger had made it so. Too soon he fell back, his mind blank, his strength for the moment having deserted him.

A voice was calling him. Coming to with a start he clambered to his feet, leaving Marjory lying content and fulfilled in the dry, grassy tufts. Her thighs were still bare, her legs still drawn up. Now the voice brought her half upright, her eyes wide, staring at a figure that had suddenly appeared on the far side of the low thorn bushes.

'Ah, there you are!' the voice said, almost on top of them.

Too late John leapt away to find himself confronted by a small, bow-legged man, grinning from ear to ear as he took stock of the little scene, Tom Baker's wife half-naked, his best friend frantically adjusting himself.

Will Randere was gazing from the lowered chaussers of the man to the naked thighs of the woman, now trying to cover herself, all the while his grin revealing more and more of his worn teeth.

'Do I see here young Marjory Baker?' he queried. 'And this be not her gallant husband with her, he still in Brentwood, but his dearest friend, if my eyes serve me aright, his best and loyalest friend, helping to take his place.'

Randere's little eyes swivelled narrowly towards his victim, now on his feet and standing like one ready to do battle, but Randere was keeping his distance.

'Was she good then, John? Sank yourself well into her, did you, the wife of your cherished friend? Such juicy fruit be sweet, be it not? I vow that cherished friend would be sore heartbroken to find who has been cuckolding him.'

John could have smashed his fist into the leering face had Randere not backed even further away into the faint glow of firelight and safety. People were still dancing and singing, still adding faggots to the flames.

Still moving away, Randere pointed across the river. 'That's what I came to tell you,' he said slowly. 'Kent has seen your signal and has made answer. I saw you come this way and hurried to tell you. I didn't dream to find you otherwise occupied, lighting a beacon of your own wi' your own friend's wife.'

John gave a roar and started after him, leaving Marjory to deal with herself, but the eel-catcher was way ahead of him now. Adam Melle noticed his son coming towards him like a charging bull, Randere having veered off a little and now standing safely to one side.

'So you've seen it too,' Adam Melle called heartily to John, his arm in its splint seeming no bother to him at this minute. 'They have answered us. 'Tis done! We all rise together.'

People were prancing in triumph, women mostly, their men elsewhere this night. The few men in the village came to slap John on the back for the hero he was. Randere, too, was being congratulated as having been the one who'd led the small band with their captive bailiff across the marsh.

John, having his hand pumped by everyone

around, saw Marjory creep out of the shadows and streak across the meadow towards her husband's house, but no one saw her go and he turned his back on her, sick at heart at what he had done.

Fifteen

'Fore God, I've seen happier faces hanging from gibbets!'

Ralph Spicer of Prittlewell, who'd managed to find a bigger horse than the palfrey John had last seen him riding, leaned across to clap him on the shoulder, jerking him away from his thoughts.

Will Randere had disappeared as the beacon had finally collapsed in on itself, sending lazy showers of dull sparks into the dark sky. Alarmed to find no sign of him, John had run to Randere's cottage, but he had already gone. The thought of galloping on to Brentwood to stop him before he told Tom what he'd seen had been prevented by a delegation of those men remaining in the village conducting him down to the alehouse to celebrate this night's victory. Had he refused they'd have seen him as odd and churlish. By the time he was allowed to leave at around two in the morning Randere would have been be well on his way. No catching him up.

So John had returned to his own home, sick at heart, lying down beside Alice to endure her hopeful fondling, hardly needing to pretend at being too weary for her after his long ride and the raising of Kent. He knew she cried silently, her back turned to him, but there was nothing he could do for her.

She'd fallen asleep to snore away what was left of the night while he lay awake, staring up at the thatch and hating the woman who had so deliberately tempted him for her own pleasure and relief; hated himself, too, for allowing it to happen, for not being strong enough to prevent it.

Spicer was leering at him. 'Why all these dreamy looks? Still in your woman's bed, eh?' He gave a broad wink at those around them. 'We had no such comforts last night, lads, Pitsea being a mite scant o' obliging women-folk.'

It seemed almost as if he knew, but he couldn't have. John felt himself cringe with guilt nevertheless.

'All I had for comfort,' called one joker, 'were our accursed minstrel here. Nigh drove me out of my wits with imaginings, he a-warbling love-lays half the night and plucking the strings of his gittern like it were a pair of maiden's ripe pubies.'

'Finish with it, will you!' John suddenly shouted, leaving them all agape. Spicer gave him a hearty thwack across the shoulders.

'Lad, we're quizzing you, that's all. Even so, I sorely miss my woman. Wed ten year come Martinmas. Never a night away from her till now. The sooner this business in London be done and I back with her, the better, I say.

Come on, lad, unbend them brows. This be not a day for glum faces. We've some fine business ahead of us.'

They left Pitsea flank to flank like lords leading an army along, with John Hurt on the discarded palfrey and Will Croume and several others variously mounted.

Where a couple of hundred men had travelled a few days before, there were now over a thousand. The road too narrow for so many, they spread across fields and through woodland, skirting both sides of the villages they passed, trampling harrowed and seeded strips, but there were few left to complain, and even some womenfolk and old men came to join them. All John wanted was to run away, dreading his meeting with Tom, but how could he? Randere had a compulsion to make mischief, to see people squirm, and he must have spoken to Tom by now.

Never was there such a spectacular sight as those running from Brentwood to meet the newest arrivals that would swell the multitude already there.

Guiding Halberdier through the back-slapping, hand-shaking, jovially tussling crowd, John heard his name called over the noise and saw his brother shouldering his way towards him. The lad looked in fine fettle and John uttered a prayer of relief as he leapt from the saddle, leaving the horse to its own devices, to embrace the boy.

No boy this, but a man now. Their few days

apart seemed to have wrought a huge change in Ned. Or was it just that they had never been parted before – had the transition from childhood to adolescence gone unnoticed? Only now, seeing him after even this short absence, did John realize how grown he was, how thickset like himself and surprisingly muscular for his sixteen years.

'Have you seen Thomas Baker?' he asked finally.

Ned thought for a while. 'I saw him with Master William Gildeborn some while ago, by the tollbooth, talking to ... Hey!' He broke off to point. 'The horse you were on...'

John turned to see several men clustered about what must seem to them an ownerless animal, each ready to claim it for himself. Forgetting all else, he thrust his way towards them, pushing aside those in his path, leaving a string of curses in his wake.

Ramming into the group, he roared, 'Hands off, you bastard turds! That horse is mine!'

'By what right?' bellowed the man he'd shoved the hardest and who immediately shoved viciously back.

'By right o' this!' John's right fist caught him square on the jaw, all of his self-hate behind the blow.

With a grunt the man fell backwards into the crowd. Some stepped aside hastily, others not so quick went down with him in a sprawl of bodies.

The stalwart clinging to Halberdier's bridle had drawn a heavy cudgel from his belt and brought it down across John's back, knocking the breath out of him, though he managed to keep his feet. The man was fairly hefty but John was young and brawny. With all his might, he swung a crooked arm back and up, the point of the elbow catching him full in the throat. There was a gurgling, wheezing sound and the man let go of Halberdier, who danced back from the melee, snickering and snorting.

John would have made a grab for the rein but three of the bystanders came surging forward looking for satisfaction. Sunlight glinted off a long-bladed knife and the curve of the other's newly polished, two-tined shack fork, while the third man brandished a stave. Behind them a ring of faces slavered at the prospect of watching blood being spilt.

Instinctively John crouched, his own knife in his hand now, but three well-armed men against one boded ill for him, with murder going unpunished on this day of wide-scale insurgence. He was suddenly and violently brushed aside as several men hurtled past him to plough into his attackers.

Realizing they were allies, he went in alongside them and within minutes two of the aggressors lay disarmed and moaning, the third knocked clean out. The original claimants to the horse, apart from the one he'd walloped, were nowhere to be seen.

He looked up to find Wat Gildeborn, Dick Elys, Ralph Peteman and Henry Sharpe standing there. 'Thank God for your timely...'

His thanks fell away as he glanced over to see if Halberdier had run off or been craftily claimed by the others. Tom was holding the animal's rein, his attention taken up with calming it.

Seeing him, John felt his insides knot. What would he see in Tom's eyes when he finally looked up? Would he find accusation in them, or would they remain still innocent and friendly? If Tom came over now and beat him senseless to the ground, kicked his body black and blue in murderous rage or broke every bone in that body, it would still not compensate for what he had done. His body might heal but it would be the terrible hurt he'd see in his friend's eyes that would never leave him.

John felt an inane impulse to fall on his knees before the cuckolded man, beg his forgiveness, saying that some devil had tempted him before he knew what he was about – as if that would make it all right! Tom deserved better than that. But their eyes did not meet, Tom seeming too intent on pacifying Halberdier. Was that a sign in itself that he couldn't even bring himself to meet John's eyes?

As though from a distance he heard Wat's appraising voice. 'That was a proper fine blow you landed this one.' He was gazing down at the man John had first caught with that tremendous, hate-filled punch, still sprawled on the floor. 'Looks like you nigh broke his jaw for him.'

233

He wanted to say that he had taken no pleasure in it, but his voice seemed to desert him. From now on he'd find little pleasure in anything.

Several men from his village had come to crowd around him, a little more dishevelled than when he'd left them, most with stubble on their cheeks and in need of a wash, all asking for news of their homes, clamouring to know how everything had gone. Without enthusiasm he told them of the beacon being lit and the answering blaze from Kent.

Word was passed around to waves of cheering. 'Kent has risen! Kent is with us! To London, men, to London!'

In all this, Tom had made no comment, remaining on the perimeter of the joyful celebrations, and John was conscious of the fact that no greeting had yet passed between them. He was still left unsure whether the eel-catcher had got to Brentwood or not, and whether or not he'd told Tom what he'd seen. If he had, then it must be tearing the man apart. It showed plainly enough in the very way he was holding himself aloof from all the noisy revelry.

By the time they wended their way to the tollbooth, John could take no more of it. Hanging back until Tom was abreast of him, still leading the animal, he said amicably, 'Tom, shall I take the horse?'

'As you wish,' came the monotone reply.

The rein was handed over but without the normal exchange of smiles one would expect between friends. Even a stranger would have offered a smile. John ran his hand over Halberdier's muzzle, steeling himself for what must be said.

'I ... I gave your message to your wife,' he faltered.

'Yes.' Tom absently patted the animal's flank, looking at those who were streaming past them.

'Something happened,' John burst out at last, his voice little more than the croak of one tortured almost to death. 'At Fobbing, I...'

He saw Tom flinch as though from a blow. 'There's no need,' he said abruptly. 'I know you were successful there.' It could have meant anything.

He was startled by a sudden and explosive laugh, and Tom seemed to spring to life like a jack-in-the-box. 'Yes, great news of Kent ready to march. We'll all be a great company. Tomorrow be Whit Sunday and many'll go to church and confess themselves. As soldiers do. Be absolved of sin and in a state of grace before battle. For the Devil be in all of us, John. And you should go, too.'

With that he moved on, leaving him standing beside the horse, staring after him, his guilt reading connotation in every word Tom had said. But above all that lay another thought: once John found him, Will Randere would not see another sunrise, of that he would make certain.

'I shouldn't fret over that bit of advice.' A full-bodied voice close to his ear made him jump. He swung round to see the bearded Tripat lounging two feet away from him against the side of the tollbooth. Tripat moved his lean frame away from the wall to grin at him. 'We've nowt to fear from them in London,' he said. 'They might muster an army to meet us but we've the weight of numbers on our side, enough to make such a noise as'll be heard all down the ages. So don't let your friend dishearten you wi' talk of confessions before battle. There won't be a battle. We'll simply walk in.' He nodded towards Tom, already being swallowed up by the moving throng. 'Best get after him. Take the tidings with you that we have a leader at last – from London itself.'

John stared at him, all else swept from his mind for the moment. 'From London? Who?'

The ex-soldier gave a low chuckle. 'All in good time. When he arrives his name will be on everyone's lips. But you can say this – our first task is to find as many documents as we can that bear green seals showing them to have been issued by the Exchequer. Every last one must be burned.'

He grinned as John raised a questioning eyebrow. 'They're lists showing the name of every man in default of paying his poll tax and many other fines and dues. Not a single one must remain.'

'And after that?'

'We make for London. Now, get along. I've errands elsewhere.'

Left to himself, John made his way through

the crowd, finding his neighbours on the far side of the market square. Squatting beside them after having relayed Tripat's message, he accepted a tiny portion of cold, stringy mutton that Dick Wodelarke had managed to find, together with a piece of the heel of a two-day-old loaf they were sharing between them. Elys wasn't being so generous, hugging a leather jug quarter-full of ale and refusing to offer it round. By the looks he was getting, John vouched he would soon have it torn out of his hands anyway, but he was more concerned that Tom hadn't asked any question of him though the others still pressed him to enlarge on anything that might have slipped his memory from Tripat's message.

Again he thought of Randere. The man must be somewhere around, but apparently no one had seen him. Keeping well out of the way, John surmised contemptuously.

It was the longest afternoon he could ever remember having spent, the day degenerating into one of restive expectancy with men asking why they were not already making for London. They sat in groups, their laughter played out. They diced. They talked, putting the world to rights. They roamed the town for food and drink. Many who had come to Brentwood on horseback guarded their animals as though they were chests of gold, continually grooming them so as to establish ownership.

John went to sit by Halberdier, tethered to a rail, nibbling some hay he had found. Here

237

he didn't have to look at Tom, and he was sitting there when Wat Gildeborn came up to him, clutching a wineskin to his bosom. It slopped as he slid down beside John to put an affectionate arm about his neck, obviously drunk, the front of his gipon splashed and stained from the rich, dark liquid he told him was 'the beshed Rhenish wine as ever ye'll tashte'.

'I have a mind t'share it wi' a good ... a good friend.' He hiccupped. 'Wi' you, John ... a goo' friend.'

Despite his depressed spirits, John felt his lips quirk into a smile. It would be good to get blind drunk, forget all else. And as night closed down on them, somehow things didn't seem so bad.

He awoke to the matins bell from distant Weald Church. His sleep had been deep and dreamless, like the sleep of the innocent. He was conscious of that irony as he opened his eyes to the pearly light of a fine Whit Sunday and the memory of all that had gone before. It had almost taken on an air of unreality.

Perhaps, having been given time to rethink, Tom might have come to view what he'd been told as no more than the mischievous lies of a spiteful man, angered at having his leadership swept from under him. That was it. It had to be. But the monotonously tolling bell spelled the truth: that it had happened, no matter which way he twisted it, and that there was a need to make confession, to receive his pen-

238

ance and be free of the Devil's clutches.

A few souls were evidently of the same mind, moving off down the main street towards the distant resonant call. In a way it was a peaceful sound, as if the recent disturbances had never been. Adding to the peace of the morning, the small exodus moved slowly, unobtrusively, even humbly, so as not to disrupt the slumber of those still asleep.

John got to his feet, careful not to disturb Wat. He found his head to be surprisingly clear considering the amount of wine he'd consumed – perhaps because it had been very good wine.

The early morning had a chill to it. Having relieved himself, he bent and retrieved his hood, which he'd used as a pillow, pulled it over his head, dragging the woollen gorget well down like a cape over his shoulders and wrapping the long end of the top of the hood around his neck for extra warmth.

Going a few yards away to where the others lay, he gazed down at the sleeping bodies. Ned and Robin were curled up like young babes and Tom, as supple in repose as he was in action, lay easy and relaxed, his fine features gentle in sleep.

John went back to Halberdier, tethered beside Wat's grey and William Gildeborn's skewbald. They dozed, heads lowered. Their saddles lay stacked nearby. Beside them stood a bucket of water.

His mouth furred, he went and ducked his head into it, drawing in a mouthful of water

239

to cleanse his teeth. The animals lifted their heads to watch his ablutions, looking now for their share. Refreshed, he took the bucket to them and, as they drank, lifted Halberdier's saddle and hoisted it over the creature's back. He would ride to church.

The movements startled Wat's fiery brute into throwing up its head and snickering. William Gildeborn's beast began dancing on the end of its tether, making Halberdier skittish, too. Trying to secure the girth, John swore mightily at the stupid beast, his voice loud enough to reach his sleeping comrades.

Tom was on his feet in a second, the transition from sleep to alertness as smooth as a cat's. 'Who's there?'

Ned, too, started up but relaxed back on an elbow, laughing. 'It's only John. What're you doing? Where are you off to?'

''Tis Whit Sunday,' John reminded, irritable at finding them all awake now. 'The matins bell's been ringing this last several minutes. Whatever you care to do, I'm to church. As Tom said...' It sounded wrong to be speaking his name. 'Afore battle a soldier should be in a state of grace...'

'You consider yourself a soldier?' Wat gave a croak of a laugh, his throat dry, and fell to coughing.

'I'll come with you,' Ned offered, several agreeing it a good idea, and soon they were all making their way towards South Weald, John deciding it better to walk with the rest of them, leaving Halberdier behind in charge of

240

an old stableman.

They were halfway down the long, gentle incline out of town when a rider came galloping towards them, kicking up clouds of dust behind him.

'The King's Commissioner comes hither!' he was yelling at the top of his lungs as he passed. 'Not two leagues back, with an armed escort.'

Whit Sunday forgotten, dozens of men were already racing back uphill to Brentwood to join those they'd left and to prepare to make a stand against this unknown force of arms, hearts racing as fast as their legs.

Sixteen

Sir Robert Bealknap, Justice of Common Pleas, came into Brentwood at a leisurely pace, being a man who frowned upon unnecessary agitation and impetuous decision. He found a formidable barrier of grim faces awaiting his arrival, a forest of scythes, axes, staves and shack forks as well as the more conventional weapons.

Another man might have quailed before such a confrontation, especially as all he had with him, beside his three clerks, was an escort of a dozen armed men. But if the sight was daunting, he did not show it.

Riding in at a leisurely walk would instill respect into these ignorant rustics – respect born of generations of serfdom since the Conqueror's time. He was gratified to see them give way as he came on, part for him to pass through to reach the tollgate. He even smiled, slowly, imperiously. Then his smile vanished as slowly as it had come.

Too late he realized his mistake as their ranks closed behind him and his men, hemming them in on all sides, the faces all around him set with grim determination. Worse, there was silence, which he knew could break into a sudden roar, and he trapped in their midst. But not one sign of his unease did he let show as he and his company moved slowly on, like a water bubble moving through oil. In this way he reached the open-ended toll-booth, dismounted with his entourage, and regarded them all steadily.

If the insurgents thought to find another puffed-up blusterer like that fool Bampton, they were to be disappointed. A large-boned man with a stern, square face and steady, smoke-grey eyes, he regarded the thousands packed tight into the square and main street, so great a throng that much of it was being forced into the side streets and alleys and unable to see him or hear his voice.

He had a fine gift for words. He'd addressed many a meeting, holding his audience spell-bound. Here, he realized as soon as he had begun that his high-blown verbosity was going over the heads of these simple people. Slowly the chant began, low at first but soon gaining in strength: 'When Adam delved and Eve span, who was then the gentleman?'

The chant grew in volume until it drowned out his voice. The chanting soon became ragged, with staccato shouts accusing him of false inquests against them, damning him for a traitor. With the taunts came missiles, and soon sticks and stones were finding their mark.

He was a judge, not a soldier. He had put himself at risk here and was now unable to retreat, at a loss to pacify this mob. All he

243

could do was raise his voice above the incensed roar as best he could, calling again and again to hear their requests. Slowly the yelling and the threats died away. Now he had them, but he must keep them appeased, even if it meant telling the odd lie.

His voice rang out. What were their requests? He would grant them if he could. Their demands were immediate: that he hold no more sessions.

'Done!' he said promptly.

That he would make no use of false inquests taken before him.

'Done!'

Nor was he to act as Justice of the Peace in this locality.

'Nor will I.'

They were simple enough, these demands, made by men who would forget them within a week or two. But he had agreed with them too readily. Nervousness had made him careless. An air of uncertainty had begun to settle over the crowd.

'Do you swear upon this, your Lordship?'

Bealknap regarded the young man who had stepped out in front of the crowd brandishing a bible. He put out a restraining hand as his soldiers stiffened in readiness to dispel any possible danger to his person.

'I shall swear on your bible, young man,' he said boldly. 'But only on condition that I am allowed to leave here without harm.'

'Done!' cried the young man after a brief pause. 'But as a token of good faith, leave us a list of them justices as have convicted folk hereabouts for tax defaulters. Also the names of those as were jurors at such sessions. We require you also to leave all official documents with us.'

This young man was bold indeed. Bealknap was already marking his features for future reference. But he bowed his agreement, adding one small proviso. 'As long as those named come to no harm.'

The man nodded, but from out of the crowd came a loud guffaw. 'Don' 'ee worry, your Lordship, we'll see 'em served orright!'

John had been separated from his companions and unable to get near the front. In the seething crowd very few of them had remained together. He had, however, been near enough to see the bible brandished aloft and had heard Bealknap swear on it to keep his word.

It was only as the multitude parted to allow the Justice of Common Pleas and his retinue through that John learned it was Tom Baker who had held up the bible. 'Waved it right under ole Bealknap's nose, he did, and forced he to swear on it.'

But it seemed that Tom's doubts were bearing fruit, a wave of uncertainty already beginning to spread through the mass of men. It had all been too simple. There was a feeling that they had somehow been robbed, that things had gone too smoothly to be true. There was an air of uneasiness that they'd

245

been duped while Bealknap summoned more armed backing and returned to put them all to rout.

'We've been cozened,' someone said. 'Played for fools. The mighty lords don't overlook an insult that easy, one of their officers being humiliated and told to swear on the bible that his word be true.'

Several nodded sourly and began to remember the clerks that had been with Bampton – spies brought back to identify certain ringleaders of the attack on Bampton.

'Us ought to catch up with 'em,' came a suggestion, 'afore they can inform on us.'

Realizing he was being pursued, Bealknap and his escort spurred their horses to a gallop, but the clerks on their small amblers, hampered by flowing gowns and pouches of documents and writing materials, were soon overtaken and brought back amid catcalls and jeers. Dragged from their saddles, they were pushed, punched and generally mis-handled back to town.

Mounted though John was, such was the eagerness of those flowing past him that Halberdier was taken further and further back until all he could see were fists going up and down, the cries of the victims lost in the confusion of yells for revenge of any sort, the centre of violence eddying further and further away from him. There was no point in forcing an already nervous horse any nearer and risk being thrown. Besides, he had already guessed the fate of the unfortunate clerks.

With Halberdier safely back in the stable by the good grace of the old stableman, John stood watching the triumphant procession parade through the town bearing poles with the severed heads of the clerks skewered on top, dripping blood on to the pole-bearers below.

A little way behind he recognized some of his neighbours, eyes wide with the excitement of blood-letting, among them Wat Gildeborn.

Seeing him, Wat called over, 'Hey, John, join us, eh?'

His morning hangover seemed to have completely left him. 'Tom with you?' he asked, falling in alongside him.

'Not since he pulled down one of them scribblers,' yelled Wat above the cacophony of men's voices raised in discordant singing to the thump of tabors, the jingling of tambourines and the occasional blare of a stolen trumpet.

'He pulled one of 'em down?' John echoed incredulously.

'Ay, went at him like the man had done him a personal injustice,' Wat shouted back and gave a raucous laugh. 'Mind, we all knew they were spies. Now we're off to winkle out them jurors hereabouts as are named in Bealknap's list. They're the ones as spoke out against innocent folk, so they too will have the honour o' joining our guests.' He lifted a long arm to point over the top of the moving throng where one of the heads could be seen bobbing along like a boiled pudding, his eyes

247

now trained on the monstrosity.

John had dropped back, allowing Wat to continue, finally dropping out unnoticed. He could hardly believe what he had been told – that Tom had helped in the clerks' murder. Tom, compassionate, deep thinking, gentle – was this now a man bent on revenge? Upon whom? Surely not just on a defenceless clerk. He shuddered despite the sweat pouring off him. Is this what he, John, had done to him?

He felt tears spring into his eyes at all that had gone wrong because of his insane obsession for a woman, the result of which was tearing to shreds a long and dear friendship.

He thought of this insane uprising – insane as his own actions had been, violence and savagery taking place of clear and careful thinking, madness instead of wise planning – doomed to failure. What would be the end of it all for these men, for him?

By Monday morning the excitement had paled. The heads of the clerks, along with those of three unfortunate jurors, were turning black on their poles, of no interest to anyone. The homes of the jurors had been thrown to the ground. There was nothing more to do here. Brentwood was fast becoming a place of boredom.

Men began to split into groups, seeking to revenge past injustices, some moving east to the manors of Dengie and the Rochford hundreds, or south to the Chafford hundred.

Yet others drifted back westward to their own villages to spread the news of their uprising and make some mischief of their own. The main body, however, remained. The name of Cressing Temple was on everyone's lips. A certain Thomas Farndon or Farringdon had arrived from London, an indication that something like organization was at last being formed. It at least stimulated the flagging spirits.

'Not only Kent, but London joins us. The whole of England is rising against injustices,' was the message being spread.

A messenger, seeking a few erstwhile leaders of the revolt, found some of the Fobbing villagers ensconced in their now established headquarters in front of the back-alley stableyard.

'I am sent by the franklin, Master William Gildeborn,' the messenger said in reply to their challenge. 'I look for his brother Walter, and for Master John Melle, Master Thomas Baker and Master Will Randere. He awaits all four of you at the tollbooth.'

'Master Randere is not with us,' John said curtly, glancing across to Tom, who had eventually joined them sometime in the night.

'What does my brother wish to see us about?' asked Wat.

'Summat to do wi' plotting the demise of that accursed Hobbe the Robber,' was the reply.

'Hales,' John mused. Sir Robert Hales,

249

prior of the Hospital of St John of Jerusalem at Cressing Temple and, since February, England's appointed Lord Treasurer, who they all held to be responsible for inflicting the most recent and unjust poll tax upon the country.

At the tollbooth, leaders of other villages had gathered. William Gildeborn stood before the narrow buildings with several others. Gildeborn introduced them hurriedly: John Stalworth, a prosperous barber of Chelmsford; William Chypenham, a wealthy Moulsham brewer; another Moulsham man – a franklin by the name of Baud, and another of Bocking whose name John did not catch, his gaze being caught by the sleek, distinguished figure standing beside Gildeborn.

The man wore a saffron-coloured doublet nipped at the waist with a belt of the softest calfskin worked here and there with gold and a purse with a large gold-encrusted green jewel for a clasp. Even his pointed, soft leather shoes were worked with gold thread. His conical hat was also in saffron and his red hose were of the finest wool. Never had John seen such dress.

'This is Master Thomas Farringdon,' Gildeborn said, seeing all eyes drawn to the man. Farringdon bowed condescendingly, his smile gracious.

'A goldsmith of London,' he enlarged. 'As you see, not all those in London are for this poll tax, and join with you all in putting it down. In my own small way I have little to

250

thank Sir Robert Hales for. A matter of a personal grudge, an inheritance lost to me through Sir Robert Hales that I shall settle in my own good time. But to wider issues, I am against this subjugation of the common man, and have vowed to do all in my power...'

'Master Farringdon will be leading us,' Gildeborn cut through what looked to become a wordy speech lest it go completely over the heads of his audience. 'We will march on to Cressing Temple...'

'So that *he* can settle his own private score with Hales?' Tom interrupted, and rudely too, considering the man was on their side. John stared across at him. This was indeed a Tom Baker he didn't know.

Farringdon's smile remained smooth and he nodded amiably. 'Your feelings are understandable, young man. I do indeed have a score to settle, as I have said, but do assure you that is not my only interest. I am here to say that London will make certain its gates are not closed to you when you reach there. We, too, have our agents. And now to business.'

He became serious, the gracious smile fading to hard-faced urgency, and John saw him now, a man accustomed to making business deals without sentiment. Here at last was a tenacious leader.

'We proceed to Cressing Temple where lies all the important green-seal documents. If they are not burned and it happens we are defeated...' He broke off as howls of protest

251

met that supposition. 'We must think of that. With any battle the impossible must ever be considered, even while confident of victory. In such a way does a king command his army, for then is the ground laid with foresight and he can meet his enemy with strength of knowledge.'

John felt inclined to disagree. To his mind, men should be confident of victory. To be otherwise was to be demoralized before he ever began – but of course he had never been in battle.

'The remainder of this day should be spent resting in preparation for our journey,' Farringdon was saying. 'Half of you are still drunk. There will be no more drinking. That is an order. We have a twenty-four-mile trek to Cressing – not a great distance for a few folk together, but we number near two thousand. By the time we reach Cressing that number will be double and such a multitude travels slower.'

His dark eyes concentrated on them all as though picking out each and every one, and every man knew he was under orders at last. No more wandering about aimlessly, each man feeling he was being seen as a soldier. 'We should come upon Cressing Temple a few days hence. Every document held there will be put to the torch, taking us two more days, and then we turn for London in time to assemble at Mile End beyond Aldgate on the day of Corpus Christi. That is ten days hence. At that time Kent, under the command of the priest John Ball of Colchester, Wat Tyler of Maidstone and his lieutenant Jack Straw, will be assembled at Blackheath on the other side of the Thames. Our two armies will number more than fifty thousand.'

Gasps of awe went around the gathered men, unable to contemplate such numbers. For truth, all England would have to be there. In all England were there that many?

'On that day,' Farringdon ended on a note of triumph, 'the gates of London will be opened to you.'

With his spirits, like everyone else's, lifted, John looked over at Tom and grinned without thinking, just in time to see him switch his glance away, although it could have been that Tom hadn't noticed. John, too, looked away, depression settling on him so that he hardly heard their leader's further orders that none should go faster than the slowest man, so to arrive at Cressing in an impressive body rather than in dribs and drabs. The drawback was that it took two days for such numbers to reach even Chelmsford, ten miles on.

Chelmsford was the county town where the King's business was often conducted. As the horde poured across the River Cam it seemed every housewife with produce to sell had set up a stall with bread, meat already cooking in open-air clay ovens, bacon, fish, pies, sweet-meats and enough home-brewed ale for everyone, and for once nothing was over-priced.

'I knew all along that folk would see us

253

proper fed,' Wat said between mouthfuls of pie.

'Not every town'll be so generous,' muttered Tom, intent on his food.

Wat gave a laugh, wiping his mouth with the sleeve of his tunic. 'By my cods, they'd better be!'

'Mind someone don't cut off your cods and make a woman of you,' Tom returned without looking up, his face expressionless as they all roared with laughter. John didn't laugh, an oversensitive mind hearing a sly dig at him.

The day was spent roaming the town seeking diversion from the boredom of tramping to Cressing. There was plenty to divert them. Following them as seagulls follow the plough, were peddlers, tumblers, jongleurs, tricksters and hedge priests and pardoners with their holy relics and pardons to buy an easy way into Heaven, though it seemed Heaven was already here on earth by way of a sprinkling of street-hardened harlots.

Over the heads of a crowd watching a cock-fight, John saw the tall figures of Wat Gilde-born and Tom Baker. But it was another who caught his interest: a small, bow-legged man glimpsed through a gap in the crowd with his arm about a fresh young wench hardly more than fourteen. Nearing forty, Randere still had a fancy for maids hardly into their puberty, demonstrated by having married his present wife then barely fifteen. Before John could reach him, the gap closed, but at least now he knew that Randere wasn't far away.

He spent a restless night thinking how he was going to deal with the evil bastard when he found him again. First beat him almost to a pulp to find out how much he had told Tom. Then put him out of his misery with a slash to the throat, let him bleed to death – he didn't deserve a quicker one. Murder and the satisfaction it would give him lay in John's heart all night, preventing sleep.

At first light he rose from the hard ground and was about to steal away from the others when Tom's low whisper pulled him up sharply.

'It might be wise, John, to leave your horse here in Chelmsford when we leave.' It was so unexpected that John turned to stare at him. But Tom had more to say. 'You'll be seen too easily up in the saddle. You mustn't let yourself be marked out by them seeking men to hang for treason. When Cressing is lit up by a blaze of documents, there'll be faces marked out a-plenty. On foot you'll be of less account.'

He managed to find his voice at last. 'Why are you telling me this?'

'I wouldn't want you to be one of them taken, that's all.'

He fell silent and, unable to answer, John was left standing where he was, wondering why Tom had spoken to him in this way. If Randere had told all, surely he would be seeking redress, not warning of danger. It was baffling. His own intention of seeking out Randere dwindling, he sank back down.

Seventeen

It hadn't been easy letting Halberdier go. John felt a deep tug of regret as he handed him to a local stableman.

The man was reluctant to stable him for small reward, but told the animal was his to keep provided he promised to treat it well, he brightened, swearing profusely by his patron saint to give it all the care due to such a fine beast. Though John ruefully suspected he'd sell it for a good profit to the next wealthy buyer as came his way, he had to bow to the inevitable and found two witnesses to declare that the man had come by the beast honestly lest he later be accused of stealing.

Wat Gildeborn wasn't so easily persuaded to give up his mount. 'Only a fool walks when he can ride,' he said, and John shrugged, leaving him to his folly as they joined the walking exodus swarming northward out of Chelmsford.

The sun's heat was moderated by thin, high cloud that promised an end to the dry heat, and already the air had a moist, enervating feel to it – not that they went any quicker, as nearly a whole day was wasted waiting for stragglers to keep up.

Following only wooded tracks and spreading across the countryside slowed their progress further, and more than once John felt restless that they hadn't headed straight for London. But Master Farringdon seemed to know what he was about and at last they had an able leader.

For John it was again a sleepless night as he lay awake thinking of that vile informer, Will Randere. There hadn't been a single glimpse of him since that first brief sighting. He wouldn't have gone skulking back to Fobbing to face all sorts of awkward questions, so he had to be somewhere here. But among all these people it was easy to hide.

He must have fallen asleep at some point, because he came to with a start to hear Wat shouting that his horse had gone. And it was daylight.

'He must have wandered,' John offered, but Wat gave him an impatient gesture.

'He were tethered proper.' But already his long nose was twitching at a distant aroma of cooking drifting through the earthy smell of the morning air. What was there in this godforsaken part of the world to cook? Those awakened by his shouts sat up to see him striding off, following the scent like a bloodhound.

'Where's he a-going?' Ralph Peteman queried.

'To find his horse,' John said, and Peteman grunted as if that were good enough for him.

Minutes later the hunter was back, his long,

angular face working with rage. 'Body o' God! The spawn of whores! Nigh two score of 'em sitting about a fire wi' their smug faces smeared with fat and their guts bloated. Not a bone, not a hoof, hide or hair – not even saddle or bridle.'

'I expect they sold those,' observed Tom quietly, almost to himself.

John hardly heard him, his mind on Halberdier and thanking God that he had taken Tom's advice.

Wat had thrown himself down on the ground to glare balefully back the way he'd come. 'Would that I'd thumped them innocent looks off their faces.'

'You accused them?' Tom asked. 'It might not have been your horse, or any horse, but a deer.'

Wat's face was distorted by a sneer. 'It were my horse orright.' He clambered back to his feet, glaring down at those still sitting there while small groups were beginning to move off. 'I'll be glad to quit this place. Do we go or do we sit here the rest of the day?'

'If I were you,' John Reede said, getting up and pulling on his hood, 'I'd call myself fortunate to be rid of that there animal no matter what its fate. Tom here said as riders could be more easily marked than them on foot. Seems them as took your horse did you a service.'

'Maybe they did,' Wat admitted ungraciously as John realized that others had also heard Tom's advice that he had thought had

258

been for him alone.

'But if it were to be roasted,' Wat continued sourly, 'then it should a' been us as roasted it and appeased our own bellies. The Devil take them sons o' harlots and give their cursed guts a belly ache!'

Cressing Temple finally came into view on the fifth day. Nestling amid wide meadows and shallow, watercress-filled streams bordered by willow and alder, it was as peaceful a scene as any could wish to see. The peace, however, was misleading. Cressing Temple had already been alerted, its monks gone into hiding, and most of the better class had left.

A hulking figure slapped John on the back as he passed him, his stride having lengthened in anticipation of spoils, calling over his shoulder, 'We'll dine well tonight, friend. That priory be well stocked. Enough for all.'

'It needs to be,' Dick Elys called after him. 'Other than at Chelmsford, we've eaten little since leaving Fobbing.'

The man slowed, waited for them to catch up. 'Fobbing, you say? Ain't that man as waved a bible in Sir Bealknap's face the baker of that village – the one as is said to be one o' the first movers o' this uprising? One of the first leaders?'

John tried to signal to Elys to mind his tongue, but with more stupidity than any man should be endowed with, Elys grabbed Tom's arm.

'This be the one. Thomas Baker, of our own

village.'

The man's eyes widened with admiration. He held out a cordial hand to Tom. 'Will Saille o' Goldhanger.'

'Where's that?' Ned's strong voice called out, making Tom glance sharply at him, mistaking the voice for John's, the two very much alike.

Saille grinned. 'A marsh village, like your own. Goldhanger be on the River Blackwater, east of Maldon.' He turned back to his hero. 'I were near you, sir, when you flourished that bible like it were a sword. I wouldn't have had the courage. Old Bealknap's face were like thunder. But he swore well enough on your bible, eh?'

A shout brought him back to the present. Seeing his friends calling to him, he excused himself and hurried on.

John wanted to round on Elys for his foolishness. Saille would tell his friends, point out his hero. Word would go around, Tom pointed out as having done a heroic, if treasonable act. If things should ever go awry, the name Thomas Baker of Fobbing would be set down in the records, a wanted man, death hanging over his head.

Despite all that had happened, his affection for Tom was still strong, borne of long friendship from childhood into boyhood and adolescence, and but for one stupid act it would have gone on even into old age.

Sir Robert Hales wasn't at Cressing Temple.

Whether Farringdon had been given the wrong information and Hales was still in London, or whether he had been alerted and had fled, the London goldsmith aired his disappointment in no uncertain way. He demanded men scout far and wide to find Hales, but most were content to raid Hales's deserted property, making straight for the manor house to see what could be looted.

It was well built, as strong as a church, with steep roofs, a belfry, arched windows tall and narrow, though a newer wing had wide, traceried, stained-glass windows, which was obviously the chapel. It was all protected by a wall and shallow, dry moat, with elm and lime trees for shade. A beautiful home once, but no longer.

Stoutly built or not, by the time John reached it, the gate had been breached and the great entrance battered down. Hospitallers in their black frocks and cowls with the white eight-pointed cross on their breasts had been outnumbered and thrust aside. Hundreds of looters were in the courtyards, ransacking outhouses, stables, kitchens, the brew-house and even the small infirmary.

Carried along on a tide of men, he arrived to find the cool, dim interior of the great hall seething with people elbowing each other out of the way to get at the rich furnishings.

John had his mind more on what wonderful food might be left as he forged his way through to the buttery. He found the place a shambles, everything edible already taken.

Beyond the tiny, open-ended room he could see men fighting over hunks of meat, pies being torn to shreds as their claimants aimed blows at each other, milk and broths spilled, turning the dust into mud as their containers were snatched from hand to hand.

Oblivious to the scrapping and bickering, men and women strutted and simpered in rich apparel. A skinny bondsman with a pitted, bulbous nose, his hands still grimed with dirt, was striding around in a plum-velvet surcoat, while a thickset, toothless peasant had perched on a windowsill of the infirmary trying to drag bright particoloured hose over his ragged chaussers, their points unable to reach his thigh, hanging down untied around his calves.

In the grounds a mound of splintered furniture had been set ablaze and was now being fed with armfuls of scrolled documents, but John was only interested in feeding himself. He wondered if the rest of his friends had found anything as he stood in the bright sunshine looking about for them.

A small, bow-legged man draped in a blue brocade houppeland was strutting and bowing to everyone, enjoying playing lord of the manor. John's smile of amusement lasted one second before realizing who it was. The next moment he was bounding through the clusters of revellers to grab a fistful of the man's fine apparel, almost dragging its occupant off his feet.

The man gave a squeal of surprise. Recognizing the identity of his assailant the squeal became a shriek of terror and he seemed to fold up inside the voluminous drapes so that John's aim went over his head. But the hand hadn't let go. Hanging in his drapes like a puppeteer's doll, his scream dissolved in a frantic gabble. 'Mercy, John. I've done no harm to you.'

'No harm?' John's face was contorted in fury and he shook his victim as a terrier would a rat.

'None!' came the cry. 'I swear...'

'Liar!' The fist was again drawn back, this time judging its mark.

Randere cringed. 'Don't strike me! I know what you think, John. I own I did go to Tom Baker, but said nowt about coming up on you and ... you with ... *her.*'

'You lie, you foul-mouthed whore's spawn!'

He realized people were looking at him and he wasn't prepared to beat this piece of offal senseless for their vile pleasure. Dragging Randere by his looted robe, he made towards the gates. Yanked off his feet, Randere tried in vain to regain his footing, rolling across the dirt like a bundle of rubbish, his terrified cries coming from somewhere inside the folds of the now dishevelled clothing.

'Mercy, John! Please, believe me. I said nothing. I was too afeared.'

'Not half afeared as you'll be seconds from now,' John grated.

'It's the truth!' Randere begged pathetically. 'All know a bearer of bad tidings be at risk from them they tell. He'd have pounded me.'

'I intend to do worse than just pound you,' John snarled, staring ahead. Beyond the gates the moat was shielded by bushes and he dragged the pleading Randere into them. Minutes from now the man's face would be a bloody mess, a knife across the throat to finish him.

Randere was still babbling when John pushed him to the ground. 'For God's sake, John, let me speak! Tom Baker doesn't know. He doesn't know!'

It stayed John's hand. 'What d'you mean, he doesn't know?' Of course he knew, his whole attitude these past days said as much. 'You told him something,' he spat. 'What did you tell him?'

Randere had calmed a little, seeing the chance of reprieve. 'I spoke of seeing you at Fobbing, giving orders for the beacon to be lit. In jest, I told him that you were merry and thought you drunk. I said that even drunk you did look powerful and commanding and...'

'Get on with it!'

'I said – in jest, John, only in jest – that you did look so strong and handsome that even his wife had to turn to admire you...'

'Christ! Have done wi' your clown's flattery. Say what you have to say, straight, no lies, else I'll slit your throat right now.' With one hand on the cringing man's chest, he drew the blade to hold it close to the other's face as if to prick out an eye. Calm deserting him at the move, Randere squealed again in terror, words tumbling from his mouth.

'It be the truth, John. I asked him, what if a woman were to gaze at such a man enough to turn his head, would it not tempt him to lust for her? I know it was wrong to pose such a question, but you did treat me badly and I could think only of revenge for it. But I saw for an instant that it made him think.' Randere's voice became a whine. 'Was it my fault if I caught you two together, she with her bared legs up around you while you—'

The words ended in another squeak as the knife jerked forward a fraction. 'I never stalked you. I came upon you by accident, it be the truth.'

'What exactly did you tell him?'

Randere cringed away from the knife now threatening his nose. 'I was angered by your ill handling of me that night, but I feared his wrath if I told him all of what I saw. But then he laughed and said there was a time when he wouldn't have put such capers past you, but that you were married now and had too fine a sense of right and wrong to be thus enticed. Without warning he ceased laughing and became angry and asked if I were implying his wife had behaved unseemly by looking at you in that way.'

Randere squirmed, seeing the knife menacing him. 'He demanded to know why I was telling him this. I began to wish I'd not approached him. He asked did I see her trying to entice you. I was in fear. How could I say his wife had cuckolded him? So I said I

265

thought it was *you* looking at *her*. I didn't dare to say more. I've caused you no real harm, John, I swear ... On the lives of my children, I swear...' He was weeping now and John knew the man had already wet himself in his crass terror. 'He seemed to change then,' he blabbered on. 'He pushed me away and ordered me to say no more.'

Finding the hold on him lessening, Randere tried to scramble away but found himself hauled back and shaken like a rat, John's enraged fist smashing into his face again and again even though he twisted this way and that to avoid some of the blows. The knife had fallen into the grass. In trying to retrieve it, John's grasp on him loosened again and this time he managed to roll clear and, scrambling to his feet, he fled.

All John had learned from Randere was that Tom, with only hints and half truths, must be confused. Even if he couldn't bring himself to believe any part of it, the seeds had been sown. Striding from the scene, his sight misted by his own tears of rage and dismay, knowing he should have finished Randere as he had planned, he heard his name called. It took a second call for him to acknowledge it.

Dick Elys was standing some way off, halfway up the bank of a small stream, only his top half visible. He was waving and beckoning to him.

'Hey, John! Over here, lad!'

John hesitated. He wanted no one's company, but he went towards the man to find several of his friends reclining on the grass bank. Wat, stripped to the waist in the midday heat, was busily devouring a piece of venison pie, the rest of the food they'd taken from the house divided between the others with quite a lot still scattered around on the grass.

'Help yourself,' Dick said, squatting down. 'There's plenty for all.'

Tom was crouched on his haunches by the stream scraping several days' stubble from his cheeks with the blade of his knife.

'So what've you been up to?' his brother-in-law John Reede asked between mouthfuls of food.

John shrugged. 'Just looking around.' He noticed Tom hadn't looked up and again he wished he'd ended Randere's life for him.

'We wondered where you'd been,' Ned said. Robin was with him, the slip of a lad looking happy, despite the rough living.

And there lies the difference, John thought, dropping to the ground to accept a portion of a mortrewe of pork and chicken bound with egg and spices. Doing his best to ignore Tom's back, he put his mind to comparing the lad's breeding to his own – he a plain smith, one of these men whose coarseness was ingrained and unalterable.

John frowned. His brain felt as if it were about to burst with the effort of thinking. Such thoughts were better left to those like Tom, who'd been taught his letters and knew

267

how to control thought. All it was doing for him was making his head spin.

He forced himself to take another nibble of the mortrewe. Eaten with watercress scooped up from the stream, a handful of liquorice and dried apricots, it made meal fit for any lord, but his appetite had deserted him. He looked towards Tom, who still had his back to him. All around, conversation was light-hearted, inane and coarse, yet Tom held himself aloof from it. Randere had been lying – he'd told him all.

Above the casually lolling men a figure suddenly appeared, making them all look up, its familiar rotund shape startling them.

'Master Rycard!'

'Ah, I've f-found you at last.' Swaying on the edge of the bank, he was very much under the influence of the leather wine flask he held. He took a step forward, slipped on the grassy slope, and came careering down on his rump to land in a heap in their midst, and all without letting go of the flask.

The wary looks that had met his appearance now turned to laughter and even Tom glanced round. Rycard no danger to them now, Wat plucked the wine from his grasp.

'By Christ! Comes our bailiff bearing gifts. Just what were needed to wash down the fine victuals we've just eaten. By your leave, your lordship.' Impudently he saluted him with the raised flask, lifting its neck to his mouth and taking a long swig before lowering it and wiping the mouth in great satisfaction with the back of his hand. 'God bless you, Bailiff, for your generosity. Here's something worth drinking, lads.'

John felt a need to vent his spleen on someone. 'How come you're here, Rycard?' he demanded savagely, without any semblance of politeness. He saw Tom's back straighten, though the man did not turn. 'And drunk as well. Not much different to the rest of us, eh?'

He saw Tom come slowly to his feet. He came over to where Rycard was drunkenly reclining, going down on his haunches beside him with a forearm resting casually across one knee, having calmed John with a touch on his arm.

'Have you been to our manor, Master Rycard, spoken to anyone there by chance?' Rycard was grinning, trying to focus. Tom spoke slowly, making every word clear for the man, using patience with him. 'We need to know of anyone you've spoken to.'

It was a good hour before Rycard was anything like coherent. No jests now as he finally began to sit up and take notice. Tom's quiet questions began to reap harvest.

After escaping, he had exchanged his gold rings for an old nag and on this had made his way home to let his wife know he was safe. John realized that he'd reached there an hour before his own arrival to find his wife in a state of terror. She told him that in his absence an investigator had come to the manor and, finding him absent, had gone into the village. When he didn't return, she'd gone

269

to make enquiries and found all the men gone, those that were left making her feel uneasy, filling her with fear.

Leaving his wife in the care of her maid-servants, he'd set his face to finding Steward Somenour, but had lost his nerve lest he be blamed for having allowed himself to be abducted, perhaps relieved of his position as Bailiff.

Some way from Pleshey he had stopped at a cottage that sold ale, first tethering his nag to the ale-stake. But when he came out the horse had gone – stolen. It was folly to continue to Pleshey on foot with the whole country up in arms, so he'd joined up with a band of men and found himself here at Cressing Temple, deciding to make the best of a bad bargain by helping himself to a drop of Sir Robert Hales's finest wine.

'It sounds fair enough to me,' John said, glancing at the man who had laid his hand on him, heartened by its gentleness, but found his glance not returned. A shout took away his attention as along the top of the little bank Randere came towards them, his battered face all but concealed by soot. Some of the others leapt up and went to meet him, wondering at his looks, and then bore him back as if he was a hero.

'He fired the priory!' John Mott yelled. 'The first to put torch to it.'

Now that they were on their feet, they could see the pall of smoke drifting on the still air. Randere was grinning despite his battered face, and again John wished he'd finished his deed. The man was a leech, slimy as the eels he caught, sucking blood like a lamprey.

They gathered around him, demanding to know more, but his eyes seemed trained solely on John, glinting with hatred and revenge.

'Ay, I be the first as put torch to it,' he said. 'Though somewhat knocked about in the doing of it, as all can see.' He fingered his blackened and bloody face gingerly, which brought their grunts of admiration. 'Till then I'd been keeping eyes and ears open for anything as others don't know about. Ay, even while others made fools of themselves.' His eyes had not left John. 'Some too occupied creeping into corners wi' their lemans and other men's wives, thinking themselves unobserved.'

He gave a chuckle and John shot an involuntary look towards Tom, shocked to see him staring back, the clear blue eyes direct and steady, with such depth of knowledge in their brilliance that John looked hastily back to Randere as if thoroughly and innocently interested.

'I did see one such fool,' Randere was saying, gazing straight at him. 'About your age, young Melle, well experienced at his task for all his youth. Ay, fit to pound his shaft through her into the very ground where she lay, her sighing and crying his name. What was it now? Ah ... I know ... nay, I disremember. But it fair made my own man stand up in

271

my chaussers. And the shamed looked when they found themselves being observed – hah! A merry thing it was to see, I can tell you.'

'Did you see any beheadings?' young Dick Wodelarke asked, licking his lips.

'I were first to fire the priory,' Randere reminded him, tiring of his tale. 'Ain't that enough for you?'

Wat Gildeborn was gazing around him. 'All are beginning to forsake this place,' he announced. 'Time we upped and left too.'

With them climbing back up the bank, John hung back. As Tom made to follow, he called to him. 'Just a word with you, Tom. It'll not take long.'

He needed to be done with this uncertainty and torment. If Randere meant to dangle threats over his head for the rest of his life, even demanding money for his silence when things returned to normal, it was best to suffer what had to be suffered now, a quick solution preferable to a lingering one.

'I can't endure this business any longer,' he began.

The ferocity with which Tom suddenly swung round made him step back. 'You'd taunt me wi' confession as if I were a priest to ease your conscience? Nay, John, I want none of your self-ease.'

Recovering, John heard himself say stupidly, 'You know, then?'

'I know nothing!' the voice scraped. 'Nor wish to.'

He tried to take a step towards him,

perhaps to beseech, and was startled when Tom put his hands out as though to stop a descending sword.

'Get away from me, John!' It was a cry of anguish more than hatred, but John felt compelled to advance. He saw hands ball into fists, both raised together to be brought down across his shoulders, over and over, pounding senselessly where any other man would have hit straight from the shoulder to smash into his face. And all the time came the anguished cries: 'Get away from me, John, my friend ... my treacherous friend...'

He would have endured the battering until he dropped, but Tom suddenly fell against him, those passing looking askance at the weeping, apparently drunken fool.

It wasn't an act of forgiveness, that strange embrace. He heard the strangled torrent of words against his shoulder that no amount of contrition would ever erase from his soul: 'You can have her ... She's no more my wife ... Will never bear a child of mine ... You my friend for longer than she was my wife and you've destroyed it – by your own hand ... I can never forgive you for that.'

John stood letting the words sink in. There was so much he needed to say to the friend he'd wronged, but it was too late.

All he could do was move away, leaving the man to collapse under his own weight, on to his knees, and at least relieved that the others had long gone out of sight and earshot.

Moving slowly at first, like a man in a

273

dream, his stride lengthened until he was running, blindly, his breath heaving from unshed tears of remorse as he wiped a small trickle of blood from his cheek.

Eighteen

All manor records, labourers' services, fines and tithes had gone up in flames along with the valuables of the Lord Treasurer's priory. But the number of writs found bearing the green wax seals had disappointed Farringdon.

'They'll be at Coggeshall,' he told the men he'd personally gathered about him. 'At the house of John Sewale.'

The Sheriff of Essex was closely allied to Sir Robert Hales. If the writs weren't here then that was where they would be. Coggeshall lay four miles northeast on a road constructed by Roman legions over a thousand years ago and still in use, known as Stane Street. On this good, straight road, the first of his men could be there in little over two hours.

Even so, they were running out of time. Already it was the eve of Holy Trinity. They had to be at Mile End outside London by Thursday, the eve of Corpus Christi, and Mile End was still forty miles away.

They arrived to find men already storming the Cistercian abbey on the far side of the River Blackwater. Distant figures could be seen scurrying amid its idyllic fish ponds,

275

streams and gardens where monks raised their vegetables, laying all to waste, the cries of the white-robed monks and the raucous yells of the raiders floating across the water. John could only feel anger at the needless destruction. What did an abbey have to do with a poll tax rebellion? Some of these men were little more than vandals.

John felt desperate need for absolution. Just to go down on one knee and bow his head and pray for forgiveness, although there was no priest, might make a world of difference to how he was feeling. Oblivious to those who swarmed past him, he did just that. Hands clasped against his bowed forehead, he let his mind run, reliving those moments in the shadow of Fobbing Church and mentally scourging himself for every thrust he had made. Dear God, if he had a lash to wield at this moment, he would need to flail every inch of his skin and still not receive absolution.

But the moment passed and, getting to his feet, he turned his mind to worldly things once more, stretching his neck to find his companions. Each time a figure remotely resembling Tom's caught his eye, his heart leapt.

Whether Tom had followed at a distance and was hereabouts or whether he'd turned off and joined the others going towards London, John had no idea. He kept telling himself that it didn't matter any more, but he knew this wound would never heal, and would remain a gaping rent for the rest of his life.

The sheriff's house was in Church Street, north of Market Hill. It was here that the crowds were thickest, for many had cause to hate John Sewale, one of his duties being to serve Exchequer writs. In the past he had brought many before the courts to face exorbitant fines for quite trivial offences.

Like Hales, the sheriff had fled. A band of rebels from Bocking had entered the town two days before. Badly mauled, he'd escaped to Chelmsford where he had a second house.

As John came up to the confusion around the door of the sheriff's house, cries from inside told him the man had been cornered. He heard Wat yelling in his ear.

'D'you see anything, John!'

'Nothing,' he yelled back. Quickly hemmed in by the swaying mob, he was glad of someone he knew.

'I can see something,' the tall shepherd bellowed. 'It's the King's escheater, Master John Ewell – they've got him!'

Something was being borne aloft over everyone's head and being passed from hand to hand. Instinctively he and Wat raised their arms to receive the burden as it reached them. John felt its weight, limp and heavy, like a bundle of sodden rags. The man's limbs threshed weakly and from the gaping mouth blood dripped briefly on to John's shoulders before the body was passed onwards.

With the dispatch of the escheater, the sheriff's house was entered, and every scrap of parchment brought out to be fed to a bonfire already blazing in the street, so many scrolls that men lost patience unrolling them so that only the ends caught fire, the centre remaining untouched.

Without waiting to express his regrets to the grieving family of John Ewell, whose body was now being carried to the church beyond the sheriff's house, Farringdon set about leading his army back to Chelmsford with promise of more writs.

'That man's fair obsessed wi' them there documents,' Wat grumbled as they left the sheriff's burning house. 'About time we made for London.'

Several houses in Coggeshall had been fired, including a fine house belonging to Sir John Gildeborough who had been with Thomas Bampton in Brentwood.

John thought of how Tom had taunted Gildeborough when they were there and how steadily Gildeborough had looked back at him, every muscle of his firm, refined face revealing controlled anger. There was no doubt that he had marked him out for recognition and probably saw him as one of the prime leaders of this revolt. Might he even blame Tom for his house being put to the torch and then seek revenge? He spoke of his fear to Wat as they turned their faces from the fierce heat of crackling wood and hissing thatch. Wat let out a laugh.

'And when will he get chance for revenge, eh? Within a week we'll be storming the very gates of London with every lord inside them walls quaking in their shoes. Do you think Gildeborough will be spending time seeking revenge on one single man like Tom Baker? He'll be more occupied saving his own skin.' His exuberance faded and his voice dropped. 'Where is Thomas Baker anyway? I ain't seen him since we left Cressing. Do you not think that odd?'

John made an effort at a shrug. 'Maybe he's grown tired of trolling about from one town to another and has made off with some as are going on to London.' He kept his eyes staring ahead as they walked with the crowds.

'But you and he be seldom apart. Why would he go on without you? God's teeth, you and he be the closest of friends. All know that. Or did...' He hesitated in his tracks. 'Or did you two quarrel?' he finished. 'I thought I did hear voices raised in anger when we were leaving that stream in Cressing. I did look round but saw nothing amiss, only your heads just visible above that bank, your arms around each other. I never did see Tom Baker after that.' He studied John's face. 'Were you bidding a farewell to each other? Is there some secret way he must go that we mustn't know of?'

John managed a flat laugh. 'No, nothing. I, too, thought he was following on.'

'Then why is he not here?'

Sudden anger caught John unaware. 'How

279

should I know why, curse you?' He rounded on his companion, instantly regretting the outburst as the man looked at him in hurt surprise.

'What have I said?' Wat asked, himself angry. 'Why curse me? I did but ask if you knew where he was, no more, and you turn on me.'

He wanted to say he was sorry, but instead strode off, leaving Wat staring after him, bewildered.

On Farringdon's orders, crowds of men trudged through the night to make up time lost, reaching Witham in the small hours to snatch some four hours of sleep before continuing on, by then the sun already well up.

It was not until Chelmsford that John finally saw a face he knew. Ned was leading a large, ancient horse pulling a creaking, somewhat unstable wagon full of purloined provisions, as well as several men who sat guarding their gains with billhooks and scythes, daring any to try and take what they saw as theirs.

Catching him up, John fell into step beside him, grateful to see him. With an arm about Ned's shoulders, his first question was, 'Have you seen any other of our friends?' He began naming a few, ending as if on a casual note with Tom Baker.

'I did glimpse Will Copyn, our hayward,' Ned obliged. 'He was with Henry Sharpe and some others. But I can't find Robin.' He seemed a little down in the mouth as he said it. 'He did disappear back at Coggeshall when I was watching the sheriff's house go up in flames. I hope he's come to no harm. I enjoyed his company.'

'He may have gone back home,' John offered, hoping to cheer him, but he wasn't concerned about Robin. 'And Tom Baker, have you seen him?'

'Nowt o' Tom Baker,' Ned answered easily.

They walked on in silence, the wagon squeaking and creaking behind them, the dull clop-clop of old sumpter-horse seeming a little uneven to John's ears.

'That beast is near to casting a shoe, I reckon,' John said absently, his mind on where Tom could be. Taken from his thoughts, he glanced at the animal, noting it had a slight limp on its front right leg. Looking down he could see the fine edge of protruding metal where the shoe had started to twist. 'We'll have to get that fixed soonest we can,' he said.

'We should gain Chelmsford within the hour,' said Ned. 'You think it will last that long?'

'I daresay,' John said, returning to his thoughts.

The horse finally cast the shoe half a mile from Chelmsford. The town crammed full, the blacksmith there was too busy hammering out rough and ready weaponry to turn farrier for one old horse. But when the two newcomers announced themselves to be blacksmiths, he happily gave them leave to select a length of iron and thrust it into the glowing charcoals beside the lengths to be turned into swords.

On a spare anvil, with Ned to help, John worked swiftly and skilfully, reaping admiring glances from his host as the open forge rang to the clang of hammers upon iron. 'That be good work you do there, lad,' he growled, his eyes on his own work.

John threw a glance at the sword taking shape under the man's hammer. ''Tis but a shoe. That there sword do discount my work.'

The smith appeared flattered. 'As best I can do wi' iron as is nowt but rust and pitted half through. No sense using best quality for them as lack the art of using such. I've made swords for knights. Sir John Gildeborough himself, Earl of Oxford.' The name instantly brought John's mind back to Tom, but the man was still talking. 'Where be you from, Blacksmith?'

'Fobbing,' John replied, plunging the now fashioned shoe into the butt of cold water, watching the steam rise, his mind still on Tom.

The man paused in his task to study him for a moment. 'Fobbing, you say? There were someone as did pass here but an hour since, asking me to sharpen a knife for him.'

John became attentive. 'Did he give a name?'

The smith shook his head, studying the edge of the sword he was holding up for inspection. 'Nay, just went on his way, though he did mention something about being a baker there. I were eating a pasty between working and he said as how it looked over-baked and as how he could have shown the one what baked it a thing or two. He were right – it were as hard as this bit of iron here – but I jested with him, asked if he was such a good baker then, but he didn't laugh. He paid for the sharpening and went on his way. Ah, one thing more – he did ask after some-one named Melle, a blacksmith.' The man looked questioningly at John. 'That wouldn't be you, would it?'

John didn't reply. 'Did you see which way he went?'

The man wrinkled his bulbous nose. 'In this lot? I ain't time to see which way a man goes. I only know they'll all be going to London by and by, and then this town might fall peaceful again.'

Neither said any more as John applied himself to fitting the shoe and nailing it in place, finally thanking the man who nodded absently, having lost interest.

The sun having long since slipped below the horizon, the night had become dotted with myriad small campfires. Perhaps Tom sat round one of them, but what had Tom been doing enquiring after him after what had happened between them? Perhaps the same as John himself was doing, still clinging to a long and once treasured friendship.

'I've a mind to take a wander,' he told Ned

283

after they'd enjoyed a share of the wagon's provisions, payment for shoeing the horse. 'I might find one or two of our friends. Better to keep together.'

The evening had finally settled down after a somewhat half-hearted attack on Sheriff Sewale's home off Bridge Street. Not so many had joined in that attack, all eyes beginning to focus on better prizes in London, others more keen on catching up with a bit more sleep, knowing they must be up and away by dawn.

Everyone settling down, John wandered the quiet groups of rustics for an hour or so looking at this one and that for the face he hoped to see, and at the same time feared to come across. Weariness forced him back to where his brother was already snoring, letting his body drop down beside Ned's to sleep like a log.

He awoke with a start to pearly dawn, aware of men amalgamating once more into one great flood southward. Those who owned the sumpter-wagon had already left. The brothers got to their feet, mouths furry, eyes bleary, to see Wat Gildeborn bearing down on them with one or two others in his wake.

'Is there anything to drink?' John asked and was handed a scuffed leather flask of weak ale, Wat seeming to have forgotten their brief quarrel. But his expression was peeved nevertheless.

'We'll be fair worn out at this rate, time we reach London,' he grumbled. 'Traipsing all about. There be only two days left to us to get there afore the others from Kent reach there. It's still more'n thirty mile.'

'Which can be done in two full days,' John said ambitiously and a little abruptly. 'So long as we start now and lengthen our stride somewhat.'

'That's what I think they're all doing,' Ned said, noticing a new, brisk determination in everyone's step.

Some forty-odd scrolls of unburned documents had been stuck on stakes stuck into the ground at intervals along the route as a gesture of the strength of the commons. Not only was their step brisk but voices were being raised in song and a large group from Ingatestone and Fryerning were heard bellowing out a familiar tune to the beat of a tambor:

Tutivillus, the Devil o' Hell,
He writeth their names sooth to tell.
Ad missam garulantes.
Better we be at home for ay,
Than here to serve the Devil's pay.
Sic vana famulantes.

These women that sitteth the church about,
They be-eth all the Devil's rout.
Divina impedientes.
But they be still, he will them quell;
With keen crooks draw them into hell.
Ad puteum multum flentes.

285

It was a tune the Fobbing men knew well, taught to them by their own Parson Rackstrawe – Jack Straw, now – who marched on the other side of the Thames, so word had come to them, alongside the Kent leaders Wat Tyler and John Ball.

Many had been the time that Rackstrawe had whipped up his congregation's enthusiasm with this stirring tune – not one that would have brought a smile to his bishop's face but their parson had never been orthodox in his approach to the Church, and, of course, now they knew why.

Even John, deep as the ache in his heart was, found himself joining in. 'Jack Straw were once our parson,' he persisted in boasting to those who he and his friends passed.

True, he'd never had much idea what the Latin words of the song meant. Tom would have known. Priest-taught, he'd once tried to convey that knowledge to him, but what call had a blacksmith to learn such things – much less the need to read and write? He remembered that Tom had finally given up in despair.

The bittersweet memories flooded over him, bringing him near to weeping even as he sang, yearning for the innocence of a past that was gone for ever.

Finally the song died away. Back towards Brentwood, but skirting it, keeping their faces turned towards London, and that night slept in the open fields, warmed by their fires, eating what they could scrounge from hamlets they passed, all fearing to be late reaching Mile End.

The following morning saw no jollity, heard no voices raised in song. Faces tightly set, the great army of commons forged on, eager to have their first sight of London.

Nineteen

'God's holy blood. Look!'

Wat Gildeborn pointed towards the distant skyline, one such as few of them had even seen – the spires of London, hundreds of them, some tall and thin as wheat stalks, some squat and fat as hayricks. And rising above all of them the soaring spire of the great St Paul's, even above the height of the solid square keep of the Tower, the royal residence of kings and now of the golden-haired boy, the fourteen-year-old King Richard II whom they all hoped soon to see in the flesh.

'That be a wondrous sight,' breathed Dick Elys, echoing everyone's thoughts.

These last days the hamlet of Mile End had seen thousands pouring in from road and field like a plague of blackfly. Tomorrow would be the eve of Corpus Christi. Those with whom most of the Fobbing men had travelled had arrived in good time.

Across the Thames, on Blackheath, those of Kent were gathering in their tens of thousands to combine with those of Essex, Cambridgeshire, Suffolk and Norfolk in such a multitude as London had never before seen.

'I cannot believe we are here at last,' John said. 'To be but one mile from London's very gates.'

'Them gates'll be locked by now,' came a slightly nasal voice that John had come to loathe. Taken by surprise, he looked back to find Will Randere standing with a small knot of men a little way behind him.

Grimly dismissing him, John turned to his own friends. 'We were told the gates would be opened to us.'

'Not until we are ready to enter,' put in Simon Rycard, who seemed to have decided to join up with them and had been accepted. He'd come too far to dare go home now. 'Like all great towns, the gates will be locked at this hour. Curfew has long since rung and they'd have taken all the cattle in from the fields. London, I regret, is closed to you for the time being and you will have to go hungry this night.' Ever a long-winded man, he still had more to say, ignoring the resigned sighs from those round him.

Coming up for breath, he gave a cynical chuckle. 'Knowing how many are here,' he went on before any of them could get a word in, 'doubtless they will remain locked on the morrow and will not open until those inside carry out their orders to have them opened to us. Until then, my fine friends, you must hunt for what food you can find.'

'And don't forget, Master Rycard,' Wat cut in before the man could draw yet another breath. 'You'll be seeing the least of whatever

289

food we find. So don't crow too soon, Master Bailiff. You'll feel as hungry as the rest of us afore them gates open. Still,' he looked him up and down, 'you've enough fat stored around your middle to live off for some time yet.'

Rycard scowled as others laughed. 'Don't be too sure of yourself, Walter Gildeborn. None know yet what awaits them on the other side of that gate. You might all find yourselves...'

But he was ignored. 'We know something as them lords don't,' Wat continued. 'That them gates will be opened whether they want or not.'

'How can we be certain?' someone asked.

Suddenly John heard Will Randere's voice strike up, far too close at hand. He swung round, but the man was still keeping his distance, his voice ringing out.

'Them gates will be opened orright. Then with us going in by Aldgate and the London Bridge portcullis lifted by them inside for Kent to enter, I doubt as London'll be able to even hold us all, much less stop us.'

'How do you know so much?' asked Dick Elys.

The eel-catcher smirked and tapped the side of his nose. John was conscious of the man's eyes on him. 'It do pay to keep eyes and ears open. I know a lot more than some think. Be that right, young Melle?'

But before eyes could turn to look enquiringly at him, John strode off, seething, tears of fury pricking his eyes. Randere still rankled from the beating he'd received at John's hands, the marks still visible, everyone thinking them a hero's wounds from his brave deeds. But Randere hadn't done with him yet and John actually felt fear, like a grinding wheel in his stomach, at the mischief Randere could yet do.

While others settled down to sleep John kept thinking about Tom and Marjory, and where Tom might be. Finally giving up, he got quietly to his feet and stood, trying to resist the temptation to wander among the dying campfires that for the most part had cooked nothing this night.

Across the river he could see countless orange pinpricks of light from identical fires. Were they on that side enjoying good mutton turning on spits? Were they far more organized than those on this side? For as far as he could tell these men were little more than a disorganized mob. Where was Farringdon? Where were their leaders? And where was Tom?

Someone was at his elbow. He felt rather than saw the man, and whirled about to face him, his heart already leaping to welcome the tall, slim figure he'd expected to see. Instead he found himself faced with a smaller man and instant hatred swept through him. Shock and disbelief numbed him and all he could say was, 'What d'you want?'

'A word, nowt else,' came the reply. There was a ring of contrition in the tone, but it touched deaf ears.

'I've nowt to say to you, Master Randere,' he spat.

'Even so, I would crave speak to you. There's no need to answer if you wish not, but I must speak. I was wrong to take pleasure in taunting you afore your friend, young Tom Baker. But can you blame me after your treatment o' me earlier? A man would seek revenge after what you did to me.'

John saw him finger the bruises on his face, but held back from the obvious question: what else had he expected?

'I were aggrieved to be so handled by a younker with enough brawn on him as could fell an ox, yet pummel the likes of a small man like me. 'Twas an unfair advantage you had over me, John Melle, and I twice your age.'

John couldn't help himself. 'And what of the advantage you took of me?' he blurted out.

Randere gave a mirthless chuckle. 'And what unfair advantage did you take of Thomas Baker, your trusting and loving friend?'

The question went into John like an arrow point, the stolen moments coming back to him so vivid that his breath caught in his throat. It was as though Satan himself stood at his elbow, laughing at him, taunting him with his own weight of sin.

'Can't you leave me be?' he heard himself plead, all the fight and the outraged anger

292

taken out of him.

'In a moment,' said Randere. 'I'm not here to harass you, but I do have a message for you.'

Now John turned on him, Tom's name hovering on his lips, but all he could manage was, 'A message – from whom?'

'I'd no chance to convey it to you afore,' Randere evaded, seemingly unable to resist the opportunity to taunt even further. 'When I did try, you did sorely batter my face.'

'Then give it now!'

Randere's expression became guarded. 'I hesitate to say lest you go at me again.'

'For Christ's sake!' John made a move towards him, but this time Randere stood his ground.

'It be from *her*. From Marjory Baker...'

'God blast you! You still dare to taunt me, you foul—'

'John, don't strike me!' He cringed now from the suddenly raised fist. 'She did give me a message, for you. I were racing homeward after finding you and...' He broke off as John loomed over him. 'I were in fear of you coming after me. I feared to go home lest you came and battered down my door to get at me and thought only to leave while I could, but she came out from behind the church and called after me. She were pale and distracted. She bade me to speak to you on her behalf.'

'I'm not interested in whatever you have to say,' John grated, but Will Randere was not a fool. He'd seen the blue-grey eyes brighten in anticipation and now he grinned slowly, an inborn need in him to harrow the young lover at least once more by drawing out the moment a while longer before delivering his message.

'She were full persistent that I give you her words exactly as she spoke them to me. I did make solemn promise to convey those very words to you when I saw you.'

'If you don't say what you have to in two seconds, they'll stay in your dead mouth for ever,' came the grating threat. Randere nodded hastily, but the leer remained.

'I were to say that her heart is lost to you, that she knows not how she can live without you.'

'You lie!' John exploded, but the eager light in his eye was turning to one of loathing for this man. 'She wouldn't be so bold, and most certainly wouldn't speak thus to you.'

'And who else would she ask to convey her love message to you?' Randere challenged, and John knew he was right. 'Her love for you made her bold,' Randere went on. 'Though she was bold enough to lie in a field with other than her husband and give herself to him with such zest as I saw...' He gasped as John's hand came out and grabbed a fistful of his grubby tunic. 'Nay, forgive me! Hear me out. I'll give her exact message.'

'Then spit it out and go.'

'I will. Of a certain I will. She did tell me to say as she swooned with love for you but knew it could not be. She could not further wrong her husband, who was kind and gentle even though she had no love for him, despite what had happened to cause them to marry, that it had been a passing thing, and it was you that her heart had always been lost to. Please, Master Melle, that were her words, not mine...'

Randere's face turned pasty-white as the grip on his gipon tightened, pulling him closer to his captor. 'I've delivered her message. I did only what she asked of me. Please, you've beaten me enough.'

The grip on his clothes loosened so abruptly that he almost fell back. Stumbling, he turned and scurried off on his small, bowed legs.

Another sleepless night, John cursed, lying awake for hours staring up at the starry blackness, the stars becoming misty. There'd be rain soon, at least in a day or two, and most likely drizzle. And indeed as darkness took on an almost imperceptible grey he was conscious of dampness in the air. There'd be no sunrise to be seen this morning, he thought, his eyelids closing heavily.

It seemed hardly a second later that he came awake with a start to the sound of someone calling, 'Wat, Ralph, Dick, everyone – rouse up, all of you!'

As John sat up sharply he saw men already astir, the dawn coming up grey and overcast. And there was Tom urging the Fobbing men to their feet. John realized that he himself was being ignored and it was Ralph Reede who had to relay the message to him while Wat, surprised to see the newcomer, had begun asking where Tom had been all this time.

Tom answered readily enough. 'With them as stormed Sir John Gildeborough's manor at Wennington. We found many more documents there than at Coggeshall.' He sounded excited, was speaking much too fast. 'A fine old riot we had, Gildeborough's house reduced to smoldering sticks in less than an hour. His lady were there wi' her children, and she shouting at us to go away and leave her in peace. God's blood, but we put them all out of countenance with our noise and commotion.'

He seemed not the least abashed that a defenceless woman had been terrorized in her own hall, her home burned down around her, her treasured possessions smashed and burned. He seemed like a different person.

John found his voice. 'You didn't molest them!'

Again he was ignored, as if he wasn't there, Tom speaking directly to the others who were all ears around him. 'We only frightened them. We did not touch them. But to see their servants run off across the fields like rabbits! If we'd intended harm to Gildeborough's lady, they'd have been no stout defenders of her.'

All John could do was to stare at him, unable to compare this brilliant-eyed rebel to the friend he'd always known as gentle and

296

caring and thoughtful. Tom had changed, and so quickly. This man, with his talk of burning, sacking and beheading, of riot and insurrection, was no longer the man he knew. Yet, sick in his heart, John knew he was the cause of all this. He wanted to run away, as far as he could from this apparition. But he would really be running away from himself and what he'd done, and even if he ran to the ends of the earth, he would never escape that.

Tom was being urged by the others to tell more and was quite ready to oblige. 'Then we came through Rainham and on to Barking and saw the great abbey. Some there had gone to join them in Kent, we heard. Then we came to West Ham and then to Bow and from there to here.'

'Did you see anything of my brother William?' Wat asked. 'I ain't seen him since leaving Coggeshall.'

'Saw him just outside Witham,' Tom supplied, stopped in his tale. 'He said he were going home, concerned as to how his animals and family were faring.'

Wat shrugged. 'Ay, that he would.'

'Who can blame him?' Tom said. 'A man with heavy responsibilities.'

The sound of cheering some distance away, towards the London walls, brought every man around to his feet. Men began to run towards it, those from Fobbing with them. John found himself running beside his friend, any dissension swept aside as several riders came swooping through the fast massing crowds, one of the riders tall and gaunt.

Seeing him, the man's name flew from John's lips. 'Rackstrawe – our parson!'

On the large roan horse, still with the same angular, grey face, the hair cut straight, but the features no longer dour, was a totally different man to the one Fobbing's parson had presented. This man, this one they called Jack Straw, had a gleam in the eye, an animated liveliness to his mouth. No longer clothed in dull brown robes but in a tunic of green with a breastplate and helm. His legs encased in metal, he wore a sword. He raised an arm again and again in greeting as men clustered about him.

With him, John recognized the London goldsmith, Farringdon. Tom was pointing wildly to another rider.

'That be John Cobbe o' Danbury. I saw him when we passed there. Going like the wind toward London, but his animal wasn't half as like that great destrier he's now riding.'

In his excitement Tom seemed oblivious to the rift that had come between them and John found himself quite at ease alongside him as he pointed to the fourth rider who carried a fluttering pennon on which was painted a single word.

'What says that?' John called to Tom.

'Elmdon,' Tom quoted without thinking. 'Not a name I've heard of. Come on!' he yelled to those around him.

Thrusting through the thickest of the press, with John just behind, they gained the small clearing created by the great roan's prancing, Tom the first of them to reach their erstwhile parson's side.

'Parson – Parson Rackstrawe!' he called up.

Seeing him, the man immediately leaned down from the saddle and briefly grasped Tom's hand while managing his wild-eyed mount with all the nonchalant ease of a trained knight. He seemed as though he'd been in the saddle all his life, and John found himself wondering what this man had been before they'd ever known him.

But there was no time for ruminating as the man's gaze alighted on him, his clear voice carrying easily above the cheering and calling out: 'Young John Melle, it is good to see you. How does your father now?'

'Well enough,' John only just had time to yell back, for already Jack Straw was casting his gaze further afield, instantly becoming a stranger to them. He threw up an arm in yet another wave to the hordes of men still gathering, and this time his voice carried sheer across their heads, even to the man furthest away.

'Harken all! The King comes to Rother-hithe, by barge, to speak with the people of Kent.'

At the same time Thomas Farringdon held an arm aloft, his voice higher pitched. 'And Aldgate will be opened to you. Get you all to Aldgate.'

There was an immediate turmoil of men scurrying this way and that as some hurried

299

to gather up what belongings they had, while others with nothing to carry but themselves made for the walls. Finally all began to flow in the one westward direction, leaving last night's remnants of campfires dotted about to mark where they had been. Within minutes a large spur broke off to veer towards the river.

'Come on!' Tom was yelling, he too veering off. 'I'm to the river to see our King arrive. Hurry! We might never get another chance.'

It was half a mile to the river. Everyone was streaking across the low-lying ground, leaping over tufts of grass, hoods flying, their long liripipes streaming out behind like thin pennons in a high wind. Even on reaching the marshy approaches to the river, their feet didn't falter. The Fobbing men had split, some going on to London to feast their eyes on the sights, with around ten or so making for the river to see King Richard.

'Them gates will stand open for us to pass in and out as we please,' Tom said to any that wanted to hear as they arrived on the banks of the river.

'Ay, Aldgate,' said someone next to him. 'Opened by an alderman, no less, name of William Tonge. So Jack Straw said this morning.'

'Seems we've high-placed friends inside them walls,' John put in, glancing at Tom, who hadn't seemed to have heard him.

'It were an alderman as opened London Bridge for the Kent folk,' said a small perky man, winking his good eye at him, the other

300

being milky-white. 'One named Walter Sibil let it up after it were lowered for the night and another as drew up the portcullis – John Horn, who went out to 'em with a standard o' the royal arms to allow 'em safe conduct right into the city.'

'Where did they come by the standard?' John asked.

The man tittered. 'One o' them city clerks, I heard tell. The mayor lent it to him wi'out even knowing the purpose and the silly clerk handed it over. Horn divided it, giving the one half to his servant for safe keeping, tying the other half to his lance to bring them of Kent into the city unchallenged. What d'ye think of that for cheek?'

John laughed sociably and glanced up at the sky. It had begun to take on a fiery hue, the veil of cloud that had hung over them all night suffused with colour. Red sky at morn, he quoted silently, shepherds be warned. Indeed, to the southwest the sky had taken on an ominous purple hue. But any rain would be welcome. Since that storm in May, the crops were in need of it. Now with the sun's rim flooding the land with light, he could see thousands on the far side of the river waiting in silent expectation. The river, the flood tide filling it from bank to bank, was clean and beautiful and flowing, whereas at low tide it was just a muddy meandering stream.

From the far bank there came a stir. Word flew from man to man: 'He comes! King Richard comes!'

They watched the swaying mass of people who could see what they couldn't, hidden from them by the river bend. But they read the signs well enough as a deep-throated cheering rolled across the water from those on the southern bank. Then from around the bend came four small craft, the royal barge in their midst. The Fobbing men began yelling themselves almost hoarse trying to attract the royal attention, but the tiny flotilla was obviously making towards the greater numbers on the southern bank.

'He'll not see us,' Tom was shouting, leaping up and down as fifty yards from the opposite bank the craft slowed, the rowers holding their oars hard so that gradually all five glided to a halt, giving the Essex side a better view than first expected.

The royal barge was a sight to behold. Bedecked with awnings, each displaying three gold leopards one above the other on red, quartered with the triple lilies of France, gold on blue. On the high forecastle, also painted with the royal arms, stood two of the King's men in particoloured hose, gold-belted blue tunics and green velvet conical hats. The King's companions within the vessel looked even more like peacocks, their elbow-length capes every colour of the rainbow and sparkling with jewels.

'Which is the King?' someone called out.

John strained his eyes, then pointed, seeing the flaxen locks among the darker ones, Richard renowned for his luxuriant golden hair inherited from his Plantagenet forebears. And there he was – a tall, slim youth, seeming to shine in the shadow of the awning as though a fragment of sun had come to rest there. But King Richard had gone to the side of the barge nearest the Kent bank. They could see people beckoning for him to come among them, but when the flotilla remained stubbornly offshore, the happy cries began to alter, subsiding at first, then breaking out afresh, this time with the high note of protest. From where he stood, John could see raised fists, frustrated and angry beckoning, and weapons being brandished.

'I think the King is refusing to meet their request for him to land,' John said.

'I don't blame him,' Tom said quietly at his elbow.

'They can't mean him harm,' John put in. 'Perhaps his accursed uncles have advised against going among his people.'

The cluster of vessels began to move and, amid jeering and shouts of rage from the bank, turned and made back towards the Tower shore. As the flotilla moved out of sight, the mass on the far bank began to change its shape like oil on a current of water, growing long and narrow as it began moving westward towards the city.

'Quick!' yelled Wat as those on this side started to do likewise. 'To London!'

Turning, they raced with the hordes streaking across the marshland, over the fields, back to the road leading them into the city. John saw the great, dark, twin towers of Aldgate loom over him, was aware of the brief hollow echo off its stone walls from their running feet and the concerted bellow of tightly packed humanity as he passed underneath. Then he was inside the wall, its lower part of ancient Roman construction, its upper part of recent brick mottled pink and grey stretching away on both sides to be swallowed up by close-packed houses and narrow streets.

To his left he caught a glimpse of the imposing bulk of the Norman tower and the King's residence, gleaming white in the early morning sun and bright with gently flapping banners and pennons. He was in London, the greatest of cities and one he had never thought he would see.

Twenty

Beyond Aldgate the street branched four ways, each as clogged as the other with folk still pouring into the city.

'Which way?' Wat called.

'This way,' Tom answered, elbowing to the left into a narrow, twisty lane that looked less congested.

'Where do it lead?' John asked innocently.

Tom didn't reply. So pointed was the rebuff that John felt he could easily have walked away. But where would he go? Tom was right, of course – in his place he'd have behaved the same – but if Tom loathed him so much, why stay? Perhaps for the same reason that he stayed: wandering alone in this strange city, away from those he knew, would be to become totally lost. He had no other choice but meekly to follow the others, keeping out of Tom's way and avoid addressing him as much as possible.

The tall wooden houses were so close together, their upper storeys overhanging, almost shutting out sunlight but also shutting in every stink, with foul odours of human waste rising from the gutter running down the centre of the cobbled street surface to become trapped.

'The quicker we find fresh air, the better,' Wat said, wrinkling his long, thin nose, but Dick Elys sniffed deeply.

'I can smell cooking. I'm starved. Let's get out of this hole and find somewhere to fill our bellies.'

It was the best idea yet. Together the six of them – Dick, Wat, Tom, Ralph, himself and Ned – broke into a run until finally they found themselves out on a crowded but far broader street. People seemed to be moving aimlessly past each other as if, now that they were in London, no one had any idea what to do. Leadership seemed to have broken down.

Wat went over to someone who looked friendly. 'Do you know what plans have been made now we're here?' he asked.

The man shrugged his shoulders. He seemed completely lost and just a little panicky. 'I be as mystified as you, friend. I hear some are gone to the Royal Palace at the Tower. Me, I just want to find them as I came here with.' With that he moved on, his eyes roaming this way and that for his companions.

'Maybe that's where we should be,' Ralph said. 'At the Tower.'

'Where we *should* be,' Dick said, 'is getting some food inside our bellies. We've money enough.'

They did indeed have money enough, having helped themselves to what they could find while ransacking certain houses. It wasn't a lot, some having got there first, but it was enough. Money had previously been virtually useless, with most villages already emptied of provisions, but here there was enough to feed the population a dozen times over, the most appetizing smells already making their mouths water.

'Come on, lads, let's buy us a feast,' Dick urged, eying a cookshop with a painted wooden board shaped like a great pie hanging by iron straps from a bracket. From inside came the delicious aroma of roast beef.

'That'll do,' Dick said, and soon they were sitting in the centre of Cheapside, meat juices running down their chin as they gnawed ribs of beef and bit into succulent pies that even Tom couldn't have boasted an ability to do better at making, though for the most part he said little these days. Even now he sat slightly withdrawn from the others. John hadn't much to say either. At least he had Ned by his side and could chat with him without seeming brash and defiant.

He looked around him. There was Poultry, through which they'd just come, with three other streets filtering into it – Lombard Street, Cornhill, Threadneedle Street – each crammed with people. Ahead, Cheapside branched out again, Paternoster Row skirting St Paul's. Further north lay the Shambles leading to Newgate Market. On either side of Cheapside he could see narrow alleys and warrens and holes called streets only by the wildest stretch of the imagination.

He didn't want to move. Sitting back, his

belly full of good food, he felt safe from this moving tide of people. If only he had Tom beside him he'd have felt more at home. If only none of that had happened. If only ... But it had.

He could hear Dick, Ralph and Wat talking between themselves but not Tom's voice and wondered if he was still there. He was conscious of Ned looking enquiringly at him, his mouth busily chewing a morsel of meat. 'Is owt wrong, John? You be very quiet.'

He managed to smile. 'There's nothing wrong with me. Daydreaming, that's all.'

He was relieved to see Ned fall to tearing off another piece of meat with his young, strong teeth. But in being tugged back to himself, he was aware of a change of mood in those passing by, a general movement westward.

Catching the mood, he got up, finding the others doing likewise. He reached out and plucked the sleeve of a passing man, a youngish fellow with cadaverous cheeks – the grey pallor of the Londoner.

'Where are they all going?'

'To the Savoy.'

'What be the Savoy?'

The lad found it interesting to enlighten these simple rustics. 'John o' Gaunt's palace. And God grant his damned guts fry in Hell. His palace stinks with riches and treasure while the likes of us poor turds cannot buy enough to eat in this great, wealthy city, for being taxed to death to keep the likes of him in comfort. Oh, yes, they try to tell us the poll tax goes to pay for the wars in France. But we know different. Huh! They go to line his purse, that's what we say.'

John knew well what people said about the Duke of Lancaster, that it was said he coveted the throne. But he hadn't realized that John of Gaunt resided at this palace outside London, called the Savoy. He'd gleaned by now the purpose of this exodus, but he let the lad ramble on.

'We'll have no King John ruling us. Come nightfall his grand palace'll be burning from end to end and all his treasures smashed to bits and him along with 'em. Mind you, word is that no one is to take anything for his own.'

'How so?' Ralph queried.

'We aren't looters but righters of wrongs,' came the reply. 'Everything is to be smashed or thrown into the river – ay, even money. That's the orders we've been given.'

'Who from?' John asked, but the man carried on talking.

'But no one says what we can't do with the man, and if we find him, we'll have his head on a poll, by Christ, we will! You come with us and you'll see a burning the like of which will make your eyes bulge. Right, I'm off then.'

They were left to gaze at each other in amusement.

'He should a' seen what we done at Cressing Temple,' Wat said drily. 'Happen that would've made *his* eyes bulge.'

309

Wiping greasy fingers on their scuffed jerkins, they made after the westward-moving tide of humanity, with Wat warning darkly, 'And we all keep together. No one strolls off on his own, in case there's trouble.'

John would have liked to have gone into St Paul's, with its famous Rose Window. What he had wanted most of all was to pray in there for forgiveness and peace of mind. Not that it would have helped. Somehow time was dulling the keen edge of what he'd done. He now found himself viewing Tom's attitude towards him as petty. If anyone was to blame it was that brazen wife of his, enticing him as she had. What man could be blamed for succumbing to his natural needs before such brazen temptation? She'd known full well what she was doing, what the consequences would be, and no doubt she was counting him as one of her conquests. Had it mattered to her that she had destroyed a deep affection between two friends, a friendship that should have lasted their lifetime? She was evil and he'd been a fool. All anyone could do now would be to ask for God's mercy. That great church would have been the place to ask for it.

He gazed longingly at it as they continued, seeing it soaring in all its magnificence above the poorly built houses, the maze of streets so narrow that a cart could hardly pass through, the serpentine alleys reeking of filth. How could such a thing of beauty stand cheek by jowl with this offensive morass of life?

The great church wasn't the only fine edifice, John realized as they moved onwards. Cheapside itself boasted some fine houses with ornate gates and gardens. But those didn't last. On they went, past the convent of the Black Friars and the King's Wardrobe, through Ludgate and then turning south to follow the Fleet River to the Thames.

'Jesu!' Ned glanced down with disgust at the Fleet's stagnant mess. 'Phew!'

All kinds of refuse blocked the flow, the dark greasy liquid trickling around mounds of rotting offal thrown in from the Shambles – even whole carcasses too foul for human consumption – together with sewage from the convents of the Black Friars and the White Friars combined, as well as from Fleet Prison nearby.

John grinned at his brother, his own problems forgotten for the moment. 'Just hold your nose. We'll be away from it soon. The wind blows to the east away from us.' But it was impossible to hurry past for so many trying to cross the Fleet Bridge.

'It fair makes you wish for the clean air of our marshes,' remarked Ned, almost on the point of retching. 'Who'd want to live in this city, great though it be? I feel we'll never find open country again.'

But beyond Ludgate they could see fields and John drew deep breaths of the fresh air that came to waft away the smell of the Fleet. There were still houses on either side of Fleet

Street, but they sat in lovely gardens shaded by large trees – the homes of wealthy merchants, most of them shuttered and bolted against the oncoming insurgents.

Excitement was rising. Before them lay Temple Bar, where the young lawyers learned and practised their legal cunning. It was already being stormed, people up on the roofs, stripping off tiles and throwing them down. Some of them were obviously drunk and as John looked, one man slid bodily down the sloping roof of a building to land among those below. Whether he was hurt or not John was unable to see as he was borne along past a house burning furiously, as was a chandler's shop nearby. This had to be the work of those only out to make mischief and line their own pockets. It was being said that many a score had begun to be settled in this city, using this uprising as an excuse.

From the Strand they could see the many-turreted main building of the Savoy, with a large tower at one end from which the Duke's pennon flapped lazily on a meagre, sluggish current of air.

That was the only semblance of tranquility. Everywhere else seethed with men as, unhindered, they went through the main arch from the Strand, the beautifully ornate gilded gates having been flattened by the first wave of rebels to have arrived.

Beyond the outer ward everywhere was like a madhouse, men flooding in and out of the kitchens and storehouses and the undefended

312

barracks, what few soldiers had not gone with Gaunt to Scotland having been quickly overpowered.

The armourer's shop had been ransacked, men strutting about clad in breastplates and helmets, brandishing axes and swords and pikes. In the mews the falcons had all been released. In the cellars, great hogsheads of fine vintage wines had been broken open, the rich liquids slopping everywhere as the wreckers guzzled, many of them already roaring drunk with the heady stuff most were unused to.

From every glazed and leaded window, furniture and linen was being flung. Men hardly able to stand had draped themselves in apparel only lately worn by the Duke before being torn to shreds to add to a huge blaze in the main courtyard, together with all the vestments from the chapel.

Caught up in the excitement, John and his companions ran through the centre ward, anxious to reach the palace itself. Mounting the marble stairs and into the Great Hall they found it clogged with people. Inside, the noise was deafening, the yells and hoots of hundreds of over-excited rebels echoing off the high marble walls, and everywhere filled with smoke from a dozen fires that had been started on the creamy tiled floor in order to burn all the Duke's possessions.

Buffeted this way and that by men forging in and out past him, John stood for a second or two in the great entrance, awed, not by the antics of his fellow countrymen, but by what this place must have looked like before they had invaded it. Through the smoke he could discern the enormous staircase, the high, painted walls that would have been hung with rich tapestries, they now burning merrily on the fires. At every turn men were tearing, smashing, spearing fine napery upon lances, crushing costly jewels on the floor tiles with hammers, every man intent on destruction, not one hoping to enrich himself with a hastily secreted jewel or two.

In fact, even as John stepped into the hall, he was grabbed by the shoulder by a burly man whose beard was dusty and speckled with charred remnants of cloth. The man thrust his face close to his.

'Harken, friend,' he blared as though John were his sworn enemy. 'We be here for the purpose o' revenge and nowt else, d'ye hear? Think to try and help yourself to a trifle – just one – and your body'll be here and your head'll be there!' He pointed out to the courtyard, and with a final shake of John's shoulder, strode past him, back into the turmoil.

His progress interrupted, John found himself separated from the others, but now he wasn't worried. They wouldn't go far. At one time he did glimpse Wat with his shoulder against a barred door, vainly heaving with several others to get it open. As he watched, the hinges gave way and the crowd fell in on top of the planks, most of them disappearing headlong into the darkness, probably down some steps.

Of Ned there was no sign, but he caught sight of Tom and Ralph both helping to feed one of the fires with parts of a large linen chest painted with figures of cherubs and leaves.

Pushing his way through, he joined the two of them as with a cry from the minstrel gallery a huge gilded cabinet came crashing down to join a mound of shattered and splintered furniture that had suffered an identical fate. That which hadn't already broken apart upon impact was being rendered into manageable pieces with hammers and axes.

'Watch out!' John heard Tom's warning and leapt clear as an enormous roll of tapestry landed with a thud heavy enough to take a man's head off. In fact, several were thrown sideways by its weight as it caught them a glancing blow. John began to wonder how many would lose their lives this day by their sheer exuberance, and not one weapon raised in battle.

His eyes stinging from the smoke of the burning tapestry, he moved off through the energetic throng to see what else there was to rend, perhaps help push whatever treasures he found through the windows and into the Thames. On the river he could see John o' Gaunt's barges, which only six weeks earlier would have been decked with flowers and ribbons for May Day celebrations, being deliberately sunk. Even as he glanced through the aperture, more of the Duke's belongings were tumbling down past him, landing in the water with mighty splashes, lighter apparel and linen floating away on the air.

Wat appeared at his elbow. Red wine stained the front of his tunic. In his hand was a silver chalice, not for holding the liquid but for pounding out of all recognition, and one side had been caved in.

'Have you seen young Ned?' John shouted above the noise of breaking and crashing, having begun to worry if his brother was safe amid all this destruction.

The gangly shepherd bent down and energetically thumped the chalice repeatedly against a marble stair, making it ring. 'Saw him up in the minstrel gallery a while ago. But then I took myself down into that treasure chamber.' He nodded below.

'I saw you breaking down the door,' John yelled above the noise.

'Full o' silver and gold dust in kegs,' Wat shouted back. 'Ornaments of all kind, like this. We're breaking every one. Come and help.'

Dragged back down the stairs, he was relieved to see Ned above him, busily helping to manoeuvre a cumbersome bundle of brocade bed hangings over the balustrade and on to the fire below. On to the same fire several men were rolling three small barrels.

One of these barrels had broken open, spilling dark powder over the floor. But John was more concerned about the state of the minstrel gallery. It couldn't stand the weight of all those men for much longer. If it collapsed, Ned could be killed.

He took a deep breath and roared up to him. 'Ned!'

His voice was powerful, carrying above all the shouting, and Ned heard it, leaning over the balustrade to call back, 'What d'you want?'

'I need you down here.'

For a moment the lad's mouth tightened, but then he moved along the gallery and came down the staircase, now littered with shards of porcelain and tattered shreds of silks and velvets and bits of shattered furniture, testily elbowing his way between those still rending and smashing. The men with the small barrels had ceased rolling them to the edge of the fire and were now guzzling wine from battered gold goblets, an experience they'd probably never have again.

One of them idly scooped up a handful of the black, gritty dust from the broken barrel and let it trickle through his fingers.

'Look at this, lads. Do this be some sort of precious stuff? Do it go to pay for wars wi' France or to buy our Duke o' Lancaster yet another castle? I tell you, lads, this is the best place for it.' He tossed the handful into the flames where it sparkled in the air above the fire with robust popping sounds.

'Afore God!' the man cried out. 'Who'd think gold'd burn so lustily?'

John frowned. Of a certainty gold would not

react to heat in that way – nor was gold ever black, as far as he knew. But he was given no more time to ponder as Tom came flying at him, grabbing his arm, dragging him from the immediate area as two of the men bent to their original task of rolling both unbroken barrels into the fire.

'Out!' Tom yelled at the top of his voice. 'Ned ... Wat ... Quick! Out!'

Even as he propelled John through the throng, he was yelling a warning to the others, the men with their barrels staring stupidly at him.

'Gunpowder! Out, or die!'

Twenty-One

With Tom screaming like someone demented, one hand gripping John's arm, the other clutching a handful of Ned's gipon, all three were halfway down the outer staircase when an unbelievable force, like a giant fist, punched John full in the back, throwing him bodily forward, pitching him helplessly down as if being transported into Hades, to land on the courtyard below, the breath knocked out of him.

He seemed unscathed, but he saw that others hadn't been so lucky as he managed to raise his head. Two men were lying not far away, unmoving, though their clothes had been torn off them and their flesh looked to be smoking.

His ears still rang from some great explosion but he could vaguely hear fearful screams and cries for God to have mercy on them.

Someone was pounding his back, which he realized felt strangely hot, scorched. He managed to sit up, finding it to be Tom. Beyond him the palace was no longer beautiful, its marble entrance shattered, men staggering through it, their garments in tatters that smoked like damp grass fire, whose faces were black and raw, their eyes staring, terror-stricken, red-rimmed in the blackened rawness.

John saw it all in the space of one heartbeat before there came a second explosion. Instinctively he twisted away to hide his face in the dirt, his arms protecting his head. Hearing a strange, groaning roar, he looked up to see the great tower crumpling slowly, buckling inwards, sinking downwards, to finally disappear, taking most of the wall with it in a smothering, upward billowing cloud of white dust and a groaning roar that sounded like some dying beast.

John sat up again, lowering his head on to his knees. His back was still a little painful but not too much so. A lazy pall of smoke was rolling eastward. There were smoldering pieces of debris drifting down, one piece settling on the leg of his chaussers, scorching the cloth. Galvanized at last into activity he smacked at it, cursing in sudden panic as he struggled to his feet, stomping around in foolish fear that the cloth could ignite and burn him to death. For a second he really thought he was going to burst into flames.

Regaining his wits, he looked around at those in various states of shock but could see no one he knew. His mind flew to his brother and a new fear clutched at him. Had Ned been killed? Had he caught the full force of that explosion?

In new panic he stared about, his eyes

refusing to focus properly. His mouth had opened, a voice issuing from it that didn't seem to belong to him, a hollow bellow that echoed inside his head, crying repeatedly, 'Ned, Ned!' as though he had no control over his voice.

Then another voice rang in his ear. 'It's all right, John, we're here.'

Faces leapt suddenly back into focus. He saw Tom, his face ashen and fixed. Ned was kneeling not far away, a stupefied look on his ravaged face. Not far from him, Wat Gildeborn sat rigid with his legs splayed out in front of him as though he'd been turned to stone and dumped there. A smear of blood traversed his forehead from a large graze. Ned was holding his shoulder but there appeared to be no blood. As for Tom, the sleeves of his gipon had been scorched away but he seemed uninjured.

It was then that John realized how little time had elapsed since the explosion, that men were still yelling, calling for help, running about, that what had seemed like silence a few minutes ago had been his ear deafened by the explosion itself.

With immense relief to find Ned safe, but still bewildered, he looked at Tom. 'In Christ's name, what happened?' Without waiting for a reply he looked back at what had been the Duke of Lancaster's wondrous palace, now a blackened ruin, and thought of those burned to death inside or trapped in cellars as the tower slowly toppled, men who a moment before had been laughing and drinking and happily establishing their right to live.

'Them kegs – gunpowder,' he heard Tom say, his voice trembling slightly. 'Some wouldn't have known that.'

'Gunpowder, of course.' His mind was beginning to come together. 'It did all that?'

Of course he knew its properties, its tremendous power. It was merely that he had never before felt its unbelievable force.

What he did realize was that but for Tom he would have been blown to shreds. Gratitude suddenly engulfed him and he turned towards the man who had saved him.

'Twice you've rescued me from harm,' he said, his tone humble knowing how little he deserved this man's aid. To his horror he saw Tom's expression grow suddenly blank.

'Old habit dies hard.' The words seemed to catch in Tom's throat. 'And so do memory.'

Any effort John could have made to try and acquit himself of his past error was interrupted by Ned and Wat coming towards them on somewhat unsteady legs, Ned throwing himself at his brother to wrap his arms about his shoulders.

'Thank God you're safe, John. What happened? What was it?'

'You can see for yourself,' John said, sharp and offhand, having no care to explain after the words Tom had spoken, unbelievable to him after all that had happened and already breaking his heart.

Others were coming, dozens of them, all

their neighbours, separated by hordes of insurgents but nearby all the time. Most of them had been by the river gate when the explosion happened and were coming to see the damage it had wrought. Others had only just arrived at the outer ward and had come running to see what they could do. But some were missing. Tom gathered them all together, once more in control, ignoring his scorched arms as John was ignoring his own scorched back.

'Know you any of us as were inside there?' he asked.

They shook their heads, frowning and racking their brains.

'Master Kirkby, I know was in there,' Tom went on. 'I saw him. Has any seen him since?'

Again they shook their heads, this time in concern. All eyes turned to the blazing ruin from where only a miracle would have any emerging now, each man crossing himself and lowering his head in brief prayer for a dead man's soul.

'Anyone else you might think of?' queried Tom after a suitable pause, and again they shook their heads, faces bleak at this first loss amongst them, where in life they'd hardly have given the man more than a passing thought.

'Well then, there's nowt we can do here.'

Everyone had begun to leave, pouring through the great arch out on to the Strand. Many looked scared to death by their experience, but others were buoyant and ready for more havoc.

The cry had gone up: 'To Clerkenwell!', though who had given the order no one seemed to know. Someone said they'd seen Farringdon sitting astride his horse and pointing across the fields in the direction of Clerkenwell where St John's Priory lay.

As John and his friends began to follow the others, they began to see why everyone was going this way. If the people could do no more where the Duke of Lancaster was concerned then they'd have the Lord Treasurer, Robert Hales – Hobbe the Robber! They would take him and nail his head to Drawbridge Gate on London Bridge, the place where the heads of all traitors ended up.

They streamed in their hordes across the fields, John yelling as loud as any, his blood up, needing to seek revenge on someone, it didn't matter who, for Kirkby's death. East to the Temple they went, past the still burning Inns of Court, John drunk on this endless atmosphere of excitement and beginning to feel he could have conquered the world, righting every wrong.

'We've set all London alight!' he shouted, pointing as he went. 'We hold sway. All them lords will be cowering behind their doors. But we'll burn 'em out, eh, Tom?'

Tom made no reply, his eyes watching the crowds pouring out from the city through northerly Aldersgate to swell the numbers of those streaming across the Clerkenwell fields.

Ahead was St John's Priory, silently waiting

to be ransacked. In the west, in a haze of high, golden cloud, the sun was making ready to retire for the night, but to the north of London, this mob would not sleep.

In the depths of the night the crowd staggered back through the several city gates, smoke-blackened, bleary-eyed, well satisfied with their night's work, behind them the dark sky lit by a lurid glow.

The rebels had been busy inside the city walls, too. As John came back through Aldersgate, men were lurching about, carousing along the dark, narrow streets, finding their way by the torches they'd lit, their faces glowing in the flickering flames.

Many with arms linked weaved from side to side, bawling out ribald songs at the top of their voices, the streets and alleyways echoing to them. They stumbled over those sprawled across kennels, oblivious to the filth, lying as they had fallen, dead drunk.

They at least moved occasionally, groaned, tried to rise and join in more of the jollity. There were others here and there who would never rise again. Singly or two or three piled together, for the most part headless, Flemings or Lombards, it didn't matter – any who spoke with a thick accent or failed to pass the test of having to say 'bread and cheese', their foreign tongue unable to get around the proper pronunciation, were fair game. John preferred to leave London to itself and so ignored the yells, the running footsteps, a sudden scream, as another victim was found.

To John's relief the screams belonged to men. Nowhere had he heard the scream of any woman. Disorderly the London upstarts might be, full of wine and bloodlust, but they appeared to be leaving the women unmolested – even the Flemish women.

'This ain't no Jacquerie,' one Londoner sneered at Ralph Reede. 'We don't rape and torture, as them Frenchies did in *their* bloody uprising agin their nobles in 1358. We be English.'

He was angry at being associated with his hated enemy, the French, and looked at Ralph in contempt that he should even presume to query why they left the women alone. 'We be Englishmen,' he stated again with drunken dignity and went on his way, puffed up with pride to seek out yet another unfortunate Fleming.

'Well,' Ralph said as the man staggered off. 'Why bother ourselves wi' Flemings?' He giggled drunkenly. 'We're after bigger prey.'

'At least we're honourable in our pursuits,' John replied. He too had had a little too much wine and he too was flushed with pride. 'We want nothing to do wi' Fleming hunters, nor them felons as was let out of Fleet and Marshalsea prisons, using us as cover for their wholesale thieving, s'long as we don't be blamed for it. 'Twasn't us as let 'em out.'

He glanced at Tom, who was completely sober while the rest of them had drunk their fill. For a split second he hated Tom – always honourable, always fair, always straight – making him feel disgusted with himself because that slut of a wife had tempted him in one small moment of weakness...

His heart suddenly filled with wine-stimulated tears. Damn the man – if he wanted to be distant, then he would not address him again. Yet Tom had saved his life. Seconds later John had forgiven him. Tom was justified, he supposed, in how he was feeling.

He began to sing at the top of his voice: 'But bring us in good ale, and bring us in good ale...' and they all began to join in. All except Tom, John noticed vaguely.

Somewhere near Aldgate, to the east of London, they met up with the rest of their neighbours in a noisy greeting. Holding each other up, they staggered out of the city through a near-deserted gate where the day before they'd entered with hardly room to breathe. With no real purpose in their direction, they blundered over a body not knowing or caring if it was dead or merely dead drunk, and out into the clean, fresh night air of darkened fields at nearly midnight.

There were still men encamped outside the walls. Probably, like them, they'd had enough of the stink of London. As the group approached the few campfires they were immediately challenged.

'To whom d'ye hold?'

'To King Richard and the true commons,'

some of them managed to reply, and soon found themselves sitting with others, trying to sing, but mostly falling asleep.

John awoke at first light to find men making ready to move. On asking where they were going, he was told, 'There's talk of laying siege to the Tower. Simon of Sudbury and Robert Hales are said to have taken refuge there, along with our King.'

So, they had the King trapped at last and would beleaguer him gently into hearing their petitions. But his advisers would not be treated so gently. This day would be theirs, the commons. St Katherine's Fields looked as they had two days before, men gathering up any belongings they had, ready to go into the city once more, at which Ralph groaned.

'I've no fancy to mix with the like o' them London people again. It do seem wrong to me, them going after them poor foreign sort as have nothing to do with our cause. They be hard, them Londoners. I've no liking for the place. The sooner this be over and I back in my own home, the better.'

John smiled his agreement as they were swept along with the rest. Moments later his smile died on his lips. Coming towards them against the flow was Will Randere, Dick Wodelarke with him, grinning from ear to ear. It was obvious at the very first glance that Randere had made a man of young Dick somewhere in the stews of London. Randere leered at John as he came up to them all, but turned away as Wat gave a great belly laugh.

'And how many of them malkins did you get through last night, there in the stews of Bankside? That's where you've been while us were storming the Savoy Palace, and poor Kirkby killed.'

Randere sobered for a moment, then brightened. He, a fisherman, had no interest in Kirkby, a forester. 'One of 'em women be enough to keep any man occupied a whole night.' He gave a lascivious chuckle, eying Wat's begrimed face and the open graze on his forehead. 'By the looks of you, you'd have been better having your fill of a lusty whore. Or perhaps I'd lay odds you wouldn't a' lasted a minute with even the least of 'em.' He glanced at his still-grinning protégé. 'Him, he astounded me wi' his stamina – his first time, too, he tells me, and him just a younker. When's the last time you had a woman, Wat Gildeborn?'

The shepherd's features tightened. 'If that's all you can think about in times like these, you lecherous old ram, then a pox on you!'

Tom looked across at them. Randere's dig hadn't been lost on him. His tone was low. 'It could come to that. Not one of them peronelles is not be-riddled with it. You could have a pox even as you gloat, Master Randere.'

'How so?' demanded Will, his fear of Tom forgotten, still reckoning he'd done no mischief. 'She did wash her parts, right in front of me so I could watch her do it, saying it did cleanse away unwholesome vapours, and she invited my help, which I gave willingly.'

He licked his lips at the memory of that pleasure.

'What did she wash herself with?' Tom's voice was calm and serious.

'Why, wi' water and a fine-smelling soap,' Randere returned, while poor Dick had begun to look concerned at what might have infected him.

'It should a' been wine,' Tom informed him with all sincerity.

Everyone looked at him. He was the learned one. He could read, and had probably read about these things.

'Wine?' repeated Will idiotically, put at a disadvantage by the other's sweet tones. 'You say she should have washed herself with wine?'

'If she didn't,' Tom said, his tone one of urgency now, 'then anything you might have caught can still be remedied.'

The older man's face was a picture to behold. He even grabbed Tom's arm convulsively. 'How? Tell me how?'

'By cleansing your own parts soonest possible, with strong wine – the stronger the better, I've heard tell. It must be held in the liquid for several minutes, taken out and shaken thoroughly, then plunged in again, three or four times at the very least.'

Will's eyes registered both horror and hope. 'Have you any such?'

'Nothing here strong enough for your needs. It must be the finest.'

'If I went back into London...' Randere suggested frantically.

Tom pursed his lips. 'No time. Some about here may have good wine as they helped themselves to when in London. But it must be the best. Make very certain of that.'

They watched Randere hurry away on his bowed legs, leaving behind a deeply anxious Dick Wodelarke.

'I should go with him,' the young man said anxiously, but Tom put out a hand to stop him.

'No need, Dick.'

'But if I've caught a pox, you did say good wine would...'

'I lied,' Tom said.

'How d'you mean? You mean it doesn't?'

Tom shrugged. 'I could not truly say if it does or not. Though if it do, then it may well become a remedy worth passing on to Old Mother Harelip.'

For a moment there was stunned silence as the significance of what he'd said sank in. Seconds later came a great burst of laughter from them all, each with a picture in his mind of Will Randere going from group to group, begging men to give him their good vintage wine – not for drinking but for some far odder application. Each time the picture sprang to mind as they again moved off towards London, there came fresh guffaws of laughter and a spate of wisecracks.

John Mott was near to tears. 'Was ever wine used to such a purpose, I wonder?'

Doubled up with laughter, Ralph Reede

clapped him across the back while his naturally deep voice took on Will Randere's higher tones. *'Kind sirs, I do crave to rub your wine on my cod and coilons*! If that doesn't invite a thump on the ear, by my oath, I don't know what would!'

'Perhaps someone'll offer to do the rubbing for him,' put in Dick Elys. 'Forsooth! I'd rather have the pox!'

In all this, Tom's face remained impassive, and again John felt that crawling of sullenness that he knew was unjustified as he walked some way behind him, keeping his distance to avoid any further contact.

He was aware as they neared Aldgate of a smallish body come flying past him to throw itself at Tom Baker, dealing him a punch to the back of the neck, throwing him forward in surprise, Randere leaping back out of range of the other's fist should he turn and lash out at him.

'That for your cunning, curse you, Tom Baker!' yelled Randere from his safe distance.

Seeing the attack, Tom with his hand clasped hard against the back of his bruised neck, John automatically called out, 'Tom! Are you hurt?'

His concern was instantly waved away, but to the others also studying him with concern, he said quickly, 'No damage done. It was probably well deserved.'

'Hardly that,' John called back angrily. 'It was he as caused mischief in the first place.' He saw Tom turn to look at him, even giving him the ghost of a smile, one that John found inscrutable, or if anything read several things into it – condemnation, resignation, pain, an ability to see inside his head, making him squirm with guilt, hating himself, hating this man's natural perceptiveness.

He wanted to shout at him to have done with it; that yes, he had made love to his best friend's wife, and to do him the favour of plunging a knife in his guts and finishing it, for he felt at this very moment that he would sooner be dead and never feel this lingering weight of guilt ever again. He was on the point of challenging his friend when a cry was heard from the vicinity of the Tower.

'Envoys! From the King!'

Twenty-Two

In the dawn light they could make out two riders. Everyone was running towards them, and as the Fobbing men broke into a run, three more riders galloped past to meet the original two horsemen. As they swept by, John recognized Jack Straw and Farringdon. The third was dark-bearded and solidly built but that was all John could see.

The onward surge of men slowed as the two sets of riders came up to each other and the dark-bearded man – apparently the leader of the three by his manner – caught the bridle of the nearest envoy's mount, halting it. His voice, full-bodied and harsh with insolence, rang out across the field.

'Ho there, sir knight! Your errand at this early hour, if you please?'

Immediately John knew he'd heard that voice before – it was the man who had confronted him at the entrance of the Great Hall in the Savoy Palace. It was the same dark, bushy beard, the same heavy features, the very same man.

The finely chiselled face of the one hailed took on an expression of haughty anger as John, nearing the riders now, was able to see quite clearly. The man lifted one hand, the other expertly controlling his nervous horse.

'We come unarmed.'

True, neither bore swords or wore armour of any kind. His companion, whose visage remained calm and composed, portrayed an air of command as he manoeuvred his horse between the two.

'Sir, to whom do I address myself?' he enquired.

The mouth, half hidden by the beard, twisted crookedly. 'Sir,' he said, parodying the other's courtly manner, 'you do address Walter Tyler of Essex, but of Kent these last eight years.'

John gaped, as did many others. He stood within but a few yards of Wat Tyler, the man whose name was on everyone's lips, from Essex to Norfolk and beyond, one that was becoming as well known as John Ball himself. And this was the very man who had thrust his face close to his so that John had been able to smell the smoke on his beard as he spoke.

Tyler had bowed low over his saddle towards the envoy, lampooning knightly courtesy, but when he straightened his face was hard, his words abrupt. 'State your business, knight, and return to Richard.'

In reply, the envoy held out a tightly rolled parchment. 'Our Lord King bids you to read. Can you read? If not, then I shall...'

He had the parchment ripped savagely from his hand. 'I read well enough, knight,' Tyler spat as he swiftly tore away the heavy royal

335

seal and unrolled the King's terms to scan them while the messengers waited.

Crowds had gathered around the horsemen. John, managing to edge his way to the front, was studying Tyler's face at leisure in the strengthening dawn light, whereas at the Savoy he'd only had a glimpse before being shoved aside. It was a rugged face but with a high, broad brow and eyes keen and glaring. Broad cheeks, a strong if crooked nose, and beneath the beard the lower lip was thrust forward aggressively. It was the face of a man one might follow into battle.

He glanced at Tom, noting by comparison the tall, slim build, the sensitive face, hardly that of a born leader, yet Tom had led them for a while with his common sense and his quiet wisdom. But he no longer needed to lead, for which John experienced a wave of relief, despite their present differences.

Some sixth sense, perhaps born of their years of friendship, had made Tom turn his head as though called to. His eyes meeting John's, there came a questioning look, a small flicker of acknowledgment as though fingers of regret drummed at the back of the man's mind, a half smile never quite brushing away the disillusionment that lay there. Then the expression went blank and he looked back towards Tyler, leaving John bewildered.

Tyler had finished reading and was staring insolently into the haughty face of the knight, his mouth twisted into a sneer. 'Do our Lord King Richard think us to accept such terms as are set out here?' Viciously he slapped the parchment with the back of one large, broad hand.

'I know not its contents,' hedged the man while his companion leaned forward to fiddle with his horse's mane as if to fill an awkward moment.

'Of a certain ye do!' thundered Tyler. 'If Richard thinks to turn us aside wi' terms ... Blood o' Christ, do he think us fools?' He half turned in the saddle to face the crowd, raising his voice as he waved the parchment for all to see. 'Good people! We are this morning given our King's terms, and this after I have sent messengers *twice* to him. We are desired to set down our demands and give them to these heralds here.'

This reference he spoke with a disparaging note and John saw both knights' heads go up in indignation at being called heralds.

'And then,' continued Tyler, his voice growing in strength, 'then we are to depart to our villages and townships, and this after all our bleeding efforts to come here. God defend us against babes on thrones! Did we come this far, achieve this night's triumph, only to be bidden to pen our wants and grievances on a bit of parchment and depart to our homes without hearing this King's reply?'

Shouts of indignant rage greeted this, flowing in waves as his words were passed back to those furthest away.

'But mark you,' he continued, 'this is young

Richard's traitorous advisers who have guided his hand this night. Hales and Sudbury, who even now crouch in the safety of the Tower in fear and trembling of the great society, huddling behind a boy's crown.'

Again came a vehement roar of angry agreement.

He lifted one thick arm high in the air to stab an accusing finger towards the grey walls of the Tower behind him. 'In there reclines our young King, and with him, his mother, the Fair Maid of Kent. And behind the skirt of a woman and the shoulders of an innocent boy, cower our fine Lord Chancellor and our brave Lord Treasurer. Brave enough to tax us unto death, but no wit brave enough to face our wrath because of it.'

Amid yet more cheering and cries of rage, he turned back to the emissary, his voice still at oratory pitch. 'Take this piddling missive back to the King. Say to him that we will not speak terms by letters passed back and forth in the night, but would meet him face to face in the light of day and put our demands to him at that time and not before. Then shall we decide if his words be his or those fed to him as milk is to a babe from its mother's breast.'

Thrusting the proclamation into the knight's hand, he leaned towards the other man, surprising him by grabbing one velvet-clad shoulder.

'And your companion shall remain our guest – a mark of our King's good faith to come to Mile End fields at the hour of terce to hear our demands.'

Amid roars of approval, John glanced at Tom without any thought of hostility. Terce was the third hour after daylight and most of one hour must have already gone by. 'Do he expect the King to attend Mile End in so short a time?'

Tom gave him a grin, taking him by surprise, most likely he also too carried away on this tide of elation to consider their present relations. 'Of a certainty he does,' he said lightly.

But there was no time for John to ruminate on this change of attitude as the knight beat a hasty retreat with orders to bring the King's reply within the hour, everyone now flocking around Wat Tyler.

They were informed by him that he and his companion were bound for the house of Thomas Farringdon in Goldsmithery for a meeting with the priest of Colchester, John Ball himself, and that as soon as the King's reply arrived it was to be brought to them there.

With a farewell salute, the crowds confident now of success, all three cantered off, their hostage knight among them, amid delirious cheering for Wat Tyler, the people's hero – cheering that must have reached the ears of King Richard and his advisers in the Royal Tower.

One more brief moment of excitement came

prior to the King's reply. A Kent woman doing her morning washing down by the River Thames had seen two eminent-looking persons clambering most secretively into a boat by the Water Gate of the Tower of London across the river from her. She'd sent her son to run the full length of London Bridge to alert the insurgents there. By the time they'd reached the river bank the boat was midstream, but, seeing several boats in pursuit, the boatman had hurriedly rowed back to the Water Gate and his passengers had gone. It was now certain that those he'd carried had been Sudbury and Hales, attempting to escape.

'They're cornered like the rats, they are,' went the word.

'What if the King refuses to hand them over?' John asked as they made their way on to Mile End, hoping to see him at closer quarters than the last time.

'Then he too condemns himself as a traitor to England,' was Wat's prompt and sweeping reply.

But John felt sympathy for the lad, forced to hand two of his highest ministers over to the people's displeasure else see his capital set ablaze from end to end, his realm in chaos and he dragged even from his throne. What a decision for a boy of fourteen to have to make.

With the sun in his eyes, the young Richard Plantagenet emerged from the protection of the Royal Tower surrounded by a small retinue of high-ranking lords bearing many banners and emblems. Following him was a large number of clerks in black caps and voluminous gowns. On every side they were accompanied by thousands of noisy commons making sure their King suffered no second thoughts.

Halfway to Mile End, Tyler and Farringdon met the entourage, Richard at its head surrounded by his own bodyguards, the Earls of Warwick, Oxford and Salisbury, who, with the help of a dozen or so soldiers, were fighting to keep the throng that had accompanied them all the way from Aldgate from pressing too close.

It was noted that Hales and Sudbury were not with them. They had certainly not escaped from the Tower, so must still be there. With a great gathering of men left behind to make sure they didn't escape, things did not bode well for the two.

'If they dare show their faces,' Wat said vehemently, 'their heads'll be on pikes before they've gone ten yards. I'd like to be there to see that. What say we go to watch?' No one took up the offer, far keener to see their King in the flesh.

'What a sight,' John breathed as the entourage drew nearer. 'What a tale to tell our grandchildren.' Though at eighteen, who cared to think so far ahead as telling tales to grandchildren? Enough for the moment just to speculate on taking home the tale of what he was witnessing this morning.

The King wasn't brilliantly dressed, not as he had been on the river only a day or two ago, but he passed by John and his friends so close that John felt he could have reached out and touched the boy's knee.

It seemed everyone was of the same mind and he found himself being jostled for position in this general elation, almost pushed under the hooves of the King's great milk-white destrier. Frantically, he leaned against the press while those guarding the King strove to fend off the enthusiastic peasants.

'Back! Back!' Salisbury was calling. 'Regard your King's safety.'

Warwick, a swarthy man in plum-coloured velvet, spurred his horse into the crowd, threatening real damage to them and calling more forcefully, 'Stand away! Stand away, all of you!'

Oxford's higher voice appealed, 'In the name of God, good people, consider your conduct!' as he repeatedly leaned from his saddle to thrust this one and that aside with a gauntleted hand.

It was Tyler who finally gained control of the excited throng. Seizing a royal standard from Sir Robert of Namur, he waved it aloft, wheeling his horse across Richard's path to stop further encroachment.

'Behold, the fair young King Richard!' he bellowed. 'Your liege lord! I command you pay homage. Kneel to your sovereign lord. *Kneel*!'

The shouting died. This was their captain. Him they would obey. Row upon row pushed back to leave a clear path for the King's progress, many bending the knee as he passed, those remaining upright standing quiet now and respectful – not only to their king but to their captain.

Passing on to the appointed place, the long line of clerks following, the people closed in behind in their thousands while King Richard rode on, not like a boy, but erect and stately and with such wonderful grace that the coarse-tongued, sweaty, bearded peasants would have fallen silent anyway in their awe.

For John, as with all of them, it was a moment he'd remember for the rest of his life. A youth so fresh and fair ... The flaxen locks, bound by a broad circlet of gold, fell heavy and curling to his shoulders. The nose was thin and straight, the chin elegantly small, the lips thin but so touched with the blush of youth they appeared gentle and sweet, and all of this balanced on a neck as slender as a maid's. In fact his beauty was very akin to a maid's.

By good fortune, John was again at the front when the crowds parted to make a clearing for the arrivals to dismount. If he'd been awed by the sight of Richard up in the saddle, he was even more so to see him afoot, so tall and as slender as a willow wand. Clad in a short, tightly belted yellow tunic worked with gold beneath a small cape of azure velvet, his hose of the same azure colour, he stood with quiet composure facing Tyler, three times his age and four times his girth in the roughest garb beneath a cuirass of dull metal. It was like seeing a delicate bloom against a looming ancient oak.

John wasn't the only one. A great sigh of admiration rippled through the spectators like a breeze. Yet as he glanced towards Tyler he saw mistrust in the man's wind-tanned face that made him frown in surprise. Here was a man not to be swayed by sweet looks – king or angel.

Perplexed, John found himself studying the smooth, pampered, gold paleness of Richard against the grim, weather-beaten commonality of Tyler, both in his own way born to lead – the boy king and the seasoned soldier, each with the ability to draw men to his side.

Looking deeper, from the wondrous lure of sweetness to the glower of determination, John suddenly knew without questioning which man he would follow, he too feeling reason to mistrust the King's sweet face.

Tyler had executed a pretentious bow, an insolent greeting, one that King Richard chose to return with an elegant but brief inclination of his head.

'God grant I see ye well, King,' Tyler said, undaunted.

It was pure, unadulterated overfamiliarity and John had to stifle a gurgle of amusement. Others were more open, chuckles breaking out here and there. To his credit, Richard remained unruffled.

'Well enough, Master Tyler,' he said smoothly, then turned from him to address those gathered, his voice carrying with the high-pitched ring of any fourteen-year-old whose voice is soon to break. There was too a slight hesitation that John guessed must be nerves. For what youth wouldn't feel nervous before this rabble?

'Good people – what lack ye?'

The crowd responded immediately, calling out their individual grievances. Confronted by the incomprehensible clamour, he held up a beringed hand, the other motioning his earls to stay back when they would have thrust at the front rank of the crowd to bring order.

'We take it that you have elected Master Tyler as your leader and spokesman. Therefore he will convey your needs to us. What will you say, Master Tyler?'

In contrast to the cultured young voice, Tyler's husky tone was thickly accented. 'We will that ye make us free. Us and our heirs, for all time.'

There was no hesitation now, royal breeding prevailing. 'That we agree to.'

'And that ye abolish serfdom.' Obviously Tyler wasn't completely convinced by this readiness to agree and began to expand his request. 'All feudal services to be remitted. Villeins to be free tenants, and none shall no more be called bondman, nor so reputed.'

This again was agreed to without reservation.

Tyler frowned in suspicion, but continued. 'That none pay more than four pence for each acre of land they till.'

Yet again there was no hesitation. 'It is so agreed,' Richard said.

'That all market monopolies be abolished,' Tyler continued.

'Agreed,' Richard said.

'A general amnesty for all reputed crimes committed during this protest.'

'Agreed.'

'That the foregoing be put down in writing forthwith.'

'It will be done straightway.'

'And royal banners be distributed to every district to show that henceforth we do march as the King's loyal subjects so that none shall lay hands upon us as criminals.'

'It will be done.'

'That all traitors against the true commons be delivered into our hands within the hour.'

For the first time those near enough saw Richard's pale eyes slip from their steady gaze. He knew this would include his Lord Treasurer and his Archbishop. He took a deep breath and shot a fleeting glance at Warwick before returning his gaze to Tyler.

'This is the total of your list, Master Tyler?'

But the shrewd Kentishman wasn't to be beguiled so smoothly. 'You have uttered no agreement to that last term, my liege. What say ye?'

'We say they shall be dealt with according to the law.'

Tyler's expression hardened. The reply was glaringly evasive. 'You quibble, my liege. Pray give your agreement to our last demand.'

'Demand, Master Tyler?' Richard's hazel eyes widened dangerously.

'Term, then,' Tyler conceded impatiently. 'What say ye to it?'

Tyler's direct demands had been ill-mannered throughout, yet Richard's youthful red lips had not once tightened against them.

'We have already said it will be dealt with,' he said, his high voice steady. 'What more? Suffice it that we will have charters drawn upon the instant and delivered to every district here present.'

An imperial finger signalled to the cluster of clerks to come forward, which they promptly did, scurrying in to the multitude that parted to make way for them, trestle tables already being set up for this use.

Richard had his horse brought and swung with supple grace into the saddle, letting the spirited animal wheel away from the steadying hand of the groom, clad in olive and scarlet livery with the white hart, Richard's emblem, emblazoned upon his breast. Adeptly bringing his mount round again to face the rustics who hadn't rushed with others to see the charters being written, Richard addressed them calmly.

'Sirs, withdraw you now to your homes. But leave behind you two or three of every village, and we will cause writings to be sealed with our seal and they shall contain everything that you demand.' Evenly he met Tyler's discerning gaze. 'And to the extent that you shall be better assured, we shall cause our banners to be delivered into every bailiwick, shire and county.'

Someone behind Tyler called out fervently, 'Sire, bless you, young Richard!'

'God bless our young King Richard!' cried another man.

Benevolently he smiled down at them, encompassing them all with his graciousness, his subjects responding wholeheartedly.

But John found himself unable to join in with the cheering. For one brief moment he had glimpsed behind Richard's smile something of what Tyler must have seen earlier – a tremble of passing contempt, perhaps? He wasn't sure. It may have been nothing more than his imagination with the boy made sensitive by Tyler's attitude, but doubt on the genuineness of the King's heart had begun to gnaw at him. He looked across at Tyler. The man was standing by as if in resignation but his expression held a mixture of perceptiveness and cunning.

Meanwhile the golden boy seemed in danger of being carried away by the adoration of these rude rustics. His young voice rang out with his delight of the moment.

'Sirs, among you good men of Kent and of Essex, you shall each have one of my banners with you. And you of Sussex, another.' As each county began clamouring for a banner of its own, he continued, 'And of Bedford, of

Cambridge, of Stafford, of Yarmouth, of Lynn, each one of you, we pardon everything you have done hitherto, so that you shall follow our banners and return home.'

'That we will do!' came the cry from all quarters.

'Fools!' came a muttered remark from close by and John turned to see the large bulk of Wat Tyler standing beside him, for the moment forgotten by the ecstatic thousands.

The man moved past John, not looking his way, his eyes trained on Richard. But Tyler's remark hadn't been directed at the King and his retinue, but at the crowds. Again John looked up at the King on his fine horse to see what Tyler had read in the boy's face.

The King was brushing aside his companions' anxious urges for him to leave as he wallowed in his hold over his subjects who had flocked to him, their sovereign. He saw himself loved, had a need to show his advisers that he was king in more than name.

John wondered if he and Tyler were the only ones to have noticed it. He made an attempt to draw his friends' attention to what he could see, but most of them were looking to make towards the trestle tables where men were collecting in their hundreds. He saw Tyler a little way off now, in a clearing made by men rushing to receive their charters. He saw him snap his thick fingers sharply towards Farringdon who was in charge of their horses. At the signal, Farringdon mounted and brought the other to Tyler, who swung himself heavily into the saddle, the animal leaning to his weight.

Throwing a last glance towards the King's party, he flicked the reins slightly and, with Farringdon close behind, began moving off. Drawing clear of the moving mass and away from the King's notice, he prodded his heels hard against the animal's flanks and broke into a gallop, making towards the city.

Watching them go, John had no illusions as to what they were about. Hales and Sudbury were still at the Tower, kept there by the great crowds around Tower Hill who were still calling for their blood. Once Tyler and Farringdon arrived to take charge, they would strike, surging into the Tower by force of numbers. Overpowered, the heads of both Archbishop and Lord Treasurer would soon be adorning Bridge Gate, he was certain of it.

'What're you gazing at?' Wat Gildeborn's enquiry brought John back to the folk now flocking en masse to collect their charters and banners. 'All will be gone, time you get yours. Most of us have ours already. Come on, John.'

Twenty-Three

The royal party had finally left, their pace leisurely.

'By the time they return to the Tower,' Wat said darkly, 'King Richard's ministers will be dead.' He had now come to the same conclusion as John, that their King had not been quite as open with them as he'd seemed. 'Too late for us to get back into London in time to see it, but I'd have liked to. I've come to have a feeling that these piddling bits of parchment are not worth the cleric's ink.'

He waved his own charter, still unread. He would have to get Tom to read it to him, when he found him, Tom having disappeared somewhere in the throng.

John too had his charter in his hand. He studied the unintelligible writing, all blotted and smudged in the clerics' haste to write and give them out. He looked at the pennon he'd been given, a dirty-white falcon on faded azure linen, its edges frayed from years of fluttering from the corner of some castle. Were these indeed worth the excitement of owning?

The crowds had thinned, though the clerics still buried under the many clustered about

351

them were still scribbling furiously. Slowly people were turning for home, charters tucked into their belts, bits of banners flying high. Others had turned back towards the city, they too growing suspicious that their King had not been as honest with them as he might have been.

'What are we supposed to do with this?' John asked, holding up his piece of parchment. 'Do we notify Buckingham – who hardly knows he owns the manor of Fobbing, much less who his tenants are – that we owe him no more fealty?'

'I've no idea,' Gildeborn sighed.

'Are we meant to have it verified at manor court? That we are truly freed from taxes, tallage and tithes? Seems to me this was all too quickly done. There must be loose ends still to be tied up.'

They were walking aimlessly, not sure what to do next. They came upon Tom along with several others. Wat Gildeborn put their questions to him, but Tom was more interested in gazing towards London, an expression of uncertainty on his face. He was fingering his own piece of parchment.

'I think we should stay here for a while,' he said slowly.

John suddenly found himself losing his temper. Tom hadn't once acknowledged his arrival, yet he'd smiled at young Ned and had nodded at Wat's questions.

'What d'you mean, stay here?' he burst out. 'You believe the promises as were made here today?' He tore the paltry bit of parchment from his belt to flourish in Tom's face. 'How much d'you think this'd be worth if our King takes a change of heart? If you wish to sit here staring at the horizon, content with kingly promises to—'

'I be not content,' Tom stopped him, turning to stare into John's enraged eyes, his own as cold as ice. 'I be no wise content, John. Not with this, nor many other things.' The emphasis on his name, the cold way he'd met his eyes, caught John off guard, but he continued on quietly.

'I've no liking for the ease our King agreed to our demands and the manner of his smile. Nor did quite a few people I've spoken to since.' He began walking back and forth, talking as if to himself. 'Golden boy – ay, but all be not gold as do sparkle, as we found out with that there gunpowder, and we ought not be caught out twice.' He stopped to look at them all. 'We know why Tyler made so hastily for London. I think it wise that we stay away from there.'

Wat Gildeborn glowered. 'Speak for yourself, Tom Baker. I for one wouldn't mind seeing what's going on. If too late to see them heads lopped off, then to witness them being nailed up on London Bridge. Just so we can be sure 'twas done,' he added.

Tom looked around at them all as they began to nod agreement. 'Have we not had our fill of violence these past days? I know I have.'

It seemed his words were falling on deaf ears as Wat and the others turned away one by one to follow those already moving past with their sights set on the city. After a moment's hesitation, seeing his brother also making off, John started to follow. After covering some ten yards or so, he looked back to see that Tom had gone to sit on the ground. Sitting there, virtually alone, he presented a lonely figure.

For a moment John was tempted to retrace his steps, to go and sit down beside him, but what would that achieve? What did either of them have to say to each other? One act would not reprieve him, would not bring back the friendship that had once been. With a miserable shrug, he turned and moved off after the others, leaving Tom where he sat.

Inside the city all was chaos. Even from Aldgate the howls for blood could be heard. It had taken some time to reach here on foot and John had expected everything to have calmed down, but apparently the victims were being stubborn, refusing to give themselves up, inciting the mob to even greater determination. Then suddenly a great howl went up and he knew they had achieved what they'd come for.

He arrived at the Tower with Ned, Wat and a few others in time to see two bound prisoners being borne out through Tower Gate. On rising ground they were clearly visible above the heads of the mobs – a tall man in fine but sober clothing, another in the brown robe of a friar. After that he could see nothing as they were pushed to the ground.

It was impossible to get any nearer because of the crush, but he could hear the bloodlust howling coming to him in waves each time the axe fell. He suddenly felt sickened. God, how many were they slaughtering? The howls went up at least a dozen times.

He began to feel ashamed of being part of this. He grabbed Ned by the arm. 'Come on, I've seen enough.'

Ned too was looking a little sick. 'So have I, John. Let's get out of this city. I want to go home.'

Yes, that's what he wanted, too. Strangely he wanted most to see Alice, to take up his old life, think more kindly towards her, his good wife, and put all this madness, including Tom's seductive wife, out of his mind.

Shoving through the crowd, they emerged into the relative emptiness of Aldgate and hurried out into fresh air once more, leaving the violence and the stink behind him, vowing never again to set foot in that great city. He could almost taste the peace of his village.

'Let's go home,' he said quietly. Ned said nothing, but he nodded, and in silence they returned to where he'd left Tom.

There was no sign of him and John experienced a moment of panic, for what reason he didn't know. But before he could think of where he could have gone, he saw Randere and a few others running towards him.

'Did you see it?' Randere squeaked with hardly concealed excitement. 'Did you see the way their heads came off?' He didn't wait for confirmation. 'I've never seen anything like it. The worst mess I've ever seen, by Christ! The one as did the chopping was no expert as an axeman, for all he said he were. Go after go he had afore he could get either head free of its body. They also lopped the heads of John Legge, a serjeant-at-arms, and a juror called Richard Somenour – nay, not our steward, but one of the Friars Minor...'

John turned on him viciously. 'I thought our grudge was against grasping noblemen, not lesser priests.'

'Not so,' Randere retorted. 'That friar were Brother William Appleton, Master of Medicine and adviser to John o' Gaunt, as much a traitor as the Duke of Lancaster himself. Had Gaunt been in London, his head, too, would be adorning Bridge Gate this very minute.'

But Randere was keen to get on with his tale. 'All London be in tumult as I came away. The London citizens are after them Flemings proper this time. I heard they did go to St Martin's in the Vintry and there beheaded nigh on forty of 'em. And not only them, but notables, too. I heard Tyler himself struck off the head of Richard Lyons, a wealthy vintner. He be still in the city.'

'It's said Tyler had a private quarrel wi' him,' put in Will Copyn as John gave a gasp.

'Ay,' agreed Randere. 'Tyler did once serve

356

him – in France – and he did strike Tyler many a time while in his service. So he had a debt to settle there, as would any thus treated.'

'Did you know who got into the Tower to bring them out?' Ned asked.

Will Randere gave him a withering look. 'Know any?' he echoed shrilly. 'Know any? Why, us of course! Tyler and his men rode straight over the drawbridge wi' hundreds of us following, so many that we overpowered them guards easy. Had 'em falling into the moat, the water all red wi' their blood. By the time we got in all were in disarray – Richard's fine possessions all strewn about, his kingly bed tipped over to see if it hid the traitors...' He broke off with a bellow of laughter. 'There was one merry incident, though we didn't see it, but we did hear women squeaking and squawking. Seems some did tip Princess Joan out of her bed trying to look under it for Hales or Sudbury.'

John could hardly believe what he was hearing. 'They handled the Fair Maid o' Kent, the King's own mother, as if she were a serving wench? And you think that cause to laugh? Had Prince Edward of Wales lived, she'd have been our Queen.'

'And young Richard not yet our King,' reminded Copyn sagaciously. 'None to advise him so wrongly in his youthfulness, and this protest of ours never need have begun. Had the Black Prince lived, then all this...'

Will Randere wasn't listening. 'She and her

women scurried from her chambers, she all huddled in her cloak, and was taken, half swooning, to the Water Gate, from there to the Queen's Wardrobe by Baynard's Castle to the west of London. When news got to the King afore he reached the Tower, he went there instead to comfort her. So we didn't see him, which was a pity.'

Being at the Tower, Randere hadn't received a charter nor seen the King, which to John seemed a just punishment, but he was shocked and angered by the way Randere was treating what had been a violent and vicious act of aggression as a great joke.

'By God, if it had been I who had known my mother so vilely mistreated, I'd be sorely inclined to withdraw all my promises.' He was thinking of his own mother, the tax inspector she had let into her house in all good faith, mishandling her young daughter before her eyes, her husband then crushing the man's skull with a hammer.

'You can scoff, William Randere,' he roared, loathing the man with all his being for the mischief he'd already brought upon himself. What sin he'd committed had been any man's natural reaction to a woman pulling him down on the ground beside her. What Randere had done had been slimy malice with no care of the damage his actions would do to others. 'Others may see it as droll and amusing, but you are nothing but contemptible.'

All the while, as Randere glared at him, he

358

kept seeing Tom sitting alone at Mile End, his loneliness self-enforced. For the rest of his life he would never be able to wholly imagine what his actions and those of Randere had done to the man. If it was anything as bad as he felt, then it was too hard to bear.

It was good to be on his way home.

Word had it that Wat Tyler, still not satisfied with the King's promises, had called for another meeting at Smithfield outside Newgate. Richard had consented to Smithfield as convenient, being that he'd be at nearby Westminster the next day to hear mass.

Randere and many of the others went back into London to witness it, while John and the rest, just four of them, turned for home, some of their neighbours, Randere said with a tone of contempt, having already departed for home. 'Faint-hearts and old women,' was the term he'd used, which no doubt included John and his party. But they'd seen enough. It was time to go home.

Leaving a pretty deserted Mile End, they were caught up a mile or two further on by Wat Gildeborn, who had decided he should be back helping his brother. He came riding a small cob, leading a second while refusing to say where he'd found them. So much havoc had gone on these past weeks that it had seemed no crime to make use of them. They had doubled up with the riding, each taking his turn to walk awhile. It was certainly quicker than all of them tiring themselves by walking.

John thought constantly of Tom, wondering where he was, hoping he was in no danger. He could have left for home or changed his mind and gone back into the city. There was no telling.

He was therefore overjoyed as they came across him by the roadside several miles further on, giving an ancient-looking, shaggy-coated horse a drink of water. He told them he had bought it for a paltry sum from two men, possibly horse thieves wanting to be rid of it. With the extra mount, there had been no need for anyone to walk, and this way they came clip-clopping into Fobbing as the sun was going down, those already home coming to greet them, every man's family glad and relieved to see them back safe and sound.

Alice's arms were flung joyously about John's neck, careless of who saw, she crying and laughing at the same time. His mother was running her fingers through his matted hair in anxious concern for him, rubbing his fair stubble as though it were a wound to be gently tended.

His sister, however, was standing back, more interested in striking a provocative pose, conscious of her blossoming woman-hood, her eyes far too bold for his liking. The incident with the tax collector seemed to have done little to diminish Cicely's awareness of her ability to attract the village lads.

He turned his eyes from her as his father came towards him, having to extricate himself from Alice's loving clutches for the man to grab his hand in both of his, the injured arm now usable to some extent.

As his father clasped him to him, John glimpsed Marjory Baker with her arms about her husband, he kissing her face repeatedly, she returning the kisses, the beguiling witch. How could she profess love for her husband, who loved her so dearly, yet lure another man into the shadows as she had done for her own adulterous pleasure?

Even as she embraced her husband she was looking over his shoulder at John and as their eyes met, hers widened as though trying to convey some message. Quickly he looked away, shocked into anger. Never again would he look at her. Never again would he be so gullible as to be lured by that oh-so-innocent smile, her sensuality beckoning him under the guise of one swooning to be comforted.

He would never forgive her for the gulf she had put between himself and his dearest friend, a gulf that would never close. To show that she was nothing to him, he tenderly took Alice back into his arms and dropped a kiss on that downy cheek, and in doing so caught the faintest sourness of her breath. But no matter. Alice was a good woman, a quiet and gentle soul, mindful of her wifely duties, whose constancy would never be in question – for who would steal her?

He hadn't meant that thought to be unkind. Rather he was lucky and thought that perhaps God had blessed him, for God's ways were strange. He now thought of Tom with sorrow. It was his misfortune to have found himself a wife with an ever restless eye. Worse, that he now knew it to be his misfortune. God grant His blessing on Tom too, John thought.

And thank God for Alice, came another thought as he went into his own home with his family around him. Familiar smells greeted him, the faint reek of yesterday's cooking, the earthy smell of the floor and the dusty one of thatching, the warm odour of their plough ox in its byre that abutted on to the house and in which also roosted the chickens and the sow with her litter. Wonderful, familiar smells.

His grandmother was sitting hunched by the hearth while the two younger children sat making themselves useful in preparation for the next day, gazing up wide-eyed as the family entered.

John drew in a deep breath. London was a memory, a tale to be told over and over, a fleeting episode that already seemed to belong to someone else. Unreal. This was real – his home, his life, a wheel turning endlessly until the good Lord saw fit for it to grind to a standstill. At last he felt content.

He sat awhile by the hearth having eaten his fill of mutton stew. He had answered all their questions, twice over. And now it was time for bed. One by one they retired. With a great feeling of relief he pulled off his clothes, the first time they'd been off since leaving home, and went naked to bed. It felt good, his pallet felt good, soft and comfortable after so much time spent sleeping on the hard ground.

After washing the dishes, Alice came to bed. Lifting the coarse coverlet, she lay silently down beside him. Then he heard her whisper, 'John?'

He knew he should have fondled her in response, but he felt worn out. Feigning sleep, he was glad when she turned over to sleep, too.

Twenty-Four

He had hardly begun to drift off when a hollering outside awakened the whole family.

Hastily pulling on his clothes, his father already making for the door, John hurried out to see several of those he had parted company with at the hamlet of Mile End – Will Randere among them – slithering from the saddles of an assortment of horseflesh flecked with foam and blowing hard, they themselves hardly able to catch their breath, having ridden so hard.

'Wat Tyler, foully murdered!' Randere was yelling. He grabbed the jug of water Tom's mother had brought out for them and drank deep before having it snatched from him by one of the others who passed it around, each man drinking thirstily.

'At Smithfield,' he went on, breathlessly. 'A valet came forward while he were addressing the King and accused him as a thief and a liar and Tyler drew a dagger...'

'Calm yourself,' soothed Adam Melle. 'Slower now, man, from the beginning.'

Randere took a deep breath and began again, though still agitated. 'We went to Smithfield, where King Richard had consented to meet Master Tyler. There, he drew his horse up beside the King's so that they were facing each other and shook him by the hand. Richard wasn't displeased by the greeting and smiled and nodded pleasant enough to Master Tyler. I did see it, being there at the front, though I could hear naught o' what were said.'

'When the valet called him a knave and a thief,' put in Will Copyn, 'Master Tyler damned the man for a traitor and there were high words.'

'A knight approached Tyler on horseback,' Randere took up the story again, glaring at Copyn, 'to take his message to the King, and Tyler were indignant and said he should approach him on foot. But the knight said, "As you be sitting on a horse, it is no insult to you if I approach you on a horse" or some such words.'

He hurried on before Copyn could add his bit. 'What wi' that, and what wi' the valet's insults, what would our worthy leader do but draw his dagger to fright the man off? Seeing it, the knight also drew his baselard and brandished it to drive Master Tyler away from the King's horse.'

'You saw all this?' Tom chimed in harshly. 'From where you were?'

Randere gave him a look, well aware that no love was lost between them, and hurried on, admitting he couldn't properly see what happened next. 'I did hear the King cry out, commanding the knight to desist from striking Tyler, but only arrest him. Tyler grew angry and said he'd come to speak with him to ask for charters to be amended as he wished, and he urged his horse forward again, but I think he must have forgot he still had his dagger unsheathed.'

He broke off suddenly. 'Pray, Mistress Baker, another drink of water. I be parched wi' talking.'

He gulped the water down while all around his neighbours fidgeted impatiently.

'Get on with it,' John snapped. He saw Tom throw him a look that had no friendliness in it. But Randere was off again.

'Afore there were any high words, I think Master Tyler could have been more courteous. 'Twas not the way I would a' greeted our own anointed King. But Richard were tolerant with him and did allow a jug of water to be brought, it being midday and most warm. And even when Tyler rinsed out his mouth before him, Richard seemed not offended. Then he called for a jug of ale and drank deep, offering the King some, but Richard declined most graciously. Who would a' thought it would come to such a pass later, and all in the twinkling of an eye? One minute all was of accord, the next...' Again he broke off, this time, it seemed, for effect, until Adam Melle himself growled at him to get on with it.

'It was the valet calling him a knave and a liar as began the trouble. Master Tyler were so indignant he drew his dagger and the Mayor of London, thinking the King in

366

danger, drew his baselard and struck Tyler a blow on the head, slashing his neck. Another of the King's household dashed forward and ran Master Tyler through twice with his sword and Tyler drew back crying that he'd been killed and fell from his horse.'

'We were stricken by the sight,' cried John Hore, one of the villagers who'd gone back into London with Randere.

'And some reacted angrily,' Randere cried. 'And there were murmurs and some even raised their bows, aiming directly at the King's heart. There could have been slaughter. But that royal boy was braver than any man and spurred his horse forward to face our angered crowd, calling us his men and asking would we kill our King, and saying he would be our captain and to follow him to Clerkenwell Field yonder and he would give us all the things for which we asked. Well, who would fight such a doughty lad, and who would pass up such an offer?'

Going on with his story before anyone else could interrupt, Randere began to tell his shocked listeners that Richard had gone ahead, leading them and they following, leaving Tyler where he had fallen.

'Did no one care that Master Tyler lay dead?' queried John in horror. Randere didn't even glance at him.

'Not dead when they left. I hear he died finally in St Bartholomew's Church nearby, taken there by some of the King's men, and after he died, beheaded for a traitor, his head was taken to London Bridge to replace Hales's.'

There was stunned silence. 'What transpired at Clerkenwell Fields?' Tom asked finally.

'Richard commanded his own party to return to London and not follow, for he would be alone wi' his subjects awhile. That made us all look on him with awe – a King alone amid all of us. At Clerkenwell he sat on his horse in the midst of us and listened most earnestly to what we asked. None of us were near enough to hear but we could see him nodding his head to all that was being asked. Then of a sudden...' Randere's voice fell as if he still lived the surprise of seeing the King's household returning with some six hundred soldiers in harness and more than a thousand on foot, all well armed, with a knight, Sir Robert Knolles, drawing them all into battle order.

'It were alarming,' Will Copyn broke in, 'us surrounded and penned like sheep. I did tremble for my life. Men began to kneel and crave mercy and threw down their staves and bows and all their arms.'

'Then young Richard,' interrupted Randere vehemently, 'bless him for a great and merciful monarch, cried out to his captains to do no harm, that many there had followed their leaders out of fear of their lives and the burning of their homes and need not be harmed.'

'So Richard be for us,' Tom said slowly. 'John Ball were right in saying it were so.'

'Tyler were a mite too forthright,' his brother-in-law added. 'Going about his demands wi' too much hardiness for his own good afore a King, and did receive his just deserts, I'm thinking.'

'Ay, he would a' done for us all,' Randere concurred. 'Even so, the King commanded all banners be handed back and we saw them rent to pieces. Then he commanded that none re-enter London as did not reside there, under pain o' death, but to return home immediately. And so we departed right quick. He could have had us all slain by all them soldiers, but didn't, and we blessed him for his clemency. That lad will see justice done.'

'And he still holds to his charter for us?' asked John.

'Ay. I have mine here.' Will drew the scrap of parchment, darkened with sweat, from his belt and unrolled it. He looked at Tom. 'Would I could read it. But you can do that, Tom.'

Tom was frowning and at first John thought it was Randere acting so forward and friendly after all the mischief he had done. Then he realized his frown was from reluctance. He must already have read his and it seemed he wasn't happy with its contents. But with everyone urging him to tell them what it said, he finally he took it and, tilting it to the light, bent his head over it and began to read in a loud, clear voice.

'Richard, by the grace of God, King of

England and France, and Lord of Ireland, to all his bailiffs and faithful men to whom these present letters come, greetings.

Know that by our special grace we have manumitted all our liegemen, subjects and others of the county of Essex; and we have freed and quitted each of them from bondage by the present letters. We also pardon our said liegemen and subjects for all felonies, acts of treason, transgressions and extortions performed by them or any of them in whatsoever way. We also withdraw sentences or outlawry declared against any of them because of these offences. And we hereby grant our complete peace to them and each of them. In testimony of which we order these letters of ours to be made patent.

Witness by myself at London on fifteenth June in the fourth year of my reign.'

As Tom let his voice fade into silence, his listeners frowned, their blank stares revealing their effort to digest these learned, high-flown words that in their everyday lives held little meaning.

Finally John steeled himself to ask directly, 'What does it mean?'

'It means,' Tom said thoughtfully, 'that Master Tyler were right after all to ask for it to be amended. They be clever words, but

370

where be the promise to withdraw the poll tax on us, and where be any promise to hold down prices and rent of land and to remit the Statute of Labourers? And what of tithes to the Holy Church? Do we still pay them? And where says it that the riches of the Church ought to be divided among common men for their own good? There be nowt in this of forest and land to become common land so we can hunt and fish at will to help feed ourselves in time of want.'

Everyone began to fidget in sudden discontent at this new revelation. 'And now Tyler be dead for his valour,' someone said. 'Curse our King!'

'It were not our King who killed him,' Tom said sharply. 'But them as were with him. Blame them. We've executed the two we sought, but our King's counsellors and advisers seem to breed like flies.'

'Ay,' cried Will while others nodded somberly. 'This had nothing to do with Richard. He proved right brave, coming into our midst, an angry crowd, and preventing an ugly moment. A mere boy! He be as fine as Great Edward, his grandfather. Perhaps young Richard will honour our other requests later.'

'Then why leave them out now?' John challenged, and had Randere viciously turn on him.

'What d'you know of wordy writings as cannot read a word yourself? Who's to know Tom Baker hasn't left some of it out to cause

371

discontent? If our parson, who also can read, were here, he could—'

'You call my son a liar?' Tom's father roared, looming towards the eel-catcher, who cowered back, gabbling in fear.

'Nay, Master Baker, I merely say your Tom is well read but maybe not well enough to see all that be written where a priest would. All I say is that maybe what is written there encompasses all these promises. It do say we be freed from bondage. I say it means we be freed of *every* sort of bondage, including poll taxes, and no need of more writing than be there. I say we ought to take it as such.'

The others were beginning to range themselves behind him – even John's father, who usually held firm views against all comers. Everyone had become content with the royal manumission as it stood and no one was listening to Tom as he tried again to let them see how wrong they were.

Slowly they drifted away to their homes, the general observation being that a youngster like that did not know enough about the world. Only John felt a need to stand by him, but when he professed his support, it was met with a baleful look from Tom from which he, too, hastily retreated to silently brood on his past actions.

It took only until morning for Tom to be proved right, as Fobbing awoke to the arrival of four more riders. Three were strangers. The fourth was Simon Rycard, the bailiff, but not the blistering overseer of earlier times, nor the bewildered, terrified man they saw at Cressing Temple, but one deeply disturbed by the news he bore. The others did not linger, anxious to convey their doleful tidings to their own villages, and left him to tell his tale alone.

After his horse had been led away and he bidden to sit outside one of the tenements to rest and quench his thirst, he began.

'Our Parson Rackstrawe, who they called Jack Straw, is arrested. To think I followed him to Sir Robert Hales's manor at Highbury to see it burn, may God have mercy on the soul of a poor fool, putting my livelihood and even my life in jeopardy when I should have returned here to see about my proper business of this manor. But I yielded to fear and weakness and shrank from reporting all to our steward...'

'What of Rackstrawe?' growled Adam Melle, who had followed his sons from the smithy, feeling he had much to worry about from his bailiff.

'As I said.' Rycard looked up at him. 'Arrested – by the King's men. God curse that young cur! He makes promises as a man then plays with them as a child with a toy. Woe to the land where a child is king.' With this Rycard's face screwed up with anguish and fear. 'And now I am as at risk as any, through no fault of my own.'

'We care not a wit for your woes!' Adam Melle thundered. 'What of our parson?

Quick, man!'

With an effort Rycard pulled his mind together. 'It was said he was pressed into saying that John Ball, Wat Tyler and himself did scheme to rule all England and to cause Richard to do their bidding, after which, when his usefulness was at an end, they would kill him.'

This was unbelievable. Not Rackstrawe, their worthy parson, the man they had looked up to, confessing to lies? Why should he do such a thing? The questions flew from everyone's lips. Rycard shook his head sorrowfully and he shuddered and sighed.

'Tortured from him, most likely. I dare not contemplate what is done in dungeons deep beneath London's gleaming towers. I've seen enough of London these three days to know that any wicked thing that can happen will happen in that terrible city.'

'Hearsay, Master Rycard,' John burst out over a barrage of questions. 'Our brave Jack Straw would never forswear ... would never be of such weak flesh...'

'Not flesh, young wight!' Rycard shot at him with a spark of his owlish pomposity. 'Not flesh. Of a certain he feared his soul to hang in Purgatory had he not made confession before he died. Thought you of that?'

'Died?' came the cries of horror.

'How died?' called John.

'His head struck off,' replied Rycard, rubbing his forehead with a gesture of weariness. 'All is lost. Your rising was for naught. John

374

Ball had fled to Coventry and will be pursued, captured and given a traitor's death. But Jack Straw's head already hangs on London Bridge beside Wat Tyler's.'

'God have mercy on us,' they all heard Tom Baker whisper while the shock of bitter sorrow prickled behind John's eyes, as it did everyone's.

Sighs died away to silence. In the warm morning sunshine women dabbed their eyes on their sleeves and turned away. Hardy men swallowed hard. Above the sense of loss, in everyone's mind were now uneasiness and doubt and apprehension. What of Richard's promises now?

Their King was indeed proving to be an unpredictable child, given to impulses as shown by his gallant but rash headlong dash into the midst of an outraged mob at Smithfield. Was he indeed untrustworthy, unstable?

Slowly the vision of the golden boy, swayed only by scheming counsellors, began to fade, replaced by a young, crouching leopard. But which way would he spring?

With two of their chief leaders done to death and a third fleeing for his life, what of those charters? They'd counted on the King's word. If that was broken, if he went back on it, must they fight on without leaders?

Should they tear up their charters and destroy all evidence of their involvement in the clamour in London? Ought they to go humbly to beg royal pardon, or just remain quietly where they were?

Over the next few days these questions and a great many more racked everyone's brain. But with no more news from London, life slowly reverted to its old pace, much as it had always been. Simon Rycard, still in fear over his part in the revolt, had left with his wife and was now living with friends in some distant corner of Essex, certain his future as a bailiff was at an end.

None was sorry to see him go, although in time another bailiff would be set over them. The manor might even have a change of tenant who would inevitably exact homage from them as he in turn would pay homage to his overlord, Thomas of Woodstock, Earl of Buckingham, who owned so much land around. So it had been and seemed set to continue. Why should their little uprising make any dent in a system that had been around for as long as any could remember?

The thought brought bitter despondency. There had been no triumph. Best those charters be thrust into the dust, and yet still they clung to a hope that these bits of parchment, mere palimpsests, might one day afford them a better life.

Some hope, John thought grimly as he dampened down the smithy hearth for the night. The sun had gone, the sky shot with reds and purples; it would be a fine day tomorrow. What they wanted was rain, but no sign of it.

He stood staring into the blackening charcoal. Ned and his father had gone into the house, leaving him to tidy up. He thought of all the things that had happened these past weeks, all for naught.

'John?'

The voice made him jump almost out of his skin, so quietly had she crept up. He whirled round to see Marjory standing there, her slender figure silhouetted by the glowing evening sky.

Quickly he pulled himself together, glancing about in case she had been seen coming here, but all was quiet. Even so, he reached out and drew her into the shadows of the smithy in case they were seen. 'What d'you want of me?' he grated.

He saw her shake her head in surprise. 'How can you speak to me so roughly, John, after what happened between us?'

He didn't want to remember what had happened between them. 'That's done with, Mistress Baker.'

'Mistress Baker?' she queried. 'You called me your sweetest Marjory that night. What has happened to alter that?'

'Much,' he said abruptly. 'You've done too much mischief.'

'Both of us, John,' she reminded him calmly. 'Both of us. That cannot be undone.'

'As far as I'm concerned,' he growled, trying to ignore the seductive huskiness of her voice, 'it is done with. If you think to tempt me further...'

'There is something I need to tell you, John,' she interrupted gently.

377

'Then say it quickly and leave.' There was every chance that Ned or his father would come to find why he was taking so long. 'You can't be seen here.'

For a reply she held up an iron pot with a broken handle. Her full lips thinned into a sly smile. 'All I have come here for, if any should question, is to have this handle mended.'

'At this hour? That could well wait until the morrow.'

She let the pot fall to her side and came further into the smithy, so near that he was sure he could feel the warmth emanating from her body. 'I had to see you, John,' she whispered. 'I am in some fear and crave your comfort.'

'I've no comfort to give.'

He knew what she meant and he felt alarm. He needed her to go – not in case she be discovered here, but because her presence was making his feelings rise, and she knew it. He hated her wiles, yet the need of her was taking over so fast that he felt out of breath. But why did she say she was in fear?

'John,' she said softly. She had come close without him knowing it, and her body was against his. He hadn't put his arms out to receive her, but hers were around him, her face lifted to his.

The womanly smell of her was so strong in his nostrils, weakening him so that, hardly thinking what he was doing, he pulled her to him. She gasped in joy, tiny, silent gasps that made him want her above all else.

378

The world about him seemed black. He could see nothing, feel nothing but this great need as, standing, he took her, she accepting him with those silent, panting gasps growing ever more rapid and urgent, until finally it was over and he felt drained as he unclasped her arms from him. Only then did reason return and he felt sick and drained.

'You must go,' he said huskily.

Slowly she moved away from him, her eyes seeking his, but he couldn't look at her, hardly able to believe that he'd let this happen again. All he wanted was for her to leave. All his vows, all his resolve, wrecked with the subsiding of passion. Now came misgivings, doubt, dilemma.

This would happen again and again, he knew it now, driving his once close friendship with Tom further and further away. All he could see stretching ahead of him was this subterfuge, this underhandedness, making furtive love in dark corners.

'This mustn't happen again, Marjory,' he told her. 'Now go.'

Obediently she moved towards the open front, then stopped and turned back to him.

'John, there is something I do need to tell you.'

She hesitated while he waited impatiently for her to be gone. 'John, I'm frightened. Not from what we have done, but something more.' Her voice trembled, sounded suddenly small. 'I've not had my monthly flow and I think I be with child.'

'It's your husband's,' he said promptly, but he knew it couldn't be. Even as he spoke he saw her shake her head.

'My husband were away. You both were both away, but it was you who came back here.'

He couldn't answer her. He felt cold with shock. He felt it break out on his skin as a cold sweat. But she was still talking, her voice low and husky and afraid.

'What shall we do?' she asked.

The question pulled him together. 'You must say it is his.'

'But he will know it isn't.'

'Tell him you knew when he went away but could not tell him then, with all that was happening.' From the house he heard Alice calling to him to come in for supper. He saw Marjory's eyes dart in that direction. 'We cannot talk about it now,' he said urgently.

But Marjory tarried. 'We could be wed, you and I.'

'How so?'

Her eyes grew cunning. 'I could proclaim to the village that my spouse cannot satisfy me in bed. It is all that is needed to end a marriage. You know that. And you could proclaim that your wife be barren. There are no sign of children as yet. And we can be wed, you and I.' She began to move towards him again but he stepped back.

'No! I'll never wed you. You are wed to my closest friend.'

Her blue eyes grew hard. He could see them even in the fading light. 'Such a close friend that you cuckold him. Twice.'

Anger consumed him suddenly. 'Get out!' he cried. 'Let me alone!'

He turned, taking the rear door of the smithy that led towards the house, leaving her to depart on her own.

Twenty-Five

Everyone's hope that those bits of parchment would afford him some measure of a better life fell apart within days as news came of a great army assembling in London.

Richard's uncles had returned, John of Gaunt from Scotland and Thomas of Woodstock from Wales. Richard had issued a proclamation concerning insurgents and had commanded it to be displayed at all prominent places around the country. One had been put in Brentwood. Tom and his father went to bring back a copy.

John was loath to see him go. It left Marjory to her own pursuits and, despite having her household duties under the eyes of her mother-in-law, it was all John could do to keep out of her way. He left Ned to clear up the smithy that evening lest she come by, while he followed his father into the house. There was little she could do during the day, but he was aware of her watching him, knowing that given the smallest chance, she would be there. It made him sick to recall how close he and Tom had once been and would never be again. How could he have let her seduce him? He'd been a fool. But she was a witch.

Worse, Tom had no idea she was.

John was heartily glad to see him and his father returning, but with mixed blessings that he'd have to face him day after day, keeping his secret close, only hoping that in time the rift would heal even though his heart told him that it never would.

He stood in the street to hear Tom read out the King's proclamation, but his inability to look his erstwhile friend in the face was swept aside as the gathering heard what the proclamation had to say.

'Because we understand that various of our subjects have risen in various counties of England against our peace and to the disturbance of the people and have formed various gatherings and assemblies in order to commit many injuries against our faithful subjects, and because they affirm and inform our people that they have made the said assemblies and risings, by our will and with our authority...'

Tom paused to run through in an undertone the mass of high-flown jargon that would have meant little to anyone, picking up again where it would make more sense to them all:

'We hereby notify you that these risings, assemblies and injuries did not and ought not to derive from our will or authority, but that they displease us immensely as a source of shame to us, or prejudice to the Crown and of damage and commotion to our entire kingdom.'

This was met with silence, everyone having half expected something like this. Whether or not they wholly understood the wording, doubt about Richard was already in everyone's mind, and these words seemed to bear out that doubt. There was just a resigned tightening of the jaw, a compressing of the lips. But there was more to come:

'Wherefore we command you to have this publicly proclaimed in the places where it seems this can best be done to preserve the peace and resist the said insurgents against our peace...'

Tom's voice grew suddenly husky with the defeat they all felt.

'...to desist completely from such assemblies, risings and injuries and return to their homes to live there in peace, under the penalty of losing life and limb and all their goods.
Witnessed by myself at London, eighteenth June in the fourth year of my reign.'

With a sense of defeat the crowd began to disperse to linger in small groups talking among themselves or to wander off to their homes, everyone of a like mind. They now knew what to do.

Richard and his court were at Waltham. They'd take the opportunity to send representation there to ask if he still planned to allow them to enjoy those privileges he had promised, his proclamation having put that in doubt. They could take comfort in discovering that much of the county had the same idea and planned to send a few worthy members of the community rather than go in a body, and Fobbing quickly selected Tom's father and his father-in-law; John's father, respected blacksmith; William Gildeborn, freeman and yeoman farmer; and John Melner, miller, who, although almost as dishonest as his father had been, was still a respected member of the village by tradition. John was concerned for his father with his still troublesome arm, but Adam Melle refused point-blank to allow it to deter him.

They returned the following morning, the King's words bitterly etched on their minds. No one knew just how bitterly until John Melner burst out, his somewhat nasal voice trembling with passion at the grievous insult to his own high standing.

'The Devil curse that traitor! Rather I had grovelled to a viper with its flicking tongue than to that *golden boy*, who spat honey from his mouth to fill it with venom towards us. Wretched men, he called us. "Oh, you wretched men, detestable on land and sea."

385

By my troth, I could have rammed his words down his royal throat. My bile came up to hear him fly into a childish rage, such fits of temper as no grown man would display. "You who seek equality with lords," he screeched, and us on our knees afore him. "You are not worthy to live." By the living Christ...'

He broke off, his words choking in his throat at the humiliation to a man of his respectability while Tom's father took up the story.

'I cannot rightly remember all our fine King said, but he did say as how he would have punished us with the most shameful death had he not been determined to observe the law concerning the safe conduct of envoys such as we were.'

He narrowed his eyes in an effort to get the words correct. 'I do recall some of it, though it sickens me to relay such a reply. "Rustics you were and rustics you are still," he said. "You will remain in bondage, not as before but incomparably harsher, for as long as we live and by the grace of God rule over this realm, we will strive to suppress you so that the rigour of your servitude will be an example to posterity." And to that I say, may God curse our King – let him have no peace or joy – let him perish at the hands of traitors as we perish by his!'

No one had ever heard their normally calm and composed baker speak with such venom and they stood quiet. As he turned and went into his house, Tom was also silent. Marjory glanced at John, who hastily looked away. To show he wasn't swayed by her glance, he put an arm about Alice's waist and she looked up into his face with unspoken appreciation of his protection at this dreadful time.

Will Copyn said it all. 'I'd soonest still have old Edward ruling us, doddering old fool that he did become, wi' his strumpet, Alice Perrers, as were talked of so. At least we knew then what was what. This half-weaned King is no better than them as advised him.'

'And as to his uncles,' Adam Melle said glumly, 'Richard vowed to send them to crush our pride. The two of 'em be coming this minute into the country – the Earl of Buckingham as holds these very manor lands among his possessions, and Sir Thomas Percy, brother to the Earl of Northumberland.'

He glanced round at his neighbours, who stood about in a fine drizzle of rain, the first rain since that paltry drop in London ten days earlier and which should have lightened the spirits but failed.

'We also learned that there be a Chief Justice of the King's Bench already appointed to try all rebels captured, trials to be held at Chelmsford town. So none be safe. For what it is worth, I say we should burn them charters as was given us, lest we be found with 'em and condemned as rebels. As I see it, it could be a hanging for any caught wi' one, proving him to be a rebel.'

Nothing could have been more designed to

bring fear into everyone's heart and instant nimbleness to everyone's feet. In minutes the street was empty and the air became filled with the reek of burning parchment.

Letters of manumission made a small flame compared to the conflagration two weeks earlier of manor records and exchequer documents, but these small blazes were great with acrimony of heart. Yet even as the ashes were kicked about into oblivion, still no one felt any safer.

Later John found himself outside at the same time as Tom. He was taken totally off his guard when Tom addressed him directly, even if distractedly, which proved the extent of everyone's feelings.

'What of them as look to save their own skins and babble of their neighbours? We no longer dare trust anyone.'

It could have been meant to apply to him, but John knew he was thinking of something totally different. He found himself saying, 'What have we to lose if we fight on?'

They'd all heard of the commissioned Justice to the King's Bench, Sir Robert Tresilian, spoken of as a man without mercy or human feeling, who had been known to condemn to death the innocent and guilty alike at many a bloody assize.

'Men might tremble,' he went on. 'But men can fight.' There was no other way and John felt desolate at that thought.

He saw Tom look at him, his young brow furrowing in contemplation. No time now for personal grudges, Tom slowly nodded in agreement.

Once more men were called to arms. Gathering what weapons they could lay hands on, they left their villages, every man who could be spared.

Word had passed from village to village like wildfire. Every horse that could be found, be it stolen or borrowed, nag, ancient ambler or sprightly palfrey, was put to use pulling food-laden, weapon-filled wagons and farm carts.

The finest place to make a stand, came the word, would be the high wooded area to the north of the village of Billericay, some five miles east of Brentwood, where the enemy would be coming from.

Any further east and they could very well be caught with their backs to the North Sea. Too far west and they would meet Buckingham and Percy's men too soon and on level ground with little chance of seeing them from a distance. But the northern and western edges of Billericay's vast woodlands gave fine views across a broad, low valley stretching almost to Brentwood and Chelmsford. They would see them coming from miles away. They needed time to dig in, erect a barricade of farm carts and a palisade of sharpened stakes upon which a charging cavalry would be impaled. Even now word was coming that Percy and Buckingham were at Galleywood, just south of Chelmsford.

The Fobbing men arrived as rain cleared

and the sun returned, to find the place filled with activity and many others still arriving. It was a great army. Many had found body protection of some sort, parts of old hauberks or coats of mail. Some had helmets, mostly ancient, but some new, probably taken while raiding manor houses on the way to London or in London itself. Some were already proudly wearing their helmets, fancying themselves as fine knights.

John called to one man almost in full armour, somewhat rusty and ill-fitting. 'You'll fry your brains in that there thing under this sun.'

The man, who was already having trouble keeping up the loose visor, held it up with one hand and grinned out through the aperture. 'And you'll regret your own attire when arrows start to fly.'

John wore only a thickly padded gambeson buckled about his chest, which would repel an arrow but probably not a lance. He did have a helm, a brass, dome-like thing that he'd found and which he'd hammered to fit better. He held it up for the man to see.

'I shall wear this when the occasion calls for it,' he said. 'The day be far too warm for it to be worn now.' But the man merely grinned and went on whittling stakes.

Wagons, quickly unloaded, were being hauled through the sparser parts of the woods to add to the barricades. Their own carts were accepted with enthusiasm and they themselves set to work helping to drag other carts to the growing lines.

A group from Southchurch and Leigh were digging a ditch, others throwing up a palisade of sharpened stakes. Beyond, the land sloped away to lower open ground, used only for pasture, it being strewn with low gorse bushes, but of great advantage to the defenders of the higher ground.

With everyone from his village hurrying to help, John recognized the bull-face of Ralph Spicer, the man he had first met at Shoebury. He went over, dragging young Ned with him, aware that Tom had followed, too.

'I know you from Shoebury, Master Spicer,' he began. 'What can we do here?'

The man gave a deep, offhanded frown, not placing him, making John feel instantly foolish as Ned giggled, the young brat.

But Tom's face didn't alter. 'Tell us what is needed,' he said evenly.

'You can sharpen that lot if you've axes with you.' Spicer jerked a heavy chin towards a stack of freshly felled saplings, green and bent. 'Both ends,' he said. 'Some of you can fix 'em in place, some can dig, and the rest of you can help bring up more carts. Leave your weapons over there.' With this he returned to pounding already sharpened stakes into the ground.

All around the woods echoed to men calling commands to each other, horses whinnying as they were made to pull carts through the undergrowth, the rumble and creak of carts being tipped on to their sides for the barricade, the clank and rattle of chains to secure them together and the dull thud of axe against wood, the splinter of falling saplings and the thump of them being hammered into the soil to form their deadly angled palisade.

The day had become hot, humid and oppressive, the sky a hazy yellow, but darker to the east with humps of low cloud. By midday men were going bare-chested, sweat trickling down cheek and torso and between shoulder blades.

Many times John glanced up to where Tom was toiling, already looking weary. His skin had the paleness of one whose work kept him mostly indoors. It gave him a vulnerable look and John felt a shudder go through him imagining it pierced by an arrow or sword in the coming battle. God keep him from harm, he prayed, pausing to gaze across the stretch of low, sparsely wooded country before it rose again to the distant ridge. The sun sinking over those ridges shone directly into his eyes, making him squint and throwing everything into silhouette. If Buckingham and Percy chose now to appear, all up here would be blinded by those slanting rays. No one would know where to fire. Arrows would be wasted, men confused. This battle would be lost ever it began. 'Pray God they come not this evening...'

'What's that you say, friend?'

A small, jolly-looking man was puffing beneath the cumbersome weight of several crooked, unstable saplings, and heaved them

392

on to the diminishing pile beside John.

Realizing he'd been caught praying aloud, John grinned sheepishly. 'I were wondering when our enemy will come.' He continued to peer west, shading his eyes with a hand. The man shaded his as well.

'Better tomorrow morning wi' the sun in their eyes rather than ours. If you have to pray, then pray for a good downpour as'll make that slope nice and slippery for 'em to get up, and sun tomorrow to blind them.' He gave a chuckle and pointed southeast. 'Them clouds look to be sent by God, right enough. We'll have our downpour tonight, and be as well advantaged here as any.'

'If only it were known the size of their army.'

'Do it matter? Up here we'll be more'n a match for they.'

John hoped so. Tom had let his mallet fall by his side, unable to progress any further with the palisade obstructed by a jut of woodland. He turned to the speaker.

'Them be stout words, friend, but have you taken note of what arrows we have?' The man shrugged. 'Well, I have. And it be poor showing. Some with a bare half dozen shafts, some with even less, and many o' them wi' broken vanes, missing cock feathers, and all as blunt as a spinster's bodkin. Share what we have and I swear there'll hardly be one apiece.'

Spicer, directing men at their tasks, whirled on Tom, his face thrust forward. 'Have done with such talk! Would you have our doughty

393

men dispirited by such words?' He swung back at those who had stopped working to gawp. 'And you, get back to your work, all of you!'

Tom stood his ground. 'I say nowt against our determination, sir. I say against our folly. I've seen none counting their arrows or any weapons we have. We've made a fine defence, but what of our offence? What of our lines of battle order? Where are the leaders to command us in our attack?'

'We have no leaders,' Spicer shot back at him. 'Our leaders be dead, or flown. We'll do our best wi' what we have.' Again he glared at those who once more paused to listen. 'I said get back to your duties!' he roared and they quickly obeyed as he stomped off towards them.

The little jolly-faced man chuckled. 'No need to fret, younker,' he said. 'We've bill-hooks and spears enough, axes and staves a-plenty for crushing skulls. And all can handle a bow. Did not the old King decree every man should practise his archery, so to be ready for them French marauders? No lack o' veterans here, lad, and fine marksmen all, as no doubt ye be. There's none as can match the English longbowman.'

'Twill be English longbowmen as'll be matching us here on this very ground on the morrow,' reminded Tom, unsmiling. 'And what good longbows wi'out arrows, and them we have old from practising at the butts for years with the same old weapon?'

'And few with manor lords as thought it worth replenishing,' John added. 'They have a duty to supply such, not us, and thought a man only needed a handful of shafts for his use in play.'

'We do not play this day,' Tom remarked acidly. 'And what we have will soon be gone.'

The little man's humour did not diminish. 'Then we only have to stand back and wait for them to fire first. Then we collect them as fall on our side and fire 'em back. Spit 'em wi' their own arrows.'

Tom turned his gaze to the makeshift barriers. 'And once they breach that lot, what then?'

At last the little man's face lengthened and he gnawed at his lips with nearly toothless gums. But his optimism was soon back. 'Then ... then we'll draw back into the forest where horse cannot penetrate. We know this country. They don't. We'll fight a furtive battle, leap out on 'em, surprise 'em, leap out of the trees on 'em. We've skilled archers and we'll pick 'em off one by one. Their archers and them men-at-arms and armoured knights won't know which way to turn. You mark my words.'

He went back to his task, laughing at his own wisdom, but Tom stood looking at the makeshift barriers. 'I can't help thinking of Buckingham,' he said idly to John. 'Lately back from the Welsh Marches, country far more difficult than any around here, mountainous.'

If then, Buckingham's army was capable of penetrating such terrain, a paltry barrier of carts chained together and a rabble of ill-armed rustics would surely not hold him up overlong. But it was best to keep such thoughts to himself.

Twenty-Six

Nothing more could be done to the defences. Everyone settled down for the night, drawing together with companions from their own village to cook what food they'd brought over small, cautious fires. Talk was hushed, laughter non-existent, a far cry from the light-hearted banter, the merry jesting of those hurling days only a fortnight earlier.

They spoke little now of the battle to come. If they spoke at all it was of everyday matters, immediate things. Thoughts of sudden death, desperately lulled by faith in God turning aside the arrow or sword or lance at the last moment, went unspoken. Death was something that happened to others, not oneself. Please God, not oneself.

Nor did they mention loved ones now, avoiding any reference to the hearth and home that might diminish what courage a man had mustered to face the coming ordeal.

Around midnight the clouds that had been threatening all day came together to let down their moisture upon those below. It was not a violent storm – lengthy pauses between pale flashes of lightning and thunder a begrudging distant rumble like the rattle in the throats of dying men – but the rain made up for it, hissing upon the embers of the fires, collecting in every narrow animal track between the trees in brown-stained pools.

In the darkness the woodland plants sucked it up in joy. The men trying to sleep, trying not to think of the morrow's battle, merely hugged their own wet bodies in misery and huddled closer to the trees for shelter.

With the approach of morning the clouds broke, leaving a heavy mist to disperse quickly in the sun's first rays. And there in those same rays the men crouching behind their barricade caught the first glimpse of the great army below them – here a brief flash as the newly risen sun caught the surface of a well-polished breastplate, there a sudden glint striking off a helm or a shield.

'They come!' came the cry. 'Make ready, lads! Bowmen, make haste! Here – up here!'

In the mad scramble, arrows good and bad were nocked excitedly and too soon, some even loosed uselessly, causing those taking command to turn upon their fellows with loud words of vituperation.

Men gripped their makeshift spears – staves to which a knife had been bound – their axes and billhooks and swords stolen earlier from many a manor house, white-knuckled, as though the enemy was already at their throats.

Finally every man got himself to his chosen place at the barricade of upended carts and, after much sorting out, the bowmen aligned sufficiently further back for better aim over the heads of those in front.

With a sickeningly beating heart, John crouched, tense, gripping an axe and rehearsing in his mind how he would slice through armour and helmet with all the power of his smith's biceps behind each swing of his axe.

Next to him, young Ned held a sharp billhook, capable of slicing through whatever bit of flesh an armour might leave unprotected, and bowmen did not wear armour such as a knight would. He took heart in the way the boy held it, firm and resolute. Behind them stood Tom with his longbow, one he kept by him for the butts and ever in meticulous condition. John glanced briefly at him, but Tom had his eyes on the horizon. He stood erect and steady. He even looked calm, his hands relaxed on the bow, the arrow ready but as yet pointing earthward until ready to take aim.

Taking his eyes off him, John turned back to those below and some way off. A man might almost imagine the countryside deserted but for the myriad glints from armour and weapons that were slowly approaching.

'A good league off yet,' John heard young Dick Wodelarke mutter, but he didn't reply. Everyone was staring ahead, all far too tense. By the time the fight came to them they would already be worn down by tension.

They were silent, the silence of apprehension broken only by an occasional in-drawn breath, a nervous clearing of a throat, a softly mouthed oath as the waiting slowly became too much to bear.

John again glanced round at Tom and this time their eyes met and he saw him smile, a brief smile of understanding. The comfort it brought made John feel that a tiny part of the old affection and friendship must still flow between them. He smiled back and turned away quickly, before it became too laboured, and resumed watching the slow, steady approach of those men-at-arms and keen-eyed archers.

But the battle was not to be fought this day, nor the next. Through the daylight hours, plagued by the heat of the sun, the humidity after the rain, and the irritation of woodland insects it caused, the men's eyes ached from their constant staring at the country below where Buckingham and Percy's armies had halted half a league from them. Tantalized by the sight of what seemed like thousands of dots moving nonchalantly about, at night they were treated to the disconcerting sight of countless campfires dotting the countryside as if taunting them.

The next day was a repetition of the first, except that an overcast sky and a persistent drizzle was as uncomfortable as yesterday's sticky sunshine and was followed by an equally sticky night and restless sleep.

After two days of waiting, they were becoming short on food, but none dare forage or leave to bring back more, for now came fears that the enemy might dispatch some of their number to creep behind their lines and capture any as might venture away from the main body. Sentries had been posted, but no man alone cared to walk straight into an ambush. So they were starting to go hungry. Thus the third day saw sleep-deprived, empty-bellied men slumped at their posts as a well-fed, well-rested enemy made its move.

Across the sloping open pastures, just as the sun climbed to its zenith, came the wavering bleat of trumpets, the faint cry of commands and the distant whinnying of horses being saddled and mounted.

Banners could be seen now, fluttering despite a desultory midday breeze as they were borne by energetically galloping horsemen up and down the now easily discernible lines of horse and foot.

'Make ready, lads! Make ready to receive 'em!' came the cry, but the men were already on their toes, every heart stepping up its beat, hunger and weariness flung aside.

'They'll send out heralds any minute now,' Wat Gildeborn growled, straining his neck above an upturned cart to see better as he gripped a gleaming, handsome sword, a prize from the raid on Cressing Temple.

'Ay,' returned young Henry Sharpe, 'and we'll be sending down one of our own to receive their proclamations.' This was in accordance with the recognized code of chivalry at the start of any battle, or so he'd heard from veterans of the French wars.

But suddenly, with no prior formality, the

ranks of horse and foot began to move forward. Once within range of their arrows, the bowmen, confident of little answering fire, calmly took their stance, each straight-legged, body held at right angle to the target. With equal calmness each nocked his arrow, drawing the bow strongly, took aim and fired, all in perfect unison. More than a hundred arrows soared together, briefly darkening the sky in a close-packed, upward arc.

'Christ's blood!' spat Will Randere, ducking instinctively before they ever arrived. 'The Devil's spawn deny us even the honour of a herald. We be not even seen as a worthy foe!'

Every man heard the swish of the steeply descending missiles. Chaos broke out as many found a target in unprotected flesh, cries of pain from those struck, at least a dozen fatally, yells of anger from the rest. One arrow fatally struck the throat of Will Randere's brother, Dick. With a stricken cry, Will fell on his knees beside him to pluck out the arrow as if that would bring him to life and, when it didn't, to clasp his brother to his breast.

As the body fell back in the eel-catcher's arms, John saw the anguish and utter disbelief in his face and all his hatred for the man flowed out of him. He remembered Tom standing out in the open, totally exposed, and swung about in terror as another volley came swishing overhead.

Already the rebels could feel the vibration of the great destriers' hooves thundering upon the earth and the sight of them sent a wave of fear through their ranks.

'We must hold,' John heard Spicer shouting from a short way off. 'We must repel 'em! No one run. Hold! Hold!' Even his voice sounded high with terror. But they held.

Every man had rushed to the barriers, ready to spear any that the sharpened palisade failed to spike, to slash and crush any who clambered over their chained barrier. Yet all knew this oncoming mass of steel closing on them with unbelievable rapidness would be impossible to turn back. Even so, if hearts had quivered before, no man showed it now.

John's whole body had become like a rigid bar of iron. His jaw ached from clenching it. Was there a man inside each gleaming carapace, or some evil thing from the bowels of the earth? He could imagine no human face behind the lowered visors of those domed helmets, no limbs of flesh and blood inside the jointed mail, no hands but cruel, hard talons beneath the steel gauntlets, each set of talons gripped about the hilt of a huge double-edged sword or a thick-shafted, iron-tipped lance.

The first rank was no less terrible, their chargers with muzzles drawn back from great yellow teeth and foam-flecked red maws. Beasts of Hell, they carried not weapons, but iron hooks on coiled rope.

All this John saw in the split second before, galloping the length of the barriers, the grappling irons were flung, ropes snaking out to catch the upended carts and the chains securing them, so many together that under the combined weight of several horses, the wagons groaned, toppled, dragging chains, palisade and all, to roll downhill leaving the way open for the next wave that was already galloping in at a tremendous pace.

The laboriously built defences breached in three places, the battle was already lost. Men reeled back before a towering wall of men and horses, each clearing the shallow ditch in one leap, and scattered in all directions, falling over those already slaughtered. But some held.

A iron-clad apparition leaned from a snorting monster, its sword describing an arc towards John. On his feet, his blood pounding with battle fever, John swung the axe behind his left shoulder with both hands and swept it round, aiming upwards. With all his power behind it, the head of the axe crashed against his assailant's arm, cutting into the metal plates. The figure let out an agonized cry, his scream mingling with the screams and shouts, the clang of steel and the squealing of horses, and toppled from its saddle. Never had John felt so elated.

There was no time to gloat. From behind he glimpsed a second attacker, saw the flail of a sword. More in instinct than with any dexterity of forethought, he leapt aside, the downward-plunging blade missing his neck by a hair's breadth, and again ducked as the sword was slashed backward at him.

It was Wat Gildeborn who thwacked the rider across the shoulders with his own sword, an unskilled blow, but from a keen-bladed sword once owned by a knight. It was Wat who felled his victim, and it was Wat who was immediately felled by another rider's well-drilled aim, the blade piercing his inferior quilted gambeson straight through the heart.

As John saw him fall, so he saw Tom standing over another fallen figure, flailing left and right with a spear on a broken shaft, desperately trying to deflect the mounted opponent's lance. Bounding to his side, John swung his axe in an almighty sweep across the aggressor's thigh, biting into the steel. With a cry of pain and surprise, the man toppled sideways.

What had appeared to be bodiless creatures inside all that steel were vulnerable men after all.

Tom was shouting. His face, streaked with blood, was twisted into a grimace of grief and rage. 'John! Your brother! Look to Ned!'

It was then John noted who the fallen man was – not man but boy – who Tom had been protecting. Blood oozed from a huge rent in the back of the peasant tunic from which the makeshift gambeson had been ripped.

With an anguished cry, John dropped the axe and flung himself at his younger brother's body, gathering it to him, calling his name. He barely heard Tom's warning shout, but turned instinctively to a shadow above him.

He saw the rider bearing down on him, the flash of the lance, and at the same time saw Tom strike upwards with his shattered spear at the raised visor.

He glimpsed the eyes, staring with blood-lust within the darkness of the slit, and then a burning agony struck his right side, throwing him forward across Ned's body.

Pain, like a great black wing, covered him, smothered him, bore him down into an abyss.

It was hard to know where he was. It was dark. A damp, cool breeze touched his forehead and he became aware of pain.

It was quiet but for the steady shuffling of feet through damp leaves. He seemed to be floating. Not floating, for small, uneven jerking movements were sending shafts of pain into his side. He was being carried on a litter. There were no sounds of battle.

Looking up, he saw Tom's face above him, looming from the Stygian darkness of leafy canopy and moonless night. He could just make out the gleam of Tom's even teeth in a wan smile. The memory came flooding back. Ned. Sweet Jesus, what had happened to Ned? Trying to lift himself in renewed fear for his brother, pain swamped him and he fell back, gasping his brother's name.

'Hush. Be still, John,' came Tom's voice, little above a whisper. But he had to know about Ned.

'In God's mercy, Tom, tell me ... Ned...'

'Quiet!' Tom hissed. 'We'll be heard.'

Gently his litter was lowered to the dank woodland floor. Faces were gazing anxiously down at him. Tom bent over him.

'John, listen to me. You musn't cry out. We're being hunted. Soldiers are combing these woods for any who escaped, killing everyone they find.'

Gritting his teeth against the agony in his side, John managed to whisper that which was gnawing at his mind. 'Ned. What of Ned? How is he?'

Tom's face was close to his, filled with sadness. 'You musn't cry out. Ned ... he be killed...' He broke off to put a hand over John's mouth to stifle the cry of grief that went on and on against his smothering hand.

He looked into John's eyes with such sorrow and understanding, but all John could see was the dead body of his brother lying back there somewhere on the ridge, everyone escaping with such urgency that the dead had been left behind.

'I know, John, I know,' came Tom's soft tones. 'But no sound. We've managed to evade them thus far, but for how much longer? We be trying to get you home. You're badly wounded and need tending.'

'Leave me here,' John moaned, wanting none of this. 'Let them find me, I don't care.'

'None shall take you, John. Adam Melle shall not lose yet another son, nor I a cherished friend. Now, quiet.'

Gently he took his hand from John's mouth, the slim fingers wet with John's tears for his brother. But even in his misery and grief, two words rang in his head. *Cherished friend.* And after all he'd done to that cherished friend...

The thought brought fresh tears and silent sobbing.

'Come, a sturdy heart now,' Tom urged, though his own voice was shaking. 'Buckingham's men are all around, so quiet, dear friend.'

But already John lay quiet, loss of blood taking its toll of him, grief and pain and all his surroundings melting away into nothingness.

Twenty-Seven

There had been fever, tossing and turning, burning pain. Faces came and went continuously, but never Tom's face.

In delirium John cried, sobbed for the loss of Ned, but it seemed it was someone else who sobbed and threw himself about on his pallet. Between bouts of derangement he was aware that his questions about Tom were met with long faces from Alice and his mother. But though he begged to be told, neither would say where Tom was.

Tom never did come to him. It was Marjory Baker who came, while he was still in a high fever.

He remembered being aware of a commotion at the door, of a woman screaming abuse, forcing entry despite his father's roars of rage. Then he'd felt the frail weight of Marjory throwing herself upon him, small fists pounding in fury at his face, his chest, the pain of it, and hearing her frantic sobs filling the room as she was dragged off him.

'You killed my husband,' he vaguely heard her screaming. 'A curse on you. The Devil curse you!'

Tom killed? How killed? He hadn't ... *couldn't* have killed his best friend. He felt confused, even as Marjory sobbed out that Tom had been taken, saving him.

Into his muddled brain came torrents of words. Tom Baker. Taken. Convicted of felonies and high treason, along with seven others of Fobbing. Thomas Baker, drawn and hung at Chelmsford on the fifth day of July, 1381.

Later, as he recovered from the wound that had almost killed him, the full story was given to him by Alice.

No one was sure if Tom Baker had been executed. It was rumoured that a Thomas Baker was in flight, that he had escaped the hangman's noose, yet he had not returned to Fobbing but had fled the country. No word was ever sent to his wife, though Tom had known about his wife and John. But the fact that there had been no word to his parents – nothing, just silence – meant he must have been executed after all. And yet...

For years John had wondered. Marjory had her baby. The baby thrived but, never a strong woman, she'd died in childbirth. He'd watched the child grow to womanhood, so like her mother but more robust. She had married, had children of her own, she and her husband taking over Bakerscroft at the death of her grandparents, who'd raised her from a baby, thinking her to be Tom's child.

But John had always wondered. Had the baby been his or Tom's? Had Marjory Baker lied? He would never know. And he wondered, too, about Tom, if he had indeed died or

410

had escaped. Until today. Now he knew.

Some other Thomas Baker had been recorded as a traitor and executed. Some believed he was a baker from Billericay, others that he came from Fobbing. It was a common enough name, and clerks were notoriously incorrect – especially if harassed by impatient judges.

But how could he, John Melle, speak of what his eyes had seen this night, of what his ears had heard, of the gnarled, beloved hands he had held? How could he tell anyone that Tom had returned? How could he condemn his old friend to a death he had managed to elude these forty-odd years?

John lay on his pallet, his sturdy young grandson and Alice at his side. The pain in his chest had not diminished. Every breath was agony and there was such a weight on his chest.

Perhaps he had only dreamt ... But no, he could have sworn he'd seen Tom coming towards him, young, tall, eager and full of life...

He opened his eyes and looked up, but there was only Alice, mopping the cold sweat from his brow. She was crying. She looked old. He hadn't noticed that before. Her eyes were red with tears. He tried to talk, to tell her not to cry, but his voice was a croak, his lips stiff.

'I did see...' he began, then fought to form the words. 'I did see Tom Baker. My friend...'

Alice's voice came no less difficult than his.

'That you did, John. But he is now dead – several days since, poor old man. He did leave here to travel to Brentwood, despite his daughter's pleas for him to stay, and was taken to Chelmsford. There they did hang him, saying he was a traitor, one of the first movers of that uprising all them years ago. An old man they did hang! After all that time. On the fifth of May in this year of our Lord, 1420...'

He stared at her through his pain, unable to comprehend. He'd seen Tom this very evening. May? How could it be May? And what did she mean by old man? It was hard to breathe, each breath drawn in painfully.

'It be July,' he croaked. 'Fourth year of King Richard...'

'It be May, dear husband.' Alice's voice seemed to be coming from a great distance, trembling with sorrow. 'This be the first year of Henry Sixth. Know you not what year it be, my dearest?'

No, he did not know. Nor did he care. What did it matter? He could see Tom and that was what mattered. Young Tom Baker, running towards him, waving, and there was sunshine and his father's forge, his father nursing a broken arm...

He was so tired of this labouring breath. Faintly he could hear Alice talking.

'Our young John, our grandson ... He and John Hacche, husband of old Tom Baker's daughter ... A commitment to them by main-prize of Thomas Aylmore and Adam Stoure.'

The names meant nothing to him. 'To keep old Tom Baker's old place, Bakerscroft, or, as it is now known, Pokattescroft. So old Tom Baker's daughter will not lose her home. Had it still been his and not his parents and she inheriting it from them, it would have been seen as his property and forfeited, and she homeless, but not now that young John, our grandson...'

She had been gabbling on, her voice becoming fainter and fainter until he heard her cry out, 'John? John! Oh, dear God!'

But John no longer heard. The pain in his chest had completely receded. His breathing no longer harassed him, but seemed to have stopped. Perhaps one more breath? But no, Tom was calling and he must make haste to be in Brentwood.

No time now for breath. No time to bid Alice farewell. He must be away ... It was a fine, sunny day and Tom was calling to him. Dear Tom...